Fueled

Book Two in the Driven Trilogy

K. Bromberg

Copyright

This book is a work of fiction. Names, characters, places, and incidents are the product of the author's imagination or are used fictitiously. Any resemblance to actual events, locales, or persons, living or dead, is coincidental.

Copyright © 2013 K. Bromberg
Fueled by K. Bromberg

Cover art created by **Tugboat Design**
with Shutterstock image # 89919298

Copy and Line editing by **The Polished Pen**

Final Proof by **Polished Perfection**

Formatting by **Hayson Publishing**

Except for the original material written by the author, all songs, song titles, and lyrics mentioned in the novel Fueled are the property of the respective songwriters and copyright holders.
ISBN: 978-0-9894502-3-2

Dedication

To J.P. -

Thanks for your patience while I take on this challenge that's always been a dream of mine. Oh and hey, it's not just a hobby anymore...

Prologue
Colton

Fucking dreams. Jumbled pieces of time that tumble through my subconscious. Rylee's here. Filling them. Consuming them. And fuck if I know why the constant sight of her in a place that's usually clouded with such horrible memories fills me with a sense of calm—of what I think might be hope—allowing me to realize that I might actually have a reason to heal. A reason to overcome the fucked up things that lurk here. That the black abyss in my heart just might have the capacity to love. Her presence here in a place so dark lets me think the wounds that claimed my soul and have always been raw and festering just might be finally scabbing over.

I'm dreaming—*I know I'm dreaming*—so how come she's everywhere, even in my sleep? She's robbing me of thoughts every minute of every goddamn day, and now she's woven her way into my fucking subconscious.

She pushes me.

Unmans me.

Consumes me.

Scares the ever-loving shit out of me.

She feels like the start of a race, stopping my heart and speeding it up simultaneously. She makes me think thoughts I shouldn't. Digs deep into the black within me and makes me think in *whens*, not *ifs*.

Fuck me!

I must really be dreaming if I'm thinking fucking shit like this. *When did I become such a pussy?* Becks will hand my ass to me if he hears me talking shit like this. It can't be anything more than just needing to be buried in her again. Have her warm body beneath me to sink into. Soft curves. Firm tits. Tight pussy. *That's all it is.* I'll be fixed then. My head will return to where it needs to be. *Well, both heads actually.* And once satisfied, I'll be able to focus on something else besides useless shit like feelings and a heart beating that I know is incapable of giving or accepting love.

It has to be the newness of her that has me feeling like a needy little bitch—so much that I'm dreaming about *her specifically,* not just the faceless, perfect body that usually frequents my dreams. There's just something so fucking hot about her that I'm losing my mind. Shit, I actually look forward to the time spent before fucking her as much as I do the time I am fucking her.

Well, almost.

Unlike the numerous chicks that throw themselves at me with their overtly sexual ways: tits hanging out, eyes offering me to take them any way I want to, legs spreading at the drop of a dime—and believe me, most of the time I'm fucking game to their willingness. With Rylee though, it's just been different from the start, from the moment she fell out of that fucking closet and into my life.

Images flicker through my dreams. That first jolt as she looked up at me with those fucking magnificent eyes of hers. That first taste of her that seared my mind, crept down my spine, grabbed hold of my balls, and told me to not let her leave—that I had to have her at any cost. The image of her ass swaying as she walked away without a backward glance, reeling me in with something I'd never considered sexy before. Defiance.

Pictures continue to circle. Rylee kneeling down to Zander, trying to coax his damaged soul out of hiding; her sitting on my lap in my favorite t-shirt and panties, straddled over me last night on the patio; showing up at her office, confusion mixed with anger warring across her incredible features from my non-refutable offer; Rylee standing before me in lacy lingerie, offering herself to me, selflessly giving everything to me.

Wake the fuck up, Donavan. *You're dreaming.* Wake up and take what you want. She's right next to you. Warm. Inviting. Tempting.

Frustration fills me, wanting her so desperately and not being able to shake this damn dream to take her sexy as sin body as I see fit. Maybe that's what it is about her. That she doesn't realize how sexy she actually is. Unlike the countless others before who spent hours staring at and critiquing themselves and their best sides, Rylee has no fucking clue.

Images of her last night consume me. Looking up at me with violet eyes, her bee-stung bottom lip tugged between her teeth, and her body instinctively responding to me, submitting to me. Her signature scent of vanilla mixed with shampoo. Her addictive taste—sinfully sweet. She's irresistible and innocent and a vixen all mixed into one tempting, curvaceous package.

The thought alone makes my dick hard. I just need another fix of her. Can't get enough. *At least until the newness wears off and I move on like usual.* There's no way I'm gonna be pussy-whipped by any one woman. Why get attached to someone that will only leave in the end? To someone who will run the other way when they really know about the truths inside of me, the poison that clings to my soul. Casual is just what I need. The only thing I want.

The only thing I'll allow.

I feel her hands slither around my abdomen, and I sink into the feeling. *Fuck I need this right now. Need her right now.* The knowledge that the tight, wet, heat I crave is just within my grasp stirs my dick awake. Sinking into the softness of her body and forgetting all of this shit in my head is just mere moments away. My morning hard-on stiffens further so that it's almost painful, begging for her touch.

My body tenses as I realize the arms encircling me aren't soft or smooth or smelling of vanilla like Rylee's always are. Shivers of revulsion streak down my spine and turn my stomach. Bile rises and chokes my throat. Stale cigarettes and cheap alcohol permeate the air as it seeps from his pores with his heightened excitement. His paunchy gut presses against my back as his meaty, unforgiving fingers spread across my lower abdomen. I squeeze my eyes shut, the throb of my pounding heartbeat drowning out all sound including my feeble whimpers of protest.

Spiderman. Batman. Superman. Ironman.

I'm so hungry, so weak from the lack of food while Mommy has been away on her last *trip* that I tell myself to not resist. Mommy said that if I'm a good boy and do what I'm told, we'll both be rewarded—that doing this for her makes her love me; she'll get her fix of "Mommy feel goods" from him, and I'll get to have that half eaten apple and plastic wrapped pair of crackers she luckily found somewhere and brought back here. My stomach cramps and mouth waters at the notion of having something in it for the first time in days.

Spiderman. Batman. Superman. Ironman.

I just have to be good. I just have to be good.

I repeat the mantra to myself as his bearded jaw scrapes against my neck from behind. I try to stifle the heaving sensation from my stomach, and despite there being nothing to throw up, my body shudders violently, trying to anyway. The heat of his body against my back—always against my back—makes tears spring in my eyes that I fight to prevent. He groans into my ear—my fear exciting him—as the tears leak through my squeezed eyelids. They trail across my face to fall on my mom's musty mattress sitting on the floor. I tell myself not to resist as his thickening thing presses against my bottom. I remember all too well what happens when I do that. Resist or not, either option is painful, is a nightmare that results in the same ending—fists before pain or just accepting the pain without the struggle.

I wonder if there's pain when you die.

Spiderman. Batman. Superman. Ironman.

"I love you, Colty. Do this for Mommy and I'll love you again, okay? A good little boy does anything for his mommy. *Anything.* Love means you do things like this. If you really love me and know that I love you, you'll do this so that Mommy can feel better again. I love you. I know you're hungry. So am I. I told him you wouldn't fight this time *because you love me.*"

Her pleading voice rings in my ears. I know that no matter how hard I scream, she'll never open the door to help, despite sitting on the other side of it. I know she can hear my cries—the pain, the terror, the loss of innocence—but the haze of her withdrawal is so strong she doesn't care. She needs the drugs he'll give her when he's done with me. His payment. That's all she cares about.

Spiderman. Batman. Superman. Ironman. Spiderman. Batman. Superman. Ironman. I repeat the names of the superheroes, my silent escape from this hell. From the fear that races through my veins, coats my skin with sweat, and fills the air with its unmistakable scent. I repeat the names again. Praying any of these four superheroes will show up and rescue me. To fight evil.

"Tell me," he grunts. "Say it or it'll hurt more until you do."

I bite my lip and welcome the metallic taste of my blood as I try to prevent myself from crying out in fear and terror. From giving him what he wants, my screams for the help that I know will never come. He grips me hard. It hurts so bad. I give in and say what he wants to hear.

"I love you. I love you. I love you…" I repeat over and over, endlessly as his breath picks up from the excitement my words bring him. My fingernails dig into my clenched fists as his hands grope and grab their way down my torso. His rough fingers find the waistband of my threadbare underwear—one of the only pair I have—and I hear them rip under his excited and jerky movements. I suck in my breath, my body shaking violently, knowing what happens next. One hand cups my crotch, squeezing me too hard and hurting me, while I feel his other hand spreading me apart from behind.

Spiderman. Batman. Superman. Ironman.

I can't help it. I'm starving but…it just hurts too much. I buck against him. "No," gurgles past my chapped lips as I fight hard to escape what happens next. I thrash violently, connecting with some part of him as I spring from the bed and escape momentarily. Fear consumes me, engulfs me as he rises off the stained mattress and comes at me, a determined grimace on his face and desire in his eyes.

I think I hear my name being called and confusion flickers through my overwhelmed brain. *What is she doing here?* She has to go. He'll hurt her too. *Oh fuck! Not Rylee too.* My frantic thoughts scream for her to run. To get the hell out, but I can't get the words out. Fear has locked them in my throat.

"Colton."

The horror in my head slowly melds and seeps into the soft morning light of my bedroom. I'm not sure if I can believe my eyes. *What is real?* I'm thirty-two but I feel like I'm eight. The chilled morning air mingles with the sheen of sweat covering my naked body, but the cold I feel is so deep down in my soul I know that no amount of heat will warm me up. My whole body is taut with the impending assault that it takes a moment for me to believe that he's not really here.

I shift my gaze, my pulse thundering through my veins, and lock eyes with Rylee. She is sitting up in my beast of a bed, pale blue sheets pooled around her bare waist and her lips swollen from sleep. I stare at her, hoping this is real but not sure if I believe it. *"Oh fuck,"* I exhale on a shaky breath, unclenching my hands and bringing them up to rub them over my face to try and wipe away the nightmare. The coarseness of my stubble on my hand is welcome. It tells me I really am here. That I'm an adult and he's nowhere near.

That he can't hurt me again.

"Fuuuccckkk!" I grit out again, trying to get a hold on the chaos in my head. I drop my hands down to my side. When Rylee moves, my vision comes back into focus. She very slowly reaches her hand up to

rub the opposing shoulder, her face grimacing with pain, but her eyes are chock full of concern as they remain focused on me.

Did I hurt her? Fuckin' Christ! *I hurt her.*

This can't be real. My nerves are shot. My mind is racing. If this is real, and that's really Rylee, then why do I still smell him? How come I can still feel the scrape of his beard against my neck? How come I can still hear his grunts of pleasure? Feel the pain?

"Rylee, I—"

I swear his taste is still in my mouth? *Oh God.*

My stomach revolts at the thought and the memory it conjures up. "Give me a fucking minute." I can't get to the bathroom fast enough. I need to rid the taste in my mouth.

I barely make it to the toilet, stumbling and falling to my knees as I empty the nonexistent contents of my stomach into the bowl. My body shakes violently as I do what I can to expunge every trace of him from my body even if those traces are only in my mind. I slide down to lean back against the tiled wainscot wall, the cool of the marble welcome against my heated skin. My hand trembles as I wipe my mouth with the back of it. I lean my head back, closing my eyes, and try to shove the memories back into hiding to no avail.

Spiderman. Batman. Superman. Ironman.

What the hell happened? I haven't had that dream in over fifteen years. Why now? Why did—*oh fuck! Oh fuck! Rylee.* Rylee saw that. Rylee was witness to the nightmare that I've never confessed to. The nightmare full of things that absolutely no one knows about. Did I say anything? Did she hear something? No, no, no! She can't find out.

She can't be here.

Shame washes through me and lodges in my throat, forcing me to breathe deep to prevent from getting sick again. If she knows the things I did—the things he made me do, the things I did without a struggle—then she'll know what kind of person I am. She'll know how horrible and dirty and unworthy I am. Why loving somebody, accepting love from somebody is not possible for me. *Ever.*

The deep-seated fear that lives just under the surface inside of me—over someone finding out the truth—bubbles up, sputters over the edge.

Oh fuck, not again. My stomach riots violently, and when I'm finished dry heaving, I flush the toilet and force myself up. I stumble to the sink and with shaking hands squeeze a heaping glob of toothpaste on my toothbrush and scrub my mouth aggressively. I close my eyes, willing the feelings away while trying to remember the feel of Rylee's hands—instead of any of the numerous women I've used unabashedly over the years to try and smother the horror in my mind—to take the memory away.

To use pleasure to bury the pain.

"Fuck!" It doesn't work so I scrub my teeth until I can taste the coppery hint of blood from my gums. I drop my toothbrush with a clatter on the counter and cup some of the water in my hands to splash onto my face. I focus on Rylee's feet through the mirror's reflection as she enters the bathroom. I take a deep breath. I can't let her see me like this. She's too smart—has too much experience with this kind of shit—and I'm not ready for the skeletons in my closet to be exposed and gone through with a fine-tooth comb.

I don't think I'll ever be.

I scrub my face with the towel, unsure of what to do. When I drop it, I look up to her. *God, she is so incredibly fucking beautiful.* She takes my breath away. Bare legs sticking out beneath my rumpled t-shirt, smudged eyeliner, hair tangled from sleep, and a crease in her cheek from the pillow do nothing to lessen her attraction. For some reason, it almost heightens it. Makes her seem so innocent, so untouchable. I don't deserve her. She is so much more than someone like me is worthy of. She's just too close right now, closer than I've ever let anyone get. And it terrifies me. I've never let someone this far in because that means secrets are shared and pasts are discovered.

And because it means you need. I've only ever needed myself—needing others only results in pain. In abandonment. In unspeakable horrors. And yet, *I need Rylee right now.* Every cell in my body wants to walk over, pull her against me, and cling to her right now. Use the warmth of her soft skin and the sound of her quiet sighs to alleviate the pressure expanding in my chest. To lose myself in her so I can find myself again—even if just for a minute. And for that reason alone, she needs to leave. As much as I want to, I can't...I just can't do this to her. To me. To my carefully constructed life and way of coping.

Alone is better. Alone, I know what to expect. I can map out situations and mitigate problems ahead of time. Fuck! How am I going to do this? How am I going to push away the one woman I've ever really thought of letting in?

Better to lose her now then when she bolts after finding out the truth.

I take a fortifying breath in preparation and meet her eyes. So many emotions swarm in her violet irises, and yet it's the pity that sets me off, that allows me to grab on to it and use it as my piss-poor excuse for what I'm about to do. I've seen that look so many times over my life and nothing irritates me more. I'm not a charity case. I don't need anyone's damn pity.

Especially not hers.

She says my name in that telephone sex rasp of a voice she has, and I almost cave. "Don't, Rylee. You need to leave."

"Colton?" Her eyes search mine, asking so many questions and yet none pass through her lips.

"Go, Rylee. I don't want you here." She blanches at my statement. My eyes trace down her face, and I watch her bottom lip tremble. I bite the inside of my lip as my stomach churns and feels like I'm going to be sick again.

"I just want to help…"

I wince inwardly at the break in her voice, hating myself for the pain I know I'm about to cause her. She's just so goddamn stubborn that I know she's not going to leave this without a fight. She takes a step toward me, and I grind my teeth in reaction. If she touches me—if I feel her fingertips on my skin—I'll cave.

"Get out!" I roar, her eyes snap up to meet mine, disbelief flashing in them, but I also sense her resolve to comfort me. "Get the fuck out, Rylee! I don't want you here! Don't need you here!"

Her eyes widen as she clenches her jaw to prevent her lip from quivering. "You don't mean that."

The quiet temerity in her voice hits my ears and tears into parts deep inside of me that I never knew existed. It's killing me to watch how I'm hurting her, how she's willing to stand there and listen to what I'm hurling at her just so that she can make sure I'm okay. She's proving now more than ever that she is in fact the saint, and I am most definitely the sinner.

Sweet fucking Christ!

I'm gonna have to destroy her with bullshit lies just to get her out of here. To protect myself from apologizing and keeping her here—from opening myself up to everything I've always protected myself against.

"Like hell I do!" I yell at her, throwing the towel in my hand across the bathroom in frustration and knocking over some stupid bottle-like vases. Her chin lifts up in obstinance as she stares at me. *Just go, Rylee! Make this easier on both of us!* Instead, she just holds my gaze. I take a step toward her, trying to look as threatening as possible to get her to leave.

"I've fucked you, Rylee, and now I'm done with you! I told you that's all I was good for, sweetheart…"

The first tear slides down her cheek, and I force myself to breathe evenly, to pretend that I'm unaffected, but the wounded look in those amethyst eyes is killing me. She needs to go—*now*! I pick up her bag off of the counter and shove it at her chest. I cringe when her body jerks backwards from the force I've used. Putting my hands on her like this makes my stomach churn even more.

"Out!" I growl, fisting my hands to prevent myself from reaching out and touching her. "I'm bored with you already. Can't you see that? A quick amusement to bide my time. Now I'm done. Get! Out!"

She looks at me one last time, her watery eyes still silently searching mine with a quiet strength before a sob tears from her throat. She turns and stumbles from my room as I brace myself against the doorjamb and just stand there, my heart pounding in my chest, my head throbbing, and my fingers hurting from gripping the doorjamb to prevent myself from going after her. When I hear the front door slam shut, I exhale a long, shaky breath.

What the fuck did I just do?

Images from my dream resurface, and that's the only reminder I need. Everything hits me at once as I stagger into the shower and turn the water on hotter than I can stand. I take the bar of soap and scrub my body violently, trying to erase the lingering feeling of his hands on me, trying to wash away the pain within from both remembering him and from pushing Rylee away. When the bar of soap is gone, I turn and empty a bottle of some kind of wash over me, and start again, my hands frantic in their quest. My skin is raw and still not clean enough.

The first sob catches me by complete surprise as it tears from my throat. *Fuck!* I don't cry. *Good little boys don't cry if they love their mommies.* My shoulders shake as I try to hold it in, but everything—all of the emotion, all of the memories, seeing all of the pain in Rylee's eyes— from the past few hours is just too much. The floodgates open and I just can't hold it back anymore.

Chapter One

As the sobs that rack my body slowly abate, the stinging on my kneecaps brings me back to the present. I realize that I'm kneeling on the coarse cobblestone in Colton's front entrance with nothing on but his T-shirt. No shoes. No pants. No car.

And a cell phone still inside on the bathroom counter.

I shake my head as hurt and humiliation give way to anger. I'm over the initial shock from his words, and now I want to give him my two cents. It's not okay to treat or talk to me this way. With a sudden rush of adrenaline, I push myself up from the ground and shove the front door back open. It slams back against the wall with a thud.

He may be done with me, but I haven't had my say yet. Too many things jumble around in my head that I might never get the chance to say again. And regret is one emotion I don't need added to my list of things to rue over.

I take the stairs two at a time, never more aware of how little I'm wearing as the cool morning air sneaks beneath the shirt and hits my bare flesh; Flesh that is slightly swollen and sore from Colton's more than thorough attention and adept skill the numerous times we'd had sex last night. The discomfort adds a quiet sadness to my raging inferno of anger. Baxter greets me with the thump of a tail as I enter the bedroom and hear the spraying water of the shower. My veins flow with fire now as his comments replay in my head, each one compounding upon the next. Each one transitioning from hurt to humiliation to anger. On a mission, I toss my bag carelessly on the counter alongside where my cell phone sits.

1

I stride angrily into the walk-in shower, ready to spew my venom back at him. To tell him I don't care who he is on the social scale, and that self-proclaimed assholes like him don't deserve good girls like me. I turn past the alcove in the shower and stop dead in my tracks, the words dying on my lips.

Colton is standing in the shower with his hands braced against the wall. Water streams down his shoulders, sagging and defeated in their carriage. His head hangs forward, lifeless and beaten. His eyes are squeezed shut. The distinct and always strong line of his posture that I've come to recognize is missing. The strong, confident man I know is nowhere to be found. Completely absent.

The first thought that flickers through my mind is it serves the asshole right. He should be upset and remorseful over how he treated me and for the abhorrent things he said. No amount of groveling is going to take back the hurt he's caused with his words or from pushing me away. I fist my hands at my side, warring within over how to proceed because now that I'm here, I'm at a loss. It takes a moment, but I've decided to leave undetected—call a cab—walk away without a word. But just as I take a step backwards in retreat, a strangled sob wrenches from Colton's mouth and shudders through his body. It's a guttural moan that's so feral in nature it seems as if it's taking every ounce of his strength to hold himself together.

I freeze at the sound. I watching this strong, virile man come undone, and I realize the anguish ripping through him is over something much bigger than our exchange. And it is in this moment, being witness to his agony, I realize there are so many different ways a person can ache. So many definitions I never realized held within such a simple word.

My heart aches from the pain and humiliation Colton inflicted with his words. From opening itself up after all this time to have it torn again with such cruelty.

My head aches with the knowledge that there is so much more going on here—things I should have noticed with my extensive training—but I was so blindsided by him, his presence, his words, and his actions that I didn't pay close enough attention.

I missed seeing the forest through the trees.

My soul aches at seeing Colton fighting blindly against the demons that chase him through the day and into his dreams to torture him at night.

My body aches to go to him and provide some type of comfort to try and ease the pain these demons cause. To run my hands over him and soothe away the memories that he feels he'll never be able to escape, that he'll never be able to heal from.

My pride aches from wanting to stand my ground, be stubborn, and stay true to myself. To never walk willingly back to someone who treated me the way he did.

I stand on the precipice of indecision, unsure which ache within to listen to when Colton strangles out another heart wrenching sob. His body shakes with its violence. His face squeezed so tight, his pain is palpable.

My debate on what to do next is minimal because I can't hide from the fact that whether he wants to accept it or not, he needs someone right now. He needs me. All of the cruel words he spat at me evaporate at the sight of my broken man. They fade elsewhere to be addressed at another time. My years of training have taught me to be patient but to also know when to step forward. And this time, I won't miss the signs.

I have never been able to walk away from someone in need, especially a little boy. And right here, right now, looking at Colton so bereft and helpless, that's all I see: a shattered little boy that's just broken my heart—is currently breaking my heart—and as much I know staying here will result in my own emotional suicide, I can't find it in me to walk away. To save myself at the expense of another.

I know if I were watching someone else make this decision, I'd tell them that they're stupid for walking back in the house. I would question their judgment and say they deserve what they get. But it's so easy to judge from the outside looking in, never knowing the decision you'd make until you're in that person's shoes.

But this time, this time I am in those shoes. And the decision is so natural, so ingrained in me to take a step forward when most others would step away that there isn't one to be made.

I move on instinct and cautiously enter the shower, *willingly walking into emotional suicide*. He stands beneath one of two huge rain showerheads while numerous jets in the stoned walls squirt water down the length of his body. A built-in bench spans the length of one wall; various bottles of product are shoved in a corner. In any other circumstance, my jaw would have dropped at the grandiose shower and thoughts of standing in there for hours would have flickered through my mind.

Not now.

The image of Colton—so magnificent in body yet isolated in emotion—as he stands there with water running in rivulets down the artfully sculpted lines of his body overwhelms me with sadness. The anguish that radiates off of him in waves is so tangible I can feel the oppressive weight of it as I walk up to him. I lean against the wall next to where he presses his hands. The scalding water that ricochets off of him tickles my skin. Indecision reappears as I reach out to touch him but pull back, not wanting to startle him in his already fragile state.

After some time, Colton lifts his head and opens his eyes. He gasps audibly at the sight of me standing before him. Shock, humiliation, and regret flash fleetingly through his eyes before he lowers them for a beat. When he raises them back to me, the uncensored pain that I see in their depths renders me speechless.

We stand there like this—motionless, wordless, and staring into the uncharted depths of each other for some time. A silent exchange that fixes nothing and yet explains so much.

"I'm so sorry," he says finally in a broken whisper before lowering his eyes and pushing himself off of the wall. He staggers back and collapses onto the built-in bench, and I can't hold myself back any more. I take the few steps to cross the shower stall and use my body to push his knees apart so I can step between his legs. Before I can even reach for him, he takes me by surprise, gripping his fingers into the flesh at my hips and yanking me to him. He finds his way beneath my now wet shirt and runs his hands up my torso, pushing it up as he goes until I cross my arms in front of me and strip it off. I toss it carelessly behind me and it lands with a loud slap against the tile. The minute I'm naked, he wraps his arms around me, and crushes my body to his. With him seated and me standing, his cheek presses against my abdomen, and his arms are like a vice gripping me tight.

I place my hands on his head and just hold him there, feeling his body tremble from the emotion that engulfs him. I feel helpless, unsure of what to say or do with someone so emotionally closed off. A child I can deal with, but a grown man has boundaries. And if I overstep my boundaries with Colton, I'm just not sure how he'd react.

I gently run my fingers through his wet hair, trying to soothe him as best as I can. My fingertips try to express the words he doesn't want to hear from me, the motion just as comforting to me as I'm sure it is to him. In this space of time, my thoughts process and begin to whirl. In the absence of his mind-numbing words, I'm able to read behind the venom of Colton's outburst. The pushing away. The verbal lashing out. Anything to get me to leave so I wouldn't witness him falling apart, trying to reaffirm to himself that he needs no one and nobody.

This is what I do for a living, and I missed all of the signs, love and hurt overriding my training. I squeeze my eyes shut and mentally chastise myself, although I know I couldn't have handled it any differently. He wouldn't have let me. He's a man used to being alone, dealing with his own demons, shutting out the outside world, and always expecting the other shoe to drop.

Always expecting someone to leave him.

Time stretches. The only sound is the splatter of the shower water against the stone floor. Eventually Colton turns his face so his forehead rests on my belly. It's a surprisingly intimate action that squeezes at my heart. He rolls his head back and forth softly against me and then takes me by surprise as he kisses the long line of scars across my abdomen. "I'm sorry I hurt you," he murmurs just above the sound of the water. "I'm just so sorry for everything."

And I know that his apology is for so much more than the verbal barbs and the cruelty in how he pushed me away. It's for things far beyond my comprehension. The angst in his voice is heartbreaking, and yet my heart flutters and swells at his words.

I lean over and press my lips to the top of his head, holding them there as a mother would a child—as I would to one of my boys. "I'm so sorry you were hurt too."

Colton emits a strangled cry and reaches up, pulling my face to his. Between one breath and the next, his lips are on mine in a soul-devouring kiss. Lips collide and tongues clash. Need crescendos. Desperation consumes. I sink down so my knees rest on either side of his on the bench as his lips bruise mine, branding me as his.

His trembling hands come up to cradle my face. "Please. I need you, Rylee," he pleads breathlessly, his voice choking on the words. "I just need to feel you against me." He changes the angle of the kiss, his hands moving my head, controlling me. "I need to be in you."

I can taste his need and can feel his desperation in his frenzied touch. I grab the sides of his face and pull back so when he lifts his eyes to search mine, he can see the honesty in them when I speak my next words. *"Then take me, Colton."*

I can feel the muscle pulse in his jaw beneath my palms as he stares at me. His tentativeness unnerves me. My arrogant, self-confident man never hesitates when it comes to the physicality between us. Thoughts about what could make him react this way fill me with dread, but I push them from my head. I can process this all later.

Colton needs me right now.

I reach down with one hand and grab his rigid cock, positioning it at my entrance. A short, sharp breath is his only response. When he makes no indication of movement, his eyes squeeze shut and his forehead creases with whatever is still haunting the edges of his memory. I run my hand up and over his impressive length. Doing the only thing I can think to help him forget, I lower myself down onto him. I cry out, surprised when he thrusts up suddenly, our bodies connecting and becoming one. His eyes flash open and lock onto mine, allowing me to watch them darken and glaze with lust until he can't resist from feeling any more. He throws his head back and closes his eyes at the sublime sensation as he fights his control—fights to push out the bad and focus solely on me and what I'm giving him. Comfort. Assurance. Physicality. Salvation. I watch the struggle as it flickers across his face, silently egging him on.

"Don't think, baby. Just feel me," I murmur against his ear as I slowly move and create the sensation needed to try and help him forget.

He exhales shakily before biting his bottom lip and bringing his hands down to roughly grip my hips. Colton rocks into me again, burying himself deeper than I ever thought possible. I whimper, so overwhelmed from feeling him tense so deep inside me.

The only reaction I can give him is to part my lips and say, "Take more from me. Take everything you need."

He cries out, restraint obliterated, and holds me still while he pistons his hips into me in a relentless, punishing rhythm. Our bodies, slick with water, slide easily against each other. The friction against my breasts heightens my ache for release. He flicks a tongue over a nipple, sliding it across my chilled skin before capturing the other one in his mouth.

I moan out in pleasure, accepting every forceful stroke from him. Allowing him to take so that he can find the release he needs to forget whatever haunts him. The volatility in his movements increases as he drives himself higher and higher, giving himself no other option but to forget. His grunts and the sound of our wet skin slapping against each other echoes off the shower walls.

"Come for me," I grate out as I slam back down on him. "Let go."

He quickens his tempo, his neck and face taut with purpose. "Oh fuck!" he yells out, crushing me against him with his powerful arms and burying his face in my neck as he finds his release. He rocks our joined bodies back and forth gently as he empties himself into me. The desperation in his strangling grip tells me I've given him only an iota of what he needs.

He sighs my name over and over, lacing absent kisses between them, his emotion transparent. His utter reverence coming on the heels of his earlier insults steals my breath and completely immobilizes me.

We sit like this for a couple of minutes so that he can take a moment to compose himself. It can't be easy for a stoic and always in control man like him to have a witness to such an emotional episode. He runs his fingers over the chilled skin of my back, the hot water running a few feet behind me sounding like Heaven.

When he finally speaks, it's of nothing we've just experienced. He keeps his head buried in my neck, refusing to meet my eyes. "You're cold."

"I'm fine."

Colton shifts and somehow manages to stand with my legs wrapped around him. "Stay right here," he tells me, placing me in the stream of warm water before leaving the shower. I look after him confused, wondering if his display of emotion was too much for him and now he needs some distance. I'm not sure.

He returns quickly, water still running in rivulets off of his skin. He takes me completely by surprise when he swoops me up in his arms, turns off the water with an elbow, and carries me out. I shriek as the cold air from the bathroom hits me. "Hold on," he murmurs against the top of my head at the same time I realize his intent.

Within moments he has stepped into the bathtub that is filling with water, and sets me on my feet. He sinks down in the overabundance of bubbles and tugs on my hand for me to follow. I lower myself, the blissful heat surrounding me as I settle between Colton's legs.

"Ah, this feels like Heaven."

I lean back into him, silence consuming us, and I know he's thinking about his dream and the aftermath. He traces absent lines up and down my arms, his fingertips trying to tame the goose bumps that still remain.

"Do you want to talk about it?" I ask, his body tensing against my back with my question.

"Just a nightmare," he finally says.

"Mmm-hmm." Like I believe it was a run of the mill monster chasing you down a dark alley type of dream.

I feel him open his mouth and close it against the side of my head before he speaks. "Just chasing my demons away." I reach my hands up and lace them with his, wrapping our joined hands across my torso. Silence stretches between us for a few moments.

"Shit." He exhales in a whoosh. "That hasn't happened in years."

I think he's going to say more, but he falls silent. I debate what to say next and choose my words very carefully. I know if I say it the wrong way, we might end up right back where we started. "It's okay to need somebody, Colton."

He emits a self-deprecating laugh and falls quiet as my remark weighs heavy between us. I wish I could see his face so I can judge whether or not to say my next words. *"It's okay to need me.* Everybody has moments. Nightmares can be brutal. I understand that better than most. No one's going to fault you for needing a minute to collect yourself. It's nothing to be ashamed of. I mean…I'm not going to run to the first tabloid I see and sell your secrets—*secrets I don't even know."*

His thumb absently rubs the back of my hand. "You wouldn't be here if I thought you'd do that."

I struggle with what to say next. He's hurting, I know, but he hurt me too. And I have to get some things off of my chest. "Look, you want to shut me out, that's fine…tell me you need a minute—that you need…" I falter, searching for something he'll relate to "…*to take a pit stop.* You don't have to hurt me and push me away in order to have some space."

He mutters a curse into the back of my hair, his heated breath warming my scalp. "You just wouldn't go." He exhales in exasperation. I'm about to respond when he continues, "And I needed you to go. I was terrified you'd see right through me and into me, Rylee, in the way that only you've been able to…and if you did, if you saw the things I've done…you'd never come back." His last comment is barely a whisper, so soft I have to strain to hear him. The words unzipping his hardened exterior and exposing the vulnerability beneath. The fear. The shame. The unfounded guilt.

So you tried to make sure my leaving was on your terms. Not mine. You had to have control. Had to hurt me so I wouldn't hurt you.

I know his confession is difficult. The man who needs no one—the man who pushes people away before they get too close—was afraid to lose me. My mind spins with thoughts. My heart squeezes with emotions. My lips struggle to find the right words to say. "Colton—"

"But you came back." The utter shock in his voice undoes me. The significance behind his admission hangs in the air. He tested me, tried to drive me away, and I'm still here.

"Hey, I've gone up against a teenager with a knife before…you're nothing," I tease, trying to lighten the mood. I expect a laugh but Colton just pulls me back and holds me tighter, as if he needs the reassurance of my bare skin against his.

He starts to say something and then clears his throat and stops, burying his face back into the curve of my neck. "You're the first person that's ever known about those dreams."

His bombshell of a confession rocks my mind. In all his therapy dealing with whatever it is that has happened to him, he's never talked to anyone about this? He's that hurt, that ashamed, that traumatized, that *whatever*, that for almost thirty years he has kept this festering inside of himself without any help? *My God.* My heart twists for the little boy growing up and for the man that sits behind me—so disturbed by whatever happened that he's kept it bottled up inside.

"What about your parents? Your therapists?"

Colton is silent, his body taut and unmoving, and I don't want to push the issue. I lean my head back on his shoulder and angle my face so it nuzzles into the side of his neck. I kiss the underside of his jaw softly and then rest my head down, closing my eyes, absorbing this quiet vulnerability from him.

"I thought…" He clears his throat as he tries to find his voice. He swallows harshly and I can feel his throat work beneath my lips. "I thought that if they knew about them—really knew the reasons behind why I had them—they wouldn't…" He stops for a moment, and I can feel the unease rolling off of him, as if the words are physically hard for him to utter. I press another kiss on his neck in silent reassurance. "They wouldn't want me anymore." He exhales slowly and I know the admission has cost him dearly.

"Oh, Colton." The words fall from my mouth before I can stop them, knowing full well the last thing he wants is my sympathy.

"Don't…" he pleads, "*Don't pity me—*"

"I'm not," I tell him, although my heart can't help but feel that way. "I'm just thinking how hard it must have been to be a little boy and feeling all alone without ever being able to talk about it…that's all." I fall silent, thinking that I've said and pushed hard enough on a topic he obviously doesn't want to address. But I can't help the next words that tumble from my lips. "You know you can talk to me." I murmur against his skin. His hands tense in mine. "I won't judge you or try to fix you, but sometimes just getting it out, getting rid of the hate or shame or *whatever* is eating you makes it a tad bit more bearable." I want to say so much more but forcibly tuck it away for another day, another time when he's a little less raw, a little less exposed. "I apologize," I whisper. "I shouldn't have—"

"No, I'm sorry," he says with an agitated sigh, leaning forward and kissing the shoulder he tagged with his elbow. "For so very much. For my words and my actions. For not dealing with my own shit." The regret in his voice is so resonating. "First I hurt you and then I was rough with you in the shower."

I can't help the smile that forms on my lips. "Not going to say that I minded."

He laughs softly and it's such a good sound to hear after the angst that filled it moments ago. "About your shoulder or about the shower?"

"Um, shower," I say, noting his attempt to digress from my comment and thinking that a change in topic is just what is needed to add a little levity to our extremely somber and intense morning.

"You surprise me at every turn."

"How so?"

"Did Max ever treat you this way?"

What? Where is he going with this? His comment takes me by surprise. When, I turn and face him, he just tightens his arms around my torso and pulls me closer. "What does that have to do with anything?"

"Did he?" he insists, the master of deflection.

"No," I admit contemplatively. Sensing I've relaxed some, he unlaces his fingers from mine and moves them back up to draw aimless lines on my arms. I look down at my hand and watch as I poke absently at the bubbles. "You were right."

"'Bout what?"

"The first time we met. You told me that my boyfriend must treat me like glass," I whisper, feeling like I'm betraying Max's memory. "You were right. He was a gentleman in every way. Even during sex."

"There's nothing wrong with that," Colton concedes, bringing his hands up to massage the base of my neck. I don't speak, shocked at myself for feeling how I do. "What is it? Your shoulders just tensed up."

I exhale a shuddered sigh, embarrassed at my train of thought. "I thought that was how it was supposed to be…that was what I wanted sex to be. He was my only experience. And now…"

"Now what?" he prompts with a hint of amusement in his voice.

"Nothing." Heat rushes into my cheeks.

"Rylee, talk to me for Christ's sake. I just fucked you in my shower like an animal. Used you basically for my own reprieve, and yet you can't tell me what you're thinking?"

"That's exactly it." I aimlessly draw circles down his thighs that cradle my sides, the admission tackling all of my modesty and throwing it to the ground. "*I liked it.* I never realized it could be different. That it could be so raw and…" *Oh my God I'm drowning here.* I don't think I even spoke to Max about sex like this, and we were together for over six years. I've known Colton less than a month, and we're discussing how I think it's a turn on to be manhandled. *Sweet fucking Jesus* as Colton would say.

"Carnal," he finishes for me, and I can hear a tinge of pride in his tone. He kisses the side of my head, and I shrug, embarrassed at my lack of experience and unfiltered admission. Sensing my discomfort, Colton squeezes me tighter. "There's no need to be embarrassed. Lots of people like it lots of different ways, sweetheart. There's a lot more out there to experience than just the missionary position with whispered sweet nothings." He breathes into my ear, and I wonder how even he can turn me on with that statement.

My mind flickers back to Colton demanding that I tell him that I want to be fucked our first time together. Of him pushing me to the brink by taking me hard and fast. Of him whispering the explicit things he wants to do to me when we have sex—lifting me up, pressing me against a wall, and grinding us toward release. Of how the knowledge of any and all of these things can cause me to ache with a need so intense that it unnerves me.

My cheeks flush at the thoughts, and I am grateful he can't see my face because he'd know exactly where my mind has wandered. I exhale a shaky sigh, trying to stifle my mortification at the direction of conversation and my own self-revelations.

"That's one of the things I like about you. You're so uninhibited."

What? I feel like looking around the room to see whom else he is talking to. "*Me?*" I croak.

"Mmm-hmm," he murmurs. "*You're amazing.*" His voice feathers over my cheek, the movement of his lips grazing my ear.

His words leave me motionless. He's echoed my thoughts of him despite the chaos and hurt from earlier. Maybe this combustible chemistry between us is because I possibly mean more than some of his others? He's sending me all of the signals to validate this claim, and yet hearing it would mean so much more.

He lathers his hands up with a bar of soap and then proceeds to run them over my arms and down the front of my chest. I suck in a breath as his fingertips slide lazily over the peaks of my breasts and his mouth licks its way up the curve of my shoulder. "I don't think I could ever get my fill of you." Proving my point exactly. *Words that say it but don't really say it.* "You're always so reserved, but when I'm in you…" he shakes his head, a low hum deep in his throat "…you lose all sense of everything, become mine, submit completely to me."

His words are a seduction on their own, never mind his thickening cock pressed up against the cleft of my backside. "How does that make me uninhibited?" I ask, angling my head back so I can rub against the coarse stubble on his jaw.

Colton's laugh is a low rumble that reverberates through my back. "Let's see...we'll put it in baseball analogies for you since you seem to be so keen on them. Almost third base in a public hallway. Twice." He chuckles. "Second base on a blanket at a beach." With each word I can feel my cheeks redden. "Homerun, pressed against the window of my bedroom," he pauses "...that overlooks a public beach."

"What?" I gasp. *Oh. Fucking. Hell.* What is it about him that makes me lose my head? My ass was pressed against a glass wall while we had sex, and anyone could have enjoyed the show. I think dying from humiliation is a viable option right now. I have no other choice but to shift the blame. "It's all your fault," I tell him as I push away and splash water at him.

A cocky grin lights up his face. It's a welcome sight from the haunted look from earlier. The dark and brooding bad boy has returned and is sitting across from me, knees and torso peeking out from above an overabundance of bubbles with a playful look on his face. Is it no wonder I've fallen for this man who's such a juxtaposition of characteristics and actions?

And fallen damned hard without a safety line to hold on to. *Fuck, I'm so seriously screwed.*

"How's that?" He splashes water back at me and catches my wrist in a quick grab when I try to retaliate. He pulls me toward him playfully, and I resist in turn. He gives up and I flop back, sloshing water out of the tub at all angles. We both erupt in a fit of laughter, bubbles floating through the air at my sudden movements. "I've been with plenty of women, sweetheart, and most aren't as sexually candid as you've been, so you can't blame me."

I'm glad that we're laughing when Colton makes his off the cuff remark because I can see him tense even though a smile remains on his face. I make a quick decision to remain playful despite the pang his remarks cause. I really don't want to think about the *plenty of women* he's been with, but I guess I can't ignore them either. Maybe I can use this slip of his to my advantage, get more information on my fate as well as make a little point of my own.

"Oh really?" I arch a brow and scoot closer, a smile playing on my lips. "Plenty of women, huh? Glad I can surprise such an experienced man such as yourself." I toy with him as I run my finger along the line of his throat and down between his pecs. His Adam's apple bobs as he swallows at my touch. "Tell me," I whisper suggestively as my hand dips beneath the water and rakes toward his already erect cock. "These plenty? How long do you usually keep them around for?"

He sucks in his breath as my fingers graze over the tip of his shaft. "This isn't the right time to—aarrgh!" He whimpers as my hand cups his balls and massages them gently.

"It's never the right time, but a girl's gotta know these things." I lower my mouth to suck on one of his flat nipples, tugging it gently with my teeth. He groans deeply, his mouth parting when I look up at him from beneath my lashes. "How long, Ace?"

"Rylee…" he pleads before I take his other nipple between my teeth at the same time I press the pleasure point just beneath his balls. "Four or five months," he pants out in response. I laugh seductively, hiding the jolt that tickles up my spine at knowing the clock is ticking on my time with him. I lick my tongue up the line of his neck and tug on his earlobe. "Ah…" He sighs when I trace it around the rim.

"Good to know…"

He remains silent, his shallow breath the only sound. "You play dirty."

"Someone once told me that sometimes you have to play dirty to get what you want." I breathe into his ear, repeating his words back to him. My nipples, chilled from the air, skim over the taut skin on his chest.

He chuckles low and deep, and his eyes alight with humor because he knows he's not the only one affected. I slide my other hand down his chest beneath the water, and I watch him watch my hand disappear. He looks back up at me and raises his eyebrows, curious as to where I'm going with this. When he just continues to stare at me, I grip the base of his shaft with one of my hands and twist it up and back on his length while the pad of my thumb on my other hand pays special attention to the crest. "Oh God that feels good, baby," he moans. The look he sends me smolders so intensely with need and lust it's enough to ignite my insides.

I stroke him a couple more times, enjoying this game I'm playing. Enjoying the fact that I can create such a visceral reaction from this man. I stop all motion and Colton's eyes that have closed partway in pleasure fly open to meet mine. I smirk slowly at him.

"Just one more thing…" I can see the confusion on his face, his jaw grinding as he silently begs for the pleasure to return.

Now that I've gotten his attention, I continue again, altering my grip and angle of stroke. Colton hisses out at the difference in sensation, his head falling back against the edge of the tub. I stop again and cup his balls in my hand.

"Look, I know you were upset, but if you ever treat me like you did this morning again..." I enunciate each word, the teasing humor in my tone gone as I gently squeeze my hand around him "...disrespect me, degrade, or push me away by humiliating me, understand now that I will not be coming back like I did today—regardless of your reasons, how I feel about you, or what's between us."

Colton meets my implacable stare and doesn't flinch at my threat. His mouth slides into a ghost of a smile. "Well it seems you have me by the balls both *literally and figuratively*, don't you now?" he taunts, mischief dancing in his eyes.

I squeeze him softly, fighting the smirk that wants to play at the corners of my mouth. "Is that understood? Non-negotiable."

"Crystal clear, sweetheart," he says to me, his eyes conveying the sincerity within his response. Satisfied he understands what I am telling him, I shift in the water and release my hold on his balls. Keeping my eyes locked on his, I slide my hands up to his rigid length and repeat the motion that rendered him agreeable moments before. Colton groans a long, drawn out, "Non-negotiable." And I don't respond to his answer because I am so turned on watching his reaction. "*Christ, woman,*" he grates out, grabbing my hips and pulling me toward him. "You like to play hardball, don't you?"

I accept his nudging and position myself over the top of his shaft. I lean forward, tunneling my fingers in his hair and place my cheek against his. As I lower myself at an achingly slow pace despite his hands urging me faster, I whisper in his ear, his own words back to him. "*Welcome to the big leagues, Ace.*"

Chapter Two

"Are you sure you can handle it?"

"Yes," he drolly calls out from the kitchen.

"Because if you can't, I can whip something up real quick."

"The image you just brought to my mind of you with a whip, high heels, and nothing else on is exactly what is going to prevent me from getting breakfast done." His laugh carries outside onto the deck where I sit.

"Okay, I'll just sit here quietly, enjoy the sun, and leave you with those images while I wait for my food."

I can hear the carefree note as he laughs again, and it lightens my heart. He seems to have tucked away the earlier nightmare and ensuing incident, but deep down, I know it's lingering just beneath the surface, always waiting patiently to remind him again of whatever atrocities he endured as a child. Nightmares. Shame. The overriding need for physicality with women. Memories so horrid he vomits with the reappearance of them. I can only hope the causes that flicker through my mind from my past work with other little boys with similar post-traumatic stress symptoms does not hold true for Colton.

I force myself to sigh away the sadness and soak up the welcome warmth of the early morning sunlight, to enjoy the fact that we've turned this morning around from the disaster that it began with. I can only hope that maybe, in time, Colton will trust me enough to open up and feel comfortable talking to me. Then again, who am I to think that I'll be the special one and make a difference in a man who's emotionally isolated himself from everyone for so long?

The speakers on the terrace come to life around me, and Baxter lifts his head momentarily before plopping it back down. Stretched out on the chaise lounge, I watch the early bird exercisers on the beach. I guess it's not that early now after our diversion in the bathtub. I swear I don't know what came over me and prompted me to act that way. That is so not me, but it sure was fun making Colton putty in my hands. And when all was said and done, with the bathwater growing cold, he made sure that my whole body ended up just as boneless as his.

And then there's the down side to our whole bathtub time. His admission that his average shelf life with a woman is four or five months. *Shit.* Tawny might be right. He's going to get bored with me and my lack of bedroom prowess. I shrug away the notion time is running out for me. The thought causes my breath to catch and panic to fill my every nerve. I can't lose him. I can't lose how I feel when I'm with him. He means too much to me already, and that's with me trying to be reserved in my emotions.

Jared Leto sings about being closer to the edge. I close my eyes thinking how I already have both feet over and beyond that edge that Colton has explicitly explained he does not want to teeter on. But how can I not plummet off it when he makes me feel so incredibly good. I try to rationalize that it's just the incredible—and it's mind-blowingly incredible—sex that's making me feel these insane feelings after only knowing each other for three weeks. And I know that sex does not equate love.

I need to remind myself of this. Over and over and over to prevent the fall.

But his words, his actions, tell me that I'm just more than an arrangement to him. They all flicker through my head—different things over the past three weeks—and I just can't see him not thinking that there are definite possibilities here. If not, then he has me fooled.

Matt Nathanson's voice fills the air around me, and I hum along to *Come on Get Higher*, my thoughts scattered and disjointed, but oddly content.

"Voila!"

I open my eyes to see Colton lower a plate onto the table beside me, and when I see its contents, I laugh loudly. "It's perfect, sir, and I so appreciate the depths of your fine culinary skills." I reach over and take a bite of my toasted bagel and cream cheese and moan dramatically in appreciation. "Delicious!"

He bows theatrically, obviously pleased with himself, and plops down beside me. "Thank you. Thank you." He laughs, grabbing a half off of the plate and taking a large bite of it. He leans back on an elbow, washboard abs bare and board shorts riding low on his hips. The sight of him is enough of a meal in itself.

We eat, playfully teasing each other, and I silently wonder what's next. As much as I don't want to, I think I need to get home and put some distance between the two of us before the night we've spent together and the feelings it solidified accidentally come stumbling out of my mouth.

"I told you to leave them," Colton says from behind me as I wash the dish in my hand. "Grace will get them or I'll clean them up later."

"It's no biggie."

"Yes it is," he whispers into my neck, sending an electric pulse straight to my sex as he slides his arms around my waist and pulls me backwards against him.

God, how I could get used to this. I'm grateful he can't see the look on my face that I'm sure is one of complete satisfaction. Adoration. Contentment.

"Thank you, Rylee." His voice is so quiet I almost miss the words over the noise of the water.

"It's one dish and a knife, Colton. Really."

"No, Rylee. Thank. You." His words are swamped with sentiment— a man drowning in unfamiliar emotions.

I set the plate down and turn off the water so I can hear him. So I can allow him the moment to express whatever it is he needs to say. I may not be very experienced when it comes to men, but I know enough that in the rare instances that they want to talk about feelings or emotions, it's time to be quiet and listen.

"For what?" I ask casually.

"For this morning. For letting me work through my shit the way I needed to. For letting me use you for lack of a better term." He moves my ponytail off of the back of my neck and places a soft kiss there. "For letting me have mine and for you not complaining when you didn't get yours."

His words, the thoughtfulness behind them, has me biting my lip to prevent me from making that verbal pitfall I was worried about earlier. I take a second to think of my next words so I don't take that stumble.

"Well, you more than made up giving me *mine* in the bathtub."

"Oh really?" He nuzzles that sensitive spot just beneath my ear that drives me crazy. "That's good to know, but I still think I might need to further remedy the unsettled situation from earlier."

"Really?"

"Mmm-hmm."

"You are insatiable, Colton." I laugh, turning in his arms to have my lips captured in a tantalizing kiss that funnels sparks all the way to the tips of my toes. His hands map themselves down my torso and over my backside, pressing me into him.

"Now let's talk about that image I can't get out of my head of you with a whip and wearing only bright red stilettos." The wicked smile on his lips has the heat flowing from my toes back up.

"Ahem!" The clearing of a throat has me jumping back from Colton like I've been singed by fire.

I snap my head up, warmth burning through my cheeks when I hear Colton shout out, "Hey, old man!" and then embrace whoever it is in a huge bear hug. They have turned, hugging so fiercely that I can only see Colton's face, his pleasure evident.

I catch murmured words in gruff tones as they hold on to each other, hands slapping each other's backs, and when I think I know who it is, my blush deepens at the knowledge that he overheard what Colton had said to me. My hunch is confirmed when the two break apart and the visitor places a hand on the side of Colton's face and stares at him intently, concern etched on his face over something he sees in his son's eyes.

"You okay, son?"

Colton holds his father's stare for a moment, the muscle in his jaw pulsing as he reins in the emotions playing over his face. After a beat he nods his head subtly, a soft smile turning up the corners of his mouth. "Yeah...I'm okay, Dad," he acquiesces before glancing over to me and then back to his dad.

They draw each other into another quick man-hug of loud back slapping before they part, and the clear, gray eyes of Andy Westin dart over to me and then back to Colton, love and I think surprise bordering on shock reflected in them.

"Dad, I want you to meet Rylee." Colton clears his throat. "Rylee Thomas."

The woman you will forever think of in correlation with red stilettos and a whip. *Lovely.* Can I die now?

Andy mirrors my step forward and reaches out a hand to me. I try to

18

act calm, to pretend like I'm not in front of a Hollywood legend who has just caught me in a compromising situation, and when I see the warmth mixed with disbelief in his eyes, I relax some. "Pleased to meet you, Rylee."

I smile softly, meeting his eyes as I shake his hand. "Likewise, Mr. Westin."

He's not big in stature like I expected, but something about him makes him seem larger than life. It's his smile that captivates me. A smile that could make the hardest of people soften.

"Pshaw, don't be silly," he scolds, releasing my hand and brushing his salt and pepper hair off his forehead, "call me Andy." I smile at him in acceptance as he shifts his gaze back to Colton, a bemused look in his eyes and a pleased smile on his face. "I didn't mean to interrupt anything—"

"You didn't," I blurt out. Colton turns to me, an eyebrow arched at my staunch denial, and I'm grateful when he lets it go without correcting me.

"Nonsense, Rylee. My apologies." Andy glances over at Colton again and gives him an indiscernible look. "I've been on location for work in Indonesia for the past two months. I got back late last night and wanted to see my boy here." He pats Colton on the back heartily, and his obvious love for his son makes me like him that much more. And even sweeter than Andy's adoration of his son is Colton's reciprocation. Colton's face lights up with complete reverence as he watches his father. "Anyway, I'm sorry I barged in. Colton never has..." he clears his throat "...Colton is usually out on the deck alone, recovering from whatever the chaos the night before has brought upon him." He laughs.

"You two obviously haven't seen each other in a while, so don't let me get in your way. I'm going to go grab my purse and I'll be on my way." I smile politely and then frown when I realize that I don't have my car to drive.

Colton smirks at me, realizing my oversight. "Dad, I've got to drive Rylee home. Do you want to hang here or I can stop by the house later?"

"Take your time. I've got some stuff to do. Stop by later if you get the chance, son." Andy turns toward me, an inviting smile warm on his lips. "It was very nice meeting you, Rylee. I hope to see you again."

The drive home from Malibu is beautiful as is expected, but the cloud cover starts to move in and smother the coastline the closer we get to Santa Monica. We talk about this and that, nothing serious, but at the same time I sense that Colton is distancing himself a bit from me. It's nothing he says per se, but it's more what's not said.

He's not rude, just quiet, but it's noticeable. Those little touches are absent. The knowing looks and soft smiles gone. The playful banter silenced.

I assume that he's taking the drive to think about his dream, so I leave him to his thoughts and stare out the window watching the coastline fly by. The radio's on low and the song, *Just Give Me a Reason* by Pink plays softly in the background as we exit the highway and head toward my house. I sing softly, the words making me think about this morning, and as I hit the chorus, I notice Colton glance over at me in my periphery. I know when he hears the lyrics because he shakes his head and the slightest of smiles graces his lips; his silent acknowledgement of my knack for finding the perfect song to express my feelings.

We remain in a contemplative silence for a bit longer until Colton finally speaks. "So um, I've got a crazy busy schedule the next two weeks." He glances over at me momentarily, and I nod at him before he looks back at the stoplight in front of us. "I've got a commercial to shoot for the Merit endorsement, an interview with Playboy, um…Late Night with Kimmel, and a whole lot of other shit," he says as the light turns green. "And that doesn't include all of the dog-and-pony shows coming up for the sponsorship with you guys."

I take no offense to the comment because I'm not too thrilled with the dog-and pony- show junket either. "Well that's good, right? Publicity is always good."

"Yeah." I can tell he's irritated at the thought as he slips his sunglasses on. "Tawn's doing a great job garnering press this year. It's good and all…and I'm grateful that there's the attention, but the more shit there is, the less time I have on the track. And that's where I need to concentrate my time with the season right around the fucking corner."

"Understandably," I tell him, unsure what else to say as we pull onto my street, unable to help the smug smile that tugs at the corners of my mouth. It's been a profound twenty-four hours with Colton. He's let me into his personal world some, and that counts for something. Our sexual chemistry remains off the charts, and I think it actually intensified after our night together. I told him about Max, and he listened with compassion and without passing judgment.

Then we had this morning. An hour filled with poisonous words and overwhelming emotions.

And not once did he mention his idiotic arrangement to me. How he'll only accept less when I'll only accept more; we find ourselves at a proverbial impasse despite his actions expressing the exact opposite.

Maybe my smile reflects my optimism over the possibilities between us. That Colton's unspoken words speak just as much to me as his spoken ones do.

I sigh as we pull into the driveway, and Colton opens the door for me. He offers me a tight smile before placing his hand on the small of my back and directing us up my front walkway. I struggle to figure out what his silence is saying, to not read into it too much.

"Thank you for a great night," I tell him as I turn to face him on the front porch, a shy smile on my lips, "and..." I let the word drift off as I figure out how to address today.

"A fucked up morning?" he finishes for me, regret heavy in his voice and shame swimming in his eyes.

"Yes, that too," I admit softly as Colton turns his attention to the absent fiddling with the ring of keys in his hand. "But we got through it..."

His gaze fixates on his keys, his eyes never lifting to meet mine when he speaks. "Look, I'm sorry." He sighs, shoving a hand through his hair. "I just don't know how to—"

"Colton, it's okay," I tell him, lifting my hand to squeeze his bicep— some form of touch to let him know I've said my piece about this morning and my lack of tolerance of it happening again.

"No, it's not okay." He finally lifts his head up, and I can see the conflicting emotions in his eyes, can feel the indecision of his thoughts. "You don't deserve to have to deal with this...with all my shit," he murmurs quietly, almost as if he's trying to convince himself of his own words. And I realize that his internal struggle has to do with so much more than just this morning.

His eyes swim with regret, and he reaches out to tuck a loose lock of hair behind my ear as I search his face to try and understand his unspoken words. "Colton, what are you—"

21

"Look at what I did to you this morning. The things I said. How I hurt you and pushed you away? That's me. That's what I do. I don't know how to—*shit!*" he grits out before turning and looking out toward the street where a teenager is making his way down the sidewalk. I focus on the thunk-thunk of his wheels as they hit the lines in the sidewalk panels while I process what Colton is saying. He turns back around and the lines etched in his striking features cause me to close my eyes momentarily and take a deep breath to prepare for what's coming next. For what I see written on his resigned expression.

"I care for you, Ry. I care about you." He shakes his head, the muscle in his jaw pulsing as he clenches his jaw, trying to find the right words. "I just don't know how to be..." He stumbles through words trying to get out what he wants to say. "You at least deserve someone that's going to try to be that for you."

"Try to be *what* for me, Colton?" I ask taking a step closer as he takes a step back, unwilling to allow him to break our connection. My bewilderment in regards to his confusing statements does nothing to squash the unease that creeps into the pit of my stomach and crawls up to squeeze at my heart. I part my lips and breathe in deeply.

His discomfort is apparent and I want nothing more than to reach out and wrap my arms around him. Reassure him with the physical connection he seems to need more than anything. He looks down again and blows out a breath in frustration while I suck one in.

"You at least deserve someone that's going to try to be what you need. Give you what you want...and I don't think I'm capable of that." He shakes his head, eyes fixed on his damn keys. The raw honesty in his words causes my heart to lodge in my throat. "Thank you for being you...for coming back this morning."

He finally says something I can latch on to, a diving board I have to jump from. "That's exactly right!" I tell him. Using one of his moves, I reach out and lift his chin up so he's forced to meet my eyes, so he's forced to see that I'm not scared of the way he is. That I can be strong enough for the both of us while he works through the shit in his head. "I came back. For you. For me. For who we are when we're together. For the possibilities of what we can be if you'll just let me in..."

I run my hand over the side of his cheek and cradle it there. He closes his eyes at my touch. "It's just too much, too fast, Rylee." He breathes and opens his eyes to meet mine. The fear there is heartbreaking. "For so long I've...your selflessness is so consuming that it..." he struggles, reaching up to take my hand framing his face in his own. "I can't give you what you need because I don't know how to live—to feel—to breathe—if I'm not broken. And being with you? You deserve someone that's whole. I just can't..."

The words to the song from the car flash into my mind, and they are out before I can stop myself. "No, Colton. No." I tell him, making sure his eyes are on mine. *"You're not broken, Colton. You're just bent."*

Despite my saying it with serious intent, Colton belts out a self-deprecating laugh at the apropos corniness of me using a song lyric to try and express myself. He shakes his head at me. "Really, Ry? A song lyric?" he asks, and I just shrug at him, willing to try anything to break him out of this rut he keeps returning to. I watch as his smile fades and the concern returns to his eyes. "I just need time to process this...you...it's just too..."

I can feel his pain and rather than just stand there and watch it manifest in his eyes, I opt to give him what he needs to confirm our connection. I step up to him and brush my lips against his. Once. Twice. And then I slip my tongue between his lips and connect with his. He won't hear the words, so I need to show him with this. With fingertips whispering over his jaw and up through his hair. With my body pressed tight against him. With my tongue dancing with his in a lazy, decadent kiss.

He slowly lets go of the tension in his body as he accepts and gives in to the feeling between us. The desire. The need. The truth. His hands slide up to cup the sides of my face, thumbs brushing tenderly over my cheeks. Rough to soft, just like the two of us. He places a last, lingering kiss on my lips and then rests his forehead onto mine. We sit there for a moment, eyes closed, breath feathering over one another, and souls searching.

I feel settled. Content. Connected.

"Pit stop," he whispers against my lips.

The words come out of nowhere, and I jolt at their sound. *Come again?* I try to pull back to look at him, but he keeps a firm grip on my head and holds me against him, forehead to forehead. I'm not sure how to respond. My heart's unable to follow the path he's just chosen while my head is already five steps ahead of him.

"A pit stop?" I say slowly as my thoughts race one hundred miles per hour.

He eases his hold on my head, and I lean back so I can look at him, but he refuses to meet my eyes. "It's either a pit stop or I tell you that Sammy will drop by a set of keys for the house in the Palisades and we meet there from here on out," he slowly lifts his eyes to meet mine "...to keep the lines from getting fuzzy."

I hear him speak the words but don't think I actually listen to them. I can't comprehend them. Did he just actually tell me that after last night—after this morning—he's going to pull this shit on me? Push me back in to the *arrangement* category of his life.

So this is how it's going to go? *Fucking hell, Donavan.* I take a step back, needing the distance from his touch, and we stand in silence staring at each other. I look at the man that broke down in front of me earlier and is trying to distance himself from me now, trying to regain his isolated state of self-preservation. His request stings but I refuse to believe him, refuse to believe that he feels nothing for me. Maybe this all spooked him—someone too close when he's used to being all alone. Maybe he's using his fallback and trying to hurt me, put me in my place, so I can't hurt him in the long run. I so desperately want to believe that's what this is about, but it's so hard to not let that niggling doubt twist its way into my psyche.

I hope he can see the disbelief in my eyes. The shock on my face. The temerity in my posture. I start to process the hurt that's surfacing—the feeling of rejection lingering on the fringe—when it hits me.

He's trying.

He may be telling me he needs a break, but he's also telling me I have an option. I either give him the space he needs to process whatever's going on in his head or I can choose the arrangement route. He's telling me he wants me here as a part of his life—for now anyway—but he's just overwhelmed by everything.

He's trying. Instead of pushing me away and purposely hurting me to do so, he's asking me—using a term I told him to use if he needs some space—so I can understand what he's requesting.

I push down the hurt and the dejection that bubbles up because regardless of my acknowledgement, his proverbial slap still stings. I take a deep breath, hoping the pit stop he's asking for is the result of a flat tire and not because the race is almost over.

"Okay." I let the word roll over my tongue. "*A pit stop it is then,*" I offer up to him, resisting the urge to wrap my arms around him and use the physicality of it to reassure myself.

He reaches out and brushes a thumb over my bottom lip, his eyes a depth of unspoken emotions. "Thank you," he whispers to me, and for just a second, I see it flash in his eyes. *Relief.* And I wonder if it's because he's relieved I chose pit stop over an arrangement or because he gets to walk away right now without being pushed any further.

"Mmm-hmm," is all I can manage as tears clog in my throat.

Colton leans forward and I close my eyes momentarily as he brushes a reverent kiss on my nose. "Thank you for last night. For this morning. *For this*." I just nod my head, not trusting myself to speak as he runs his hand down the length of my arm and squeezes my hand. He pulls back a fraction, his eyes locking on mine. "I'll call you, okay?"

I just nod my head again at him. He'll call me? When? In a couple of days? A couple of weeks? Never? He leans forward and grazes my cheek with a kiss. "Bye, Ry."

"Bye," I say, barely a whisper of sound. He squeezes my hand one more time before turning his back and walking down the walkway. Pride over the small step he took today tinged with a flash of fear fills me as I watch him climb in the Range Rover, pull out of the driveway, and until he turns the corner from my sight.

I shake my head and sigh. Taylor Swift's definitely right. Loving Colton is like driving a Maserati down a dead end street. And with what he just said to me, I feel like I just slammed into it head first..

Chapter Three

Haddie and I have been like ships passing in the night the past couple of days, but she is awfully curious as to my cryptic notes about my night with Colton. I'm still confused as hell at what happened between leaving Colton's house and arriving at my doorstep. The two differing vibes have left me confused and moody and desperate to see him again, see if what I thought was between us was real or if I'd imagined it. At the same time, I'm angry and hurt and my heart aches at what I want so badly to be but am afraid never will. I have over-thought and over-analyzed every second of our drive home, and the only conclusion is that our connection unnerves him. That my willingness to return when all others would have run scares him. And even with that knowledge, the past few days have been unsettling. I've shed a few tears from my doubts and Matchbox Twenty has been on repeat on my iPod. It has also helped that I have a job where I have to work twenty-four hour shifts to occupy my time.

I take a sip of my Diet Coke, singing along to *Stupid Boy*, and finish adding ingredients to the salad when I hear the front door slam. I can't fight the smile that spreads on my lips when I realize just how much I've missed Haddie these past few days. She has been so busy working on projects for a new client that PRX is trying to land she's basically been sleeping at the office.

"My goodness, I've missed you, silly girl!" she announces as she comes into the kitchen and wraps her arms around me in soul-warming hug.

"I know." I hand her a glass of wine. "Dinner's almost ready. Go get changed and get your butt back here so we can catch up."

"And you better not hold back on me," she warns with one of her looks before leaving the kitchen.

Our dinner has been eaten, and I think we are on our second or third bottle of wine. The fact that I've lost track tells me it's been enough for me to relax and tell Haddie everything. Her no-holds-barred responses to my replay of events have left me gasping for breath from laughing so hard.

As *Should I Stay* plays softly on the speakers around us, Haddie leans back against the chair behind her and stretches her legs out on the floor. Her perfectly manicured toes are a bright pink. "So, have you talked to him since then?"

"No. He's texted me a couple of times, but I've only given him one word responses." I shrug, not having any more clarity after relaying everything to her. "I think he might have a clue I'm hurt about something but he hasn't asked."

Haddie snorts loudly. "C'mon, Ry, he's a guy! Which means first of all he has no clue and, secondly, he's not going to ask even if he does think you're pissed."

"True," I concede, giggling. The aura of sadness that's been around me for the past few days continues to dissipate with my laughter.

"But that's no excuse for him being a dick," she says loudly, raising her glass up.

"I wouldn't exactly call him a dick," I argue, silently chastising myself for defending the one person that is responsible for my current confused and miserable state. Haddie just arches an eyebrow at me, a smarmy smirk on her face. "I mean, I am the one who told him to take a pit stop if he needed to deal with things instead of push me away. I just don't understand how he's kissing me one minute and then the next minute asking for one."

"Let me think about it a minute," she says, a look of amused concentration on her face. "My head's a little fuzzy from all this wine."

I giggle at her and the determined look on her face as she tries to work through everything. "Okay, okay, I got it," she shouts victoriously. "I think that…hmmm…I think that you freaked him the fuck out, Rylee!"

I throw my head back laughing hysterically at her. A drunk Haddie means a fouled mouth Haddie. "That's very astute, Had!"

"Wait, wait, wait!" She throws her hands up and luckily her wine doesn't slosh over the side. "I mean from what you've told me, you opened up to him, you talked about stuff, he fucked you seven ways from Sunday—"

I have to stop myself from spitting my wine out of my mouth at her last words. "Jesus, Haddie!"

"*Well, it's true!*" She shouts at me like I'm a dumbass, holding my gaze until I nod my head in compliance. "Anyway, back to what I was saying…you guys were flirty and fun and serious and had a great time. He found himself liking you in his surroundings. He saw himself being okay with you in his element. And then in walks his Dad. Having someone else see you there…with him…made it real for him. All of it combined probably freaked Mr. I-Only-Do-Casual out, Rylee!"

I eye her over the rim of my glass, adjusting my knees that are pulled up to my chest. Her words ring true to me, but it doesn't dissipate the hurt I feel. The ache that only reassurances from him can soothe. I need to do a better job of guarding my heart and pulling back more. I need to not give so freely to him when he isn't in return.

"God," I groan, laying my head on the back of the couch. "I've never been this wishy-washy in my life over something like I am over him. I'm driving myself crazy sitting here whining like one of those chicks I swore I'd never be. The ones we make fun of. " I sigh. "*Shoot me now!*"

Haddie giggles at me. "You are kind of all over the place when it comes to him. Shit, the two of you are giving me fucking whiplash."

I continue to stare at the ceiling, expressing my agreement of Haddie's unsolicited opinion by giving a non-committal grunt before I lift my head back up and look at her. "You're probably right about the freaking out part," I muse, taking a sip to drain the rest of my glass, "but in all fairness, he told me from the start that he couldn't give me more."

"*Screw fairness!*" she shouts, raising her middle finger emphatically.

I laugh out loud at her. "I know, but it's my own damn fault for falling in lov—"

"I knew it!" She jumps up, pointing at me. I close my eyes and shake my head, cursing myself for slipping. "Shit, I need some more wine after that revelation!" She starts to walk past me and then steps back to look me in the eye. "Listen, Ry, have you cried over this? Over him?"

Uh-oh! She has her "I'm going to get to the bottom of this" look on her face. I just stare at her and my silence is enough of an answer. "Listen. I know he looks like a damn Adonis and probably fucks like a stallion, but, sweetie, if he's what you want, then it's time to make him sweat a little."

I snort at her. "That may be easy for you. You've played these games before, but I have absolutely no fucking clue what to do."

"You turn the tables on him. You've shown him what life's like when you're around…now that he's into you, you need to show him what it's like when you're not. Let him know that he's not your every breath or thought—even if it fucking kills you." She sits on the arm of the chair and stares at me. "Look, Ry, *every guy wants to be him and every girl wants to fuck him.* He's used to being wanted. Used to people pursuing him. You need to act like you did in the beginning—before you went and fell in love with the bastard—and let him chase you." I just stare at her, shaking my head at her frankness. She tilts her heads and twists her lips up as she thinks. "I know he made you cry, but is he worth it, Rylee? I mean really worth it?"

I stare at her, tears pooling in my eyes, and I nod my head. "Yeah, he is, Haddie. He…he has this side to him that is the exact opposite of the brooding, bad boy player the media portrays him as. He's sincere and sweet. I mean it's more than just the sex." I shrug, a smile tugging at the corners of my mouth when she arches her eyebrow at me. "And yes, *it's really that good—*"

"I knew it!" she shouts and points her finger at me. "You've been holding out on me!"

"Shut up!" I shout back, giggling along with her. She stands, wobbling a bit before grabbing my empty glass.

"C'mon, spill the deets for dried up old me. How's his Aussie kiss? How many times did he make you come when you went to his house?"

I blush a deep crimson, loving and hating her at the same time. "*Aussie kiss?* What in the hell are you talking about?"

She lets out a naughty laugh and has an impish gleam in her eyes. "How's his mouth *down under?*" she laughs, deliberately looking down at my crotch and then back up at me with a raised eyebrow. I just stare at her with my mouth agape and a giggle I can't help bubbling out. "Let me live vicariously through you. *Pretty please?*"

I squeeze my eyes shut in embarrassment, unable to look at her. "Well I'd say he speaks Australian like a damn native."

"I knew it!" she yells, wiggling her ass in a little victory dance around the family room. "And…" she prompts.

"And what?" I play stupid.

"His stamina, baby. I need to know if he deserves the Adonis label in more than just the looks department. How many times?"

I twist my lips as I mentally run through the various times and places Colton and I had sex. "Hmmm…I don't know, eight times maybe? Or nine? I lost count."

Haddie stops mid-dance and her mouth falls open before spreading into a wicked grin. "And you were able to walk? You little vixen. Good for you!" She turns and teeters before heading toward the kitchen to grab another bottle of wine. "Fuck, I'd put up with a whole lot of shit from a guy if he can perform like that. I guess I was right about the stallion part," she teases from the kitchen, making a horse neighing sound that has me doubled over in laughter.

My phone rings and for the first time in several days. I don't jump up to get it. I've had enough to drink and have had enough false alarms that I know it's not Colton. Besides, according to Haddie I need to make him sweat a little.

Easier said than done. My resolve lasts two rings before I start to get up, stumbling in my inebriated state. I tell myself that I'm not answering it. No way. Haddie will kill me. *But*...even if I'm not going to answer it, I still want to see who it is.

"Well if it isn't the man of the hour," I hear Haddie say as she beats me to it and reads the screen of my phone. I stare at her with confusion as she flips on the stereo and picks up my phone to answer it.

This is not going to be pretty. Haddie drunk and being protective of me is not a good combination. "Give me the phone, Had," I say but know it's no use. *Oh fuck!*

"Rylee's phone, can I help you?" She shouts as if she's in a club, her voice rising with each word. She grins at me and raises her eyebrows while he must be speaking on the other end. "Who? Who? Oh, hey, Colby! Oh, I'm sorry. I thought you were Colby. Who? Oh, hiya, Colton, this is Haddie. Rylee's roommate? Mmm-hmm. Well look, she's a little drunk right now and a lot busy, so she can't talk to you, but I'd like to." She laughs loudly at something he says. "So here's the deal. I don't know you very well, but from what I do, you seem like a decent guy. A little too much in the press from your shenanigans if you ask me as you make jobs like mine a little harder, but hey, no press is bad press, right? But I digress..." She laughs, making a non-committal sound at Colton's response. "Wine for starters, but now we've moved on to shots," she answers him. "Tequila. Anyway, I just wanted to tell you that you really need to get your shit together when it comes to Rylee."

I think my mouth just fell to the floor. I wish I could see the look on Colton's face right now. Or maybe I don't want to.

"Yes, I was talking to you, Colton. I. Said. You. Need. To. Get. Your. Shit. Together." She emphasizes each word. "Rylee's a game changer, babe. You better not let her slip through your fingers or someone else is going to snatch her right out from under your nose. And from the looks of the sharks circling tonight, you better kick that fine ass of yours into high gear."

I'm so glad that I've had a lot to drink because if not, I would be dying of mortification right now. But the alcohol does nothing to diminish my pride in Haddie. The woman is fearless. Regardless of how I feel, I still glare at her and hold out my hand asking for my phone. She turns her back to me and continues making agreeable sounds to Colton.

"Like I said, she's quite busy right now, choosing which guy will buy her next drink, but I'll let her know you called. Uh-huh, yes. I know, but I just thought you ought to know. Game. Changer." She enunciates and laughs. "Oh and, Colton? If you make her fall, you better make damned certain you catch her. Hurting her is not an option. Understood? Because if you do hurt her, you'll have to answer to me, and I can be a raving bitch!" She laughs deviously. "Good night, Colton. I hope to see you around once you figure your shit out. Cheers!" Haddie looks over at me, a smug smile on her face as she switches off the stereo.

"Haddie Marie, I could kill you right now!"

"You think that now." She snickers, the neck of the wine bottle clinking against the rim of our glasses as she refills them. "But just you wait and see. You'll be kissing my boots when this pans out."

We finish our wine quotient for the night and are sitting on the couch, mellow, relaxed, and a little drunk, talking about the other events of the week. The local eleven o'clock news is wrapping up on low in the background when a spot for what's next on Jimmy Kimmel Live runs. I'm listening to Haddie when we both hear Colton's name mentioned as a guest. Our heads snap up and we stare at each other in surprise. With the events of the past couple of days, I'd completely forgotten his mentioning it to me.

"Well this will be interesting." She raises her eyebrows at me as she shifts her focus to the television.

We watch the opening monologue, and although the jokes are funny, I don't laugh. Maybe it's the somberness from too much wine or the apprehension of what's to come, but Jimmy's just not making me laugh. I know that Jimmy will mention the array of women on Colton's arm, and I'm not in the right frame of mind to hear it tonight.

"So our next guest is, how do I describe him? A master of many talents? *A man in the driver's seat?* Let's just say he's one of Indy's brightest talents—being listed as the driver to bring the circuit back into the spotlight—and one of Hollywood's hottest bachelors. Please give a warm welcome to the one and only Colton Donavan." The crowd in the studio erupts into a frenzy of female screeches with a few mixed in *I love yous.*

I suck in a breath as Colton walks out on stage in a pair of black jeans and a dark green button up shirt. Every part of my body leans forward in my seat as I drink him in. Study him. Miss him. The camera is at a distant angle, but I know firsthand the effect that his shirt will have on his eyes. How it will darken the circle of emerald around the exterior of the iris, leaving the center almost a translucent light green. He waves to the crowd as he walks, his megawatt smile in place.

Haddie makes a soft noise in the back of her throat. "Damn. That face is a definite work of art. You need to make sure you frame it between your legs every chance you get."

I choke on my drink as I look over at her and catch the wink she gives me. I burst out laughing. "Where in the hell do you come up with this stuff?"

"I have my sources." She shrugs with a naughty smirk on her lips.

I just laugh at her and shake my head as I turn my focus back to the interview. As Colton rounds the desk, one of Jimmy's papers flies off of it, and Colton bends over to pick it up. The slew of women in the audience go ballistic at the sight of Colton's ass in tight jeans, and Haddie laughs out loud. Colton turns around, shaking his head at the audience and their reaction.

"Well that's a way to make an entrance!" Jimmy exclaims.

"Was that planned?" Colton asks as he plays to the audience.

"No. There was such a large whoosh of air from the exhales of your female fans in here that they blew that paper off the desk."

The audience laughs and a woman screams, "Marry me, Colton!" I want someone to tell her to stick a sock in it.

"Thank you." Colton chuckles. "But none of that will be happening for a while."

"And the audience keels over in sorrow." Jimmy laughs. "So, how's it going man? Good to see you again. What's it been? A year?"

"Something like that," Colton says, leaning back in his chair and crossing his ankle over his opposing knee. The camera pans in for a close up of his face, and I breathe deeply. I don't think I'll ever get used to how striking he is.

"How do you not just stare at him all day when you're with him?" Haddie asks. I smile but don't respond. I'm too busy watching. "My God he's fine." She groans in appreciation.

"And how's your family?"

"They're doing good. My dad just got back a couple of days ago from being on location in Indonesia so I got to catch up with him, which as you know is always a good time."

"Yes, he's quite the character." Colton laughs at the comment and Jimmy continues. "For those of you who don't know, Colton's dad is Hollywood legend, Andy Westin."

"Let's not give him a big head by using the word *legend*," Colton says as Jimmy holds up a picture of his dad with his arm around him at some event. "There he is," he smiles with sincerity.

"So what have you been up to lately?"

"Just getting ready for the upcoming season to start. First race is at the end of March in St. Petersburg, so we're getting ramped up for that right now."

"How's the car running?"

"It's looking good so far. The guys are working hard to get it dialed in."

"That's great. Now tell me about your new sponsors this year."

Colton rattles off names of several of his advertisers. "And we picked up a new one this year in Merit Rum."

"Smooth rum," Jimmy says.

"Yeah, I can't complain about getting paid to drink good alcohol," Colton smiles, rubbing his thumb and forefingers over his shadowed jaw.

"I think we have a snippet of your new commercial for them."

I whip my head up to look at Haddie. "Have you seen it yet?"

"No." She looks as surprised as I do. "I've been so busy on this new client I haven't even caught up to speed with our other accounts."

"We just shot this the other day," Colton says.

The screen fills with Colton zipping his Indy car across a track, the Merit Rum logo splashed across his car's nose. His sexy rasp of a voice overlaying the scene. "When I race, I drive to win." The scene switches to him playing football on the beach with a bunch of other guys. Bikini clad women are on the sidelines cheering them on with drinks in their hands. He's shirtless with a pair of low-slung board shorts on. His chiseled torso is misted in sweat, sand sticking in some patches here and there, and an arrogant grin is on his face. He stretches out, dives for a pass, and catches it as he crashes into the sand. His voice says,

"When I play, I always play hard." The commercial switches to a scene in a nightclub. Lights blaze and the crowd dances. Shots flash across the television. Colton laughing. Colton holding a drink and taking a sip while relaxing in a booth surrounded by gorgeous women. A shot of whom you assume is Colton dancing among a couple of women because all the screen shows is hands on hips, fingers gripping in hair, and mouths meeting in a kiss. The camera switches to a picture of Colton, his arm wrapped around the waist of a beautiful woman, the camera filming at their backs as they leave the club. He turns and looks over his shoulder, a smirk on his face saying "you know what happens next." The camera cuts to an empty Merit Rum bottle on the table at the club. "And when I party?" Colton's voice says, "I only drink the best. Merit Rum. *Like no other.*"

"Wow." Haddie breathes. "The ad turned out great."

I know she's looking at it from strictly a public relations perspective, and she's right. It's a great ad. Sex appeal, product placement, and an environment that makes you feel like you are there. Makes you want to be like him.

And his lips are on another woman's. I cringe at the thought.

"Great spot," Jimmy says as the audience's applause dies down. "I bet you had fun making that one." Colton just smirks at him, a sliver of a laugh escaping his lips that says it all. "The camera loves you, man. How come you've never hit up your old man for a job? I bet the ladies wouldn't mind seeing you on a jumbo screen somewhere."

The audience shouts out in agreement. Colton just curls the corner of one lip and shakes his head. "Never say never." He laughs and my stomach clenches thinking of millions of women getting to see him in action in some love scene. Theaters would sell out just for that.

"So tell me, Colton, what other things do you have going on?"

"Well we have a little something else in the works right now that legal doesn't want me to officially announce yet because it's still being wrapped up," the crowd "*awws*," and Colton holds his finger up in a just wait moment. "But, since when have I ever done what I'm supposed to?" Colton's smirk is lopsided and mischievous as the audience laughs. I suck in my breath, shocked and pleased that Colton is going to give public notability to my company. "All I'll tell you is my company is working with a corporation who cares," he says, putting quotation marks on both title words of my company, "and we are uniting to raise money to benefit orphaned kids by providing better living situations for them...to give them more of a stable family environment on a permanent basis."

"A cause near and dear to your heart."

"Absolutely." Colton nods, leaving it at that.

"How fantastic. Can't wait until its official so we can learn more about it. But, I know you are not supposed to tell me." Jimmy rolls his eyes to the audience. "How are you going to be raising the money?"

Colton goes through the whole explanation, answering Jimmy's questions, and I just watch mesmerized, trying to decipher the Colton I know against the one that is on television before me. I see the same person and the same personality, but little nuances are different. I can see him holding back some. Playing up to the audience, and he definitely does it well.

"Well we're running out of time," Jimmy says and the audience grumbles, "but I think the audience might run me out of the studio if I don't ask the question that they want to know the most."

Colton looks around the audience, my favorite boyish smile spreading across his face. "What's that?" he prompts.

"Well, every time we see you in print or on television, you always seem to have a buxom beauty on your arm." Jimmy holds up the several magazine pages of Colton with various glamazons. "What's your status now? Are you dating? Is there a special lady in your life right now? Or perhaps *several special ladies?*"

Colton throws his head back laughing, and I wait with bated breath for his answer. "C'mon, Jimmy, you know how it is—"

"No, actually I don't." The audience laughs. "And please don't tell me you're dating Matt Damon," he deadpans.

This time I laugh at the startled look on Colton's face over Jimmy's long running joke over Matt Damon. "Definitely not Matt Damon." He laughs and then shrugs. "You know me. I'm always dating," Colton says, leaning back in his chair, hands gesturing casually to the crowd. "There are so many beautiful women out there, it'd be a waste to not enjoy them." Colton flashes his panty-dropping smile to the audience. "I mean look at all the beautiful women in the audience out there tonight."

"So in other words," Jimmy says, "you're avoiding the question."

"I wouldn't want to give away all my secrets," Colton smirks, winking at the audience.

"Sorry, ladies. That's all the time we have so I can't delve any further." The audience gives a collective groan. "Well, it's been great seeing you again, Colton. I can't wait to see you tear up the track this year."

"Hopefully you can make it out to a race."

"You can count on it. Best of luck to you."

Colton stands and shakes Jimmy's hand, saying something to him off mic that has him laughing. "Ladies and gentlemen, Colton Donavan." Colton waves at the audience and the show cuts to a commercial.

Haddie sits up and flips off the television. "Well," she muses, "That was entertaining."

Chapter Four

"That sounds great, Avery. All of the paperwork has been approved by HR, so I'd love to welcome you to the team. We'll see you next Monday." I hang up the phone and grab a pen, crossing that item off of my list. New girl hired, check.

Now, if I can just get the rest of my list completed. I glance at my week's schedule in my day planner, ignoring the inevitable date that looms tomorrow, and figure I can power through my "to dos" as I have no more shifts at The House this week.

That is if I can get motivated.

I have no one to blame for my lethargic pace this morning except for myself. Well and Haddie since she instigated the fourth, or was it fifth, bottle of wine. At least my headache has abated some so I can think without the hangover pounding in the background.

I grab the pile I've been avoiding, budgetary crap that takes too much time and in the end just gets overruled by the bosses upstairs, but I need to get through it. I sigh in fortification when I hear a tap at my door. I swear the next few moments take place in slow motion but I know they didn't.

When I look up, I cry out loudly and jump up in shock as I meet eyes that mirror mine. I round my desk and run full force into the arms of my brother. Tanner wraps them around me, spins around once, squeezing me so tight I can't breathe. All of the fear over his safety, anguish over not hearing from him, and loneliness from not having him near, vanish and manifest themselves in the tears that run down my cheeks in happiness.

He sets me back down on my feet and eases his hold on me, but I cling to him tightly and bury my face in his chest needing this connection with him. When I can't stop crying, he just holds on and kisses the top of my head. "If I knew I was going to get this kind of welcome, I'd come home more often," he says before grabbing my shoulders and pulling me back, his eyes searching mine. "What is it, Bubs?"

I smile at hearing the name he's called me our whole lives. I think I'm in shock. "Let me look at you," I manage, stepping back and running my hands over his arms. He looks a little older and a lot tired. Fine lines fan at the corners of his weary eyes, and the creases edging his mouth have deepened some in the six months since I have seen him last. His copper hair is a little longer than usual, curling up at the collar. But he is alive and whole and in front of me. The wrinkles make him more attractive somehow, adding a little ruggedness to his dynamic features. "Still ugly I see?"

"And you're even more beautiful," he recites, an exchange we've said at least a thousand times over the years. He holds out my arms to look at me and shakes his head as if he can't believe I am standing in front of him. *"God is it good to see you!"*

I grab a hold of him again and laughter bubbles up. "Do Mom and Dad know you're in the states?" I pull on his hand, bringing him into my office, not wanting to let go of him just yet.

"I flew in to San Diego and stayed with them last night. I'm leaving for Afghanistan this afternoon on a sudden assignment—"

"What?" I just get him back and now he's going to leave me again. "What do you mean you're leaving again?"

"Can you leave? Go to lunch with me and we can talk?"

"Of course."

Tanner's only request for his meal is that it be somewhere he can see and smell the ocean. I drive up the coast, deciding to take him to the beachside restaurant Colton took me to on what I consider our first date. It's perfect for him.

On the drive Tanner explains to me that he had taken a last minute week off to come home and visit us from his post in Egypt covering the unrest there. Once home, a fellow colleague had fallen ill and so now his trip was cut short so that he could head back to the Middle East to cover for him.

"So you flew all the way out here for two days just to see us?" I take a sip of my Diet Coke and stare at him. We're seated on the same patio where Colton and I ate just a couple of tables to the right. Rachel wasn't working but the hostess that is, heeded our request and set us out of the way from the steady flow of the lunch crowd.

Tanner just looks at me and smiles broadly, and I realize how much I've missed him and the calming effect he can have on me. He tilts his bottle of beer up to his lips and leans back, looking out at the waves beyond. "God, it's good to be home." He smiles. "Even if it's just for a day."

"I can't even imagine," I tell him, afraid to take my eyes off of him for just a second since my time with him is so fleeting.

Over food, we talk about the things going on in our lives. He tells me all about his living conditions and the things going on in Egypt that aren't making their way into the mainstream media. I learn he is casually dating another journalist but that it's nothing serious despite the softening of his features when he speaks of her.

I love listening to him. His passion and love for his job is so apparent that even though it takes him thousands of miles from me, I can't imagine him doing anything else.

I tell him about work and Haddie and everything in between. Except for Colton. Tanner can be a bit overprotective, and I figure why even mention something that I'm not sure even is a something. I think I'm doing a damn good job of it until he tilts his head and stares at me.

"What?"

His eyes narrow as he studies me. "Who is he, Bubs?"

I look at him perplexed, like I don't understand, but I know his investigative instincts have kicked in, and he won't back down until he gets the answer he wants. Hence why he's so good at his job. "Who's who?"

"Who's the guy that's got you tied up in knots?" He takes a draw on his beer. A smirk on his lips, his eyes never leave mine. Cocky son of a bitch. I just sit there and stare at him wondering how he knows. "Spill it!"

"Why would you even think that?"

"Because I know you *that well*." When I just fold my arms over my chest, he laughs at me. "Let's see, you are purposefully avoiding the topic rather than talking about it. You're twisting that ring around your damn finger like a worry stone. You keep biting the inside lip of yours like you do when you're trying to figure something out, and you keep looking at that table over there like you expect someone to be sitting there. Either that or you're remembering something that you and he did there." He arches an eyebrow at me. "Besides, you have a fire in your eyes that's been missing since…before," he muses, reaching out, grabbing my hand and squeezing it. "It's good to see." I smile at him, so happy that he's here. "So?"

"There is someone," I say slowly, "but it's confusing and I'm not sure what it is yet." I twist my ring around my finger and don't realize I'm doing it until Tanner raises an eyebrow at me. I stop immediately and give him the gist of things without giving him Colton's name. "He's a great guy, but I just think he's not looking for anything more than dating without commitment." I shrug, looking out at the scenery before looking back at him, a hint of tears in my eyes.

"Shit, Ry, any guy that makes you cry isn't worth it."

I bite my bottom lip and look down at the napkin I'm shredding mindlessly. "Maybe if he makes me cry it's because he *is* worth it," I say softly. I hear him sigh and I look back up at him. "It's a first step at least," I whisper with a trembling voice.

The compassion in his eyes almost undoes me, breaking the hold I have on the tears burning in the back of my throat. "Oh, Bubs, come here," he says, turning my chair and pulling it toward him. His pulls me into his arms where I just hold onto him, the one person I can always count on.

I close my eyes, my chin resting over his shoulder. "I know why you're here, Tan. Thanks for coming to make sure that I'm okay."

He squeezes me one more time before holding my arms and pushing me back to look at me with concerned eyes. "I just wanted to make sure with everything going on this week…I worry about you. I had to be here in case you needed me," he says softly. "So that if she calls, I can deal with her."

A surge of love rushes through me for my brother who has just flown halfway around to world for a day to make sure that I'm okay. It's hard to fathom the brother I grew up with, who I fought like cats and dogs with, has turned into such a thoughtful, caring man now. That he wants to deal with the fallout of the inevitable phone call I will receive from Max's mother tomorrow.

I reach up with both hands and hold my brother's cheeks and smile at him. "How'd I ever get so lucky to have you for a big brother?" Tears glisten in my eyes as I kiss him softly on his cheek. "You're the best, you know that?"

He smiles, uncomfortable with my affection for him. I stand up. "I'll be right back. I've gotta go to the bathroom." I start to leave the table and then without thought turn back around and grab him in a quick hug, wrapping my arms around his shoulders from behind as I stand behind him while he's sitting.

"Whoa, what's that for?" He laughs.

"Just because I'm going to miss you when you leave." I release him just as quickly as I hugged him and walk into the restaurant. The kitchen door shuts quickly as I walk past it toward the bathroom at the far side of the dining area.

When I emerge from the bathroom, I am preoccupied watching an adorable curly haired toddler trying to use a fork. One hand instinctively moves to rest on my lower abdomen and presses there. The pang hits me harder than usual watching her, and I can only assume it's because of what tomorrow's date signifies. The anniversary that took everything from me. Robbed me of the one thing I want more than anything in the world.

The one thing I would give up everything—everything—I have, if I could only have the chance again.

I'm so wrapped up in memories that I don't notice the commotion toward the patio until I hear, *"What the hell are you doing?"* It's my brother's voice, and it takes me a couple of seconds to maneuver around the tables to try and get in the line of sight of our table.

"The lady's with me, asshole. Keep your hands to yourself."

My heart stops.

I'd know that rasp of a voice anywhere. I rush quickly to the doorway, my pulse pounding and incredulity in my expression. I emerge out onto the patio to see Colton's hand fisted in the front of my brother's shirt, his jaw clenched, eyes full of fire. Tanner, who is still seated, is looking up at him, a smarmy look on his face. His shoulders are rigid, hands clenched quietly at his sides. The testosterone is definitely flowing.

"Colton!" I shout out.

He glances over at me and locks onto my eyes, a mixture of anger, jealousy, and aggression vibrating off of him. Tanner glances over at me, an eyebrow arching in question, his tongue tucked in his cheek.

"Colton, let go!" I demand as I stride toward him. "It's not what you think." I pull on his arm, and he shrugs out of my grasp, but he finally releases his hold on my brother. My heartbeat slowly decelerates. Tanner rises from his seat and squares his shoulders to Colton, an indiscernible look on his face. "Ace, meet my *brother*, Tanner."

Colton's head whips over to look at me, annoyance and hostility giving way to recognition. I can see a myriad of emotions flickering through his eyes: relief, discomfort, irritation.

I look at my brother, still unable to read him. "Tanner, this is my…" I falter, unsure what to label him. "Meet Colton Donavan." I watch Tanner as his synapses start firing, realizing who is standing in front of him. Who I'm dating.

The tension in Colton's shoulders relaxes some and a disbelieving smile tickles the corners of his mouth. Unapologetically, he reaches his hand out to shake Tanner's hand. Tanner looks at Colton and his outstretched hand and then over at me. "So, Bubs, this is the asshole?" he asks, his eyes silently imploring if this is who is the current cause of my tears.

I look at him, a timid smile gracing my lips. "Yes," I murmur answering both spoken and unspoken questions and glance over at Colton.

"Well shit," Tanner says, grasping Colton's hand and shaking it vigorously. "Have a seat man." He exhales. "I need a fucking beer after that." I stare at both of them, mystified at how men operate. Ready to go to blows one minute, in complete understanding the next.

"I'd love to, but I'm late for my afternoon meeting." He emits a sliver of a laugh. "Nice to meet you though. Maybe another time?" Colton turns his gaze on me. "Walk me out?"

I look at Tanner and he nods at me as if to tell me to go. I exhale, not realizing I'm holding my breath, suddenly nervous to be alone with Colton. Nervous to play the disinterested and aloof card. "I'll be right back," I tell Tanner, feeling like a little kid asking for his consent.

"Tanner." Colton nods at my brother in goodbye before placing his hand on the small of my back and steering me through the kitchen and out the side door of the restaurant.

The brief time it takes to walk toward a staff exit, I think of how we ended things the last time we spoke. Of the two options he gave me, *pit stop* or *arrangement*. That I gave him his pit stop, but I still feel unsettled. That because I've been swimming in lack of reassurance, regardless of the term, I still feel like one in a long line of bedtime companions.

I shake the thought away, forcing myself to step outside of my overemotional, over-analytical head and acknowledge that with most, success comes in baby steps. And even though Colton hasn't expressed wanting anything more than an arrangement with me, he took a baby step in calling 'pit stop'. *No more wishy-washy*, I tell myself as I recall Haddie's advice on how to interact with him. Aloof, unattainable, but desirable.

As Colton pushes open an exit door and ushers me outside, I'm preparing myself for the question of why I've not called him back. He's called me twice and I've physically forced myself to not react and pick up phone.

Colton shuts the door and turns around to face me. *Screw being unattainable.* It takes all of my dignity to not push him up against the wall and kiss him senseless. The man makes me absolutely irrational and completely wanton.

He crosses his arms over his chest and stares at me, his head angled to the side. "So your brother's in town?"

I give an unladylike snort. "I think we already established that," I answer dryly, fighting the urge to gap the distance between us. "Got a short fuse, do we?"

I can't read the look that passes through his eyes because it flashes quickly. "When it comes to you, yes. I saw his arms around you." He shrugs—the only explanation I receive. "Is he here for long?"

I stare at him for a moment, confused by his nonchalance in regards to a fight he almost had with my brother over nothing. Finally, I glance down at my watch and rest my hips back against the retaining wall behind me, figuring I'll let it go for now. "Yeah, just for today. He's due at the airport in an hour and a half." I pick a piece of lint off of my tunic sweater as a means to keep my eyes and hands occupied before smoothing it down over my leggings.

Colton leans a shoulder against the wall in front of me, and when I look up I see his eyes run the length of my legs. They travel up the rest of my body, stalling when they come to my lips and then moving back up to my eyes. "Been busy?" he asks.

"Mmm-hmm," I answer vaguely. "And you?"

"Yeah, but this is the calm before the storm with the season just around the corner." He stares at me, his green eyes penetrating into mine. "Did you have a good night out?" he probes.

I give him a deer in the headlights look but recover quickly when I realize he's referring to Haddie's little performance on the phone the other night. "From what I remember of it, yes." I flash a sassy smirk at him, hoping my acting is convincing enough to fool him. "You know how it is when you go out…too many guys thinking they're way too cool, too much alcohol, and too little clothes—it all becomes a blur."

I see anger flicker through his eyes at my too many guys comment, and I like the fact that he's bugged by the idea. I like that he's thought about it enough to ask. And after his little altercation with Tanner, it's more than obvious that Colton has a little jealous streak running rampant through him.

It's kind of hot that such a streak is flaring over me.

He angles his head and studies me for a beat. For once, I don't avert my eyes under his severe scrutiny. I hold his gaze with boredom written in my expression. "Why do you seem so distant? Unapproachable?" He grunts, surprising me with his comment.

"Unapproachable? Me? I didn't realize I was being that way." I feign innocence when all I want to do is reach out and touch him.

"Well, you are." He sighs, exasperation glancing across the features of his face.

"Oh, well I guess I'm just trying to abide by your parameters, Ace. *Be exactly what you want me to be.*" I smile sweetly at him.

"Which is what?" He huffs, confusion on his face.

"Emotionally detached, sexually available, and drama free." I can see the muscle in his jaw pulse as he takes a step near me, irritation flashing in his eyes at the defiance in my tone. "What are you doing here?"

He stares at me long and hard with such intensity that I nearly cave and tell him how bad I want him. Screw the mind games. "Luckily I escaped without the paps following me. Kelly let me up on the roof away from the crowd for some peace and quiet to eat my lunch." I arch a brow at him. "The owner," he says, breathing out an exasperated sigh at either the unease between us or for feeling like he needs to explain. *Maybe a bit of both.* I look down and focus on the chip in my manicure, desperately wanting to approach him. Kiss him. Hug him. "It's a good place to sit and mull things over."

"And what exactly are you mulling over?"

"The shit that I'm supposed to be getting together," he responds wryly. My eyes flash up to see a mixture of amusement and sincerity in his.

We stare at each other for a moment, my pulse accelerating from his proximity. I try to read the look on his face. *Is he serious?* Is he really trying to get his head straight or is he just mocking Haddie? I can't tell. "I-I sh-should get back inside. I don't have much more time until Tanner has to leave again." I push myself up and stand.

Colton takes a step closer to me, and our bodies brush against each other's briefly, his touch sending sparks of need spiraling through my system. I bite my bottom lip to stop myself from leaning in against him. "Can I see you later?" he asks, trailing a finger down the side of my face.

Does that mean the pit stop's over? Or he just needs to get laid? Either way, I need some clarity here. I fight the urge to lean my cheek into the feel of his fingertip on my cheek.

Stay strong, stay strong, stay strong, I repeat to myself. I struggle with how to answer. What to say?

"I'll send Sammy by the house at six to pick you up," he answers for me in my warring silence.

Wow, I guess he thinks that I'm a sure thing. And then the notion hits me that maybe all along he's wanted his arrangement with me, went further than he'd anticipated, and used the pit stop comment to try and put me back in my place. To put distance back between us.

Haddie's advice runs through my mind mixed with the notion that he thinks I'm going to just step back into this without a further explanation strengthens my resolve. "Sorry." I shake my head and avert my eyes so he can't see through my lie. "I have plans tonight."

I feel his body tense at my words. "What?" His tone is forced but quiet. It's obvious rejection is foreign to him.

"I have plans with Haddie," I volunteer, afraid he might think that I'm out with another guy. And if he thinks that I'm out with another guy then it'd be okay for him to be out with another girl. My stomach twists at the thought, and I realize I'm not very good at playing these types of games because all I want to do is tell him that yes I want to see him tonight. That I'd change any plans I have to be able to see him. And then I'd press him up against the wall and take with frustration everything that I want without a second thought of spooking him or crossing imaginary boundaries.

Colton lets out a dissatisfied grunt. "We're just having dinner at home," I tell him, "but it's a big deal because we haven't seen each other." Stop rambling, Rylee, or he'll know you're lying. "I can't go back on my promise to her."

Colton places a finger under my chin and lifts my head up to meet his green irises, studying me. "Well you're not trying very hard then," he admonishes despite humor alight in his eyes.

Confusion flits through me, unsure of what he's talking about. "Trying hard at what?" I shake my head not understanding.

He smirks arrogantly at me. "At being what I want you to be." The breath I exhale is audible as his eyes remain locked on mine. "Because if you were really trying," he explains, finishing the game I'd started, "you'd be where I want you. Wet, warm, and beneath me tonight."

I hold his stare while I try to think of what to say next. My body quivers at his words. It takes a few seconds for my brain to recover from his comment, and when it does, I take a step back from him.

Distance is essential when dealing with him.

"Yeah, I guess you're right." I exhale, watching the surprise on his face from my admission. "Why would I want to be someone's beck and call girl? *Predictable is boring, Ace.* And from what I hear, you seem to get bored real quick."

When he just stands there and stares at me, a bewildered look on his face, I skirt around him. He reaches out and grabs on to my arm, turning me to face him. "Where are you going?" he demands.

"To see my brother," I tell him, looking over at his hand and then back at him. "Let me know when you get your shit together." I shrug from his grip and yank the door open to the kitchen without looking back. All I hear before the door shuts is Colton laughing and swearing at the same time.

Chapter Five
Colton

Fucking temperamental women!

My lungs burn. My muscles ache. My feet pound into the treadmill belt as if I'm trying to punish it. It doesn't matter. No matter how hard I push, my head is still fucked up. Rylee's still mucking up my thoughts. Constantly.

What the fuck is wrong with me? I asked for the goddamn pit stop. Took my shot at putting it back on more familiar footing. So why am I the one that feels like she's left me behind?

Fucking women. Complicated. Temperamental. Necessary. Fuck me.

The music pounds in my earbuds. The driving beat of Good Charlotte pushes me harder, but the pressure in my chest doesn't dissipate. I count my footsteps when I run. Only to ninety-nine and then I start over again. I swear to God I've restarted the count a hundred fucking times so far and nothing has helped.

I've never played fucking games with women before, and I have no intention of starting now. I say when. I say whom. I give the terms.

I take what I want. When I want it.

And any and all of my previous bedside companions abide by my parameters without so much as a fucking flinch. No questions asked except for "Baby, how do you want me tonight? Knees or back? Cuffs or restraints? Mouth or pussy?"

All except for Rylee.

Fucking frustrating. First, I almost go to blows with her brother today, and then she walks away refusing to see me tonight. I know she

47

wants me. It's written all over her ridiculously hot body. It's reflected in those magnificent eyes that draw you in and swallow you whole. And fuck me, if I don't want her every minute of every hour. But what the fuck? She walked away, left me there, and didn't even hesitate at saying no about tonight.

No? Are you fucking kidding me? When is the last time I heard that? Oh yeah. Right. From Rylee. Shit. Now all I can think about is her. Seeing her. Hearing her. Burying myself in her until she sighs that little sound right before she's about to come. It's so goddamn sexy it's ridiculous.

I am not pussy-whipped. No way. No how. Not even close.

So why not call somebody else for a quick, uncomplicated fuck then? Why does the thought not even sound appealing? You're losing it, Donavan. I must've dipped my wick in the pool of crazies one too many times, and now it's fucking up my head.

I shove a finger at the screen and bump up the incline, forcing myself into ignoring my own damn thoughts. The song switches to Desperate Measures but the sarcasm in the lyrics I usually love does nothing for me.

Goddamnit! Nothing works. Music. Incline. Speed. Fuck! I keep seeing her in the bathtub, fingers firm on my balls, eyes heated with intensity, lips telling me how exactly she deserves to be treated. What she won't put up with from me again.

That's a first. Someone setting parameters for me. Has hell frozen over and no one told me? She had my balls in a fucking vice, and all I could think of was how much I wanted her. In my bed. In my office. At the track. In my life.

And not just on her back.

She must have a voodoo pussy or something. Reeling me up and snagging me in her hooks without realizing it. I'm just fucking horny. That's gotta be why my head's all fucked up. A week's a long time for me to go without sex. Shit! I can't remember the last time I've had a dry spell like this.

So why'd you pit stop her then the other day, dumbass? She'd have been beneath you tonight if you hadn't. Why'd you open your mouth?

I groan in frustration at my stupidity. At my need for release that this stupid-ass treadmill is definitely not helping with.

I can't stop rehashing the other morning. Fuck! It's official. Rehashing shit? I'm without a doubt a goddamn chick now. I must have lost my balls somewhere in the past week.

Only chicks rehash shit, but I keep thinking about standing with her on her porch…how I was just trying to do the right thing—protect her by pushing her away from the train wreck in my head. Trying to allow her the chance to find someone else that can give her what she needs—what she deserves—but I couldn't get the words out no matter how hard I tried. And then she stepped up and kissed me. Kissed me with such honesty and reassurance that I couldn't breathe. All I could do was feel. The moment was too real. Too raw. Too close.

Yep. I have a pussy. No doubt about it now.

But fuck if that simple taste of her didn't make me realize I've been starving for so very long.

And then I knew I had to put some distance between us and the foreign feeling of need that flashed through me. The need to covet. To protect. To care for. I had to push back from the one thing I know for fucking sure I don't want.

Love. Love and the things required of you with it.

Crying pit stop was like crying fucking wolf. Trying to tell myself I needed space to bring us back to the only set-up I'll accept. Back on arrangement status. I may have used her term to soften the blow, but my only thought was if I get us back to set parameters, then I'll be able to get the control back I felt slipping away. Regain the need to rely solely on myself.

I push a finger to the screen and wait for the treadmill to stop. I stand there, chest heaving, sweat dripping, and feeling no better for the hour of punishment I just put in. I glance out through the wall of glass at the shop down below, watching the guys finish with some engine adjustments we'd decided on yesterday before scrubbing the towel over my face and through my soaked hair.

My body feels like I'm floating a little when I hit the floor after being on the treadmill for so long. I head through the door on my left and into the bathroom that connects the gym to my office. I take a quick shower, glance in the mirror deciding to forgo the shave, and throw some shit in my hair.

Does she know how fucked up I am? Does she have any idea what a bastard I am? How I usually take when I need to and then discard? I need to tell her. Somehow. Someway. I need to warn her of the fucking poison inside of me.

I'm pulling my shirt over my head when it hits me what I need to get out of my funk. I walk out into my office and head straight to my desk to grab my cell to make some calls and get the ball rolling. But first I need to send her a text. Need to give her a warning the only way she'll hear it.

I pull up her name on my phone and type: Push – Matchbox Twenty. Then I hit send, my mind running the lyrics over and over in my head: "I wanna take you for granted. Well I will."

"What crawled up your ass?"

Despite its familiarity, I jolt at the sound of the voice. I whirl around to see Becks sitting in one of the chairs in front of my desk with his feet propped up on another.

"You scared the shit out of me," I bark out, running a hand through my hair. "Fucking A, Becks!"

"From the looks of it, you need to fuck a B brother. It's got an extra hole and you sure as hell look like you can use the added release," he drawls out, amusement in his eyes as they narrow and study me trying to figure out what's going on.

A sliver of a laugh escapes my lips as my heart begins to decelerate. I sink down in my chair and prop my feet up on my desk, mirroring him. We just stare at each other, years of companionship allowing there to be comfort in the silence as I weigh what to say and he measures how much to ask.

He finally decides to break the silence. "It's a lot easier and cheaper to get it off your chest, Wood, than to break the fucking treadmill, you know." I just give him a measured nod before glancing down at the garage again, one of my obsessive habits. "You gonna go all rogue on me with the silent treatment now?" When I look back at Becks, his eyes are now staring at the guys below, ignoring the sneer I'm giving him. "Or are you going to explain why you sat through that entire meeting after lunch with your head up your ass, giving little to no input and just being a dick in general. Only to end it without a decision so you could go break the treadmill?" He slowly moves his gaze back to mine with eyebrows arched in question and an appraising look in his eyes.

Leave it to Becks. The only person that can put me in my place. The only person I'll allow to call me on it. The only person that knows me well enough to know I'm pissed and to ask in our guy speak what the fuck's wrong.

"It's nothing," I shrug.

He chokes out a long laugh and shakes his head at me. "Yeah. It's nothing alright," he says, unfolding himself from his chair, his eyes never leaving mine. "Since you're so talkative, I think I'll be on my way then."

Fuck this. Before Becks reaches the door, I'm shoving my wallet into my back pocket, grabbing my cell, and striding toward the door. "Let's go," I mutter as I walk past him, knowing that he'll be right behind me. And I'm right because I hear his quiet laugh behind me. The one that says yep, I was right.

I give the universal 'another round' motion to the waitress with the nametag stating Connie. If she's just going to stand there and stare, she might as well do something to earn the free show. Shit. My buzz is humming now and I'm just starting to relax. I'm not drunk enough to push away my shitty mood, but I'm making progress.

Connie swivels her hips as she comes over to the table with our drinks in her hands. She leans over the table to set them down, making sure that I get the eyeful of tits she's putting on display. She's unquestionably hot in all of the right ways and in all of the right places. I'd definitely hit it—another time, another place, maybe—but I stifle back the smartass comment on my tongue about how all of a sudden from the drink request to the drink arrival her shirt just got lower and her skirt just got shorter. "Is there anything else I can get you two gentlemen?" she asks with a suggestive tone to her voice and her tongue licking over her lips.

"We're good here," Beckett deadpans, shaking his head and breaking her attempt at flirting. He's used to this shit and is a fucking saint for dealing with it all these years in his subtle, calculating way.

A text pings on my phone, and I reach for the fresh bottle as I look at it. "Smitty's on board," I tell him. I should be happy that Smitty's coming to Vegas with us. We've shared plenty of wild outings in the past. He'll definitely help get rid of my fucked up mood.

If I'm so happy, then why am I disappointed that it isn't Rylee's name on my phone's incoming text?

"Cool. Almost the whole gang then," Becks says, leaning back in his seat and taking a long pull on his beer. I can feel his eyes on me, waiting patiently for me to talk.

I lean forward and place my head in my hands for a moment, trying to shake my head out of where it keeps returning. Fucking Rylee.

"You want to tell me what the fuck we're doing here, Colton, at almost six o'clock on a Friday night? Who the hell put that stick up your ass?"

I just shake my head as I peel the label on my bottle and keep my eyes down. "Fucking Rylee," I mumble, knowing I've just opened the proverbial can of worms by admitting it to him.

"That so, huh?" he muses. I lift my head up slowly and meet his eyes, surprised by the lack of smartass comments that are his typical style. He peers at me over his beer bottle as he takes another sip, and I just nod my head. "What the fuck'd you do to her?"

"Thanks for the vote of confidence, Becks." I laugh. "Who says I did anything?"

He just gives me a look that says look who we're talking about here. "Well…"

"Nothing. Abso-fucking-lutley nothing," I bark out, tossing back my shot to help bury the fact that I'm lying to my best friend. "She's just frustrating."

"Like that's a fucking news flash. We're talking about a woman here, aren't we?"

"I know. She's just gotten under my skin and now she's playing the hard to get card. That's all." I sigh, leaning back in my chair so I can meet Beckett's stare.

"She told you no?" Becks coughs out in shock. "Like no, no? Are you shitting me?"

"Nope." I catch Connie's eye again for another round.

"Well shit, Wood. We are leaving for the city of sin in a couple of hours. I'm sure there's a hot piece of ass there that you could tap for the night to forget about her. Or for that matter, several hot pieces." He shrugs and a slight, antagonizing smirk curls up the corner of his mouth. "Since all you're doing is just fucking Rylee…because that is all you're doing, right? Fucking her? There's no commitment there to ruin. No voodoo pussy hex."

I know he's trying to push my buttons. Get a reaction one way or another as to where I stand when it comes to Ry. But for some reason I don't take the bait. It's gotta be the alcohol running through my veins. Instead, I shrug at him in agreement about finding someone else for the night, but for some reason I have no desire to. None. And why the fuck does that kind of comment—that I'm just fucking her—piss me off. This is Beckett I'm talking to. My best friend and brother for all intents and purposes—the man I discuss everything with, and I mean everything—so why does his off the cuff remark bug me?

It's like she still has my balls in her grip.

Fuck me.

"She's got a hot friend."

Becks looks at me as if I've grown two heads. "Come again? I'm not following you."

"Well, we can swing by Rylee's place on the way to the airport and the two of them can come with us." The words are out of my mouth before my brain can process the thought.

Beckett chokes on his swallow of beer and starts coughing. The look on his face is one of complete shock. Apparently I did grow an extra head.

I ignore him and turn my concentration back to my beer's label. Where the fuck did that come from? Taking Rylee to Vegas with me? The one place I can most likely forget about her for a while? The ultimate place to use pleasure to bury the pain. Taking a girl to Vegas with you is like taking a wife to your mistress' house. That's why I've never done it. Never even thought about it. Avoided it at all costs. Companions, dates, whatever they're called, always stay home. They never even know I go. No exceptions. So why in the hell did I just suggest it? And more importantly, why the hell do I want her to go more than anything?

I must be outside of my fucking mind. Voodoo pussy.

Motherfucker.

"Holy shit…" Beckett says on a long drawn out drawl. "I never thought I'd see the day that Colton Fuckin' Donavan would say that." He whistles out a sigh, and then I swear I can hear something click in that head of his. "You're barebacking, aren't you?"

I can't help my eyes from snapping up to his with the comment. Our universal guy speak for sticking with one woman. For thinking of more than just sex without strings. For fucking without a condom because you have complete trust in the other person.

For being pussy-whipped.

Neither of us have ever barebacked. Ever. Kind of a silent solidarity we have between us. Neither of us that is, until now.

"Motherfucker!" Becks jumps up in his seat. "You are, aren't you, you cocksucker!"

"Shut the fuck up, Beckett." I growl as I toss back the rest of my beer and raise my empty shot glass up to Connie who hasn't stopped waiting attentively five feet away. Becks just sits and looks at me in silence until the newest round of shots are placed in front of us. I sit and stare back at him a while longer and let my comment settle between us, get comfortable rolling the idea around in my head…and then it hits me.

Fuck yes, I want Ry to go with us. Now what the fuck does that mean? I throw back the shot, hissing at its burn before scrubbing my hand over my face as numbness spreads into my lips. Beckett keeps looking at me like I'm some kind of circus show freak. I can tell he's biting his cheek to keep from grinning at me, from saying the shit that's flying through his eyes at a lightning pace.

He holds his hand up to his ear and leans over the table. "I'm sorry. I don't think I heard you correctly. What the fuck was your answer?"

I can't help the grin that pulls up one corner of my mouth. This is being tame for Beckett, so I'm grateful that he's keeping himself in check against my obvious discomfort.

"Well fuck me!" he says, shifting in his chair to stare at me for a little while longer with disbelief on his face. He looks down at his watch. "Well, if we're going to take off on time, loverboy, we best be going."

"That's all you're going to say?" I ask incredulously.

"I haven't even started yet, Wood! I need time to process...it's not every day Hell falls below zero."

Fine by me. If I can get away with only that being said right now, I'll take it. I nod my head at him and start typing away on my phone. "I'm texting Sammy to come get us." I tell him. The background music in the bar is playing, and I laugh at the fucking song playing. Of course it's Pink. Rylee and her fucking Pink. I send my text to Sammy and then hover over her name on my phone. Before I know it, I've entered a quick one to Rylee as well.

I'm in this far, might as well go balls deep.

Chapter Six

"You really said that to him?" Haddie asks incredulously, the look on her face over-exaggerated and hilariously funny.

"I swear!" I told her, holding up my hand in testament. I look down at my phone where a text just pinged. It's from Colton, and all it says is: *Get this Party Started – Pink*.

Haddie doesn't notice the odd look on my face when I read it because she is concentrating on filing her nails. What the hell? First the text about Matchbox Twenty today, which threw me for a loop, and now this? He's a little all over the place and a lot confusing.

"Shit! I'd have loved to see his face when you shut that door."

"I know." I laugh. "It felt kind of good to leave him stunned for once rather than the other way around."

"See, I told you!" she says, pushing on my knee.

"Besides the testosterone fest with Colton, did you and Tanner have a nice visit?"

"Yeah." I smile softly. "It was so good to see him. I don't realize how much I miss him until—" a knock on the door interrupts me. I look over at Haddie, my eyes asking her who could be knocking on our door at seven o'clock on a Friday night.

"No clue." She shrugs, getting up to answer it since I have a slew of work papers strewn across my lap and on the couch beside me.

Moments later I hear laughter and voices and Haddie exclaiming, "Well look what the cat dragged in!"

Curious, I start to clear my papers when Haddie enters the family room, a broad smile on her face. "Someone's here to see you," she says, a knowing look in her eyes.

Before I can ask her who it is, Colton comes barreling into the room in a less than graceful stride with a laughing Beckett right behind him. Something's amiss with Colton, and I'm not sure what it is until he sees me. A goofy grin spreads across his face and it looks out of place against the intensity of his features. Luckily, I'm shuffling up my papers because he unceremoniously plops down right beside me.

"Rylee!" he exclaims enthusiastically as if he hasn't seen me in weeks. He reaches out, calloused fingers rasping against my bare skin, grabs me, and pulls me onto his lap. All I can do is laugh because I realize that Mr. Cool and Always in Control is a tad bit drunk. No, make that well on his way to being drunk. And before I can even respond to his sudden appearance, Colton's mouth closes over mine.

I resist at first, but once his tongue delves into my mouth and I taste him, I'm a goner. I groan in acceptance and lick my tongue against his. It's only been a few days but God, I missed this. Missed him. I forget that other people are in the room when Colton tangles his hand in my hair and takes possession of me, holding me so all I can do is react. All I can do is absorb the feeling of him against me. He tastes of beer and mints and everything I want. Everything I crave. Everything I need. I bow my back so my chest presses to his, my nipples tingling as they brush against the firm warmth of his chest. Colton swallows the moan he's coaxed from me when his arousal pushes up through my thin pajama pants and rubs against me.

"Should we clear the room?" I hear Haddie say before she clears her throat loudly, shocking me back to reality.

I pull my head back slightly from Colton's, but his hand remains fisted in my hair holding my curls hostage. He rests his forehead to mine as we both draw in ragged breaths of need.

After a beat, he throws his head back on the couch and laughs loudly, his whole body shaking from its force, before choking out, "Shit, I needed that!"

I start to scramble off his lap, suddenly aware that I'm wearing a very thin camisole tank with some very aroused nipples sans bra, and Beckett—whom I've only met once—is sitting across from me, studying us with a quiet yet amused intensity. Before I can even cross my arms over my chest, Colton's hands grip me from behind, wrapping his arms around me and pulling me back against him.

"Hey!" I shout.

"I got it!" he shouts playfully in response. "And Colton's inebriated."

What? I shift in his lap, trying to turn and look at him. "Huh?"

He chuckles and it's such a carefree boyish laugh—so at odds with the intensity he exudes—that my heart swells at the sound. "Ace," he states confidently. "And Colton's inebriated."

He busts out laughing again, and I can't help but laugh along with him. "Nope." And before I can say anything else, Beckett jumps in.

"You're drunker than I thought. Inebriated starts with an 'I', you douchebag. Spell much?"

Colton flips him the bird, his boyish laugh returning again. "Whatever, Becks. You know you love me!" he says pulling me back against him. "Now, back to business," Colton announces loudly. "You're coming with us."

Haddie raises her eyebrows, amusement on her face at my flustered expression. "Colton, let me go!" I sputter loudly in between laughs, trying to wriggle out of his iron tight grip on me. He simply holds me tighter, resting his chin on my shoulder.

"Nope! Not until you agree that you're going with us. You and Haddie are going on a little road trip with Becks and me." I start to wiggle again, and I feel Colton's free hand slip up to cup my breast through my shirt, his thumb brushing over my nipple. I suck in a breath at his touch and embarrassment floods my cheeks.

"Uh-uh-uh," he teases, his breath feathering over my cheek. "Every time you fight me, baby, I'm gonna cop a feel." He nips at the skin between my shoulder and my neck, his arousal thickening beneath my lap. "So please, Rylee," he begs, "please, fight me."

I roll my eyes despite the shock wave of need that's reverberating through me at the sound of his bedroom voice, and I can't help the laughter that bubbles out, Haddie and Beckett joining in. Drunken Colton equals a very playful Colton. I like this side of him.

"Typical male," I tease. "Always misguided and thinking with the head in your pants."

He pulls me tighter against him, one arm around my shoulders while the other is around my waist. "Well then, don't be afraid to blow my mind," he murmurs, a low, seductive growl in my ear that has me laughing from the corniness of the line all the while tensing at the suggestion of it.

"So get your asses up, pretty ladies, and get ready!" he suddenly orders, breaking our connection, pushing me to my feet, and swatting my backside.

"What are you talking about?" I ask at the same time Haddie pipes up asking, "Where are we going?"

Beckett laughs out loud at Haddie's all-in reaction before bringing a bottle of beer to his lips. "Hey!" Colton shouts. "Don't be drinking my beer you bastard or I'll take you down."

"Chill out, Wood." He chuckles. "You left yours on the table by the front door."

"Shit!" he grumbles. "I'm a man in need of a beer and of women to get their asses moving. Time's a wasting!"

"What in the hell are you talking about?" I turn to him, arms across my chest.

A slow, roguish grin spreads across his lips as he stares at me. "Vegas, baby!"

Mysterious text solved.

"What?" Haddie and I shout, but both with different meanings. There is no possible way I am going to Las Vegas right now. What in the hell?

Colton holds up his phone, biting his lip as he tries to concentrate on its screen, and I realize he's trying to tell the time with his alcohol-warped mind. "We'll be back in the morning, but wheels up in one hour, Rylee, so you better get that fine ass of yours moving!"

What? We're flying? What am I even thinking? I'm not going anywhere. "Colton, you can't possibly be serious!"

He pushes himself up from the couch, and looks a little wobbly before getting control. He looks down at me, an errant lock of hair falling over his forehead with his shirt untucked on the right side. "Do I need to pick you up over my shoulder and haul you to your bedroom to show just how serious I am, sweetheart?"

I look over at Beckett for some kind of help. He just shrugs his shoulders, silently laughing at our banter. "I'd just give in, Rylee," he drawls, winking at me. "He doesn't give up when he's in this mood. I suggest you go get changed."

I open my mouth to speak but nothing comes out. I look over at Haddie who has excitement dancing in her eyes. "C'mon, Ry," she prompts. "It couldn't hurt to escape with everything that's going on tomorrow." She shrugs. "Have some fun and forget a little." I nod at her and her smile widens. She whoops loudly. "We're going to Vegas, baby!"

Beckett stands from the chair asking for the bathroom. Haddie offers to show him on the way to her room to get ready. I turn to face Colton but am caught off guard as he swoops me up and over his shoulder, swatting my butt as he carries me rather unsteadily toward the hallway.

"Colton, stop!" I shriek, smacking his ass in turn.

His only response is a laugh. "Which room is yours?" I squeal as he tickles my feet. "Tell me, woman, or I'll be forced to torture you some more!"

Oh, I definitely like drunk and playful Colton!

"Last door on the right," I screech as he tickles me some more before throwing me unceremoniously onto my bed. I'm out of breath from laughing, and before I can even speak, Colton's body is flanking mine. The feeling of his weight on me, pressing intimately against me, creates a crack in my resolve. So much for being aloof. That card was thrown out the window the minute he wobbled into the family room with that playful and captivating grin on his face.

His mouth slants over mine and his tongue plunges into my mouth. I slide my hands up and under the hem of his shirt and run them up the planes of his back. The kiss is full of greed, angst, and passion, and I know I'm losing myself in it. To him. His hands roam, touching every inch of my bare skin he can find as if he needs this connection to tell him everything is alright between us. That our union is reassuring him, confirming that whatever's between us is still there.

I freeze when I hear a knock on the doorjamb. "C'mon, loverboy." Beckett chuckles uncomfortably. "Rein it in. You can do that later. Right now we've got a plane to catch."

Colton rolls off of me, groaning as he adjusts his arousal in his jeans. "You're such a buzz kill, Becks!"

"That's why you love me, brother!" He laughs as he retreats down the hall, giving me some privacy to get ready.

Colton props his hands behind his head and crosses his feet at the ankles as I scoot off of the bed. "God, you look sexy right now," Colton murmurs, his eyes focused on my nipples pressing against the thin cotton of my tank.

"She'll look sexier in about twenty minutes, Donavan, if you get the hell out of here and let her do her thing," Haddie says unabashedly as she breezes in my room holding a handful of barely-there dresses on hangers for me to try on.

"Well shit," Colton says, pushing himself up off of the mattress, "I guess I've been told. Beckett?" he bellows down the hall, "Time for another beer."

I twirl a lock of Colton's hair absently with my fingers as I stare down at his head resting in my lap. He's just fallen asleep and I shake my head watching the peaceful calm on his face. I'm still in shock at the direction the evening has taken. I smile, recalling the look on Colton's face when Haddie and I walked into the living room in our sexy Vegas outfits. The bottle of beer that was angling towards his lips stopped in mid-air when he saw me. His eyes ran the length of my body in a lazy perusal, a diminutive smile ghosting his lips before they met mine. What his eyes told me in that one look was everything that I'd needed to hear from him but hadn't heard over the past couple of days.

Desire. Need. Want.

And then unbeknownst to me, when Colton had mentioned flying, little did I know that there was a chartered jet waiting for us when we arrived via limo at the Santa Monica Municipal Airport. Haddie and I just looked at each other and shook our heads at the lavishness of it all. And when we boarded, in addition to Sammy sitting quietly at the rear of the plane, there was a flight attendant willing to fill any drink or meal order we desired. While Haddie, Becks, and I took advantage of the offer for a drink, Colton declined everything and crawled up on the couch beside me, laid his head in my lap, and declared he needed a quick nap to be ready for the night to come.

I shake my head thinking of it all, a wisp of a smile on my face when I look up to see Haddie and Beckett in a hushed conversation across from me. Haddie's heels are off and her feet are curled underneath her. Beckett's long legs are stretched out in front of him, and his fingers absently draw lines on the condensation of his bottle. He's quite handsome in a non-typical way. I stare at him, realizing that he has definite sex appeal, more than looks. His sandy blonde hair is cropped close to his head and spiked up with gel. His crystal clear blue eyes are fringed by thick lashes. They are quiet eyes that take in and observe in a reserved fashion. He has broad shoulders and a lean build like Colton.

I stare at him, the best friend of my lover, and there is so much I want to ask him about Colton. So many things I think he can shed light on but know he would never betray his buddy by telling me.

Whether by chance or because he feels the weight of my stare, Beckett looks up and meets my eyes, his sentence to Haddie faltering on his lips. He angles his head to the side and twists his lips up as if he's trying to decide if he should say something or not.

"You know why we're here right now...why Wood got drunk tonight, don't you?" His southern accent drawls out as he looks down and shakes his head at the sight of his friend before looking back up me.

"No," I say.

Beckett leans forward resting his elbows on his knees and looks me straight in the eye. "Because you told him no, Rylee." He shakes his head, a smile growing on his face. "And nobody, except me, ever tells him no."

"That's absurd," I tell him, looking over at Haddie, who's arched her eyebrow at the turn in conversation, a pleased smirk on her lips. I realize that Beckett is telling me I am the first female to tell Colton no. To not ask how high when he says jump. I glance down at Colton and back up to Beckett. "Surely one of his *many others* have told him no before."

He thinks in silence for a moment before answering. "Not that I know of," Beckett says, tipping the bottle to his lips, "and if they have, I've never seen Colton care like this." He leans back and stretches out again, and I try to read the unspoken words in his eyes. "He came back from lunch one surly S. O. B., Rylee. I actually felt bad for the people on the other end of our meeting today." He smiles at the thought. "And then the next thing I know, he was pounding out his frustration on the treadmill. Pulling me to the bar with him to sulk and started making phone calls. Hatching a plan. Telling people we'll be in Vegas by ten, to get their asses there, and to meet him at the usual place."

The usual place? "You guys do this often?"

"Every couple of months." He shrugs like it's not a big deal. "But here's the thing, Rylee, no matter who he's with, I've never—never— seen him bring the woman he's seeing, or whatever the hell he's doing with them, along with us." He tips the bottle of the beer at me. "Now that's something to think about."

Beckett eyes hold mine until he knows I understand. There's something different between Colton and me that he hasn't seen before. I nod my head at him.

He leans forward again. "I've known Colton for a long time, Rylee. He can be cocky as hell and a stubborn ass at times, but he's a good guy. A really good guy." I can sense the sincerity in his voice and the brotherly love he has for Colton. He looks down at his slumbering friend and back at me. "He may not always go about things the right way, or even know how to go about them at all, but he usually has the best intentions behind his actions." When I don't say anything he just nods and continues. "I'm telling you this because you matter to him. More than he's willing to admit or can acknowledge right now, but it's important for you to know. Because if he matters to you like I think he does…really matters…not just for the recognition of being with him, but because of who he is, then you need to hear it. *Shit,*" he swears, running a hand over his jaw and leaning back shaking his head. "I must be drunk if I just told you that. *Fuck.*" He sighs. "He'd throttle me right now if he knew I was telling you any of this."

"Thank you," I tell him, my voice barely a whisper as I try to digest everything he's just told me—everything I wanted to ask him but was afraid to. My head is reeling with his confession. I try to keep a rein on the hope and possibilities that bubble up inside of me. I matter enough that his best friend notices the difference in him. I just need to remember that unless Colton acknowledges it, these feelings still mean nothing.

Haddie looks over at me and smiles softly, knowing how much I needed to hear this. That these words justify the depths of emotion I already feel for Colton.

He thanks the flight attendant as she hands him another beer. "I've said this much, I might as well finish," he mutters to himself with a sheepish smile spreading on his lips. Colton shifts and turns into me, his face nuzzling my abdomen, and all I want to do is bend down and kiss him. "Trying to control Colton is like trying to grab the wind. Don't even bother…" he shakes his head "…he's gonna fuck up, Rylee. He's going to make a lot of mistakes and say all of the wrong things because he doesn't know how to do anything other than what he's been doing."

Beckett takes a pull on his beer and sighs. "He'll never admit it Rylee. And unless you are one of the few that are close enough to him to see it, you'd never guess that he's a man drowning in his past. To accept that there might be more than just the usual arrangement per se with you—and by you being here, there obviously is—he might just pull you down so that you're drowning with him." He shifts some in his seat, eyes never breaking from mine. "When that happens, Rylee, more than anything he's going to need you to be his lifeline. He's going to be so consumed and obsessed with preventing his past from meeting his future that he's going to need everything from you to keep him afloat."

He holds my eyes for a minute longer and then eases back into his seat, a slight smile playing the corners of his mouth. "I love him to death, Rylee, but some days I hate him too." He shrugs without apology, "That's just Colton."

I look back up at Beckett and smile softly, a silent agreement to his assessment. "I'm beginning to understand that," I mutter.

The flight attendant comes over to fill our drinks one last time and to inform us that we will be beginning our descent into Las Vegas shortly. I look down at Colton and a feeling of warmth spreads throughout me as I realize how much I've come to care for and love—yes love—him. I shake my head and Haddie catches my eye, her happiness for me brimming in hers.

Chapter Seven

It's been several years since I've been to Las Vegas, and I can't believe how much the city of sin has changed in that time. New hotels have sprouted up while old ones have been torn down. Aging ones have been renovated and made over to match the caliber of the new ones.

I'm dying to get a moment alone with Haddie. We haven't really had one since this whole adventure started, and I need her advice on how I should act in light of Beckett's revelations. We had a quick moment alone in the airplane while we were freshening up, but not nearly long enough to have a real discussion about the night's events.

Lights and sounds surround us, assaulting our senses as we exit the limo. Sammy nods discretely to Colton and takes the lead as we walk up a set of stairs into an entrance at the Venetian. Within moments we are walking into TAO. Colton's hand is on the small of my back, and I notice conveniently that Beckett's hand is doing the same on Haddie's. I wonder if he's just being a gentleman or if there's something else possibly going on. *Interesting.*

I realize that people are starting to stare at us as Colton's name is hurriedly murmured around the Friday night crowd who've gathered in hopes of seeing a celebrity. Camera phones flash and I look up at Colton to see his reaction. He's all smiles with the crowd, but when he looks over at me, his eyes warm up with what's missing from his public one. His nap has sobered him up some, but I can still sense that playful Colton is just within reach.

We skirt around the long line of people waiting for the chance to enter. As we near the hostess podium, a woman steps out from behind it and motions for us to follow her. Wow, life must be nice when you're Colton Donavan. *No lines and women at your fingertips.*

Colton leads me by the hand as we walk past the giant Buddha on the way to our private table. Heads turn and flashes explode against the darkened atmosphere of the room as we pass through. I hear Colton's name murmured a couple more times within the crowd before he stops and turns to face me.

I look at him, a puzzled expression on my face as he steps toward me and unexpectedly captures my mouth with his. At first I freeze—I mean we are in the middle of a very swanky and completely packed restaurant—but as Colton deepens the kiss, as his fingertips cup my face and hold my head still, I succumb to him. His taste is just too devouring and his pull on me too magnetic to resist.

The sounds of the restaurant's patrons fade away. Colton kisses me like a man drawing his last breath and I am his air. It's passionate and possessive and provocative. *And holy fuck his addictive taste drags me under and takes hold.* My mind starts to come back to reality when the whistles and hollers of onlookers begin to register in my brain.

The crowd around us gets louder as they urge on our public display. Colton keeps his hands cupping my face but tears his lips from mine. His eyes register unfiltered lust, but the grin he flashes me is arrogant and mischievous. The only thought in my head is *wow*, but he's left me so breathless that forming that simple word isn't even a possibility. I give him a questioning look.

He just cocks his head to the side, a gleam lighting up his emerald eyes. "If they're gonna stare, Ryles, we might as well put on a good show!" He wags his eyebrows at me and brushes a chaste kiss on my lips before grabbing my hand and following the hostess standing off to the left of us. The dumbfounded look on her face reflects exactly how I feel.

Playful Colton has reappeared.

Cheers follow us out of the main room into our private dining area, and it is only then that I can read the stunned thoughts dancing across Haddie's expression. I shrug at her and she just grins back at me, eyes wide and dimples deep.

We reach our table and Colton pulls me into his arms before I have a chance to sit in the chair he's pulled out for me. "I haven't told you yet how absolutely stunning you look tonight." He breathes into my ear. "And now every guy in this restaurant knows you're mine," he says in case the claim he'd just staked wasn't clear enough. He presses his lips at the spot just below my ear. "You look sexy as hell in that dress, but I must confess that all I can think about is getting you out of it." He chuckles—a seductive sound that wraps its way inside my body and causes the fingers of desire to tickle in my lower belly. "Thank you for coming tonight, Ryles."

Dinner is delicious and seems uneventful compared to the whirlwind of the past couple of hours. The conversation among the four of us flows easily, and I can see why Colton likes Beckett. He's funny and witty and really grounded, having no trouble putting Colton in his place when he needs to be. They banter back and forth like little old women, but their affection for one another is obvious.

Sammy sits at a table near us with eyes wary at all times. He's prevented our meal from being interrupted a couple of times from eager ladies wanting pictures with Colton, if not something more.

I catch myself staring at him randomly during dinner. His charisma and enthusiasm are infectious, and I love watching how his face lights up when telling a story or relaying an event. He's polite and attentive to everyone during the meal, making sure that all of our needs are met. He steals little kisses here and there coupled with the squeeze of my hand or the trace of a fingertip on my bare shoulder. I wonder if he has any clue the fire he is stoking within me with his casual affection.

I sip the last of my Tom Collins and realize I have a slight buzz going when Colton's phone alerts an incoming text. He looks down and laughs at the message. "Gotta hot date, Ace?" I tease him with a smirk on my face. He looks up from his phone to meet my eyes at the same time Haddie snorts at my nickname. He just raises an eyebrow and flashes that mischievous grin I adore. In the midst of staring at me, I see the moment his brain registers why Haddie's laughing.

"You," he says across the table pointing at Haddie.

"Me?" she says coyly as she takes a sip through her straw.

"You know what A.C.E. stands for," he says with excitement, and I can see the cogs turn in his head as he figures out how to play this.

"Now why would you think that?" Haddie flutters her eyelashes with feigned innocence.

"Spill it, Montgomery," Colton demands playfully. Haddie's eyes dart over to me and her smile widens, but she says nothing. "What can I bribe you with?

"Well," Haddie replies in her best bedroom voice. "There's definitely a lot of things you could do to me to make me talk." She breathes out, licking her bottom lip and pausing. "You know Ry and I like to play a little on our own together," she says suggestively, eyeing him up and down. The look on Colton's face is utter shock and, being the guy that he is, unfiltered lust. It's taking everything I have to not burst out laughing. "If you want me to talk, you could always join us," she suggests, "and play a little…"

He works a swallow down his throat, his eyes darting back and forth between us before a lascivious smirk turns up that skillful mouth of his. "Very convincing, Haddie…And as much as my dick's enjoying the thought, I'm not taking the bait, sweetheart," he replies while Beckett barks out a laugh.

"Damn, Haddie." Becks shakes his head. "You had me going for a minute there!"

We all laugh as Haddie throws her napkin at him and turns to me with a smile on her face. "He'll never get it."

"Attractive, charming, and exquisite," Colton guesses and then blows on his knuckles and rubs them against his chest.

"Nope." I smirk at him as I play with the straw in my drink.

"More like all consuming ego," Beckett mocks.

"Nope," I repeat, my standard response.

"Saved by the bell!" Colton says as the waiter places dessert plates filled with chocolate confections in front of us.

We enjoy our dessert, the playful banter continuing, but no matter where my eyes wander, they always come back to Colton. He looks up as I'm admiring his devilishly handsome face and smiles softly at me.

"You ready?"

I return his smile and nod.

"Haddie? Becks? You game?" They both agree and gather their things. I start to stand up and find myself tugged backwards so I land on Colton's lap. I catch a glimpse of his wicked grin before his lips close over mine. His tongue slips between my lips and teases mine with tantalizing slow licks and sweeps into my mouth. He tastes of mint and rum, and all I can think of is how these little kisses here and there are not enough to last me all evening. They are a cruel tease when I've already had the real thing and know it's mind-blowingly better. His hand slides slowly up the outside of my thigh, fingertips gliding underneath the hem of my dress, kneading my soft skin with his roughened fingers.

Teasing me.

Before I can even process a coherent thought, he pulls back and kisses me on the tip of my nose. I release a frustrated sigh, needing so much more to soothe the ache he's seated in me.

He chuckles softly at my response. "Let's go," he says, nodding his head toward the door.

We've spent the last hour and a half occupying the casino floor with a flamboyant flair. Much to Sammy's dismay, Colton decided that he wanted to play some Craps. After some initial losing, Colton ended up at a table surrounded by a crowd as he rolled again and again to their cheers of encouragement and the benefit of his wallet.

His adrenaline is still amped up, and I can feel it vibrating off of him as our car pulls along a back entrance of the Palms Casino a little after midnight. We've all had a lot to drink and I'm more than ready to release some energy on the dance floor.

"Now the fun really begins, ladies!" he exclaims before tipping back the rest of his drink and grabbing my hand.

We exit the car and are whisked via a side door through the hotel and into a back entrance to the nightclub, Rain. The energetic beat of the song *Animal* fills the club and reverberates through my body. An employee leads us up a stairway and moves a velvet rope with a sign that notes *reserved* so we can pass into the VIP area.

Such an odd feeling to be treated as the only patrons in a club filled with hundreds of other people just feet away.

We're led onto the mezzanine level, and when we enter, a roar of cheers startles me. Colton doesn't seem surprised, and I realize that the thirty plus people in front of me are who Colton's been coordinating all night long. He is suddenly pulled into the crowd of people, collecting pats on the back from the guys and overly long hugs from the women.

I step back, allowing him to have the attention of his friends and look at our surroundings. I count six rooms on this level that overlook the dance floor and it seems as if Colton has rented them all out for the night. I step toward the railing and watch the mass of people below gyrate and move with the pulse of the music.

"You doing okay?"

I look over at Haddie, relieved to have her here, and smile. "Yes. It's just all a bit more than I'm used to."

"I guess he's a little over the top, huh?"

"Just a tad." I laugh. "So, Beckett?" I ask, arching my eyebrows.

"He is hella cute..." she shrugs "...but you know how that goes." She laughs in her typical carefree Haddie way. If she wants, she'll have him eating out of her hand by the night's end. *That's just Haddie.* "You wanna dance?"

I look for Colton to tell him that we're going down to the floor, but he's in the middle of a wildly animated conversation. He'll figure it out. Within moments we've made our way downstairs, and have worked ourselves into the crowd moving on the floor. It feels so good to let go and move with the beat, to get lost for a moment and forget the anniversary that started the minute the clock passed midnight.

After a couple of songs, I look up toward the balcony above us to see Colton standing at the railing. He searches the crowd and it takes a few moments before he finds me. I have a déjà vu moment when our eyes lock—a different club this time but the same intense heat between us. His face falls into shadow momentarily, and I can't help but remember wondering on our first date if he was an angel fighting through the darkness or a devil breaking into the light. Right now, looking up and completely consumed by him, he is most definitely my struggling angel. And yet I know the devil in him is always just beneath the surface.

I continue moving despite our irrefutable connection—the one that stops my breath and kick starts my heart every time he looks at me. I smile and motion for him to come down. He just shakes his head in a measured acceptance of whatever it is that he's thinking and smiles before disappearing from sight.

The song changes and I hear the opening notes to Usher's *Scream*. I throw my arms up and swivel my hips to the beat, letting the music wash over me. I sing my favorite line. *"Got no drink in my hand but I'm wasted, getting drunk on the thought of you naked."* I snap my eyes open on the last word when I feel hands slide around my waist from behind and pull me backwards. Haddie's smile tells me that it's Colton, and I relax against him as I see Beckett and a few more of his friends from upstairs join us.

The soft curves of my body fit against the hard edges of his, and I close my eyes as we start to move together. Every movement against each other has my skin prickling and my insides igniting. Each nerve in my body is attuned to the feel of him against me. His strong hands map the lines of my torso: urging, grabbing, enticing. His hips move with mine, the ridge of his erection tempting me with each movement. We mimic each other in unfulfilled need, in mounting desire.

He turns me around to face him, the demand of his hands forcing me to do what he wants arouses me further. It evokes images of his skillful fingers running the length of my sex before parting me and slipping into me. I groan at the thought and somehow he hears me despite the music because the sexy smirk on his face and darkening eyes tell me he feels the same. I know he wants more than just this frustrating but sensual as hell petting with our clothes on.

Chapter Eight

We dance a few more songs. Each brush against him adds to the mounting need within me. A seductive game, that's tantalizing, sensuous, and felt by both of us despite the lack of words. The opening notes of Ginuine's *Pony* filters through the speakers, and the suggestive tone of the song is too much for Colton to handle. He grabs my hand and pulls me with obvious purpose through the crowd on the dance floor. Impatience, need, and determination radiates off of him and vibrates into me as he stops at the foot of the stairs. Every part of my body is on high alert when he puts his hand on my back to urge me up the steps. I'm on the first riser when he spins me around and captures my mouth in a blistering kiss filled with urgency.

He attacks my mouth with a definite purpose, thoroughly obliterating all hopes of self-discipline when it comes to him. But before I can give in to the temptation at my fingertips and react wholeheartedly, he ends the kiss just as abruptly as he began it, leaving me wanting for more and on the cusp of begging.

Colton starts up the stairs, my hand in his as I follow. When we reach the top where Sammy stands, Colton leans over and says something in his ear that the music drowns out. Sammy nods his head and turns on his heel, Colton and I right behind him.

We reach the sixth and last VIP room on the balcony, and I follow Colton's lead, stopping and looking out over the club below. I glance over my shoulder to see Sammy ushering his friends out of the last room before I look back to Colton. His eyes are focused on the crowd below, his jaw clenched, and I wonder if I've done something wrong to piss him off.

I'm a little taken aback. What in the hell did I do? He's going to choose right now to be pissed? I guess I should be used to his confusing, back and forth moods, but I'm not. We remain silent waiting for whatever Sammy is doing, and I resign myself that there is most likely a fight on the horizon for us. Can't we just have one night without it?

Sammy leans into Colton's ear and tells him something, and then we are on the move again. Colton leads me by my hand into the sixth and now vacant VIP area. The minute we clear the wall and are away from anyone's view, Colton's body crashes into mine instantaneously, forcibly pinning me against the wall.

I only have time for one coherent thought before the taste of Colton pulls me under. He's not pissed at me. *Not hardly. He's consumed with desire.*

All of the heat and urgency in the kiss on the stairs is intensified and then some. Our teeth clash and bodies mesh as his tongue pushes through my lips and licks into my mouth. His hands are everywhere on my body at once, each touch flaring my need and shooting desire like a mainline to my core.

I need him in me, filling me, moving inside of me, right now like I need my next breath.

His tongue continues its tormenting assault on my mouth, his hands seeking my bare flesh as the words of the song fuel the desire raging between us. He reaches down and pulls my leg up to his hip, his hands sliding up and under my hem. Desperate fingers dig into my willing flesh. His hand is so close yet so far away from where I need it to be that all I can do is groan out in a mixture of frustration and need. He nips my bottom lip, followed by the soothing lick of his tongue, prompting me to tighten my grip on his hair. I tug on it, my silent way of saying I need him too. Want him just as desperately.

Right here. Right now.

He drags himself away from me, his chest rising and falling with his labored breaths and his eyes bore into mine despite the fog of lust in them. "I don't like all of those guys dancing around you," he says, his strained voice is playful despite the violent desire I see raging in his eyes.

"It got your attention, didn't it?" I tease in a pant of breath, surprised by his jealousy.

"Sweetheart, if you want my attention..." he smirks, his hands cupping my ass and yanking me into him, the ridge of his erection pressing deliciously into my softness "...all you have to do is ask."

"And pull you away from your adulating *throng* of friends?" I tease, arching my eyebrows at him, my sarcasm apparent.

"So you'd rather go dance amidst a *throng* of random men?"

I suck in my breath as he moves his hands up the sides of my torso and stops beside my breasts. My body is so pent up, so on the edge of need that it responds instantly when it gets the touch it craves. His thumbs connect with my nipples and they pebble instantly as he rubs up and down. I lean my head back, closing my eyes, and allow myself to be swallowed in the sensation the stroke of his thumbs create. My head clouds, trying to think of a witty comeback to this bantering foreplay between us. "It got you out there, didn't it?" I bait, running my tongue over my bottom lip. "Just think of it as a means to an end, Ace."

Colton brushes his thumbs up and down once more, making sure he has my attention. "Oh, baby," he murmurs, "the only end that's going to be sticking into your means, is mine." He leans in to nip at my bottom lip before pulling back to meet my gaze, one hand squeezing over my breast possessively. "*Mine.*"

The intensity in his eyes prevents me from laughing. I lean into him, my hand reaching out to run over the ridge of his arousal and cup him through his pants. And I'm not sure where my brazen confidence comes from, but I bring my mouth up to his ear and whisper just above the noise. "Prove it."

Colton emits a strangled groan, and in a flash he grips my head and holds me still while his mouth crashes against mine before breaking apart way too soon.

"Come," he says, pulling me with him as he walks backwards to one of the chairs toward the back of the room. He sits down and pulls me onto him. "Straddle me," he commands, and the need in me is so overwhelming I obey without a second thought. I hike my dress up my thighs and place my knees on either side of him, lowering my center over his lap.

He looks at me, a wicked grin on his face that makes me want to earn the look he's giving me. Eyes locked on mine, he places his hands on my bare knees and runs his hands up my thighs. When he reaches my hem, he just keeps pushing my dress up. My lips part at their wanton progression, and in a quick moment of modesty, I twist my head over my shoulder to look at the doorway to make sure no one is watching.

"Don't worry," Colton whispers, unfettered need straining his voice, "Sammy's guarding the door. He's not letting anyone back here."

I'm relieved and yet uncomfortable with the thought that Sammy knows or can assume what we're doing in here. My worry falls to the wayside because Colton's hands squeeze my thighs, and I instinctively spread them wider as need thunders through my body.

"I've wanted to fuck this sweet pussy of yours all night," his voice growls in my ear. "Ever since I saw your nipples tight and pressed against your tank top. Since I watched you dancing, teasing me with this sexy body of yours." His thumbs brush over my dampened panties and I shiver, his touch like a lightning strike to my sex. "I want to feel you on the inside. I want to feel your cum coat me when I fuck you. Want to hear that sound you make when you lose it. And. I. Just. Can't. Wait. Any. Longer," he grits out between taunting kisses.

And then he finally gives me what I crave. His mouth captures mine, parting my lips and claiming my every reaction. At the same time one thumb pulls my panties to the side and the other connects with my clit. A blast of indescribable pleasure jolts through me with his touch, his lips smothering the moan he coaxes from me.

I dig my fingers into the muscled flesh of his shoulders, not caring if my nails mark him. His tongue delves into my mouth, a languorous exploration that is thorough and seductive while his fingers part my cleft and tease skillfully so that every part of me tightens in a frenzy of need. His hand slips down to where my legs are spread, and he wets his fingers with my obvious arousal before sliding them back up to coat me. On his caress back down, he doesn't stop but rather tucks two fingers into me.

I gasp out a broken breath at the sublime sensation, desperate for this and the anticipation of what is to come. His fingers start to move inside me and I flex my hips as best as I can, opening myself up to him so he can have complete access. I close my eyes, my head falling back as the ecstasy of his touch threatens to overwhelm me.

"Fucking Christ," he groans against the soft skin of my throat. "Baby, you are so fucking wet for me. So ready. Makes me so fucking hard for you. Come for me. Come so I can sink myself into you when you're still riding your orgasm."

His blatant words seduce me, pushing me higher toward the edge. The sensations his fingers incite make me forget we're in a public nightclub, but at the same time, I know. I know because the exhilaration of being where we can be caught so easily, heightens my arousal, makes me notice every brush and sweep of his body against mine. Every graze of flesh against flesh.

His lips tease the curve of my neck as his other hand gives me the friction I need on my clit to push me over the razor thin edge of sanity.

The intense rush of heat hits me, pulling me under its rolling waves as I splinter into what feels like a million pieces. I drop my head on Colton's shoulder, my heartbeat racing and body pulsing with the orgasmic pleasure that washes through me. I suck in short, sharp breaths as he withdraws his fingers and fumbles with his zipper between my legs.

Before I have time to recover, Colton is guiding my hips up and positioning himself at my entrance. I'm so lost in the moment, in the pleasure, in Colton, that the outside world ceases to exist.

Right now it's me and Colton and the carnal need igniting an inferno between us. When we're like this—connected as one and absorbed in each other—I forget everything else. His taste, his scent, his domination of my senses, are my only focus.

I sink slowly onto him, feeling every thick inch of him as I lower my hips until fully seated. Colton's rough growl of a response and his fingers digging into my hips are the only reaction I need. I lean forward and cover his mouth with mine as I rock slowly onto him, his body tensing as mine tightens around him in acceptance. I continue my movement, sliding up and down his tortured length. My hands fan over the taut muscles of his back, and my tongue coaxes and demands for him to take everything from me because I want nothing less than all of him.

His hands push and pull me on each of his thrusts. I am so focused on giving him everything that he needs, everything that he wants, I don't even realize my body drowning in the liquid heat that fills me. Colton's face tightens and nostrils flare, a sure sign of his ratcheting pleasure and impending climax. His length thickens inside of me, expanding me so when he pushes into me the next time, I detonate in an explosion of sensation. He surges inside of me a couple more times and then his hands grip my hips forcibly, holding me still as his orgasm rushes through him. He throws his head back, his mouth falling open as his shattered moan fills our immediate space before being drowned out by the cacophony of noise in the club.

I watch his face, the reactions to his release flickering across his features when it hits me what I've just done. *Holy shit!* What in the hell am I thinking, and who took the real me and transplanted this wanton woman in my place? I start to shift off of Colton when he stops me from breaking our connection. Instead, he reaches up and gathers me against him, holding me for a sweet, unexpected moment before kissing the top of my head and then the tip of my nose.

We clean up and fix our disheveled appearances without speaking. I start fidgeting and fussing when Colton grabs my hand and squeezes it until I look up at him. A slow grin curls the corners of his mouth as he pulls me into him before pressing a chaste kiss on my mouth. He shakes his head at me. "You're constantly full of surprises, Ryles."

And you're the biggest surprise of them all.

I sip my drink as I sit back with Haddie in the VIP lounge, my body swaying subtly to the beat of the music below. I need a quick break from being on my feet, my shoes starting to take their toll. I see Sammy guarding the stairs and avert my eyes immediately, embarrassed about any conclusions he's drawn as to the less than innocent nature of Colton and my time alone.

I hear a high-pitched shriek as Sammy tries to avert someone from coming up the stairs. Colton, who's immersed in a conversation, turns his head toward the commotion. He steps back to see who it is and a wide grin spreads across his face before he motions for Sammy to let whomever it is up. My curiosity is definitely piqued when I see one of the guys he's talking to nudge him in an atta-boy manner.

Both Haddie and I turn our heads just in time to take in the longest pair of legs I've ever seen in what I think is the shortest skirt ever made strut toward Colton. The rest of the woman is just as spectacular as she tosses her head, throwing her long mane of blonde hair over her shoulder so that it falls just above her perfectly showcased backside.

She grabs Colton in a longer than necessary hug, her lips kissing the corner of his mouth as she leans back, a huge smile on her perfect face. It's when I see her that I suck in a breath, realizing who she is. Recognition dawns on Haddie at the same time, and we both look at each other in surprise. She is Cassandra Miller, the current darling of Hollywood as well as Playboy's latest celebrity centerfold. And despite completing their greeting, her hands are still resting on Colton's bicep, and her perfectly enhanced body is rubbing up against his with his hand resting politely on the small of her back.

I'm surprised by the twinge in my gut at the sight of them together. I've never been a jealous person, but then again, I've never been with someone as all-consuming as Colton Donavan.

I don't like her hands on him. *At all.*

Mine. He tells me that all the time. It's one of those possessive statements that I oddly find to be so damn arousing. And right now, I'd like to do nothing more than waltz up between the two of them and stake my claim on Colton as he did earlier to me in TAO.

But I don't move. I just sit and watch them interact, talk, her giggle stupidly and bat her eyelashes at a ridiculously fast pace while she keeps her hand on him. Why don't I move?

And then it hits me. They're stunning together. Absolutely stunning and this is who most would expect him to be with: the blonde bombshell, fantasy for many a men with the devastatingly handsome playboy, the desire of women everywhere. The picture perfect couple by Hollywood standards. He may have come here with me, and will be leaving with me, but like every woman, I have my own insecurities about my looks and my sex appeal.

And right now, looking from the blonde beauty then back to myself, those insecurities have just been put on display for everyone to see. For everyone to scrutinize. Even if I'm the only one who seems to be doing it.

I bring my fingers to my lips in thought and a cat ate the canary grin starts to spread across my face.

Fuck insecurity.

Fuck perfect, long-legged blondes.

Fuck playing it safe.

I close my eyes momentarily, remembering the feel of Colton's stubble scraping against the skin of my neck; his fingers bruising my hips as he helped me move over him; the look on his face as he came; the slight desperation with which he held me to him afterward in the room right next to where we're sitting now.

I remember Beckett's warning; trying to control Colton is like trying to grab the wind. He's gotten the playboy title for a reason. The short time we've been together isn't going to change that. Women are always going to be attracted to him, want him.

Cassandra obviously does. She's a dead giveaway with her constant touching and monopolizing demand on his attention. With how she leans in to speak to him, her hand pressed to his chest, leaving it there as he puts his mouth to her ear in response.

I'm not going to be irrational and deny the fact that I'm a tad bit jealous—alcohol most likely fueling my insecurity. Or maybe I'm just hormonal…I don't know. I'm a woman; insecurity is just par for the course in the grand scheme of things.

I snort out a laugh. Haddie looks over at me like I've lost it. "You're okay with…" She lifts her chin in the direction of Colton and

Cassandra.

I look at them a moment longer before I nod my head. "It's not like I have to worry about him seeing her naked." I laugh, referring to her Playboy centerfold spread. "A huge portion of the male population has already done that and probably jacked off to her."

Haddie laughs out loud and shakes her head at me. I think she's a little surprised by my lack of a reaction. "*True*. At least you don't have staples in the middle of your body."

"Exactly." I smirk. "I have Colton *in me* instead." I love the look of shock on her face as I suck down the rest of my drink. "I need a shot and I wanna dance. You coming?" I walk out of the alcove without looking to see if she's following or not.

After downing our signature double shots of tequila, Haddie and I descend the stairs and enter into the rhythmic chaos of the dance floor. Songs come and go as we dance, and after a couple, I stop looking up at the balcony above to see if Colton's watching me. I know he isn't. That tingling of my skin telling me his presence is near is absent.

I'm thirsty and in need of a respite, so I motion to Haddie that I'm going to the bar to get another drink. Something to help dampen the dull edge of insecurity that is still holding my thoughts hostage.

I finagle my way up to the bar squeezing myself through the crowd, and prepare myself for a wait when I notice the numerous people in line. The guy beside me tries to start a conversation with me in his slurred voice, but I just smile politely and angle my body away from his. I focus my attention on watching the bartenders slowly inch their way back down the bar one order at time.

The man beside me tries again, grabbing onto my upper arm and pulling me toward him, insisting he'll buy me a drink. I shrug my arm out of his grasp with an irritated but polite refusal. I think he's gotten the hint, but I'm proven wrong when he places his hand on my hip and forcefully tugs me against his side.

"C'mon, gorgeous." He breathes into my ear, the stale alcohol on his breath repulsing me. My discomfort grows, the hair on the back of my neck starting to rise. "Baby, I can show you a good time."

I push against his chest, trying to separate myself from him, but he just tightens his grip on my hip. I turn to search the crowd for help from Haddie when the guy's arm is suddenly yanked off of me.

"Get your fucking hands off of her!" I hear the growl a beat before Colton's fist connects with his jaw. His head snaps back and the guy stumbles and trips over someone's leg, landing on the ground. Despite my distaste for violence, a shiver of relief courses through me at the sight of Colton.

Before I can even react any further than shouting, "Colton, no!" one of the guy's buddies takes a swing at him. His fist glances off of Colton's cheek. I try to rush toward him, but my feet are cemented to the ground. Adrenaline, alcohol, and fear course through me. With lightning speed, Colton cocks his arm back to take another swing, murder in his eyes and an expressionless face. Before he can retaliate, Sammy's arms close around him and pull him back. Colton's rage is obvious. A vein pulses in his temple, his face is grimaced in restraint, and his eyes burn a threatening warning.

"Time to go, Colt!" Beckett shouts at him, a resigned look on his stoic face. "It's not worth the lawsuit they'll try to slap you with…" And then I see Haddie and several other guys from the crew in my periphery. The guys grab a still fuming but more collected Colton by the arms and take him from Sammy. Once Sammy knows that Colton's taken care of, he turns to the men, dwarfing them with his sheer size, a look of amused contempt on his face as if he's telling them, "Take a shot, I dare you." They look at him and then back at each other before scattering quickly as security makes its way toward us.

I stand there shaking until Sammy puts his arm around me and escorts me out of the club.

Chapter Nine

When Sammy pushes open the door for me, the cold air of the night hits me like a refreshing blast after the stuffy, smoke filled club. He leads me to the outskirts of the parking garage where the lone limo sits apart from the rest of the cars in the lot. As we get closer, I see Colton's back, his hands spread wide on the retaining wall bordering the edge of the garage, his weight leaning on them, and his head hanging down between his shoulders. I can sense the fury radiating off of him in waves as we draw near.

Beckett, who's leaning against the open door of the car, meets my eyes as we approach, uncertainty evident in his before nodding his head at me and sliding into the car next to Haddie. Sammy stops, but I continue forward toward Colton.

The click of my heels on the concrete alerts Colton that I'm near, but he remains facing away from me. I trace the lines of his body's silhouette against the expansive glitz of the Vegas strip, his imposing figure painting a striking contrast to the sparkle of lights beyond. I stop a few feet from him and watch his shoulders rise and fall in rapid succession as his tension slowly abates.

When he finally turns to face me, his shoulders squared, his eyes dancing with fire, and his jaw rigid with tension, I realize I'm wrong in thinking his anger is gone.

"What the fuck did you think you were doing?" His voice is ice cold.

His words hit me like whiplash, taking me aback with unbelievable force. I thought he was angry at the guy he punched, not with me. Where the hell does he get off being pissed at me? If he was paying attention to his date, he'd know the answer. "What do you think I was doing, Colton? That I was—"

"I asked you a question, Rylee," he grits out.

"And I was trying to fucking answer it before you so rudely cut me off," I spit at him, having no problem going toe-to-toe with him tonight. Maybe my intake of alcohol has taken a bit of the edge off, so I'm not intimidated by his intensity. His eyes pierce through the darkness and into mine. *Then again, maybe not.* "I was buying a drink, Colton. *A drink.* That's it!" I throw my hands up as I shout at him, my voice echoing off of the concrete walls.

He looks at me, the muscle in his jaw pulsing as he regards me. "Buying a drink, Rylee? Or flirting around to get someone to buy a drink for you?" he accuses, taking a step closer to me. Despite the lack of light, I can see the fire burning in his eyes and the rage fueling the tension in his neck. Where is all of this coming from?

What. The. Fuck? How dare he accuse me of paying attention to other guys when he was up there preoccupied with Ms. Bunny of the Month? I was being cool, not getting pissed off about how touchy-feely Cassandra was with him, trying to forgo the juvenile emotions I wanted to feel over it. *But fuck it.* If he's going to get mad about a guy offering to buy me a drink and touching me even though I said no, then I'm sure as hell going to be pissed about her blatantly displayed attraction to him. Attraction that he certainly didn't reject.

I'm done with this conversation. Alcohol and anger only result in words you can't take back in the morning. And we've both had way too much to be rational. "Whatever. We're done here," I huff as I turn on my heel, intent on heading back to the limo.

"Answer me," he commands as he grabs my upper arm, stopping me in my tracks. I see Beckett step back out of the limo, a wary look on his face as he stares down Colton over my shoulder. The silent warning is obvious, but the message behind it is unclear.

"What's it to you?"

"I'm waiting," he says, keeping his hand on my arm but stepping around to block my path toward the car.

"I was buying *myself* a drink. *That's it.* Big fucking deal!" I jerk my arm out of his grasp, fatigue from the night's events suddenly hitting me like a bat to the back of the head.

Colton's eyes bore into mine as if he's looking for my betrayal or confession of wrongdoing. "There was plenty of alcohol up top. Was that not good enough for you?" he taunts. "You had to go trolling for a guy to buy you one?"

His words slap at me, knock the wind from my sails. What the fuck is his problem? I can't believe that he'd even think that first of all, but second—and shockingly so—I'm surprised by the quiver in his voice that hints at a touch of insecurity.

Like I could want something more after having him.

I take a step toward him, my voice low but implacable. "I don't need a man *or* bottle service to make me happy, Colton."

He arches an eyebrow at me. "Uh-huh." He snorts derisively, cleary choosing to not believe me. *He's obviously dated some choice women.*

I sigh, frustrated already with our conversation. "You've spent enough money on tonight. On me. On everything." I huff. "You may be used to all of your *women* needing that to be satisfied. Not me."

"Of course not." He snorts sarcastically.

"I'm a big girl." I continue ignoring his flippant comment. "I can buy my own damn drinks and pay my own way, especially if when you pay it means that you have some kind of ownership over me."

His eyes widen at my words. "You're being ridiculous."

Does he not realize he does this? That he gives so charitably in exchange for people to like and love him? "Look, you're a very generous guy. More so than most people I know, but why?" I place my hand on his arm and squeeze. "Unlike most people in there, I don't expect you to pay my way."

"No girlfr—no one I'm with pays when they're with me."

"That's very chivalrous of you." I run my hand up his arm and lay it on his cheek, my voice softening, relieved that we have seemed to skirt around having this argument. "But I don't need any of that pomp and circumstance to want to be with you." He just stares at me, emerald irises trying to comprehend the honesty in my words. "You have so much more to give to someone than material excess."

I think my words have hit their mark because Colton falls silent, a war of emotions flowing through his eyes before they break from mine and look out at the city of sin. The muscle in his jaw tics as he pushes down whatever demons he's fighting internally. I notice his posture stiffen as he shakes my hand off his face, and I can sense his discomfort with the direction our conversation has taken. "You let a guy put his hands on you," he says in a dangerously quiet voice.

At first I'm hurt by his accusation, but when I look in his eyes, *I see it.* I see the truth behind Beckett's revelations about his feelings for me. I see that he's scared by it and unsure of how to handle it. I see that he's looking for a reason to pick a fight as a way to deny his feelings.

He wants a fight? I'll give him a fight because just below my surface is the fear that maybe I'm just what he needs and he might never acknowledge it. That he is exactly what I need and someone like Cassandra just might take that chance away from me. My mind flashes back to the thought of her hands on him. "And your point is what?" I counter with more confidence than I feel. "I'm not going to apologize because someone else finds me attractive." I shrug. "*You sure as hell weren't paying any attention to me.*"

He ignores my comment as only he can, shrugging it off as if I'm at fault here. "I've told you before, Ry, *I don't share.*"

I cross my arms over my chest. "*Well neither do I.*"

"What's that supposed to mean?" The bewildered look on his face tells me he really has no clue as to what I'm talking about. Typical, clueless male.

"Oh c'mon, Colton. Most of those women in there want you, and you were more than willing to be touchy-feely with them." I throw up my hands in frustration when he looks at me as if I've gone crazy, so I figure I'll give a specific example. "You seem to have no problem having your hands on Cassandra and hers on you," I accuse, flipping my hair like her and placing my hand on his chest, batting my eyelashes.

"Cassie?" he stutters incredulously. "Oh please."

"Really? It was obvious to every person up there that she wants you. Roll your eyes all you want and pretend you didn't notice, but you know you loved every minute of it—Center of attention, Colton. Life of the party, Colton. *Playboy, Colton,*" I accuse, turning my back to him, rolling my shoulders and shaking my head. I briefly lock eyes with Beckett who's still standing against the limo, arms crossed over his chest and stoic face devoid of judgment. I turn back to face Colton. "Why is that okay for you? Isn't turnabout fair play? At least I told the guy you punched to get his hands off of me. I didn't see you asking Cassie to stop…"

Colton takes a step toward me, lights from beyond playing against the shadows on his face. The devil has once again surfaced and is indeed trying to pull me into his darkness. "I believe it was you I was *fucking* up there tonight. Not any of them." His voice implacable and holding just a hint of edge as he watches for a reaction. I cringe knowing that Beckett just heard that.

"Yeah, you're right. You were with me, but I find it funny minutes later you were with her!" I shout back at him. "You punched a guy for touching me tonight and yet you stood there and let her rub up against you without so much as a thought to pushing her off you. Well I don't share either. The irony, huh?"

Colton's jaw flexes before he raises his eyebrows, a ghost of a smile gracing his lips. "I didn't take you for the jealous type."

"*And I didn't take you for my type at all*," I counter, my voice icy with contempt.

"Watch it," he warns.

"Or what?" I goad, taking a fortifying breath. "Like I said, I can take care of myself. The guy offered to buy me a drink. I was in the process of telling him no thank you in so many words when you stormed up to save the day." I'm not sure why I feel the need to lie about this. Maybe I'm trying to prove to Colton that I can in fact take care of myself. That I don't need the macho bullshit. I'm not sure, but I've thrown it out there, I might as well follow through with it. He doesn't have to know that I was getting a little unnerved at the situation. "The guy didn't deserve to be hit."

Colton's head snaps up as if I've just punched him. "Now you're defending him?" He brings his hands up to his neck and pulls down on it in frustration. "You're fucking unbelievable!" he shouts out into the empty garage.

"And you're drunk, irrational, and out of control!" I yell back.

"*No one touches what's mine without consequences*," he grates out.

"You have to have me first, Colton," I say with a shake of my head, "and you've made it quite clear that all you want from me is a quick fuck when it's convenient for you!" My voice is firm but betrays me when it wavers on my last words.

"You know that's not true." His voice is quiet with an undertone of desperation.

"I do? How's that?" I throw my hands up in exasperation. "Every time I get too close or things go beyond your stupid rules, you make sure to put me in my place."

"Jesus. Fucking. Christ. Rylee." He exhales through gritted, running his fingers through his hair and turning from me to walk a few steps away.

"A *pit stop* isn't going to save you this time," I state calmly, wanting him to know that he can't cop out now to avoid the rest of this discussion. I *need* answers and deserve to know where I stand.

He hisses out a loud exhale of breath, his hands clenching and unclenching at his sides. We stand there in silence for a few moments as I look at his back, and he looks at the city beyond. After a moment he turns around and holds his arms out, his eyes full of a nameless emotion I can't decipher. "This is me, Rylee!" he shouts. "All of me in my fucked up glory! I'm not Max—*perfect in every way*, never making a goddamned mistake. I can't live up to the incomparable standard he's set, to the pedestal you've placed him on!"

I suck in a breath, his words hitting their target. How dare he throw Max and what we had in my face. Thoughts don't process. Words don't form. Tears well in my eyes as I think about Max and who he was and Colton and what he is to me. Confusion swamps me. Drags me under. Drowns me.

"How dare you!" I growl at him, hurt surrendering to anger before succumbing to grief.

Colton's not finished though. He takes a step toward me, pointing his finger at his chest. "But I'm alive, Rylee, and *he's not!*" His words rip into me. A tear slides down my cheek, and I turn my back to him, hiding from his words, thinking if I can't see the plea and hurt in his eyes, I won't have to accept the truth in his statement. "I'm the one here in front of you—*flesh and blood and needing*—so either you accept that it's you that I want. No one else," he rants, his voice echoing off of the concrete surrounding us and coming back to me twice as if to reinforce his words. "You need to accept me for who I am, faults and all..." his voice breaks "...or you need to get the fuck out of my life...because right now—*right now*—this is all that I can give you! All I can offer."

I can hear the pain in his voice, can feel the agony in his words, and it tears at me until a sob escapes my mouth. I bring my hand up to cover it while I clutch my other hand around my abdomen.

"That's enough, Colton!" Beckett's voice pierces through the early morning hour when he sees my anguish. "It's enough!"

In my periphery, I see Colton whirl toward him, fists clenched, emotion overwhelming him. Beckett doesn't flinch from Colton's imposing stare but rather takes another step toward him, taunting him with his eyes. "Try me, Wood," he challenges, his voice hard as steel. "You come at me and I'll knock you on that drunk, pretty-boy ass of yours in a heartbeat."

My eyes meet Beckett's for a fleeting second, the ice in his eyes surprising me before I turn to look at Colton. The features on his face are tight, and his dark hair has fallen over his forehead. The angst in his eyes is so incredibly raw. I study him as he glares at Beckett. His eyes flicker over to mine and whatever expression blankets my face holds his stare. I can see his pain and fear and uncertainty in them, and I realize that as much as his words sting—as much as they hurt me to hear—there is so much truth to them.

Max is dead and never coming back. Colton is here and very much alive, and he wants me in his life in some form or another despite his inability to acknowledge or accept it. I see the plea in his eyes for me to choose him, to accept him. Not my ghost of memories. Just him. All of him. *Even the parts that are broken.*

And the choice is so easy, I don't even have to make one.

I step forward toward the eyes that flit frantically back and forth like a lost little boy. I glance over at Beckett and give him an unsure smile. "It's okay, Becks. He's right," I whisper, turning back to Colton. "You're right. I can't keep expecting you to be like Max or compare you to what I had with him." I take another timid step toward him.

"And I don't want you to think that you have to be like Cassandra," he says, taking me by surprise that his inference about my insecurity is spot-on. I reach out my hand to him, an olive branch to our argument, and he takes it, pulling me into him. I land against the firmness of his body as he gathers me to his chest, his strong arms wrapped around me a reassurance after the cruel and callous insults we've just hurled at each other. I press my face into his neck, the beat of his pulse beneath my lips. He runs a hand up my back, tunneling it into my curls and just holds my head there. He kisses the top of my hair as I breathe in his scent.

"You. *This,*" he murmurs in a ragged exhale, "it scares the shit out of me." And my heart stops and breath catches as he falls silent, his pounding heartbeat the soundtrack to my thoughts. "I don't know *how* to...I don't know *what* to do..."

And if I hadn't already known, the raw emotion in his voice would have pushed me over the edge. My heart starts again, tumbles inside of me, and falls gloriously. I only hope he'll catch it. I fist my hand into the back of his shirt, his confession rocking me with hope and possibility. Offering us a chance. I close my eyes, taking a minute to score my memory with this moment. "*Me too, Colton,*" I murmur into the skin of his neck. "*I'm scared too.*"

"You deserve so much more that I'm capable of giving you. I don't know how or what to do to give you what you need. I just..."

I grip my fist tighter into his shirt, the fear so transparent in his tone it wrenches my heart and tugs at my soul. "That's okay, baby," I tell him, pressing another kiss against his neck. "We don't have to know all the answers right now."

"This is just..." He chokes on his words, his arms tightening around me as the sounds of Vegas swirl in the air around us. In this city of rampant sin and immorality, I have found such beauty and hope in the man holding me tight. "...so much...I don't know how..."

"We don't have to rush this. We can just take our time and see where this leads us." Desperation laces through my words.

"I don't want to give you false hope if I can't..." He shakes his head softly with an exhale to finish his statement.

I lean back and look up at the face of the man that I know has captured my heart. The heart I thought would never heal or love again. "Just try, Colton," I plead. "Please just tell me you'll try..."

Emotions war over Colton's features, his resistance to need. So much unspoken swims in his eyes. He leans down and brushes a soft, reverent sigh of a kiss on my lips before burying his face in the crook of my neck and just holds on.

I hold him there in the depths of a concrete garage. Giving as much as I am taking from the man consuming every part of me.

And it's not lost on me that he never answered my question.

The horizon is just starting to lighten to the east as we drag ourselves off of the plane and climb into the awaiting limo in Santa Monica. We are all exhausted from the whirlwind night.

I glance over at Colton's profile as we wait for Sammy to finish whatever he's doing. His head is leaning back against the headrest and his eyes are closed. My eyes track over the silhouette of his nose to his chin, down his neck and over his Adam's apple. My heart swells at the sight of him and what he's come to mean to me in such a short amount of time. He's helping me overcome some of my fears, and I can only hope in time he will trust me enough to let me in on his.

Beckett was right about Colton. He evokes such extreme emotions. He's easy to love and hate at the same time. Tonight was a breakthrough of sorts—for him to admit that I scare him—but I know in no way shape or form does that mean he's in love with me. Or that he's not going to hurt me in the end.

His lack of an answer tells me that his words and his heart are still in conflict. And that he's not sure if he can get them on the same page. He wants to. I can see it in his eyes, his posture, and the tenderness in his kiss.

But I also see the fear, sense the trepidation and inability to trust that I won't abandon him. That to love is not to give up control.

It seems like every time he gets too close, he wants to push me further away. Holding me at arms length keeps his fears at bay for a bit. Helps him push them down. Well, what if I just don't cower at the comments? Worry about his silent distance? What if instead of letting it get to me, I just shrug it off and keep going like nothing's been said? What will he do then?

Colton shifts his head over and looks at me with a softness in his eyes that makes me want to curl into him. How could I ever walk away from this face? Nothing short of him cheating on me would make me give up on him. He looks sleepy and content and still a bit buzzed.

Haddie hums the song that is playing softly on the speakers in the car. I strain to hear and meet her eyes when I recognize it as *Glitter in the Air*. Of all the songs to be on, of course it has to be this one.

"Fuckin' Pink," Colton snorts out in a sexy, sleepy voice that widens my smile.

Haddie laughs sluggishly in the seat across from us. "I could sleep for hours," she says resting her head on Beckett's shoulder.

"Mmm-hmm," Colton murmurs, shifting so he lies across the seat and places his head in my lap, "and I'm going to start now." He chuckles.

"You need all the beauty sleep you can get."

"Fuck you, Becks." Colton yawns. His voice is slurred from the mixture of both alcohol and exhaustion. "Should we finish what we started earlier?" He laughs softly as he tries to open his eyes. He is so exhausted they only open a fraction.

Beckett bellows out a laugh that resonates in the quiet of the car. "It'd be no contest. Us southern boys know how to throw a punch."

"You've got nothing on some of the fists that have been thrown my way." Colton nuzzles the back of his head into my abdomen.

"Really? Being bitch-slapped by a girl pissed off at finding out she's a one-nighter doesn't count," Beckett replies, meeting my eyes and shaking his head to tell me that he's making it up just to goad Colton. I have a feeling he might be lying.

"Mmm-hmm," Colton murmurs and then falls silent. We all assume that he's asleep, his breathing evening out, when he speaks again in an almost juvenile, dreamlike quality. "Try having your mom taking a bat to you..." he breathes "...or snapping your bone right through your fucking arm." He grunts. My eyes whip up to Beckett's, the same look of surprise I feel reflected in his. "Now that? That beats the one fucking punch I'd let you land before I knock you on your ass." He emits a sliver of a laugh. "It most definitely beats your fist any day, you cocksucker," he repeats before a soft snore slips from him.

My mind immediately flashes to the jagged scar on his arm—the one that I'd noticed last week. Now I know why he had changed the subject when I'd asked about it. I think of a little boy cowering in fear, green eyes welled with tears as his mother unleashes on him. The ache in my heart that moments before was because of my feelings for Colton has now shifted and intensified over something I can't even begin to understand or fathom.

The look on Beckett's face tells me that this is news to him. That even though he's known Colton for all these years, he hasn't had an inkling as to the horror his friend had endured as a young child.

"Like I said," Beckett whispers, "*Lifeline.*" My eyes snap up to his and he just nods with a quiet intensity. "*I think you're his lifeline.*" We exchange a silent acknowledgment and acceptance before looking back down at the man we love snoring softly in my lap.

Chapter Ten

The house is quiet and still despite the bright sun shining through the kitchen windows. It's close to noon but everyone is still asleep except for me. I'd awoken, hot and claustrophobic, with a dead to the world Colton haphazardly draped across my body. As delicious as his body felt against mine, and as much as I willed myself to go back to sleep, I couldn't. So despite Colton lying on the pillow beside me, I slowly extricated myself from him and the bed without waking him in search of Advil for my aching head.

I sit at the table, the soft snoring of Beckett asleep on the couch drifting into the kitchen. I swallow a big gulp of water hoping it will chase away the alcohol-induced fuzziness that clouds my head. I yawn again and rest my forehead on my arms that are folded on the table. *God, I'm tired.*

The distant and distinct ringing of my cell phone seeps into my dreams. I'm trying to help him. The little boy with dark hair and haunted eyes being pulled away from me by some unseen force. My hand is gripping his but my fingers are slipping ever so slowly as my muscles tire. He's pleading with me for help. The ringing of the telephone starts, startling me so I jerk and he slips away from me, crying out in fear. I scream at the loss and jolt myself awake, disoriented from my position at the kitchen table.

My heart is pounding and my breathing labored as I try to steady myself. *Just a dream*, I tell myself. Just a meaningless dream. I drop my head into my hands and push their heels into my eyes, trying to rub away the image of the little boy I couldn't save.

I hear the rumbling timbre of Colton's morning voice from my bedroom. I stand and start to walk to him when the inflection of his voice rises. "You've got a lot of nerve, lady!" resonates down the hallway.

It takes a moment for my mind to register what's going on...what day it is...the sound of my cell phone interrupting my dream. I shove the chair back and run down the hall to my bedroom. "Give me the phone, Colton!" I shout, my heart racing and my throat clogging with panic as I enter my doorway.

My eyes zero in on my cell phone at his ear. *On the bewildered look on his face.* My heart lodges in my throat, knowing the words filled with hatred that are assaulting his ears. I pray that she doesn't tell him. "Please, Colton," I plead, my hand outstretched for him to give me my phone. His eyes look up to meet mine, searching for an explanation as to what he's hearing. He shakes his head abruptly at me when I keep my hand held out.

He sighs loudly, closing his eyes before speaking. "Ma'am? Ma'am," he says more forcefully, "you've had your say, now it's time I get mine." Her voice through the speaker quiets down at his stern tone. Colton runs a hand through his hair, his V of muscle that sinks below the sheets flexes as he tenses up. "While I am truly sorry for the loss of your son, I think your accusations are sickening. Rylee did nothing wrong besides survive a horrible accident. Because she lived and Max died doesn't mean that she murdered him. No, you let me finish," he says sternly. "I understand that you're grieving and always will be, but that doesn't make Rylee guilty of killing him. It was a horrific, accident with circumstances beyond anyone's control."

I hear a litany of words in response that I can't decipher through the earpiece, my body still tense as I guess what she's revealing to him.

"And you don't think she feels guilty enough that she lived? You're not the only one who lost him that day. Do you really think a day goes by that she doesn't think about Max or the accident? That she doesn't wish it were her instead of him that died that day?"

Tears well in my eyes, Colton's words hitting too close to the truth, and I can't fight them. They slip down my cheeks and images flash through my head that will forever be burned there. Max struggling to live. Max struggling to die. My thousands of promises to God those days if we could just make it out alive.

All of us.

Something flickers through Colton's eyes at her words, and the tears come harder. There is silence between the two of them for several moments as Colton digests what she has divulged. They flash over to mine, and I'm unable to comprehend the enigmatic look they hold before darting back to look out the window outside.

"I truly am sorry for your loss, but this will be the last time you call Rylee and accuse her of anything. Do you understand?" he says with authority. "She picks up the phone because she feels guilty. She lets you bash her and accuse her and demean her because she loved your son and doesn't want you to hurt any more than you already do. *But no more.* You're hurting her, and I won't allow it. Understood?"

Colton blows out a large breath and tosses the phone onto the end of the bed where he stares at it for several moments without speaking. My heart pounds, the sound reverberating through my ears as I stare at him, emotions racing through me, tearing me apart as I wait.

Finally after what feels like hours, he shakes his head and looks down at his hands in his lap. "You are the most selfless woman I know, Rylee. Carrying around your own guilt. Allowing her to take her grief out on you. Giving everything of yourself to the boys…" My body trembles in anticipation of what he'll say next, of why he's looking at his hands and can't meet my eyes. So many emotions overwhelm me, thunder through me as I wait for him to collect his thoughts.

He looks over at me slowly, his eyes filled with a mixture of confusion and compassion. "Why didn't you tell me?" he asks gently, his eyes searching mine for an explanation.

I shrug, averting my eyes from his, trying to hold back the damn that threatens to break. I fail miserably, the damn splintering and the tears turn to sobs as he reaches out a hand and pulls me toward him. I sink onto my bed as he wraps his arms around me and gathers me to him. He smoothes a hand over my hair repeatedly, trying to soothe away my pain with reassuring words while I cry. He releases me momentarily, propping pillows behind him before lying back and pulling me with him so my head rests on his bare chest, my hand covering his heart.

The constant rhythm of Colton's heartbeat calms me. I realize that being here with Colton takes some of the sting out of today's date. It doesn't hurt any less, but it's getting easier. I realize that for the first time, I can think of Max and see him in good times, not just the final images I have of him broken, bloody, and dying. I can smile about the teenager I fell in puppy love with and the man I promised to spend my life with. I can remember the anxiety in his face the day he proposed and the surprise, love, and excitement in his eyes when I told him I was pregnant. God, I was so scared to tell him—hell I was scared myself— but when he hugged me and told me he was ecstatic and that everything would be alright, I allowed myself to feel the hope and wonderment I'd been holding back.

Colton places a soft kiss on the top of my head. "Do you want to talk about it?"

I almost laugh at his words. They sound so hypocritical coming from someone who never talks about his past. A few tears escape, falling onto his chest, and I quickly wipe them away. "I'm sorry," I apologize. I can't look at him. "I'm sure after last night, the last thing you want to deal with is a blubbering idiot."

He lifts his arm and runs his hand through his hair, sighing out loud. "I'm not good at this kind of thing, Rylee. Shit, I don't know what to do or say here…"

I can sense his discomfort at a woman falling apart in his arms. He hates drama. I know. I stroke my hand down his chest. "You don't have to do anything. You being here, sticking up for me with Claire…" I breathe out "…that's enough."

"How come you didn't tell me?" I can hear a trace of hurt in his voice, and it surprises me.

And I know he is referring to the baby. *My baby*. The part of me that forever died that day. The place that will forever be empty inside of me.

"It's not like you're exactly forthcoming about your baggage," I offer, the words hanging between us in silence. "You're so adamant about no children, I didn't think it was important for you to know. I didn't think you'd care."

I can feel him draw in a breath. "*Christ, Rylee.*" His voice strains, his hand fisting against my back. "Do you think that little of me? Just because kids are a deal breaker for me doesn't mean that I'm not sympathetic to your situation. To your loss."

I turn my head to prop my chin on my hand. I keep my eyes averted from his though by following my finger as it traces the lines of his tattoo that spans a portion of his rib cage. "I was…" I stop, trying to map out my memories. "I was shocked the day I found out I was pregnant. I mean I'd just graduated college. I was very black and white back then. I had a plan. First college, then marriage, and then a family," I smile softly.

"But you know what they say about best laid plans." I sigh shakily. "I was so scared of what Max's reaction was going to be. And when I told him, he looked at me in awe. I can still see him in my mind. He admitted he was scared but told me that it didn't matter because it was going to be okay. And I wondered how he could be so sure when everything was going to change so drastically."

I'm silent for a moment, my memories flashing through my mind like a slide show. I turn and shift my head to look at Colton as a tear slips silently from the corner of my eye. "She," I say on a shaky breath, "the baby was a girl." He nods his head at me and reaches out to wipe away the tear. "I was still scared and panicked at the thought of having a baby, but then I felt her kick." I stop, my chest tightening as I remember the feeling that I'll never experience again. "And I immediately fell in love with her. All of my reluctance faded." I clear my throat as Colton sits patiently, eyes locked on mine. "I was seven and half months along when we had the accident. I knew that first night she didn't make it, but I refused to acknowledge it. I was bleeding profusely and the cramping was...it was out of this world painful. I willed her to move. To kick me just once."

A shudder runs through me, those silent bargains I had made to God that night flickering through my head. "On some level, I knew the hope that she might still be alive is what kept me fighting to live."

"I'm so sorry, Rylee," he whispers.

"It took so long to be rescued that I got an infection from the bacteria. From what doctors saw, the damage was extensive enough that it essentially ruined my ability to get pregnant." I clear my throat before continuing. "Max's mom, Claire, blames me for everything."

"That's asinine," he interjects.

I shrug at his comment, agreeing but still letting guilt make me think differently. "She thought that if we hadn't been having premarital sex, this would have never happened."

Colton snorts at the comment. "You were together, what six years?"

I smile softly at him. "Almost seven."

"And she expected you to be abstinent that long?"

"To each their own beliefs." I shrug. "We went on the little trip because it was our last chance to get away. I was stressed about everything and the doctor was getting worried about my blood pressure. Max wanted to try and calm me down. To spend some time together before chaos ensued. So she blames me for killing him and her granddaughter."

"You know that's not true, Rylee."

"I know, but it doesn't take the guilt away. On the anniversary of the death and his birthday she calls me to vent her anger and sadness." I close my eyes momentarily, fighting away the horrible images that creep into my dreams. "It's her therapy I guess...and even though it tears me apart, listening to her is the least I can do." He pulls me farther up his chest and comforts me by wrapping his powerful arms around me and resting his chin on my head. "Oddly enough, meeting you, spending time with you, has allowed me to realize that I'm slowly coming to terms with what happened. Time has allowed me to remember Max and how he was before the crash, not just after. I think the hardest part is the baby." I exhale brokenly. "I will always cherish the feeling of a life growing inside of me, especially since I'll most likely never get that chance again." I nuzzle into the warmth of his neck and sigh. "She would have been two years old."

I catch the sob before it slips out, but Colton feels it. He squeezes me tighter, his even breathing and ability to listen is just what I need. I feel like a burden has been lifted off of me. All of my skeletons have been exposed. Now he knows. Everything. I cling to him because for some reason, his presence here completes the transformation for me.

I don't want to be alone anymore and am so sick of being numb. I want to feel again—in the extremes that Colton makes me feel.

I'm ready to live again. Really live. And in this moment I know that it is only Colton that I can imagine sharing these new memories with. I close my eyes and snuggle into him, the sleep I couldn't find earlier slowly claiming me now. I am just starting to drift off when his voice stirs my eyes open. "When I was six years old," he says so softly that if it weren't for the vibration in his chest, I wouldn't know to listen for his words. He stops for a moment and clears his throat. "When I was six, my—the woman who gave birth to me—beat me so badly that I ended up unconscious and in the hospital." He exhales loudly while I withhold my breath.

Holy shit! He's talking and hearing the pain in his voice I know that his wounds are still raw and wide open. Infected. How can you heal from your mother beating the crap out of you? How can you accept love from anyone when the one person that is supposed to protect you from everything is the one who harmed you the most? I'm at a loss for words, so I wrap my arms around him and squeeze before placing a soft kiss on his sternum. "Did the hospital call the police? Social services?" I ask timidly, unsure of how much he is willing to share with me.

I can feel him nod his head in assent. "My mom was the one who called 9-1-1. She told them my dad had done it. That she was the one who walked in and stopped it." He pauses, and I let him take a minute to compose himself and clear the emotion swimming in his voice. "I've never met my dad so...I was too scared of what she'd do to me to say otherwise...too young to know that life could be any better than what I had. She pulled me from school after that. Moved around a lot so social services couldn't check up on us..." His words drift off and there are so many thoughts running through my head, so many things I want to tell him to console him. That it wasn't his fault. That love doesn't have to be that way. That he is a true survivor for coming out of it and thriving. But I know my words will do nothing to take away the years of abuse that he must have endured or lessen its psychological after effects. Besides, I'm sure he's heard it all from psychiatrists time and time again.

I look up at him and the haunted look in his eyes tells me what he's just admitted is the least of his childhood nightmares. Do I tell him what he confessed last night in the limo? I struggle with the decision and choose not to. Sharing his past has to be on his terms. I open my mouth to speak, but he cuts me off before I can begin. "Rylee, please don't feel sorry for me."

"I'm...I'm not," I stutter, knowing that's the last thing he wants, but he can see right through my lie. How can I not feel sorry for the little boy he once was?

"That life was a long time ago for me. That little boy—he is a different person than I am now."

Bullshit. He is who he is because of what happened to him. Does he not see that?

I press a soft kiss on the center of his chest. "Do you know what happened to your mom?" I say in a hesitant voice, almost afraid to ask but also wanting to know as much I can since he is talking.

He's quiet for a moment. He lifts his hand from my back and runs it over his stubbled jaw before exhaling loudly. "After my dad found me on the steps of his trailer...he brought me to the hospital. Stayed with me," he retells, utter reverence in his voice. "Little did I know he was this big time director. Not that I would have even known what that meant though. Later...much later, I learned that he'd wasted a whole day of studio time sitting with me in the hospital. At the time, all I remember thinking was he had the gentlest voice and his eyes. They didn't look mean even though I flinched when he touched me..." He trails off, lost in memories, and I let him for a moment.

"...and he ordered me every kind of food imaginable and had it delivered to the hospital room. I'll never forget the look on his face as he watched me eat things I'd never had. Things every boy at that age should have had many times over by then. I remember pretending to be asleep when the police told him they found my mom and were bringing her in for questioning...that the x-rays and exams had shown years of..." He pauses, trying to find the right word as I hold my breath wondering which one of the horrific options he'll use. "*Neglect*. And it is the only time in my life I've ever heard my dad use his stature to get what he wanted. I heard him ask the police officers if they knew who he was. To clear it with whomever they needed to, but that I was going to be under his custody from then on. That he'd get a team of lawyers if need be, but that's how it was going to be." He shakes his head with a soft laugh.

"That's…" I'm at a loss for words. I don't want to cheapen the memory by saying the wrong words, so I just leave it at that.

"Yeah." He breathes. "I saw my mom once more, but it was across the courtroom. I know she went to jail, but I don't know anything more than that. Never wanted to know. Why do you ask?"

"I just wondered how you left it. I thought maybe if you found out what happened to her…fill in any blanks you want to, that it might help. The nightmares might go away and—"

"I think that's enough *sharing* for today," he says, cutting me off and shifting our bodies abruptly so that I'm on my back and he's lying half on me, his legs scissored with mine.

"Oh really?" I smile when I see the tension ease from his face and pain fade from his eyes. "Is the only way to get you to talk, a trade? Tit for tat so to speak?"

"Well…" he smirks pressing me into the mattress with his hips "…you have seen my tats." He arches his eyebrows suggestively. "It's only fair…"

Colton's sudden change of subject is not lost on me. His inherent turn toward making things physical between us when I delve a little too deep. Normally I'd hesitate at using intimacy to ease the ache of sadness within, but this morning I just want him to help me forget for just a little bit the tears left in my soul from that day two years ago.

I wriggle beneath him, my body humming with need for his, loving the playful side that has reemerged to lighten the dark of our morning. "And I thought you said we were *done with sharing* for today." The sound of his laugh is welcome as it rumbles through his chest into mine. I lift my head up and capture his bottom lip and pull on it. The low growl of desire in the back of his throat stokes my craving for him.

His hand brushes against my ribcage and palms my one breast not covered by his chest. He grazes a thumb over my already pert nipple, his touch a ripple of sensation slowly swelling through me. He leans down and presses a soft kiss to my lips. "Now about that tit," he murmurs, a smile curling the corners of his mouth. He squeezes my nipple between his thumb and forefinger and my gasp is absorbed by his mouth on mine.

"Will I ever get enough of you?" he asks against my lips. And I wonder the same thing. Will I ever tire of him? *Of this?* Of his taste or his touch or the rumble in his throat expressing how I make him feel when I touch him? Will he always bring me to such an aroused fever pitch? Surely my desire has to be sated at some point. From his touch alone, my thoughts are lost with only one remaining. Flickering through my mind.

Never.

Chapter Eleven

Avery smiles at me as I go over some of the schedules and our standard rules and procedures. "I know it's a lot to take in, but once you get familiar with it, you won't have to think twice about it."

She nods her head at me and looks over at Zander. He's sitting on the couch, tattered stuffed doggy clutched to his chest, watching television. "What's his story?" she asks quietly.

I look over my shoulder at Zander and smile. While still not talking much besides sporadic words here and there since the racetrack, he seems to be doing better. He is interacting a bit more with the boys, and I can see traces of emotion on his face whereas before it was blank. The therapist says he's starting to participate, starting to interact with her.

It's a start. Progress takes time.

Protective of my kids like a mother hen, I rarely share their backgrounds until a new employee has been with me for a while. "That's Zander. He doesn't talk much, but we're working on it. He was in a rough situation that he's dealing with internally. He'll get there though."

She gives me a quizzical look, but I ignore her interest and begin reviewing the next set of procedures. The doorbell rings and the unexpected interruption startles me. Jax is at baseball practice with Shane and Connor, so I rise to get the door.

When I look through the peephole, I'm caught off guard at the sight of Colton's sister. I open the door cautiously, curiosity getting the better of me. "What a surprise! Hello, Quinlan." I try to smile brightly at her all the while my heart beats rapidly at her presence. I marvel at how such a sweet looking, beautiful woman can instill such anxiety in me.

"Rylee." She nods, her perfect lips not quite forming a smile. "I came to get a tour of the place before I make a donation to the new project. I want to know exactly what my money is going to be used for."

Well, hello to you too! I smile tightly, inviting her in. She could at least grace me with a little warmth—anything to melt her icy façade. *What the hell have I done to her to deserve this deliberate chill?*

"I'd be glad to give you a tour," I force, wishing I could pawn her off on another counselor to show her around, but my manners and professionalism win out. Besides, something tells me this little visit is about more than checking out the facility for a donation. I plaster a fake smile on my face. "Please follow me."

I inform Avery that she's in charge of watching the boys and then proceed to show Quinlan the entire facility and explain its benefits. I'm probably rambling but she hasn't asked any questions. Rather she has just stared at me the whole time with a quiet yet critical appraisal. And after about twenty minutes, I realize the inspection isn't being done on The House or what we have to offer my boys. It's solely on me.

I've had enough.

I glance to make sure that all of the boys are still outside playing with Avery before turning to face her. "Why is it you're really here, Quinlan?" My tone matches the fuck you, no nonsense that I feel.

"To see if the facility is worthy of my donation," she responds too sweetly to be true. She holds my gaze but I see something flicker in the ice queen's eyes.

"I appreciate it as the facility and the kids are worthy of it," I tell her, "but let's be honest, why are you here? To see if the facility is worthy of your donation or if I'm worthy of your brother?" Quinlan's eyes flash as I hit a direct bull's-eye. Being protective of your brother is one thing. *I understand that.* Being a complete bitch is a whole different story. "Which one is it?"

She cocks her head and looks at me. "I'm just trying to figure out your angle."

"My angle?"

"Yes, your angle." Her voice is implacable and her eyes are right up there with Colton's on the intensity scale. "You're not the typical bimbo that Colton goes for…so I'm trying to figure out what exactly it is you want out of this. From him." She twists her lips as she stares at me. I'm sure the shocked look on my face is something to stare at.

"I beg your pardon," I sputter, more than offended.

"Are you a race groupie? Are you looking to land a part in my dad's newest film? An aspiring model looking to sleep your way up the ranks? I can't wait to hear what yours will be."

"*What?*" I just stare at her for a moment, shock ricocheting through me until it churns to anger. "How dare you—"

"Oh, I get it now." She smirks, sarcasm dripping from her words, and all I want to do is throttle her. "You need his money to finish this little project of yours," she says, motioning to the space around her. "You're using him to get your notoriety that way."

"That's uncalled for." I take a step forward, pushed to the point that I don't care that she's Colton's sister. I'd like to say something a lot worse, but I'm at work and I never know when impressionable ears are listening. But I can only be pushed so far before I throw my manners out the window, and she just shoved. "You know what, Quin? I've tried to be nice, tried to overlook your shitty attitude and your condescending sneer, but *I'm done.* Colton pursued me—not the other way around." She arches an eyebrow at me as if she doesn't believe me. "Yeah..." I laugh "...I find it hard to believe too, but he did. I don't want a damn thing from your brother except for him to open up to the possibility that he deserves more than what he's allowed himself thus far in his life." I step back, shaking my head at her. "I don't need to explain myself to you or justify your asinine accusations. Thanks for your false pretense of a donation, but I don't want your money. *Not in return for your judgment on me.* I think it's time you leave." I point toward the hallway, my body vibrating with anger.

She smiles broadly at me, her face dropping its guard and filling with warmth for the first time since I've met her. "Not yet. We're not done here."

What? Great, can't wait for the rest of this stimulating conversation.

"I knew you were for real." She smirks, pulling in a deep breath. "I just needed to make sure that I was right."

Whiplash.

Did I miss something here? I'm so confused right now that my mouth opens as I look at her like she's bat-shit-crazy. The schizophrenic changing of subjects like Colton does must run in the family.

When I just stand there staring at her with disdain she continues. "I've never seen Colton like that at the track before. He brings his bimbos, they flit around like arm candy, but he disregards them. He never lets someone distract him when he's in the car. *You distracted him. I've never seen him so...*" she searches for a word "*...smitten with someone before.*" She crosses her arms across her chest and leans against the wall. "And my dad tells me you were at the Broadbeach house? *Then to top it off Becks tells me you went to Vegas with them?*"

What is it with the women in Colton's life keeping tabs on me and passing judgment?

Smitten? Colton may have said that I scare him, but in no way did he infer love or even hint at that. Definitely not smitten. I'm something different than his typical in-your-face, I-want-something-from-you-in-return type of girl. *I burn him. I scare him.* But for some reason despite all of that, I don't make him want to try for something more than what he's used to. I'm not enough to make him change his ways. He's not going to confront his demons when he's not even willing to talk about them. And that's the only way I think he'll be able to give into the emotion I see brimming in his eyes and feel in the worshiping actions of his touch.

I shake myself from my thoughts and focus on Quinlan. She stares at me. Really stares at me causing me to squirm under her silent scrutiny. "And your point is what, Quinlan?"

"Listen, as much as Colt tries to play Mr. Aloof and think that I don't—shit my whole family..." she exhales "...doesn't know about his little *arrangements...*" she rolls her eyes in disgust as she says the word, "It's no secret to us. *His stupid rules and sexist ways run amok.* And as much as I disagree with him and his antics, I know it's the only way he thinks he can have a relationship...*his necessary* way of dealing with his past." Her eyes hold mine and I realize she is apologizing for her brother. For what he thinks he can't give me. Over the fact that he's afraid to even try.

"*Was it that horrible?*" I whisper, already knowing the answer.

Finally a softness plies her steeped countenance as a true sadness fills her eyes. She nods her head subtly. "He rarely speaks of it, and I'm certain there are parts that he's never spoken about, Rylee. Experiences that I can't even begin to fathom." She looks down at her pink painted nails and twists her fingers into each other. "Having parents who don't want you is hard enough to come to grips with when you're adopted. Colton...Colton had so much more than that to overcome." She shakes her head and I can see that she is struggling with how much to tell me. She looks up at me, eyes clear yet conflicted. "An eight year old boy so hungry—locked in his room while his mom did God knows what for days—that he somehow escaped and went in search for food, luckily collapsing on my dad's doorstep."

I suck in a breath, my heart quickening, my soul wrenching, and my faith in humanity crumbling.

"That's just a small snippet of his hell, but it's his story to tell you, Rylee. Not mine. I'm only sharing so you have an iota of what he's been through. Of the patience and persistence you're going to need."

I nod in understanding, unsure of what to say next to a woman who moments before was berating me and who is now giving me advice. "So…"

"So I had to make sure you were for real." She offers me an apologetic smile of resignation. "And once I did, I wanted to get a good look at the first woman that might be the one to make him whole again."

Her words stagger me. "You've taken me by surprise here," I admit, unsure of what else to say.

"I know that I may be coming off a little strong, presumptuous even in being here…but I love Colton more than anything in the world." She smiles softly at his name. "And I'm just looking out for him. I want nothing less than the best for him."

This I can understand.

She pushes off the wall and straightens herself in front of me. "Look, if you look past the gorgeously rough exterior…there's a scared little boy inside that's afraid of love. That for some reason he associates love with horrific expectations one minute and then thinks he's not worthy of it the next. I think he's afraid to love someone because he knows that they'll leave. He'll most likely hurt you to prove that you will…" she shakes her head "…and for that hell alone, I apologize because from what I can tell, you deserve better than that."

Her words hit me in their full force. I understand the little boy inside because I have a backyard full of them right now with issues of their own. I just wish they had the unconditional love that Colton seems to have in Beckett and Quinlan. Someone who stands up for them and looks out for them because they want nothing but the best for them. This love—this protective feeling—I understand.

Quinlan reaches out and places her hand on my arm and squeezes to make her point. "I love my brother dearly, Rylee. Some would say that I worshiped the ground he walked on growing up." She reaches in her pocket and pulls something out, averting her eyes from mine. "I'm sorry for my intrusion. I really shouldn't be here…interfering." She seems embarrassed all of a sudden as she steps toward the door. She reaches out her hand and places a check in mine. Her eyes look up to meet mine, and for the first time I see acceptance in them. "Thank you for your time, Rylee." She takes a step past me and then hesitates and looks back at me. "If you get the chance, take care of my brother."

I nod in acknowledgement and all I can manage is a stilted, "Bye," as my head is in a whirlwind of chaos over her unexpected revelations.

Chapter Twelve

The scream wakes me in the dead night. It's a strangled, feral plea that goes on and on, over and over before I can even get out of the bedroom door. I race through the house toward the sound of unfettered terror, Dane and Avery right behind me, our footsteps pounding with urgency.

"Moooooommmmm!" Zander screams. I bolt through the door of his room as the soul shattering sound ricochets against the bedroom walls. He thrashes violently in his bed. "Nooooo! Noooo!"

I hear Shane's panicked voice in the hallway, trying to help Dane settle down the little guys who have woken up and are now frightened. The thought flits through my mind on how sad it is that night terrors are such a regular visitor in this house that Shane's no longer phased by them. But I focus solely on Zander now, knowing that Dane will take care of Shane and the rest of the boys. I hear Dane tell Avery to help me if I need it. *Welcome to your first night at The House, Avery.*

I cautiously sit on Zander's bed. His body twists and writhes beneath the sheet, his face wet from tears, his bedding damp with sweat, and fearful whimpers escape from deep in his throat. The unmistakable smell of his terrifying fear suffocates the small room.

"Zander, baby," I croon, careful to not raise my voice and add to the violence already haunting his nightmare. "I'm right here. I'm right here." His crying doesn't stop. I reach out to try and shake him awake and am taken aback when he thrashes ferociously, his fist connecting with my cheekbone. The pain registers just beneath my eye, but I shake it off, needing to rouse Zander to prevent him from hurting himself.

"Daddy, no!" he whimpers with such heartbreak that tears spring to my eyes. And despite it being a dream that cannot be used legally, Zander just confirmed the suspicion that his father killed his mother. Right before his eyes.

I struggle to wrap my arms around him. Despite his small size, the strength he has from the adrenaline induced terror is heightened. I manage to wrestle my arms around him and pull him into my chest, murmuring to him all the while. Letting him know I'm here and that I'm not going to hurt him. "Zander, it's okay. C'mon, Zand, wake up," I whisper over and over to him until he wakes with a start. He struggles to sit up and get out of my grip, searching the bedroom with hollow eyes to orient himself to his surroundings.

"Momma?" he croaks in such desperation that my heart shatters in a million pieces.

"It's okay, I'm right here, buddy," I soothe, rubbing my hand up and down his back softly.

He looks at me, eyes red and raw from crying and falls into my arms. He clings to me with such despair that I know I'd do anything to erase his memory of that night if given the chance. "I want my mommy," he cries, repeating it over and over. It's the first sentence I have ever heard him say and yet there is nothing to be excited about. There is nothing to encourage or celebrate.

We stay huddled together, arms wrapped tight for the longest time until his even breathing convinces me that he's fallen back asleep. I slowly shift him to lie down on the bed, but when I attempt to withdraw my arms from around him, he clings even tighter.

It's not until the sun's rays peek through the closed mini-blinds that we both fall into a deep sleep.

Chapter Thirteen
Colton

The shudder of the motor vibrates through my body as I flick the paddle coming into turn four. *Fuck.* Something doesn't feel right. Something's off. I ease up more than necessary as I cross over and into the apron coming out of the turn.

"What's going on?" Becks' disembodied voice fills my ears.

"Fuck, I don't know," I grate out as I bring the car back up to speed to try and decipher what she's telling me. Every shudder. Every sound. Each jolt of my body. My attention straining to try and pinpoint what feels off—something to substantiate why she doesn't seem to be handling how she should. I can't figure out what I'm missing, what I might be overlooking that could cost us a race.

Or put me headfirst into the wall.

My head pounds with stress and concentration. I pass the start/finish line, the grandstands to my right one big stretch of mixed colors. *The blur I live my life in.*

"Is—"

"How much preload in the differential?" I demand as I hit another paddle heading into turn one. The rear of the car starts to slide as I press the gas coming out of it, accelerating the car up to top speed. My body automatically shifts to compensate for the pressure imposed on it by the force and angle of the track's bank. "Possibly the clutch plate? The ass end is sliding all over the place," I tell him as I fight to get the car back under control on the chute before heading into turn two.

"That's not poss—"

107

"You driving the fucking car now, Becks?" I bark into the mic, my hands gripping the wheel in frustration. Beckett obviously reads my mood, because he goes radio silent. My mind flickers to the nightmares that plagued my sleep last night. Of not being able to talk to Rylee this morning when I called. Of needing to hear her voice to help clear the remnants from my mind.

Goddamnit, Donavan, get your head on the track. Irritation—at myself, at Beckett, at the fucking car—has me pushing the pedal down harder than I should down the back straightaway. My fucked up attempt at using adrenaline to drown out my head.

I know Becks is probably beside himself right now, thinking I'm gonna burn her up. Trash all the time and precision we've dialed into the engine. I'm nearing turn three and a part of me wishes there was no turn. Just a straight stretch of road where I could keep going, drop the hammer, race the wind, and outrun the shit in my head—the fear squeezing at my heart.

Chase the possibilities just beyond the reach of my fingertips.

But there isn't one. Just another fucking turn. Hamster on a goddamn wheel.

I come into the turn too hot, my head too fucked up to be on the track. I have to consciously remember to try and not over-correct as the ass end gets too loose on me and slides to the right, drifting too high. A shiver of fear dances at the base of my spine for that split second when I'm not sure if I'll be able to pull the car out in time to avoid kissing the barrier.

Beckett swears on the radio as I narrowly escape, and I shout out one of my own. The only way to voice the high of fear that just jolted through my system. Adrenaline, my momentary drug of choice, reigns until the realization of my stupidity will take over in the moments to come. It always takes a few seconds to hit.

Fuck me. *I'm done.* I shouldn't be in the car right now. It's stupid of me to be here when my head's not right. I ease into turn four, decelerating when I hit pit row and stop where my crew stands behind the firewall. I silence the engine and blow out a loud breath. They all just stand there, no one stepping over, as I unbuckle my helmet and detach the steering wheel. I pull up on my helmet and it's yanked from my hands.

"You trying to kill yourself out there?" Beckett shouts at me as I remove my balaclava and ear buds. Now I know why the crew stayed behind the wall. They're used to the volatility and brutal honesty between Becks and me. They know when to stay clear. "Then do it on your own goddamn time. Not under my watch!" He's pissed and has every right to be, but fuck all if I'm telling him that.

I just stare at him, a slight smirk turning up the corners of my mouth at my oldest friend. My attempt at provoking him so that he doesn't notice the trembling of my hands. A surefire way for him to know I scared the shit out of myself as well and add fuel to his own fire. What the hell was I thinking getting in the car with a fucked up frame of mind? He just glares at me, jaw clenched and shoulders square before shaking his head, turning his back to me, and walking away.

The minute Becks turns the corner, my crew clears the wall and begins doing their various jobs as I climb out. I'm glad they steer clear of me, all obviously accustomed to my moodiness by now when testing goes to shit.

I scrub my hand over my face and through my sweat-soaked hair. I head the same way as Becks, knowing he's had enough time to calm down so that we can talk. Maybe. *Fuck.* I don't know. When things are off between the two of us, the rest of the team feels it. I can't have that coming into a new season.

I follow him to the RV and climb up the steps. He's sitting in the recliner across from the door, leaning forward, elbows on his knees. He just looks at me and shakes his head, causing a twinge of guilt to hit me for taking years off of his life with my careless stunt.

"What the fuck was that?" he asks in an all too quiet voice—the voice of a disappointed parent to their child.

I unzip my suit to the waist and let the sleeves hang, before peeling off my shirt and falling back onto the couch. I close my eyes, swiveling so that my head rests on one armrest and my feet on the opposing one. I am so tired. I need sleep that's not filled with all the fucked up dreams that've been coming repeatedly since that morning with Rylee. I'm a fucking mess. Can't think straight. Obviously can't drive worth a shit. "I don't know, Becks," I sigh out. "My head wasn't in the right place. I shouldn't have—"

"You're goddamn right you shouldn't have," he yells at me. "That was a stupid fucking stunt, and if you ever pull one like that again—get in the car when you're head's not straight—you can find yourself another goddamn crew chief." The squeak of the chair tells me he's just unfolded himself and stood. The motor home rocks with his movement and the door slams shut as he leaves.

I keep my eyes closed, sinking into the lumpy ass couch, just wanting to forget, wanting to talk to Rylee but knowing that she's probably sleeping herself after the events of her night.

I don't know why I got so panicked this morning when I couldn't reach her. My mind immediately veered to thoughts of her in an accident. Trapped in a mangled fucking car somewhere. Alone and scared. My chest tightened at the thought until I got a hold of Haddie who gave me the number to The House's landline. I felt better—and worse—after speaking to Jackson about the chaos of Zander's nightmare.

Poor fucking kid. Nightmares can be so fucking brutal. Cause such a setback and fuck with your memories even more. Make them worse. Make you relive them in the worst possible way. Remember things you shouldn't. *Otherwise wouldn't.* Don't ever want to. But at least he had Rylee to comfort him, stay with him, and keep the demons at bay with her soft voice and reassuring touch.

Exactly what I needed from her last night. What I still need from her today.

I sigh at the thought of her, wanting her in the worst way...*in the best way*. I laugh out loud at myself in the vacant RV. I can't figure out what I want more, a dreamless sleep or to hear Rylee's voice.

Shit, my head must really be fucked up if all I want from Rylee is to hear her voice. I shake my head and scrub my hands over my face, feeling pussified from the thought. What I wouldn't give to go back to a couple of months ago when sleep came easy.

When my dick and balls were firmly attached and in charge of my thoughts. When the choice between sleep, sex, or wanting to hear a specific woman's voice was a no brainer; a few hours of uncomplicated sex led to the sleepless oblivion. Two down with one shot. *And the woman's voice?* Who cared if she talked or what she did with her mouth as long as she opened wide and swallowed without a gag reflex.

Rylee flashes through my mind. Her dark hair on the white pillow as I hover over her. The look on her face—lips jolting apart, eyes widening, cheeks flushing with color—as I sink inside of her. How she tightens like a vice around me as she comes. Fucking voodoo pussy.

My dick stirs at the thought—wanting, no needing her—but my exhaustion overwhelms, and swallows me whole into its oblivion.

Spiderman, Batman, Superman, Ironman.

Spiderman, Batman, Superman, Ironman.

I jolt from the nightmare with a start, disoriented from the unknown passage of time. My heart thunders in my ears. My stomach churns. My head forgets specifics instantly, but the nightmare's clutches of fear still hold me against my will, dragging me backwards through poisoned memories.

"Fucking Christ!" I yell out to the empty RV as I force myself to calm down and breathe. To try and forget the fear that'll never go away. Never. Fear gives way to anger as I pick up the closest thing to me, one of the crew's hackey-sacs and chuck it across the aisle as hard as I can. The thud it makes does nothing to abate the feelings clawing through me, embedding themselves in every fiber of my being, but it's all I can do. My only source of release.

I'm helpless and hostage to the poison within me. Sweat trickles down my cheek. I'm fucking drenched with it. The smell of fear clings to me and my stomach twists in protest again. *Shit!*

I shove up from the couch and strip out of my fire suit as if the fabric is on fire. I need a shower. I need to clean the grime from the track and the stain of his imaginary touch from my unwilling flesh.

The water scalds. The soap does nothing to wash away the memories. I press my forehead against the acrylic stall, letting the water burn lines as it slides down my back. I will my brain to shut off and rest for five goddamn fucking minutes so I can have my own temporary radio silence.

Rylee's words keep looping through my head, badgering me, questioning me, making me wonder if it's a solution to the constant poison that I'm afraid is going to consume me. I pound a fist against the wall, the sound resonating through my fucked up thoughts. I drag myself from the shower, drape a towel around my waist, and grab my cell. I need to do this before I lose the courage. Before I puss out and think of the ramifications. The answers I'm afraid to find. The truth I fear will crumble me. I punch the number in my phone and swallow the bile threatening to rise, preparing myself with each passing ring of the phone.

"Colton? I thought you were testing today?"

Warmth spears through me at the sound of his voice, at the concern flooding into it. And then fear. How is he going to handle the questions I need to ask? The ones that Rylee thinks might help me, might ease the weight on my soul and torment in my mind.

I labor to ask the man who gave me possibilities about the woman who robbed me of everything. My youth. My innocence. My trust. My ability to love. My self.

Of the concept of unconditional love.

"Son? Is everything okay?" Concern creeps into his voice as a result of my silence. "Colton?"

"Dad…" I choke out, my throat feeling like it's drowning in sand.

"You're scaring me, Colt…"

I shake my head to get a grip. "Sorry, Dad…I'm fine. I'm good." I can hear him exhale audibly on the other end of the line, but he remains silent, allowing me a moment to gather my thoughts. He knows something is amiss.

I feel like I'm thirteen and I've fucked up again. That adolescent fear fills me—the anxiety that if I push too hard or screw up one more time, they'll send me back. They won't want me anymore. The funny thing is I thought I'd conquered this fear a long time ago, but as the question weighs heavy on my tongue, it all comes back. The fear. The insecurity. The need to feel wanted.

Dread strangles my words.

"I…uh…just had a question. Don't know how to ask it really…"

Silence fills the line and I know my Dad is trying to figure out what the hell has gotten into me. Why I'm acting like the little boy I used to be.

"Just ask, son." It's all he says, but his tone—that soothing, acceptance at all costs tone—tells me that he knows something has brought me back to that place in time. And even though all I feel is fear and uncertainty, all I hear is patience, love, and understanding.

I suck in a breath of air and exhale it shakily. "Do you know what happened to *her*? Where she is? What became of her?" My fingers tremble as I bring a hand to run through my hair. I don't want him to worry or think that I want to find her and…*I don't know what with her.* Reconcile? *Fuck no.* Never.

But it scares the fuck out of me that the idea of her—just the thought of her—can get me this worked up. Can fuck with my head more than the dreams. "Never mind, I—"

"Colton…It's okay." Reassurance fills his voice.

"I just don't want you to think—"

"I don't think anything," he soothes in a way only a father can to a son. "Take a breath, Colt. It's okay. I've waited a long time for you to ask—"

"You're not mad?" The one fear I have bubbles out of my mouth.

"No. Never." He sighs, resigned to the fact that a small part of me will always worry regardless of the passage of time.

I feel like a hundred pound weight has been lifted from my chest. Freed me from the fear of asking. "Really?"

"It's natural to wonder," he assures. "Normal to want to learn about your past and—"

"I know all I need to know of my past..." The words come out in a whisper before I can stop them. Silence hangs through the line. "I just...fucking Rylee..." I mutter in exasperation.

"You're having dreams again, aren't you?"

I struggle to answer. I want to tell him because I feel obligated to be honest after everything he's done for me, and at the same time feel the need to lie so that he doesn't worry about the memories that debilitated me as a child. So he doesn't remember how detrimental they were. So he doesn't find out *everything* that had happened. "I saw it in your eyes when I got back from Indonesia. Are you okay? Do you need—"

"I'm fine, Dad. It's just that Rylee had asked if I knew what had happened to *her*. That maybe if I knew I might get some closure. Be able to shut some old doors..."

He's silent on the connection for a moment. "I kept tabs on her for a while. I wanted to make sure when she got out of jail that she didn't come back to find you or make trouble for you when you were just starting to do so well. I stopped about ten years ago," he admits, "but I'll call the PI that I used, he'll know her habits better than anyone— and we'll see what he can find. If that's what you want..."

"Yeah. Thanks. I just..."

"No need to explain, Colton. You do what you need to fill in that piece you've always felt is missing. Your Mom and I knew this day was coming, and we want you to do whatever you have to do to find peace. We're okay with it."

I pinch the bridge of my nose and close my eyes, fighting the burn that threatens within. "Thanks, Dad." There's nothing else I can say to the man who gave me life after being dead for the first eight years of my existence.

"Sure, son. I'll call you when I have any news. Love you."

"Thanks, Dad. Me too."

I'm just about to hang up when he speaks again. "Colton?"

"Yeah?"

"I'm proud of you." His voice wavers with emotion, which in turn makes me swallow the lump in my throat.

"Thanks."

I hang up the phone, toss it on the table, and lean my head back against the wall. The loud breath I exhale into the silence does nothing to ease the overwhelming emotions swimming through me. I sit there for a bit, knowing I need to apologize to Beckett and wanting Rylee in the worst way. Needing something to clear my head.

The idea hits me like lightning, and I'm up, dressed, and climbing out of the RV in less than five minutes. I see the guys working in the garage off to my right, but I can't talk to anyone right now. Don't want to. I walk into the open bay where the favorite of all my babies is parked—*Sex*.

I don't even take a second glance to appreciate the F12's clean lines and flawless fire engine red perfection, but I sure as hell will enjoy her speed in about one minute. I climb behind the wheel and when the engine rumbles to life, I feel a piece of myself return. Spark back.

I zip past the garage, noting Beckett's refusal to meet my eyes— *fucking stubborn bastard*—and exit the track. I crank up the volume as *The Distance* comes through the speakers. Great fucking song. The minute I hit the 10 and see it's unbelievably empty for this time of day, I drop the hammer and fly. Fly faster than is safe but the feeling—luxury cocooning me, perfection in my hands, and an engine that talks to me—clears my head, and eases the self-inflicted tension pulling from all directions.

Sex never disappoints me when I need her the most.

By the time I approach traffic, my head is a little clearer and my mind is made up. I pick up my phone and make the call.

Chapter Fourteen

As I look across the kitchen at Zander and his tutor working on his spelling words, I hear the front door slam open. The excited chatter of the boys fills the hallway. They are usually animated when they get home, but today the noise is off the charts. So much so that Zander looks up from his paper and raises his eyebrows at me.

Zack comes barreling around the corner, so excited he stutters—as he normally does when overly excited—for a second. "Ry-Rylee and Za-Zander…Hurry up and get your stuff!"

"No running in the house, Zack," I warn. "What are you talking about?"

The other boys come flying into the great room before he has a chance to respond. I look over at the boys to scold them for running in the house when my voice falters.

Standing at the entry to the room is Colton. Reckless. Sexy. Devastating. The three words hit me at once at the sight of him.

I know it's silly. It's only been four days since I've seen or talked to him, but now that he's in plain sight, I'm staggered at how much I've missed him. How much I've wanted to see him. Be near him. Hear his voice again. Have a connection with him again. *So much for needing space to clear my head.*

I drink him in, my eyes dragging their way up his body. When I meet his eyes, a slow, lopsided grin curls up one corner of his mouth making that dimple I find irresistible deepen. I swear my heart skips a beat at the smoldering look in his eyes. I swallow loudly trying to gain the equilibrium that he's just knocked out from underneath me.

115

We stare at each other, the boys' raucous noise fading to white as we speak without talking. Kyle grabs my hand and tugs on it, breaking the trance between us.

"Colton's taking us to the go-kart track!" he exclaims, excitement dancing in his eyes.

"He is, is he?" I ask, raising my eyebrows and looking over at Colton.

"Yep, he is," Colton says as he takes a step toward me, his lopsided grin now at its full megawatt capacity. "Go put your stuff away guys and get in the van. Jackson's waiting." My eyes widen at his comment, and I wonder how he coordinated this.

Colton turns and meets Zander's hopeful eyes. "Hey, Zander, I thought you guys could use a break from all of this school stuff. I know it's really important, but sometimes a guy needs a break, don't cha' think?" Zander eyes grow as big as saucers and his mouth spreads in a huge grin. It's a small miracle how the grace of a smile can ease the severity of the nightmare's effects on his precious face. "Let's go get your shoes and we can meet everyone in the van. You game?" he asks.

Zander jumps up and races toward his bedroom, and I bite back the inherent scold of no running. I apologize to the tutor and send her on her way with eyes dazed from the sight of Colton. Poor thing.

When she exits the room, I can hear the boys making their way to the front door with gusto. It is only then that Colton approaches me and backs me up against the kitchen counter. He presses his hips into me at the same time his mouth captures mine in a mind-altering, head-dizzying, soul-emptying kiss. *God, I missed the taste of him.* The kiss is too brief to fulfill my four days of missing him. When our lips part, he wraps his arms around me in a tight hug that I could lose myself in— one teeming with a quiet desperation. He holds me to him, his face nuzzled in the side of my neck, and I can feel him breathe me in drawing strength from our connection.

"Hey," I murmur softly as his hands press into my back. "You okay?"

"Yeah." He breathes. "Now I am."

His murmured confession rocks me. Hits those parts deep within in me, unjaded and still full of hope and possibility.

He finally releases me when he hears sounds in the hallway. I gaze up at his face and look beyond the handsome features that still make my breath catch in my throat. I notice darkened smudges under his tired, wary eyes. He's not sleeping. More nightmares? I don't know and I don't want to ask. He'll tell me if he wants to. When he's able to.

I stare at him for a beat and try to figure out what's different about him. It's only when he angles his head to question my silent appraisal that it hits me. He's clean-shaven. I reach up and run my hand across his jaw, his face leaning into my touch. And it's something about that little gesture mixed with his earlier confession that causes my heart to swell.

"What's this?" I ask, averting my eyes to prevent him from seeing my emotional transparency. "So smooth and clean-shaven."

"It doesn't bode too well doing a razor commercial with a five o'clock shadow," he smirks, running his palms up and down the sides of my torso. Licks of desire flicker low in my belly at his touch.

I laugh out loud. "Understandably. I like it though," I tell him, running my fingers over it again when he frowns. "It's okay, Ace, you still ooze bad boy without the stubble. Besides, I'll get to sleep with someone different than this scruffy-jawed man I've been wasting my time on."

He flashes a wicked smile. "Wasting your time, huh?" He takes a step toward me, lust clearly edging the humor out of his eyes.

Every part of my body tightens at the predatory way his body moves toward mine. My God. *Take me*, I want to tell him. *Take every part of me that you already haven't stolen, taken, or claimed.*

"Oh, most definitely. He's a rebel..." I scrunch my nose up, playing along "...and I definitely don't do the bad boy type."

"No?" He wets his lips with a quick dart of his tongue. "What type exactly, *do you do?*" A devilish grin snakes up the corner of his lips as he reaches out to touch my face, and in an instant it disappears. His eyes narrow upon noticing the bruise from Zander on my cheek. My cover-up has obviously worn off. "Who did this to you?" he demands, his hands cupping my neck, angling my head to the side so he can see the severity of the bruise. "Is this from Zander last night?"

I startle at his words. "Yeah, it goes with the territory." I shrug. "How'd you know about it?"

"Poor fucking kid." He shakes his head. "I called you this morning. You were still asleep after being up with Zander all night. I hadn't heard from you and got worried." He pauses and those words—his admission that he cares for me coming on the heels of him telling me in so many words that he needs me—ignites my soul and makes my lips curl automatically. "So I called the house and Jackson answered. He told me what happened." He angles my chin up to look at my cheek again. "Are you sure you're okay?"

"Yeah." I shake my head, his concern endearing.

"So, I figured the kids might need a break to shake off last night." He leans in and brushes his lips against mine again. "And I really wanted to see you," he murmurs breathlessly, his words shooting straight into my heart and embedding themselves into my every fiber.

How can he say he doesn't subscribe to romance when he says things so casually when they're least expected?

"I have a work function tonight, so I don't have much time, but I wanted to go have some fun and release some stress." He subtly shakes his head, and I can see a hint of sadness creep back into his eyes. "Besides, it's been a rough day and I needed to get away. Do something to relax."

"Everything okay?"

"Nothing for you to worry about." He forces a tight smile, leans in, and kisses the tip of my nose. "Besides, I thought the boys might enjoy it too."

"I'm sure they will," I tell him. "I've gotta go get my purse." I start to head toward the staff's room when I hear Zander call my name from the opposite side of the house. I pause, a wide smile spreading across my face over hearing him call my name like all the other kids in the house do. It makes my heart happy. "What's wrong, Zand?" I ask.

"Shoe." It's only one word. But it's a word. And he's actually communicating so that makes it even better. I smile broadly and Colton follows suit in understanding.

"Go get your purse," he tells me. "I'll go help him."

"You sure?" I ask, but he's already turning the corner to the hall.

I gather my stuff, lock up the back door, and get ready to leave. When I near the hall, I hear the murmur of voices. I take a few steps and then stop when I realize that Colton and Zander are talking about last night.

I know I shouldn't eavesdrop—that I should walk away and leave them some privacy—but my curiosity is piqued. And when I hear Colton say, "You know, I used to have really bad dreams too, Zander," I know that I won't be going anywhere.

I can't see them but I have a feeling that Zander acknowledges Colton somehow because he continues. "When I was little, I had some really bad things happen to me too. And I used to get scared. So scared." I can hear Colton sigh and some shuffling. "And when I'd get that scared, do you know what I'd say to try and make me not so scared? I'd repeat in my head, '*Spiderman. Batman. Superman. Ironman.*' I'd say it over and over. And you know what? If I squeezed my eyes really, really tight—just like this—it would help."

I stand in the hallway. My heart melting as I listen to a man who is so damaged he's sworn off ever having children but is so unbelievable with them. Especially the broken ones. The ones that need him the most. The ones he understands better than anyone. I feel a phantom pang in my abdomen, and I push away the thoughts of what can never be. For me. And with him.

Then the best sound pulls me from my self-pity. It's meek but it's a laugh that warms my insides. I wish I could see what Colton's doing to make him laugh. What barrier he's breaking down to get that sound from Zander. "You know what? I'll let you in on another secret…even now—even though I'm an adult—when I have a bad dream or am really scared, I still say that. I promise I do…" Colton laughs and I take a step forward toward the open doorway. And what I see steals my breath. Colton is sitting on the bed and Zander is sitting sideways on his lap, looking reverently up at him. A soft smile on his lips. Colton glances up for a split second when he notices me, the gentle smile on his face widening, and then turns back to focus on Zander. "And it still helps. Now, are you ready to drive a go-kart and beat me?"

Zander looks over to me and smiles widely. "Okay, then go get in the van!" I tell him. He looks back toward Colton and nods his head once before hopping off and running toward the front door.

Colton stays seated for a moment, and we just stare at each other. A silent exchange that tells him I heard everything and that he's glad I did. That exchange—watching him with Zander—has the protective wall around my heart fracturing into a million pieces and love seeping from the cracks. I shake my head to clear it of all of the things I want to say to him in this moment and hold my hand out to him instead.

He rises slowly and gives a half smile. "C'mon." He takes my hand and tugs it. "Do you think you can beat me in a race?"

"I know I can beat the pants off of you," I reply suggestively.

He chuckles at my comment. "As much as I like your line of thinking, Ry, we're gonna be surrounded by a crowd of people."

I release his hand and wrap my arm around his torso, wanting the feel of his body against mine. It's me who needs to feel close to him now. He laughs at my sudden assault of him. "I thought being dirty in a crowd turned you on," I whisper against his ear.

"Sweet Jesus, woman." He groans. "You know what to say to get me hard."

I place an open mouth kiss at the spot just beneath his jaw. "I know. Too bad we're going to be surrounded by seven little boys who hang on your every word or I'd let you scratch this itch I seem to have."

"God, you're such a cock tease," he laughs as we walk out of the front door of the house. He releases me so I can lock the front door, a look of desire clouding his eyes as he watches me.

"You think so?" I murmur coyly, batting my eyelashes at him as he nods. "Maybe I'll have to show you just how good of a cock tease I am," I quip as I sashay down the walkway in front of him, swinging my hips back and forth. I know that sex is off of the agenda for the evening because he has to leave right after karting with the kids, and Saturday night will be the next time I get to see him.

I turn back to face him, taking a step backwards as I watch him. "Too bad you shaved," I say, fighting the smirk I want to give him. "I kinda liked the roughness of it between my thighs." I raise my eyebrows as he sucks in a breath.

This could be fun. A buildup of anticipation. I can spend the week taunting him and ramp up the expectation so that by Saturday night we can't keep our hands off of each other. *As if we need help with that anyway.*

"C'mon, Rylee! You have to beat him. You're our last hope!" Shane yells across the railing at me as I stand beside my kart waiting for my rematch.

The past two hours have been a blast. From the racing to the boys' laughter to the constant banter between Colton and me, I couldn't have thought of a better way for the boys to let off steam and reconnect after the chaos of Zander's nightmare last night.

After an hour of free-for-all racing, the boys begged to race one on one against Colton. He willingly obliged and in turn set up my current situation. Colton beat all of the boys, everyone that went up against him, except for me. I accused him of letting me win, which had him instantly calling for a rematch. The second race went in his favor. Now we're in the tiebreaker.

"Best out of three, Thomas. Whoever wins next gets bragging rights," he calls over to me, amusement in his eyes and challenge in his smile. *God, I love him.* Especially when he has this look about him: confident, carefree, and downright sexy.

"You're all talk, Donavan. Your win was a total fluke." The arrogant smile he flashes goads me further. "Big, bad professional racer like you has to maintain your dignity, you know. Can't have rookies like me showing you up! Especially a woman."

"Oh baby, you know me, I'll let a woman do whatever she wants to me." He smirks and raises an eyebrow suggestively.

I laugh out loud as I walk the ten feet between us. I look back over my shoulder at the boys who are egging me on and wink at them to show I'm on their side. As I approach, Colton turns to face me, his hand holding his helmet against his hip as if it's the most natural stance in the world for him, and the fingers of his other hand rubbing together as if he is itching to reach out and touch me.

Good, it's working. My subtle brushes against him. My little suggestive comments whispered to him here and there. My slow perusal of his body so he notices. Despite having to do them all under the detecting eyes of our audience, I'm glad to know that none of them have gone unnoticed. I can see it in his eyes and the pulsing muscle in his jaw as I approach him.

"You worried you're going to lose, Ace?" I smirk. My back is toward our audience so I bend over and tie my shoe, purposefully putting my cleavage on display. When I look up, Colton's pupils have darkened and his tongue darts out to wet his lips.

"I know what you're doing, Rylee," he murmurs softly from beneath his smirk, "and as much as your little antics have had me wanting to push you up against that wall over there and take you hard and fast more than once since we've been here—regardless of who's watching—it's not going to work." He flashes his megawatt smile at me. "I'm still gonna beat that fine ass of yours to the finish line."

"Well as much as I could use a good spanking..." I breathe out, looking up at him from beneath my lashes and catch his sharp intake of air at my words "...I was just coming over here to see if you needed any help getting your motor revved up." I smile innocently at him, although my body language says anything but.

I watch his throat constrict as he swallows, his lips twisting as he tries to prevent himself from smiling. "Oh, my motor's running just fine, sweetheart," he teases as his eyes travel the length of my body again. "Revved and raring to go. Do you need any help getting yours tuned and ready to race?"

I bite my bottom lip as I stare at him and angle my head to the side. "Well I seem to be running a little tight in the ass end. Nothing a quick lube job wouldn't fix," I toss over my shoulder as I walk back to my car, wishing I could see the reaction on his face.

The boys keep up their shouting and heckling as we put our helmets on and get strapped in our carts. I glance over at Colton and nod my head as I rev my gas pedal. And then we are off, racing side by side through the twists and turns of the track. My competitive nature surfaces as Colton noses past me. I can't hear the boys cheering me on over the sound of the motors, but I catch passing glimpses of their arms waving frantically in my periphery. We come to the next turn and I edge the nose of my cart in first, taking the corner at full speed and powering past him. We race down the straightaway toward the finish line, edging back and forth. When we finally cross it, I'm pretty sure that I won by the hysterics from the boys and Jackson on the sidelines.

I screech my kart to a stop and jump out, unable to suppress the wide grin on my face. I pull off my helmet at the same time Colton does and when I turn to him, I swear his grin is as wide as mine. I do a silly, little victory dance around him to amuse the boys who are doing their own celebrating. He just shakes his head, laughing at me with a genuine, carefree smile on his face.

"Ha!" I smirk at him. "How do you like them apples?" I taunt as I follow him to the little office at the edge of the track and out of the spectators' view. The minute we're out of the boys' line of sight, Colton spins me around and has me pinned against the wall. His long, lean body presses against every curve of mine as if we fit together like yin and yang.

"Do you have any fucking clue how turned on I am, Rylee?" He growls at me. "How much I want to take what you've been flaunting in front of me all afternoon?"

It takes every ounce of my concentration to appear unaffected by him. Every ounce. I arch my eyebrows at him in nonchalance. "Well I have a feeling that your dick pressing into me is an indication."

"God, I want to fuck that smirk off your face right now."

His words alone incite my core muscles to clench at the mere thought. I never realized that the act of seducing can provoke equal parts of desire in both parties.

My nipples harden at the feeling of his firm chest pressed against them. His breath feathers over my face and his eyes remain locked on mine. He tilts his head forward and meets my lips, his tongue licking between them, and tangling with mine. There is a quiet passion to his kiss, and I groan as he releases me, leaving me wanting more.

"I couldn't agree more, Ryles, but I gotta get going…and I have a feeling your fan club is going to come barging through that door any moment." He takes my helmet from my hand and places it on the table at the same time the door opens up and the boys come barreling through. Colton looks over at me and arches his eyebrows as if to say *I told you so.*

I bite back a careless giggle when I see all of the boys carrying bundles of cotton candy. My thoughts revert to my more than memorable experience with the confection and Colton. He groans, his own little acknowledgement, causing my lips to twitch with a devious little smirk.

"One second, guys!" I yell above their raucous noise as I take a pinch from Ricky's funnel. I step back toward Colton and deliberately run my tongue over my lips before placing the fluff of sweetness on my tongue. I close my eyes and play up savoring its taste. When I open them back up, Colton's eyes have darkened and his jaw is set with frustration and desire—just the response I was looking for.

I lean close to his ear, purposefully withholding any touch of my body against his, my voice a seductive whisper for his ears only. "Hey, Ace?" He looks over and arches a brow at me. *"I'm not wearing any panties."* I smirk. He audibly sucks in a breath in acknowledgement before I sway my hips a little more than normal as I walk away from him.

What he doesn't know, won't hurt him, I think as I picture the pair of white cotton underwear I'm wearing beneath my Levis.

Chapter Fifteen

Colton glances over at me as he listens to his publicist give him the order of events for the evening. We're gliding through Los Angeles in a limo headed toward a charity gala. This is the first of several events in the coming weeks where Colton and I will make the rounds, formally promoting our companies' joint venture, and hopefully enlist some participants for the car's lap sponsorship program.

I stare at him unabashedly as I hum to *Hero/Heroine* floating gently through the background from the speakers. I take in everything about him that has become so familiar, so addictive, so *everything* to me in such a short period of time. He's so striking in the formal tuxedo—the clothing that he's already confessed to detesting several times—and I can't stop thinking what a lucky girl I am. His face is clean-shaven again, and yet even without the usual shadow of hair, he still *exudes* the aura of careless bad boy.

It's just something that oozes off of him regardless of what he's wearing. He's almost sexier with his look tonight because I know that beneath his sophisticated exterior lies a reckless rebel at heart.

Colton glances over me again, feeling the scrutiny of my stare, and a salacious smirk spreads on his lips. His eyes meet mine and I know he is aching just as bad as I am to feel our bare skin connect. The remainder of our week since the go-kart track has been filled with provocatively taunting emails and texts explaining in depth what we want to do to one another once this evening is over. *My God, with words alone the man can make a woman need, crave, desire—and most likely beg if it takes too long—like I've never known possible.* But I'm pretty confident that the unfulfilled ache goes both ways though, from the hissing of his breath when I answered the front door in my sexy, red dress.

"Okay, so we'll be there in about five minutes. I'll jump out before your call time and get into place while the car circles around the block," Chase says, looking at both of us above her black-rimmed glasses. I hold a hand to my stomach at the thought of being photographed on the red carpet in front of all of those people. *Yikes!* I thought this was a little function. I didn't realize it was a full-blown Hollywood filled gala with questioning press. The publicity will be good for the charity, but can't I just sneak in the back door and avoid the spotlight?

Obviously that will never be the option if I'm with Colton.

He reaches over and squeezes my hand. "Don't be nervous." He winks at me. "I've got you covered."

"That's what I'm afraid of." I smirk at him, our eyes doing the talking for us. I swear I can see the electricity crackle in the air as sexual tension fills the limo. Chase busies herself by keeping her head down, her cheeks staining red at our silent yet obvious exchange.

"Well, here's my stop," she mumbles, gathering her papers as Colton rubs the back of my hand with his thumb.

"Thanks, Chase. We'll see you in a few minutes," he tells her, never taking his eyes off of mine.

The minute the limo door shuts, Colton shifts and has me pressed against the backseat. His hand tangles in my loose curls, and I arch my chest off the back of the seat, aching to feel the heat of his body against mine, but he stops inches from my face. My lips part and my breath quickens as I look into his eyes. The quiet intensity held within that flash of green undoes me.

Strips me.

Fuels me.

"Do you have any idea how many times this week I've wanted to do this to you?" He ever so slowly lowers his lips to mine, just a whisper of a touch that has me groaning with a teeming desperation.

"Colton," I plead as his lips withdraw a fraction, leaving my body focused solely on the slow slide of his hand up my ribcage to just below the underside of my breast before it makes the slow descent back down. My breath exhales in a shuddered sigh that has his lips turning up and eyes crinkling at the corners.

"Is there something you want?" he whispers against my lips as he pulls my hair gently back so my neck is exposed. His tongue glides a slow trail down the column, clearly drawing out the anticipation that we've built over the past couple of days, but I'm so addled with need, I just want him inside of me. Now. To fill the void aching for him.

"Yes. I. Need. You. In. Me. Colton. Now," my splintered voice pants as his tongue licks at my proffered cleavage.

His laugh is low and throaty, the tenor of it filling my ears, stoking my fire of need until his tongue leaves my skin. I open my eyes, looking at him from beneath eyelids weighted with desire to find his gaze trained on my face. "You didn't think I'd let you off—or rather *let you get off*—that easy did you?" He smirks and I can see the mirth dancing in his eyes. *Oh shit!* My body already taut with need tenses further. "You've given me blue balls all week, and I think turnabout's fair play." He smirks. *"To use your term."*

As much as I want to take pride in the fact he's confessed that I've successfully driven him crazy, the knowledge that my itch is not going to be scratched any time soon causes me to groan in frustration. Colton's smile only widens at the sound, and the mischief in his eyes has my own narrowing at him in turn.

"You've been killing me softly all week, Rylee, with your little suggestions…little teases…and so it's time to show you exactly how it feels."

Oh fucking hell! *Seriously?* What does he have in mind here? "I *do know how it feels*," I try to emphasize but only succeed in sounding breathy. Desperate. "Your responses have done the same to me."

He kisses my neck softly, working his way to my pleasure point just below my ear lobe. His whisper of a touch makes me slick with arousal. "No. I don't think so, Rylee," he murmurs, his lips moving to my ear. "Do you know how hard it is to concentrate on a meeting, trying to hide my hard-on because I can't get your texts out of my head? What an idiot I look like when I draw a blank at a question about wing adjustments to the car because all I can think about is savoring the sweet taste of your pussy again?" He brings a hand up and lays his palm on the base of my neck, holding my head still, so that I have no option but to meet the challenge in his eyes. *"Did it feel the same for you, Rylee?"*

I bite my bottom lip and shake my head no, our eyes, violet to green, in a silent exchange. "Say it."

"No." I take in a shaky breath, completely under his spell. Captivated. Mesmerized.

"Then tonight I'll show you," he tells me, sinking to his knees on the floor of the limo as he moves between my legs and captures my mouth again. His tongue licks in and slowly moves with mine as his hand slides up the outside of my thigh, pushing my dress up as he goes. "Sweet Jesus." He exhales as his fingers skim over the garter belts I wore specifically with seducing him in mind. For some reason though, I seem to think the tables have turned now.

I'm the one being seduced.

"Now I'm going to think about undressing you all night until you're standing in your heels and these and nothing else," he says, pulling on a garter strap so it snaps back against my thigh. The slight sting mainlines a jolt straight to my already quivering sex.

"I think you're a little overdressed." He smirks, the devilish look back on his face. I look at him with trepidation, all my focus on the carnal look in his eyes, until I feel his fingers dancing over the dampened silk of my panties. The slight fabric barrier mutes his touch, and I instinctively lift my hips up, begging for more.

"Colton," I gasp.

"And I'm a little underdressed," he murmurs, a teasing quality to his voice. I have a quick second to wonder what the hell he means by his comment, but then the limo's cool air bathes my heated flesh as he pulls my panties to the side and the question falls from my mind. I keep my eyes on him, body humming with uncontrollable need as he ever-so-slowly trails one finger up and then down my slowly swelling folds. And I am gone—my thoughts lost to the dance of fingertips, the searing heat of desire, and the unyielding ache of need.

He leans in and teases me with a soft, tantalizing kiss—fucking my mouth with reverence—that pulls all the way from my toes and back up. He's assaulting all my senses, hindering all coherent thoughts, manipulating my body with a focused purpose.

I cry out and into his waiting lips as he tucks three fingers into me, circling them around so that they rub all of my sensitive walls. I throw my head back without shame and emit a strangled moan, his fingers invading the depths of my sex and manipulating me in the way I so desperately need. I angle my hips up, straining to be closer, his fingers to delve deeper, needing this release brought on by him. The connection.

My body climbs. Tightens with the anticipation of my mounting orgasm. I'm so close to free falling into ecstasy that I can't hold back the moan that falls from my lips.

And then suddenly I'm empty.

"What?" I cry, flashing my eyes open to see Colton's green ones filled with humor and a heavy dose of lust before me.

"Not 'til later, Ry." A lascivious smirk finds its way on to that gorgeous mouth of his. "When I can take my deliriously slow, sweet time with you. Take you to places you don't even know exist yet," he says, reiterating his promise from the first night we met, except right now I have no witty comeback for him. I just want him. Now. Any way possible.

Because this time I know he can fulfill that promise. *And then some.*

When I start to protest, he brings a finger up to my bottom lip, and coats it with my own arousal before capturing my mouth with his. His tongue licks his way into mine, the hum in the back of his throat is sexy as hell. He frames my cheeks in his hands and then pulls back a fraction, laving my bottom lip again upon retreat. He looks into my eyes—that hum rumbling through his throat again. "My two favorite tastes in the whole world."

I groan in frustration. Is he fucking kidding me? He can't talk to me like that and not think I'm going to jump him and take what I want.

"Shhhh," he whispers. "I told you it's your turn to be tortured with need." I close my eyes momentarily, resigning myself to having this deep, fastidious craving remain unfulfilled for the time being. "And I intend to show you just how exquisite that torture can be *all night long,* sweetheart."

The dark promise of his words has my entire body thrumming with an unrequited desire and my pussy pulsing in anticipation. I have a feeling that this is going to be a very long, very frustrating evening.

"Starting now," he murmurs, flashing me a wicked grin while he slowly moves himself down my body, and lowers his mouth to take a slow, sweet taste of me. I groan wildly at the soft swipe of his tongue that immediately renders me defenseless and leaves me his for the taking.

He slides his tongue back and forth momentarily, his fingers whispering across and spreading my swollen flesh.

"Colton," I say in a drawn out whimper as an earthquake of sensation rocks me when he plunges his tongue inside of me. I can barely breathe. Can't even focus. My fingers grip into the flesh of my thighs—urging, pushing, building toward the earth shattering release just within reach.

"That's it, Ry." He blows on my seam, my head falling back against the seat, eyes closed and body willing. "I want you just like this all night."

I hear, rather than feel the snap of fabric as Colton falls back on his heels. And I'm so pent up with my denied release that I don't even find it amusing that he's claimed yet another pair of my panties. The low, guttural groan he emits has me flashing my eyes up just in time to see him wipe my moisture from his mouth with the remnants of my red silk panties. I just stare at him, lips parted, eyes wide, breath panting, and heart racing.

And frustrated.

"Is there something you want?" He smirks.

My head is clouded with need. Screw the game he's playing. All I want is him. Right now. Urgently. "Yes. Please, Colton. Please." I basically beg and don't care one bit that I did.

Our silent stare is broken when his phone chirps a text. He looks at it and then up to me with amusement dancing in his eyes. "Perfect timing. It's our turn in line."

I just shake my head at him as my body remains in its suspended state of negligence. He smirks, smoothes my gown back down over my legs, sans panties, and sits back in the seat next to me.

And in this moment I can see it in his eyes. The razor thin edge his control is teetering on. How his body is driven with such an incredible need and fueled by such an intense, overwhelming desire. How much this little seduction of his is killing him as much as it is me.

"A single word," he says, slowly leaning forward so one of his hands can cup the side of my face. He brushes the pad of his thumb back and forth over my bottom lip. "*Anticipation.*"

The simple word sends a tingle of awareness through my body. He grazes his lips tenderly against mine before pulling back a fraction. I lean in wanting to deepen the kiss and drown in the taste that I've been craving, but he withdraws, denying me with a seductive chuckle and a mischievous yet naughty gleam in his eye.

And for some reason, my mind picks this moment to remember the comment he'd made moments ago. "*Underdressed?*" I ask, my eyes narrowing in thought, trying to figure out what exactly he means.

He holds up my panties and works his tongue inside his mouth as he figures what words to taunt me with. "You see, now these have been exactly where I've wanted to be nestled all fucking week long. And since I haven't been allowed to be there, neither will these." He leans in to place the most tender of kisses on my lips before resting his forehead against mine. "Tonight, Rylee," he murmurs against my lips, "I want you thinking about me all night long. More specifically everything I plan on doing to you later when I have you alone." He breathes out, his voice a seductive whisper that has the desire within me igniting into a raging inferno. "Where my tongue is going to lick. Where my fingers are going to grip. Where my mouth is going to taste. Where my cock is going to stroke. How my body is going to worship every incredible inch of yours."

My hands reach out to squeeze his biceps as my mouth goes dry and my sex gets wet from the provocation of his words. He has to know I'm affected—has to know that I'm desperate for his touch already—but he continues.

"I want to know that while you are talking to all of these potential donors, looking so poised, elegant, and fucking breathtaking, that beneath this dress you are wet and dripping with need for me." I draw in a ragged breath, his words almost too much to hear in my current state. "That you ache so much it hurts. That your pussy pulses at the thought of how later tonight my cock is going to be buried in it. *For hours.*" His voice is pained as he says the last words, and I have some degree of satisfaction that he is suffering as deliciously as I am. I can't help the hum of desire in the back of my throat, as I feel his mouth curl in a smile at my response.

"Every time I look at you I want to know that I'm killing you slowly on the inside while you look so perfectly proper on the outside." He angles his head forward and gives me the kiss that he's been withholding from me. I'm breathless by the time he releases me. "And knowing that will leave me wanting just as much as you will be."

He pulls back from me and shifts in the seat beside me. I've said nothing this entire time, and yet I feel exhausted and totally overcome from our conversation. "Underdressed," he says, a mischievous grin tugging at the corners of his mouth as he holds up my panties and starts folding them. "You are no longer overdressed with these taken out of the picture..." He tucks the scrap of red silk into his pocket square opening and winks at me. "and now I'm perfect."

I stare at him wondering what depths of desire he is going to bring me to tonight. A blush spreads over my cheeks and he smirks, knowing that I'm more than along for the ride. I shake my head softly at him. "You can really be naughty, you know that?"

Something flashes through his eyes which I akin to fear, but I know that's not possible. What does he possibly have to fear from me? "You have no idea, Rylee." His jaw clenches as he looks at me, the mood is suddenly serious and I'm confused as to why. We sit staring at each other in silence for a moment before he turns to look out at the passing scenery. His voice is eerily soft and contemplative when he finally speaks. "If you were smart...if I could let you...I'd tell you to walk away."

I stare at the back of his head, confusion bewildering me. What does he think is so horrible within him that he's not worthy of me? The fact that after all of this time he still feels that he's tainted by his childhood kills me. If only he would let me try and help him. I reach out and lay my hand on his back. "Colton, why would you say that?"

He looks back at me, his face guarded. "I like your naivety way too much to give you the sordid details."

Naivety? Does he not know the horrors I have seen working at The House? Either that or it's another excuse to run from his past. "Whatever it is Colton, it doesn't affect how I feel about you. I need you to know that—"

"Colton?" I startle as the intercom from the front of the car buzzes to us in the back.

"Drop it, Ry," he warns quietly. "Yeah, Sammy?"

"ETA two minutes."

He lowers the privacy partition dividing us. Sammy turns his head toward Colton. "Sammy, please get Sex here. I feel like driving tonight."

Sex? Driving? What the fuck is he talking about?

"Sure thing," Sammy says, a crooked smile lighting up his face before the partition slides back up.

"*Sex?*" I look at him like he's crazy, glad for the change of topic to add some levity to the sudden heaviness of our conversation.

"Yeah. My F12. *My baby.* That's her name." He shrugs as if it's the most perfectly normal thing in the world, but he lost me at F12, baby, and sex.

"Ummm, can you explain that in a language for those of us with dual X chromosomes?" I laugh bewildered.

He gives me a boyish grin that would melt my panties if I had any on. "F12 is my favorite of all of my collection. She's a Berlinetta Ferrari. The first time Beckett drove her he told me that the feeling was equivalent to the best sex he's ever had. It was a joke at first, but the name stuck. So…" he shrugs his shoulders, and I just shake my head at him "...Sex."

"*Collection?*"

"Women have shoes. Men have cars." It's the only explanation he gives. I'm about to ask more when he announces, "We're here." He shifts in his seat so that he's closer to the door and butterflies take flight in my stomach. "Show time."

Before I can mentally prepare myself any further, the door to the limo opens. Even though Colton's body standing in the doorway partially blocks the flash of cameras, I am temporarily blinded by their intensity.

Colton calls out a casual laid-back greeting to the paparazzi as he buttons up his jacket before turning to help me. I take a deep breath as

I take his hand and scoot out of the limo. I exit the car and look up at him, a reassuring smile on his face. Gone is the brooding guy in the car from moments before. *Hello Hollywood playboy.*

"You okay?" he mouths to me and I nod my head subtly, overwhelmed by the onslaught of people yelling at us along with the repeated camera flashes. He pulls me toward him, his mouth resting against my ear. "Remember to smile and follow my lead," he murmurs. "You look stunning tonight." He pulls back, squeezing my hand and graces me with one of his panty wetting smiles before turning to walk the carpet.

And the only thought that breaks through the buzz surrounding us is that from this point forward, I am no longer anonymous to the press.

Chapter Sixteen

My eyes still have bright white spots in my field of vision, but I survived the red carpet. I feel so disoriented and oddly taken advantage of by the press' invasive questions and incessant picture taking. I have no idea how Colton can be so relaxed in such a situation. *Maybe years of practice.* He was calm and polite, and avoided answering the questions thrown at him—were we an item, how long had we been together, what was my name?—and deflected them with the flash of his smile, giving them the perfect picture for their cover page instead.

Colton squeezes my hand in sympathy. "Sometimes I forget how nerve wracking that can be to someone who's never done it before." He gives me a quick, chaste kiss on the lips before directing me toward the ballroom. "Forgive me. I should have prepped you for it before hand."

"Don't worry about it," I tell him, relaxing at the warmth of his hand on my back. "I'm fine."

The red carpet is one thing, but I don't think anything could have prepared me for what I'd feel entering a room with Colton. It seems as if every head in the room turns when we walk through the doorway, all of their attention focused on the man beside me. The man is just simply magnetic in every sense of the word: looks, attitude, charisma, and personality. I falter at the sudden attention. Colton feels my hesitancy and pulls me closer against his side, a not so subtle demonstration of ownership and possession to the assessing stares. The unexpected action both surprises me and warms my heart. He leans his mouth to my ear. "Breathe baby," he murmurs, "you're doing just fine. And I can't wait to fuck you later." My eyes flash up to his and the smirk he gives me tames the nerves.

The next hour or so goes by in a flash. Colton and I mingle throughout the crowd, and I'm in awe of the number of people that he knows or is acquainted with. He is so unpretentious that I find myself forgetting the circumstances in which he grew up—where celebrities are family friends and tuxedos are everyday wear.

He's really quite charming, always knowing the right comment to make or when to add a little levity to the conversation with a light joke. He subtly works the sponsorship program into each conversation and patiently answers questions about it in a laid-back fashion that has people committing to the cause without feeling propositioned or badgered.

And he wears my panties as a pocket square—a constant reminder to me of our little interlude in the limo and the seductive promises he made.

I glance around the room and notice several women talking together and stealing glances our way. At first I assume that they're looking at Colton because let's face it, it's hard not to gawk at him. And then when I take a second look, I realize that their gazes are not in admiration of Colton but rather in judgment of his date—me. They eye me cattily, sneers on their faces before turning back to each other to carry on. *Criticizing me, no doubt.* I try to not let it bother me or to let my insecurity get the best of me, but I know what they're thinking. I see Tawny's observations echoed in their looks.

I am so immersed in my thoughts that I didn't realize Colton has maneuvered me behind a tall a bistro cocktail table. He turns his back to the room behind us and kisses me to renew my torturous need for him. He pulls his face back to watch me as his hand, blocked to the crowd beyond by his dinner jacket, cups the V between my legs. "Fast and hard? Or nice and slow, Rylee? Which way should I fuck you first?" he murmurs quietly, the timbre of his voice carrying to my ears. My breath catches in my throat as one finger presses between my folds through the fabric of my dress—not enough pressure to set me off, but just enough to cause a ripple of sensation to travel throughout my body.

"Colton?"

A voice interrupts us from over Colton's shoulder. I jolt in awareness from what he was just doing, while a smooth smile slides across his mouth as he turns to address the acquaintance. He greets the gentleman and introduces me even though he knows I most likely need a moment to regain my wits. I'm sure the flush of my cheeks can tell him that much, but when I glance over at him, he's immersed in his conversation about some event they'd attended together in the past. His eyes flick over to me, a lopsided, ghost of a smirk on his face and his eyes suggesting so much more.

I watch Colton, only partially listening to what he's saying, until the couple is called elsewhere, all the while my body humming with desire. To have him so close to me—at my fingertips really—and not be able to touch him? To slide my hands up that sculpted chest beneath that dress shirt? Run my tongue down the V at his hips and taste him? Absolute torture. He leans into me, obviously guessing where my thoughts have drifted off to, and his face brushes against my hair. "God, you're sexy when you're aroused," he whispers to me before pressing a kiss to my temple.

"This is so unfair," I chastise him, pressing a hand against his chest, a foolish grin on my lips. My smile falters momentarily as I catch a nasty look from a passing female out of the corner of my eye. *What's your problem?* I want to ask her. *What have I done to you?*

"Do you want another drink?" he asks, breaking through my mental dress down of unknown bimbo number one. I figure I should number them because I have a feeling there might be more than a few here tonight. I nod my head to his request, knowing the night's just begun and I need a little liquid courage if I'm going to remain at Colton's sexual mercy. "I'll be right back," he tells me before squeezing my hand and heading off to the bar.

I watch him and see several A-list actors stop him on his way to shake his hand or pat his back in greeting. A statuesque blonde sidles up to his side trying to get his attention. I observe Colton, curious as to how he'll interact with her and noting their level of familiarity—the way she touches him, the lean in her body language towards him, the way he looks at her, but at the same time seems annoyed by her presence—makes me wonder if he's slept with her before. I can't tear my eyes away from watching them because deep down I already know the answer.

I know that he's had his fill of women, and I accept that, but at the same time, my acknowledgement does not mean that I'm okay with it. That I want to be privy to it with my own eyes. I watch him dismiss the blonde and continue across the room. By the time he actually makes it to the bar, he is surrounded by a group of people, all vying for his attention, ranging from young to old, men to women.

"He's not going to keep you around you know," an accented voice beside me says quietly.

"Excuse me?" I turn to look at the stunning beauty beside me with the requisite straight, blonde hair.

Hello, bimbo number two.

She smirks at me, her head shaking side to side in disapproval as she sizes me up. "Just what I said," she deadpans. "He doesn't keep us around for long."

Us? As if I want to be any part of anything with her, let alone the newest member of the Colton Donavan Cast Off Club. *Great! Another of his women scorned.* "Thanks for the heads up," I tell her, not hiding my disdain for her presence, "I'll make sure to keep that in mind. *Now if you'll excuse me.*"

When I start to walk away she grabs me by my upper arm. Anger fires in my veins. Every polite bone in my body riots to not whirl around and show her that underneath this glamorous dress is a scrapper willing to fight for what's mine. And right now, Colton is *mine.* My hand itches to reach out and slap her hand off of me. *Or to just slap her in general.*

"Just so you know, when he's done with you and tosses you aside, I'll be there to take your place." With these words, I successfully shrug out of her grip and turn to face her. When I just stare at her with icy contempt, shocked into silence from her audacity, she continues. "Didn't you know Colton likes to dabble with his exes when he's in between women?"

"So what? You just sit around and wait? Seems pathetic to me," I say, shaking my head at her and trying to hide the fact that her words unnerve me.

"He's that good," she rebukes.

As if I didn't know already.

And with her words, I realize that is why all of these exes are so possessive of him, even if in memory. He's the total package in more ways than one. *Less the ability to commit of course.* Suddenly, the sneer on her face is replaced by a dazzling smile. I notice her body language changing and shifting, and I know that Colton is behind me even before my body hums with the awareness of his proximity.

I turn and give him a smile, my countenance one of gratitude for saving me from this woman's talons. "Teagan." He nods to her, a reserved smile on his face and indifference in his voice. "You look lovely as always."

"Colton," she gushes breathlessly, her demeanor completely changed. "So good to see you again." She steps forward to kiss his cheek, and he absently brushes her off by placing his hand on my waist and pulling me tighter into his side. I can tell she is hurt by his lack of attention, so she tries again without success.

"If you'll excuse us, Teagan, we have a room to work," he says politely, dismissing her by steering me away.

He nods to another acquaintance and continues once we are out of earshot. "She's a nasty piece of work," he says before taking a swallow of his drink. "I'm sorry I didn't rescue you sooner."

"It's okay, she was busy informing me that when you discard me, she'll be your in-between-girl until you find someone new. That you always dabble with your exes while searching for your next conquest." I roll my eyes and try to make my tone lighthearted as if her words didn't bug me, but I know later they'll hit me full force when I'm least expecting it.

Because I'm more than sure she was speaking the truth.

Colton throws his head back and laughs loudly. "When Hell freezes over!" he exclaims, brushing off her remarks. "Remind me to tell you about her later. She's a piece of work."

"Good to know. I'll make sure I steer clear of her."

We mingle a bit more, talking up our joint venture in a room filled with deep pockets. We are separated here and there, different conversations tugging us in opposing directions. In those instances when we are apart, I can't help but look over at Colton, my soft smile is the only answer I can give to his wicked smirk.

I find myself alone for a moment and decide to head to the bar to refill my drink. I'm waiting in the rather long line when I hear the three women a couple of patrons behind me. At first I don't think they realize that I can hear them. The rude comments about my choice in dress. About how I am so not Colton's type because I'm not exactly *sample size*. How I'd benefit from a nose job and some lypo. How I wouldn't know how to handle Colton in bed even if he gave me a road map. And it goes on and on until I know for sure that they're saying it loud on purpose, in the hopes of getting to me.

No matter how much I know that they're just jealous and trying to get under my skin, they've most definitely burrowed deep and are succeeding. They've gotten to me despite the knowledge in my head that I'm the one Colton's with tonight. I decide the drink refill I want— that I currently feel like I most definitely could benefit from—isn't worth the mental angst that these bitches are inflicting.

I opt out of line and take a deep breath in fortification, planning to ignore them as I walk by. But I can't do it. I can't let them know they've succeeded. Instead I stop just as I pass them and turn back. I don't care how I feel on the inside. I'm not letting bimbos numbers three, four, and five know that they've gotten to me. I look up to meet their judgmental eyes, take in their condescending sneers, and shrug off their disapproving glares.

"Hey, ladies." I smirk, leaning in closer. "Just so you know, the only road map I need is the little moan that Colton makes as I lick my way down his delicious happy trail that points straight to his obscenely large dick. Thanks for your concern though." I flash a catty smile of my own before walking away without looking back.

My hands are shaking as I walk, veering towards the hallway near the restrooms for a moment to collect myself. Why did I let them get to me? If I'm with Colton, isn't that the only answer I need? *But am I really with Colton?* I see it in his eyes, hear it in his unspoken words, and feel it in his skillful touch. In Vegas he told me that he chose me, but when I asked him to try and give me more than his stupid arrangement, he never answered me, never gave me any of the security a simple, "Yes, I'll try," would have given me.

Maybe it's noticing all of, what I assume to be, his cast-offs here tonight—seeing them still want what they can no longer have and parading around in front of me. Couldn't he have at least warned me?

And then the thought snakes into my psyche. Is that going to be me in a couple of months? One of the many women scorned by the notorious Colton Donavan. I'd like to think not, but after seeing them here tonight, why do I think that I even have a shot at taming the uncontrollable man? Why would he change for me when the myriad before didn't even tempt him to?

I can think that I'm different all day long, but my thoughts mean nothing when his words could mean everything.

I sigh, my nerves calming and unsettled simultaneously as I look down into my empty glass. I let out a little shriek as hands slide around my waist from behind. "There you are," Colton's voice murmurs into my ear, his lips grazing the curve of my shoulder up to my neck. "I couldn't find you."

"*Well hello there, Ace,*" I say back to him, the whisper of his lips momentarily quieting my doubts.

"*Ace,* huh?" He chuckles and I try to turn into him, but he keeps his body ghosted to mine with his arms around my torso. He starts walking forward, my legs instinctively moving from the momentum of his. With each step, I can feel him hardening against my lower back. The ache that never really left roars back to life.

Colton's resonating chuckle against my ear snaps me out of thoughts of what I want him—no need him—to do to me right now. It's just too much for me to have our bodies connected from thigh to shoulder. Begging is within the realm of possibilities right now.

"A closet experience?" he asks, and it takes me a moment to get that he's offering up another lame attempt for the meaning behind Ace.

"Nope," I laugh at him, "Where'd that one—"

"God, it couldn't be any more fucking perfect if I'd planned it."

And I see it the minute the words are out of his mouth. He's walked us down toward the isolated end of the janitor's alcove, and ironically we are standing in front of a door marked *Storage*.

I start to laugh but before it can even escape, he has me turned around and pinned against the wall, his body pressing into me, his steel into my softness. Colton props his hands on either side of my head and leans his face into mine, stopping a whisper from my lips. Our chests press together as our desperation to taste one another consumes our air, hijacks our ability to breathe, and steals the process of reason.

Despite our close proximity, our eyes remain open, the connection between us unwavering. *Electric. Combustible.* "Do you have any idea how desperate I am to fuck you right now?" he murmurs, the movement of his lips brushing ever so slightly against mine.

I drown in the liquid heat his words evoke, begging him to pull me under and take me there, but all I can do is exhale an unsteady breath. He leans in and tastes me. My hands itch to fist in his jacket and rip open his shirt, buttons be damned.

Colton pulls back when he hears the click of heels but pulls open the closet door and presses me inside. The minute the door shuts to the darkened closet, Colton has my arms pinned above my head. The only illumination in the closet is the light seeping through the crack of the doorjamb. My mind never once registers my internal demons—the claustrophobia from the accident that usually smothers me at the first inkling of being confined. My only thought is Colton. Fear ceases to exist. I shudder, anticipating the moment his body will crash into mine, push me against the door, and take from me what we've both been so desperately needing.

Release. Connection. Intensity.

But it doesn't happen. The only connection between us is his hands holding my wrists hostage above my head. The closet is too dark to decipher the outline of his body, but I can feel his breath feathering over my face. We stand here like this for a moment, so close that the hairs on my arms stand up, every nerve in my body itching to feel the touch he's yet to give, suspended in this hazy state of need.

"Anticipation can enhance," he whispers, and right now, it is most definitely the definition of Ace. *No doubt.* But I don't have any time to comprehend let alone respond because his lips finally meet mine. And this time, they do more than just taste. They devour. Take without asking. Brand the claim being staked.

The world on the other side of the door ceases to exist. The doubts rioting in my head fall silent. Everything is lost to the sensation of his mouth worshiping mine.

Our tongues dance. Our reverent sighs meld. Our bodies succumb, but never touch. Besides Colton's hands on my wrist and lips on my mouth, he doesn't allow any other part of our bodies to connect.

And I so desperately need to touch him, feel the tightened buds of my nipples rubbing against his chest, feel his fingers trailing up my thighs and touching my most intimate of places.

But he refuses me that silent request, completely in control of the satiation of my detonating desire.

He pulls back on a groan from both of us. "Christ woman," he swears. "You're making it incredibly difficult to pull away from you."

"Then don't." I pant as lust coils so intensely, having him so close yet so far from me in more ways than one.

He growls in a frustrated response and just as quick as we entered the ironic storage closet, we are out of it. I momentarily close my eyes at the sudden wash of light. When I open my eyes again, Colton stands a few feet in front of me, the tension set in his shoulders a result of what I assume is the slippery hold he has on his restraint.

He looks back over his shoulder at me, his jaw set and his eyes warring with something within. "Colton?" I ask, trying to figure out his state of mind.

He just shakes his head at me. "I'm gonna hit the head. Meet you out there?"

I just look at him, a stuttered, "Okay," falling from my lips.

He starts to walk away but stops and turns back and steps toward me. Without preamble, he grabs the back of my neck and pulls me into him for a chaste kiss on the lips before walking away. I hear him call over his shoulder. "I need a minute."

And I need a lifetime.

I'm immersed in a conversation about the merits of my organization and what the new facilities will have to offer when I'm interrupted.

"Rylee!" a voice booms behind me, and when I turn around, I find myself swallowed up in a big bear hug by the arms of Andy Westin. I return the hug, his affection contagious, and then he leans back and holds my arms out to take me in. He whistles. "Wow! You're looking absolutely stunning this evening," he compliments, and I can see exactly who Colton learned how to charm from.

"Mr. Westin, so glad to see you again," I tell him, and I am surprised that I really am. In a room full of pretension, he brings vibrancy and sincerity.

He waves a hand in the air. "I told you, please call me Andy."

"Alright, Andy then. Does Colton know you're here? Can I get you a drink?"

"Nonsense. I'll get myself a drink in a moment," he says, patting my arm while searching the crowd. "We haven't seen him yet. We've been busy seeing old friends and hearing about this great cause."

"Kids Now definitely is," I muse.

He grins widely. "Speaking of good causes, I hear you and my boy are working on a little something together for your own organization."

"Yes we are!" I exclaim, a thrill shooting through me at the sudden realization that this is really happening. I am actually here promoting the new facility and its culmination. "With Colton's help—"

"There you are," a sultry voice interrupts me. I turn to see its owner and find that I am face to face with Dorothea Donavan-Westin. She is absolutely stunning, and there is a gracefulness about her—in her movement, in her smile, in how she holds herself—that makes you want to just watch and admire.

"Dottie, sweetheart! I didn't know where you went off to," Andy says as he kisses her cheek.

Dorothea looks over to me, her sapphire blue eyes alight with humor. "He's always losing me." She laughs.

"Dottie dear, this is Rylee…"

"Thomas," I finish for Andy.

"Thomas. Yes," he says, winking at me, thankful for my assistance. "Please meet my wife, Dorothea…" he turns to her "…she's the one that

Colton is working with on—"

"Yes I know, dear..." she pats his arm affectionately "...I am on the board after all." She turns to face me and extends a perfectly manicured hand. "So glad to finally meet you in person, Rylee. I've heard such great things about your work through the committee."

I reach out to shake her hand, surprised by my nerves. Where Andy is warm and inviting, Dorothea is reserved and regal. A person who makes you want to have their approval without so much as saying a word. Commanding. "Thank you. So lovely to meet you as well," I smile warmly at her. "Your husband and I were just talking about that. Your son's generous donation has made the facility become a tangible reality for us. Once his team figures the total lap match sponsorship, we just might be able to start pulling permits."

Pride fills Dorothea's face at the mention of her son, and I can see the unconditional love in her eyes. "Well I guess it was a good thing I fell ill and forced him to attend in my place then." She laughs. "Despite the incessant grumbling I had to listen to about being forced to wear a tux."

I can't help but smile at her words; I heard the same grumbling earlier. "We are overwhelmed by his generosity. Words cannot express how much it is appreciated. And then to go above and beyond and try to get sponsorships to complete the funding..." I place my hand over my heart. "It just leaves us—me—speechless. Overwhelmed, really."

"That's our boy!" Andy exclaims, reaching for a flute of champagne from a passing waitress and handing it to Dorothea.

"You should be so proud of him. He's a good man." The words are out of my mouth before I even realize it, and I find myself slightly embarrassed. My unexpected admission to his parents is insight into my feelings for their beloved son.

Dorothea angles her head to the side and regards me over her champagne flute as she takes a sip. "So tell me, Rylee, are you here with Colton tonight on a professional or a personal level?"

I must look like a deer in the headlights at her words and I look from Dorothea to Andy and back again. What am I supposed to say? That I'm in love with your son, but he still thinks of me as a woman he fucks because he refuses to accept that he might have feelings for me? I hardly think that's an appropriate thing to say to one's parents regardless of its truth or not. My mouth opens to say something when Andy intervenes.

"Don't badger the girl, Dottie!" he says playfully, winking at me as I silently thank him.

"Well..." she shrugs in apology, although I doubt she's remorseful "...a mother likes to know these things. In fact, I think—"

"What a pleasant surprise!" I hear the smooth rasp of Colton's voice, and relief floods me that I won't have to answer her question.

"Colton!" Dorothea exclaims as she turns to face her son. I'm surprised when he grabs his mom in a huge bear hug, rocking her back and forth before kissing her on the cheek, his face lighting up with love for her. She accepts his affection openly and places both hands on his cheeks and looks into his eyes. "Let me look at you! It feels like forever since I've seen you!"

He smiles at her, his adoration apparent. "It's only been a couple of weeks." He smirks at her as he pats his dad on the back in greeting. "Hey, Dad!"

"Hey, bud," Andy says, putting an arm around Colton's shoulders and squeezing momentarily. "What's this?" he asks, bringing a hand up to playfully rub Colton's cheek. "You actually shaved for tonight? Your mother was surprised when she saw the picture from the event the other night of you and—"

"You looked so handsome, Colton. All clean-shaven..." She cuts her husband off with a warning glance before smiling adoringly at her son. "You know how much I like when you shave that scruff off of your face. You look much better without it!"

Colton looks over at me, a crooked smirk on his face, his eyes telling me that he remembers my comment about just how much I enjoy the scruff against my inner thighs. "I see you've met Rylee?" he says as he slides an arm around my waist and pulls me against him, leaning over to brush his lips to my temple. I instinctively lean into him, not missing the look of surprise that's exchanged between his parents. Over what I'm unsure, but Andy's look to Dorothea appears to say *see what I mean*.

"Yes, we were just speaking about her company's new project," his mother replies, studying him closely, a bemused look on her face.

"Rylee's done a great job," he says, the pride brimming in his eyes surprises me. "If you saw the boys—the ones that are currently under her charge—what great kids they are, you'd understand why becoming involved was a no-brainer. Why this project needs to be completed." His enthusiasm is heartfelt and that is endearing to me. "But you already know that, don't you, Mom?"

We speak for a few moments before Andy excuses himself to go get a drink, and I do the same heading for the restroom. I take a few steps away when Colton places his hand on my lower back and stops me with the murmur of my name. His body presses up behind me, connecting us together like puzzle pieces.

"Don't even think about getting yourself off in that bathroom." He growls quietly into my ear causing spirals of need to electrify my every nerve. "I know you're desperate to feel me buried inside you as much as I am. I know the ache is so intense it burns. But, baby, I'm the only one allowed to take you there." He runs his hand up the side of my ribcage. "Not your fingers. Not a toy. Not any other fucker in this room." He exhales and I'm envious of his ability to breathe at this moment. "Just me. And I'm nowhere near done with you yet." He presses a kiss to the back of my head. "Mine. Understood?"

I swallow, trying to find my voice. His words were just so seriously hot that I swear I can feel the moisture pooling between my thighs. I nod my head and only when I am several feet away from him—when I can actually think without him clouding my coherency—am I able to draw a breath.

The bathroom is empty when I enter, and I head to the furthest stall against the wall. I just need a moment to myself. I'm finishing my business when I hear the door creak open and two pairs of heels clicking on the concrete floor, and their laughter echoing off of the tiled walls.

"So who's he here with tonight? He seems pretty serious about her seeing as his eyes aren't wandering astray as usual."

The other woman laughs a throaty reply and something about the familiarity of it causes me to pause with my hand on the door to the stall. "*Oh her?* She's absolutely nothing to worry about."

I hear the smack of lips as if someone is blotting their freshly applied lipstick. "Well by the looks of Page 6, you seem to be right."

"You saw that?" throaty-voiced girl says.

"Yes! You and Colton looked so great together. Like the perfect fucking couple." I bristle at the words when I recognize that throaty-voiced girl, the one saying that I am nothing to worry about, is Tawny.

"Thanks, doll! I think so too. It was such a great evening, and as usual Colton was his ever-attentive self."

Whoa! What in the hell is she talking about? Evening? As usual? My conversation with Colton's parents comes back to my mind. Andy telling Colton that his mother saw a picture of him and someone else before Dorothea cut him off. The picture was with Tawny? I swallow the bile that rises in my throat, trying to calm my thoughts from getting too far out of whack and reading into the comments. I try to push away the pounding rush of my pulse filling my ears, desperate to eavesdrop some more. I feel nauseous, so I back up and sit back down, fully clothed, on the toilet seat.

"I can't believe you ever let him get away in the first place!"

"I know." She sighs. "But he's a man that's definitely hard to sway once he makes his mind up. I've made sure that he knows without question that he can no longer use the excuse that I'm like a sibling to him though." She giggles suggestively. "And I've made sure to be there every step of the way so that in the end he'll turn to me."

"Shut-up! No you didn't..."

"Someone's gotta whip that boy into shape." My stomach revolts at her words.

"Well, I don't think it'll take him much longer now by the looks of that picture," her friend says, and I can mentally see the smirk she has spreading across her lips.

"Yeah, I know." Tawny replies. "She can't give him what he needs. She's so damn naïve. The two of them are like Little Red Riding Hood and the Big Bad Wolf. He's going to eat her alive, spit her out, and then move on to the next."

He does have quite the sexual appetite. Big Bad Wolf...hmm, that fits. Definitely some of the best sex I've ever had. *Wait a minute! Colton's been with the friend too? Deep breath, Rylee. How fucking many of his exes are there here tonight? Deep breath.*

I hear the zipper of a purse close. "He'll tire of her soon enough when she can't fulfill him. I mean look at her...she doesn't have a seductive bone in that body. She's too boring...too plain...*too blah* to keep his rapt attention. And if she's like that on the outside, I can't imagine how utterly lackluster she is between the sheets. You know how he is, predictability is one thing he doesn't tolerate." She laughs. "Besides, I dropped a few hints to him the other night to let him know I was still game. And more than willing to be anyone or do anything he wanted."

Her friend hums in agreement. "Who wouldn't be when it comes to him? *The man's a tireless fucking God in the sack.*"

"I know that better than anyone." Tawny chuckles, the sound crawling up my spine. "Besides, I can be patient. Time is most definitely on my side."

"You ready?" I hear a second purse zip and the clicking of heels again until the door closes shut, bathing me in silence.

What the hell? I fumble in my purse for my phone. I click on Google and type in "Page 6, Colton Donavan." I click on the first link that pops up and brace myself when the image fills the screen. It is a picture of Colton walking out of the Chateau Marmont. His hand is placed on

145

Tawny's lower back, who is decked out in a stunningly sexy, red dress. She is turned, looking up at him, her hand on his lapel, adoration filling her eyes, and a suggestive smile on her face. Colton is looking down at her, his face crinkled in laughter as if they've just shared a private joke. When I can finally tear my eyes away from the obvious chemistry between them, I glance at the date of the photo.

The date is this past Wednesday. The same day that Colton took the kids and me to the go-kart track. I groan out loud in the empty restroom at the realization that I got him all riled up in sexual frustration, and then I sent him off to a function with Tawny. *Fucking great!* I glance at the photo again, hoping maybe it is a stock photo the paper used to fill space, but then I take a closer look and notice that Colton is clean-shaven. He's never clean-shaven. Wednesday was the first time since I've known him that he's been like that. I feel a sharp pain in my gut as I stare at the picture again. Colton had told me that he had a work function to go to. At the Chateau Marmont with Tawny? What the hell type of function were they at, and why were they leaving together looking so damn cozy?

I take a deep breath, my thoughts rioting violently around in my head as Tawny's verbal digs enter my conscience again and take hold.

I start to feel suffocated in the confines of the bathroom stall. I fumble with the lock on the stall and hurry past the vanities. I glance at myself in the mirror quickly and am shocked that my appearance is so calm and collected when my insides twist over this newfound information.

I force myself to calm down and not jump to conclusions. Tawny is a family friend and a business associate. Of course they have to go to functions together. The picture was probably snapped at just the right moment to capture a scene people could talk about. One they could make assumptions about. There are probably twenty other pictures in that scene that are boring and non-gossip worthy. Besides, the fact that Tawny still has a thing for Colton shouldn't surprise me; she let me know as much at the track.

When I exit the bathroom, I'm still trying to talk myself down from the ledge of insecurity. I can't find Colton, so I head toward the bar, needing another drink to soothe my frayed nerves. I tell myself that I know Colton's had his share of women, but he told me in Vegas that I'm who he wants. It'd be so much easier to accept if he'd just admit to me that we were something more—that we were exclusive—anything to tell me verbally that emotions are a part of the picture. That I'm not just his physical plaything.

Get that out of your head, Rylee! I have to accept that he shows me with actions, not words. That's all he's willing to give me, and I have to accept this or walk away. I sigh in frustration. I thought I was mentally okay with this. Really I did, but then you add the mix of bimbos tonight and my insecurities have resurfaced. And having them thrown in my face repeatedly by Tawny and then tonight by Teagan—as well as bimbos three through five—makes it that much more difficult. Colton's the total package. I should be flattered that other women want to be with him.

Keep telling yourself that, Ry, and maybe someday you'll believe it.

I order a drink from the bar and when I turn to walk away, I spot Colton talking to some gentlemen across the room. I smile, the sight of him dissipating all of my doubts. As I start to walk toward him, his conversation ends and before he turns to walk away, a woman walks up to him and embraces him in a hug that lasts a little too long for my liking. And of course she is a blonde, breathtaking beauty that rivals him in the stunning looks department. When she turns so I can see her, it's none other than bimbo number five from the bar line earlier.

The flames of irritation flicker to life inside of me.

Here we go again. I stop in my path and watch their interaction. Whereas Colton's exchange with Teagan was pleasant but detached, his conversation with bimbo number five is anything but distant. When I see him smile sincerely at her and leave his hand pressed to her lower back instead of moving it, I bite back the jealousy that streaks.

He's done nothing wrong or improper, but the familiarity between them is obvious. I force myself to look away, and it is then that my eyes meet Tawny's from across the room. Her blue eyes hold mine, contempt and condescension thrown at me in the simple glare. She crosses her arms across her torso as she flicks her eyes over to Colton and then back to mine. A derisive smirk lifts one corner of her mouth as she shakes her head. She makes a show of looking down to her watch and tapping on the face of it before looking back up at me. *The clock's ticking, Rylee. Your time is almost up.*

I turn back toward Colton, careful not to give her any reaction in my facial expression despite my surmounting anger. There's not enough alcohol in this room right now for me to hold a conversation with her. I could use a good Haddie-pep-talk right now. *Where the hell is she when I need her?*

I start to make my way toward Colton when the blonde he's with lifts her eyes from his to meet mine. She gives me the same quick but appraising look she had earlier, but this time it's followed by the flash of an insolent smile. Yet another female that wants me out of the picture so that she can make her move. Then again, it doesn't seem like anyone's waiting. They don't seem to have any problem making their moves right in front of me.

I need a break from all of this frickin' drama and the inferno of irrationality that's smothering all of my oxygen. I decide to head outside to get some fresh air and regain my sense of self that these blonde leaches seem to be sucking from me bit by bit.

Colton's gaze follows bimbo number five's and meets mine. A smile lights up his face as I approach, but it falls slightly when he sees the look on my face. "You okay?"

"Mmm-hmm," I murmur, purposely avoiding looking at his companion. "I just need to get some air," I say and continue right past him without stopping to answer the questioning look on his face.

I hurry out of the ballroom, making it to the exit unscathed. I push open the doors and draw in the fresh, night air. It's cold but more than welcomed. I need it after the stifling atmosphere inside. I walk hastily toward the gardens I'd noticed on the way in, hoping that they're empty at this time of night.

Needing solitude.

Chapter Seventeen

"Rylee!" Colton calls my name but I keep walking, needing some momentary distance from him. "*Rylee!*" he repeats, and I can hear the heavy fall of his footsteps on the sidewalk behind me. They echo off of the concrete walls, confirming how I feel—that no matter how far I go, Colton will always be there. In thought. In memory. In everything. He's ruined me for anyone else. I have no other option but to stop when I come to the end of a path.

"Stop running!" He pants from behind me as he catches up. "*Tell me what's wrong.*"

Colton's technically done nothing wrong tonight, but all of my angst and insecurity brought on by the various women from the night boils inside of me. Even the most confident, self-secure woman would be affected by his many admirers tonight. I know I should be confident in the notion that Colton came here with me—will be leaving with me—but then again, isn't that what Raquel thought the night of the Merit Rum launch?

I need words from him. I need to hear it. And he hasn't given me that yet. Actions can be misconstrued. Words cannot...and let's face it, I'm female. Aren't we programmed to read into things?

When he reaches out to touch my arm, it all comes to a head. I whirl around. "How many, Ace?" I shout at him, my breath turning white against the cool night air.

"*What?*" His face is a mixture of confusion and surprise. "How many what?"

"How many of your exes are here tonight?"

"Rylee—"

"*Don't Rylee me,*" I yell at him, stepping back so I can have the space I so desperately need to keep my head clear. "If you're going to bring me here tonight and parade your bevy of blonde beauties in front of me—all the women that you've fucked—the least you can do is give me a heads up." When he starts to interrupt me, I meet his eyes and the look in mine causes the words on his lips to falter. "It's bad enough that you have Tawny—your permanent go-to-girl—who still wants you and is around constantly. Working for you. Pushing her perfectly manufactured tits in your face. Making sure you know that she'll be there for you when you tire of the current flavor of the month." The look of utter shock on his face is priceless. He looks as if I've told him the sky is yellow. Has he never noticed this? Her willingness? A part of me sags in respite knowing that he doesn't see Tawny this way, but *what about all of the others from tonight?* "And then you bring me here tonight and parade more in front of me? The least you could have done was forewarn me…prepare me for the onslaught of nasty looks and catty barbs. So how many, Ace?" I demand, *"or do I even want to know?"*

Colton looks at me and shakes his head, the corners of his mouth turning up sheepishly. "C'mon, Ry, it's not that bad. Tawny's just an old friend—she works for me for fuck's sake—and the others…we just run in the same circles. We're bound to see each other sometimes." He takes a step toward me, a lascivious smirk spreading across his gorgeous face. "You're just frustrated because you're on edge…" he moves closer, his voice suggestively smooth "…and you have needs. You're sexually frustrated."

I stare at him, my mouth falling open. *Did he really just say that?* That's his fucking response to my reasons for being so upset? To why I'm going off the deep end? *I need to come and it will make everything better?* After that all of his whores will go back and bury themselves in the holes they've been hiding in?

"C'mere, let me take care of that for you." He reaches out, unbeknownst to him how angry I am at his callous comment and tries to pull me toward him. And as much as I want him to take care of the ache burning deep inside of me, as much as intimacy with him would assuage my doubts for how he feels about me, my anger and dignity override my needs. I shrug my arms from his grasp and take a step back.

Colton's face blankets with shock, his mouth parting slightly as he stares at me. *"You're telling me no?"* he asks incredulously.

I snort out in disgust. "A new concept for you no doubt, *but yes."* I sigh. *"I'm telling you no."*

He stares at me for a moment, his eyes narrowing and then his face softens into acknowledgment. "You have more restraint than me. I see what you're trying to do here," he murmurs, shaking his head, and for some reason I get the sense that he thinks I'm toying with him. That I'm telling him no, just to play hard to get.

"Sex isn't going to fix things, Colton." I huff at him, rubbing my hands up and down my arms to ward off the chill.

"It might just a little bit," he jokes, trying to get a smile out of me. While I continue to glare at him, shaking my head and sighing deeply, he mutters a curse and walks away from me a few steps. He brings a hand to his neck and pulls down while angling his head up to the night sky and exhaling loudly. "Shit!" he mutters before falling silent for a beat. "I can't change my past, Rylee. I am who I am and I can't change that. You knew that going into this when you started all your goddamn talk about not being able to accept the *only thing* I can give you."

"What? So now we're back to that? An *arrangement*? I'm not one of your whores, Colton. *Never have been. Never will be.*" My voice cuts through the silence of the night around us.

He steps back toward me, lowering his head and looking at the ground in front of him, his jaw clenching as he finds his next words. When he finally speaks, his voice is unbending. "I told you I'd fuck this up."

His words—his excuse—followed on the heels of everything tonight, enrage me. "Don't be such a martyr!" I shout at him. "Grow the fuck up and quit using your so-called goddamn defense mechanism as an excuse, Colton!" The words are out before I can stop them, anger overriding common sense. He snaps his head up, his eyes blazing with anger as they meet mine. He takes a step back from me, the physical distance just emphasizing the emotional detachment I can sense happening. I know I'm probably overreacting. But that knowledge does nothing to stop the freight train of emotions running through me. "*Fuck. This,*" I mutter. "If you've had your way with me and don't want me anymore…if you want one of your cookie cutter blondes inside…then man-up and just tell me!"

He says nothing to me, just sits there, jaw clenched, shoulders tense, and eyes staring at me, a mixture of reactions crossing his shadowed face. I'm not sure what I expect him to say, but *I'd hoped that he'd at least say something.* I thought that maybe he'd put up a fight to keep me with him, to prove to me that I'm worth it.

I guess if I'm going to make ultimatums than I'd better be prepared to stand by them. Fear snakes down my spine when he doesn't utter a sound. I stare at him, willing him to speak. To prove my words wrong. To prove them right. *Anything.*

But he says nothing. Just a shell of a man staring at me with eyes emotionless, lips silent, and patience wearing thin.

Anger fills me. Hurt consumes me. Regret weighs heavy. I knew this was going to happen. He predicted it, and I ignored it. I thought I was *enough* to change the outcome. "You know what, Colton? Screw you!" I yell, the only words I can verbalize to portray how I feel. Not very intelligent sounding, but it's all I have. "Just tell me one thing before you walk away and move on to the next willing candidate…*besides the obvious,* what does screwing all of these women do for you, Ace?" I step closer to him, wanting to see the reaction in his eyes, needing to see some type of response from him. "What need does it fulfill that you refuse to acknowledge? Don't you want more? Deserve more out of that connection than just a warm body and a fleeting orgasm?" When he doesn't respond but rather has irritation flash across his face, I continue.

"Fine, don't answer that question…but answer this one: *Don't you think that I deserve more?*"

I see pain in his emerald eyes and a flicker of something darker, deeper, and I know that I've churned something within him. Hurt him. *But I'm hurt too.* He remains silent, and that pisses me off even more.

"What? You're too chicken shit to answer that?" I goad. "*Well I'm not!* I know I deserve more, Colton! I deserve so much more than you're willing to even try for. You're missing out on the best part of being with someone. All of the little things that make a relationship special." I throw my hands up to emphasize my point, all the while he stares at me, stone faced and jaw clenched. I pace back and forth in front of him trying to contain my pent up frustration. "Your four to five month time limit doesn't give you any of that, Ace. It doesn't give you the comfort of knowing someone cares for you so much that they are there for you even when you're being irrational. *Or an asshole.*" I sneer at him, my blood pumping and thoughts coming so fast I can't spit them out of my mouth fast enough. "You rob yourself of knowing what it's like to surrender yourself—mind, body, and soul to someone. To be completely naked—exposed and selfless—when you're *fully clothed*. You don't understand how special any of that is," I rant, realizing how sadly deprived he is with his choices. "Well I do. And that's what I want. Why has this always been about what you want? *What about me?* Don't I deserve to feel how I feel and not hold back because of some implied rules?"

He just stares at me, his body tense, his voice silent, and I can feel him slipping away. A tear slides silently down my cheek, my breath panting out in white puffs after my verbal diatribe. I don't feel any better because nothing's been solved. The wall he's hid behind for so long—that he's been slowly peeking over—is suddenly reinforced with steel.

I look at him, *the man I love*, and my chest tightens and heart twists in pain. This is what I was afraid of. What my head and heart fought over and against. And yet here I am, scared and scarred, but still fighting for him, because Teagan is right. *He's just that good.* His words run through my head.

You burned me, Rylee.

You. This. It scares the shit out of me, Rylee.

I can't seem to get enough of you.

I step forward, wanting to touch him. Craving any kind of connection with him, needing to remind him of that spark between us when we touch and to try and prevent him from slipping through my fingers. *Like trying to grab the wind.* I reach my trembling hands out, his eyes following their movement, and lay them on his chest. I feel him stiffen in response, a proverbial slap at my attempt to connect with him that pushes me over the edge.

My eyes flash up to his, and I see that he knows how much he just hurt me with that small flinch—the nonverbal rejection that just spoke volumes. He instinctively brings his arms up to wrap them around me, to try and placate me, and I can't let that happen. I can't let him pull me into the one place I want to be more than anywhere else right now because nothing between us has changed. And I know if I'm wrapped in his arms, I will succumb to everything all over again so I won't lose what I fear the most—*him*. But I deserve the whole him that he's unable—*no, unwilling*—to give me.

I push against his chest, but his hands tighten their grip on my shoulders. He tries to pull me into him, but I struggle against him. When he doesn't react…I lose it. "Fight damn it! Fight, Colton!" I yell at him, desperation seeping as my voice wavers and tears threaten. "For you. For us. For me," I plead. "You don't get to pull away from me. You don't get to walk away without a second thought." I'm still trying to resist his hold, but the dam breaks and the tears overflow. "I matter, Colton. I deserve the same *more* that you do. *What we have is not inconsequential.*"

Overcome with emotion, I succumb to my tears, my fears, the emptiness looming. I stop resisting him and he gathers me in his arms and pulls me to him, his hands running up and down over my back and arms and neck. The feeling is bittersweet because I know it's fleeting. I know that the words I so desperately want and need to hear—that this is something…that we are something…anything to him—are never coming.

I consciously etch this moment to my memory.

His warmth.

The rasp of his calloused fingers across my bare skin.

The clenching of his jaw against my temple.

The timbre of his hushed murmurs.

His scent.

I close my eyes to absorb it because I know I've scared him. I know I'm asking for too much when there are so many others willing to settle for so much less.

"Rylee…" My name is a whispered hush over my now tearless sobs.

I fall silent, my hitching breath the only sound in the night. I lean back, his hands on my shoulders guiding me so he can see my face. I steel myself before looking up to meet his eyes. I can see fear and confusion and uncertainty in them, and I'm waiting for him to verbalize what's on the tip of his tongue. His internal struggle plays out on his usually stoic face before he reins it in. My chest aches as I try to draw in a breath and prepare myself because what I see makes me panic. Has me resigning all of my fate because I know he's preparing himself to walk away.

To say goodbye.

To break me apart.

"*I deserve more, Colton.*" I breathe out, shaking my head as a single tear trails down my cheek. His eyes follow it before looking back at me, and for a moment they soften with concern, his throat working a swallow as he nods his head in agreement. I reach a hand out and place it on his jaw, his eyes cautiously tracking my movements. I feel his jaw muscles tighten beneath my palm. "I know this is the whole reason you have your rules and stipulations, but I can't abide by them anymore. *I can't be that girl for you anymore.*"

I lower my head at my last comment, avoiding his eyes because I can't bear to see the reaction. Wanting and not getting one or wanting and being rejected—either one will shred my heart more than it already is. I sigh deeply, eyes focused intently on his impromptu pocket square and my mind marveling how simple things seemed just a couple of hours ago when he was underdressed and I was overdressed.

He tenses his fingers on my biceps, and I force myself to look back up at him—glad I did because the look in his eyes takes my breath away. My gorgeous bad boy looks like a child—panic stricken and petrified. I struggle to find words to speak because standing there with that look in his eyes; he looks just like one of my damaged boys. It takes a moment, but I'm finally able to find my voice.

"I'm sorry, Colton." I shake my head. "You did nothing wrong tonight but be the man that you are...but seeing your exes here tonight still wanting more..." I sigh "...I don't want to be them in three months. *On the outside looking in.* I can't stand by and blindly obey the parameters you dictate anymore. I want to have a say." He shakes his head back and forth, automatically rejecting the idea, and I don't even think he realizes he's doing it. The grip of his hands tightens on my arms, but he says nothing to refute what I'm saying.

"I'm not asking for love from you, Colton." My voice is barely a whisper when I speak, but my conscience is screaming that I am. That I want him to love me the way I love him. His eyes widen at my confession. His sharp intake of air audible. "I'm not even asking for a long-term commitment from you. I just want to be able to explore whatever this is between us without worrying about overstepping imaginary boundaries that I don't even know exist." I stare at him, willing him to hear my words. Really hear what I'm saying, not just what he wants to hear. "I'm asking to be your lover, Colton, not your happily ever after or your structured arrangement. All I want is a chance..." My voice trails off, asking for the impossible. "For you to tell me you'll try…"

"You were never an arra—"

"Let's call a spade a spade." I arch my eyebrows at him, trying to summon the fire that coursed through my veins moments before that has since been replaced with desolation. "You have an uncanny way of putting me in my place any time I overstep one of your asinine boundaries."

We stare at each other, unspoken words on our lips, and he is the first to look away and break our connection. He shrugs out of his dinner jacket, and wraps it around my shoulders, ever the consummate gentleman even in the midst of turmoil, but where his fingers would normally linger on my skin, he recoils instantly.

"I never meant to hurt you, Rylee." His voice cracks with a quiet vulnerability I've never heard before. I'd never expect from him. He lowers his head, shaking it subtly, and mutters *fuck* under his breath. Déjà vu hits me from the night in the hotel room, and all the air punches from my lungs. "I don't want to hurt you any further."

This is it.

He's going to end it right here, right now. Doing what I can't for the life of me do myself. I press the heel of my hand to my chest, trying to press away the ache that sears through me. He runs his hands through his hair, and I tremble in anticipation, waiting for him to continue but hoping he doesn't. He lifts his head and reluctantly meets my eyes. He is stripped bare—haunted, desolate—the emotion so transparent in his eyes it's hard to hold his gaze.

And in this moment, it hits me. I realize that I've been chastising him for not fighting for me, but has anyone ever really fought for him besides his parents? Not for his material possessions or his notoriety, but for the little boy he was and for the man he is now? For the years of abuse and neglect I'm sure he endured. Has anyone ever told him they love him not despite it but rather because of it? And that all of those experiences combined have in fact made him a better person. A better man. That they accept all of him regardless— every maddening, confusing, heartwarming, piece of him.

I bet no one has.

And as much as I'm hurting and want to lash out at him in return, a part of me wants to leave him with something no one else has ever given him. Something to remember me by.

"For you, Colton..." My voice may be soft when I speak, a resignation to our fate, but my honesty comes through loud and clear. "...I'd take the chance." I can visibly see his body stiffen at my admission. His lips part slightly and the tension leaves his jaw, as if he is shocked that I'd be willing to take the chance on him. *That I believe he's worth the risk.*

He takes a step toward me and reaches a hand out tentatively to frame my jaw. He stares into my eyes with an unfettered intensity, his lips opening several times to say something but closing without a sound. I inhale a sharp breath at the resonance of his touch as he rubs the pad of his thumb over my bottom lip—the roughness of his calloused fingers against the softness of my lips. A horrible sadness takes hold when I realize rough and soft is in a way a lot like us.

"For you, Rylee," he whispers, his voice breaking. His usually steady hands tremble ever so slightly against my cheeks, and I swear I can see fear flicker through his eyes before he blinks away the moisture that pools in them. "*I will try.*"

He will try? My mind has to switch gears so quickly that I'm left disoriented. Talk about going from an unbelievable low to an unexpected high. "*You'll try?*" my broken voice asks, not believing my ears.

Just a trace of the crooked, roguish smile that I find irresistible curves up one side of his mouth, but I can hear the trepidation in his tone. "*Yes,*" he repeats. His eyes burn into mine until my eyes flutter closed as he leans in and gives me the gentlest, most reverent kiss I've ever received. He then kisses the tip of my nose before resting his forehead against mine. His breath whispers against my lips, and his heart pounds a frantic tattoo against my chest all the while my insides are leaping for joy, bubbling over with hope.

Holy shit! Colton is going to try. He is going to fight for us. For me. For him. There is so much unspoken beneath his declaration. So much promise, fear, vulnerability, and willingness to overcome whatever plagues his dreams at night and incessantly haunts his memories—just to try and be with me.

He dips his head down and kisses me again. A slow, soft brush of lips and dance of tongues that is so packed with unspoken words it causes tears to well in my eyes. He finishes by kissing my nose again and then pulling me into him in a crushing embrace. I sigh, welcoming his warmth, his strength, and enjoying how the long, lean line of his body fits perfectly against my curves. I drink in his scent and the sound of his heart beating beneath my ear. He leans his face down, his cheek rubbing against my temple, as he emits a sigh that sounds similar to a muttered oath. And I swear it sounds like he mutters something about a *voodoo pussy*, but when I snap my head up to look at him, he just shakes head and smirks.

"What am I going to do with you, Rylee?" He holds me tighter, chills dancing up my spine. "What am I going to do?" He sighs again and I suppress a smothered chuckle as I wriggle against him. The mixture of his body on mine, the relief in knowing he is going to try, and the anticipated buildup of the evening has me more than desperate for just a platonic hug in a garden.

How can such a simple statement leave me breathless with anticipation and desperate for his touch—emotionally and physically? He trails a finger down the line of my neck before dipping it down into the bodice and then descending the long torturous path downward, parting the draped slit of my dress to my hypersensitive sex. His deft fingers find me weeping and wanting, and when he touches me I swear I'm ready to splinter into a million pieces of pleasure. I gasp a strangled moan from its effect.

I lean into him, my forehead pressing against his chest, my hands gripping his biceps. I'm not sure if my responsiveness is from Colton's willingness to try or the onslaught of sensation, but my body climbs the precipice quicker than normal. I am so close. So close to the brink that my nails dig into his arms.

Colton slides his fingers back and forth one more time before emitting a feral growl. "Not yet...I want to be buried in you when you come, Rylee," he murmurs against the crown of my head. "I'm desperate to be."

I suck in an audible breath, my muscles so taut and nerves so aware of the feeling of his body against mine that I can't contain myself. I launch myself at him like an addict needing a fix. One hand grips the back of his neck, automatically fisting his hair, and pulls his face lower so I can meet his mouth. My other hand reaches down to rub the hard length of his growing erection against his slacks. His guttural moan tells me he's bound with as much need as I am.

I kiss him with a hungry desperation, passion unfurling between us, as I pour everything I've been holding back into our melding of mouths. He snakes his hands between his jacket that I'm wearing and my dress, his hands mapping the lines of my backside and hips, inciting a need so strong that it rocks me senseless and leaves me breathless.

"Colton," I moan as he laces open mouth kisses down the line of my throat, sending earthquakes of sensation rocketing through me.

"Car. Parking garage. Now," he says between kisses with a teeming desperation, restraint non-existent.

I agree with a non-coherent moan, but my body doesn't want to let up or let go. His hand fists my hair and pulls it down so my face is forced up. The dark desire that clouds his eyes has my thighs clenching together, begging for relief. "Ry? If we don't walk right now, you're going to find yourself bent over that bench right there in plain view of all of these hotel rooms." His husky warning has me swallowing loudly. He leans down and kisses me chastely, his tongue tracing the line of my bottom lip. "You've annihilated my control, sweetheart. Elevator. Now," he commands.

He pulls me to his side, his hand clamped on my hip as we walk quickly. With his free hand, Colton pulls his iPhone out of his pocket. "Sammy? Where's Sex?" He listens for a moment. "Perfect. That works." He laughs loudly, the timbre of it echoing off of the concrete walls we walk past. "Like you read my mind. You're fucking awesome Sammy...Yeah. I'll let you know." He slips his phone back in his pocket as we reach a path, and I'm mystified as to the conversation he just had. Colton looks left and then right, weighing his options with a forced urgency before veering right.

Within moments we are in an elevator at the outskirts of a concrete parking garage. The drab grey doors shut, Colton's presence dominating the small space, and before the elevator starts to move upwards, Colton has me pinned against the wall with his hips and his mouth feasting on mine with a raw carnality. I don't even have time to catch my breath before the car pings. He drags his mouth from mine, leaving me shaken by his consuming desire.

Chapter Eighteen

When we exit the elevator, a giggle escapes my lips. Who in the hell is this girl that I turn into when I'm with Colton? This brazen, wanton woman so sure of her sexuality? I definitely wasn't her an hour ago. I swear it's the *Colton effect*.

I jolt in surprise when we turn the corner and Sammy is standing there. "Hi, Sammy," I say shyly, for once again he's seeing me in my Colton-induced path to indecency. He nods at me, his face remaining stoic as he hands a set of keys out to Colton.

"Thanks. All clear?" Colton asks.

"All clear," Sammy nods before stepping onto the elevator car.

"Come," Colton commands as he pulls my hand so I land against him forcefully before his lips meet mine again in a greedy kiss. I push him back momentarily despite his protests and glance around at our surroundings to make sure we don't have an unsuspecting audience. My eyes focus immediately on a sexy-as-sin, sleek, red sports car in the far corner. I'm not really into cars, but all I know is that if that's her name? It most definitely fits her.

When I pull my eyes away from the car, I'm surprised to find the monochromatic garage completely vacant. "How'd...?" Colton just smirks at me with that *it's good to be me* kind of smirk and I shake my head. "*Sammy?*"

"Mmm-hmm." His hand roams up my waist and cups my breast through my dress. I exhale a soft moan at the muted sensation, wanting his body, naked and moving, on mine. In mine.

"Oh, Colton..." I sigh, turning into putty in his hands as his finger dips beneath the fabric. "That man needs a raise," I murmur as we pseudo-walk, pseudo-grope each other across the desolate garage. Colton laughs loudly at my comment, the sound mixed with the click of my heels echoing off of the walls. I push away the niggling feeling in my head that I wonder just what else Sammy has seen under Colton's employment. That was the past. His past.

And now, he's my future. All that matters now is that Colton's willing to try.

We reach the car, relief that we can get out of here flooding through me. Right now I'm being selfish. I'm not thinking about the gala below or my charity or anything. All I can focus on is the feelings coursing through me. The ones I need met as I steer our bodies toward the passenger side.

But Colton stands still—*doesn't budge*—just keeps my hand in his, our arms outstretched from the connection. I look over at him, his eyes trailing over the front of his car and then looking back to me. The lascivious smirk that turns up the corners of his mouth rocks my world off its balance. "Uh-uh," he tells me, confusion filling me.

What? Now he doesn't want to…*oh*… *Oh! Oh fuck!*

He recognizes the minute I understand his intention. "You. Here. " He points to the sleek, red hood of his car. I blush and hesitate, remembering my off the cuff comment in Starbucks that now feels likes years ago about how I wanted to *take him on the hood of his car.*

"Now!" He growls.

Me and my big mouth. I glance around and swallow before my eyes come back to meet his. *Always back to his.* "Here?"

"Here." He smirks as a thrill chases through me. "*I'm gonna corrupt you yet.*"

"But…"

"Don't question it, Rylee. If you obey all the rules, baby, you miss all of the fun." *Only Colton could quote Hepburn at a time like this and make it sound seductively sexy.*

His eyes dance with the thrill of what we are about to do. There is no way in hell that I am going to pass up the chance to be with him. After everything tonight—the limo, the buildup of anticipation, the fact that he'll try—wild horses couldn't drag me away.

I don't even have a moment to be concerned with our location because he grabs me and brands his lips to mine. I can taste his desire. His hunger. His impatience. His willingness. Their mixture is a heady combination that sends chills up my spine and causes goose bumps to cover my skin as he leads me backwards. Our lips part only for him to whisper the naughty promises of what he wants to do to me.

How hard he's going to fuck me. How loud he wants me to scream. How many times he plans on making me come. How insanely beautiful I am. How he craves the taste me.

The backs of my knees hit the front bumper of the car, and he slips his jacket off of my shoulders. He takes the jacket and lays it inside out on the hood of his car behind me as I fumble with the zipper on his pants, my dexterity ruined by the liquid heat that fills me.

"Hurry," he demands, his voice laced with anguished need.

I laugh, hysterics tingeing the sound from my desperation. His hands still as he pulls back from our close proximity and looks into my eyes. *A moment of calm amidst our storm of need.* He reaches up and runs his fingers down my cheek, a smile of disbelief on his face and a look in his eyes—one that says he can't believe I'm real. *That this is real.* He shakes his head and his mouth curls up to one side, his dimple winking. And with his eyes locked on mine, he runs his hand back to my hair and fists it, angling my head to the side, exposing the curve of my neck.

And then need and desire take over as he lowers his mouth to that expanse of bare skin. The feelings, the sensations, the emotions pull me under, consume me.

My eyes close. My body softens and heats up simultaneously. I feel Colton pulse against my hands and they spring to life, finally working so I can pull his pants down far enough to release his engorged length. He hisses out an incoherent litany in appreciation as my fingers encircle him and dance over his heated flesh.

"Rylee. Please. Now." He pants between open mouth kisses. My hands continue their pleasurable torture as I feel Colton's hand bunch the length of my dress up until his hands are beneath it, cupping my bare ass in both of his hands.

I feel the warmth of Colton's fingertips as they part my legs, and I tense, knowing that his touch is all I'll need to push me over the edge. His fingers smooth across my skin, and his deft fingers find their destination, making me cry out as they tease and torment.

My nails dig into his shoulders as my legs start shaking from the mounting pressure within me. "Colton." I breathe as pleasure rakes over me, a low keening in the back of my throat the only other sound I can make as he pushes me higher and higher. His mouth catches mine again as I throw my head up, the heat from his skillful fingertips ripping through me and searing every imaginable nerve in my body. My fire ignites as he slips two fingers in to invade the depths of my sex with one hand while the other grips my hip possessively. Fervent fingers digging into willing flesh. I'm so worked up—so on the cusp—that it doesn't take long until I crash over the edge into a rapturous free fall.

All of the anticipation, flirting, highs, and lows from the night intensify the mix of sensations that splinter through me. Colton brings a hand up to cup my neck with one hand, his thumb resting just under my chin as my eyes flutter open. The simple brush of his thumb there is like adding gasoline to a roaring fire. My body tenses again as another ripple of pleasure pulses through me, all the while his gaze on mine.

Colton's eyes flicker and flame with lust as he watches me regain some semblance of equilibrium from the earth he just helped to move beneath my feet. Before I can even comprehend what's happening, Colton's control snaps, and he pushes me back on to his jacket on the cool, polished metal of his hood. He grabs my hips, pushing my dress up so I am clothed from the waist up and bare from the waist down, except for garters and stockings. He lifts my hips up to meet the height of his so that just my shoulders and neck are resting on the cool silk of his jacket.

His eyes roam over my bared flesh. "Sweet Christ, woman," his voice husky with desire murmurs as I close my eyes to revel in the need he's about to fill because even though I've come, my body is aching so desperately to have him in me, filling me, and stretching me to sublime satisfaction. "Open your eyes, Rylee," he commands as he places his steely head at my entrance. I gasp at the feeling, needing more. Always needing more and never being able to get enough of him. "I want to watch you while I take you. I want to see those eyes of yours turn hazy with desire."

My eyes flash open to lock on his. My mouth goes dry from the absolute lust reflected in them. In this moment, the calm before the storm, I am irrevocably his.

I cry out in unison with his guttural groan as he enters me in one slick thrust, holding himself deep as he grinds his hips against my pelvis. The heels of my shoes dig into his backside as I tense at his invasion, my slick channel clenching onto him with every swivel of his hips. "Oh, Rylee." He grunts, his head thrown back, lips parted, and face pulled tight with pleasure.

He starts moving now. Really moving. Fitting himself to me—in me—so that each drive devastates my senses. All I can do is absorb the impossible sensations he draws out of me with each thrust, ride out the blistering onslaught with him.

The jacket beneath me serves as a slide of sorts. With each drive I glide back and up the hood, only to be pulled back onto him to start the delicious descent and thrust back up all over again. The motion causes a myriad of overwhelming sensations that only serves to coax my orgasm to come faster. Harder. Quicker.

My muscles clench around him as I lift my head to watch our union. To see my arousal coating him as he withdraws from me before plunging back in. And the sight of what I do to him, of what he does to me, is unbelievably hot. "Colton," I moan in a stilted breath as one of his fingertips grazes over my clit. My body shudders from his touch.

"You. Are. Mine. Rylee," he growls between thrusts. "Tell. Me. Tell me you're mine, Rylee," he demands.

"Colton." I gasp as my body is pulled under the pleasure swamping me. His fingers dig into my hips as his muscles tense up and I'm able to resurface momentarily. "Yes. Yours. Colton." I pant between thrusts. "I'm. Yours!" I shout as I drown in the liquid heat of ecstasy the same time he climaxes with a hard groan, my name spilling from his lips.

Several moments have passed but our chests are still heaving for air. Our bodies are still pulsing with the adrenaline from our union. I open my eyes first. Colton is still gripping my hips, his cock still within me, but completely clothed otherwise. He stands before me, so tall, so imposing. It's no wonder he dominates both my thoughts and my heart. My everything.

My whole world.

His eyes flutter open slowly, looking down at me through heavy lids, a Cheshire cat grin lazily spreading across his lips. He exhales a sated sigh, and we both wince as he withdraws before slowly lowering my legs. He grabs my arms to help me up before the jacket beneath me slides me off of the too low hood of the car. My dress makes an odd sound against the immaculate paint as he pulls me up, and I gasp aloud. In my desperate need to have Colton, the thought never crossed my mind that I might scratch—or even worse, dent—the car. A car that probably costs more than I make in several years.

"What is it, Rylee?" he asks, looking over his shoulder thinking someone has just been voyeur to our escapade, and then looking back at me after seeing no one.

"Your car...*Sex*." I cringe but at the same time feel ridiculous calling the car that name. "I hope I didn't scratch it."

Colton angles his head and looks at me as if I'm crazy before he throws his head back, a full bodied laugh flowing from his mouth. He tucks himself back inside his slacks and zips them up. "Relax, baby, it's just a car."

"But—but it's worth a small fortune and—"

"And it can be fixed or replaced if damaged." He leans in and catches my mouth in a dizzying kiss and then pulls back with a smirk. "Then again, if it's damaged, I may just have to keep it just like it is as a reminder..." He lifts his eyebrows at me as he straightens his vest before reaching up to straighten his bow tie.

"A souvenir of sorts," I muse, smoothing my dress down over my hips.

He cocks his head and looks at the car over my shoulder before looking back at me. "That's one helluva souvenir, sweetheart." He whistles between his teeth, a lascivious smirk on his handsome face. "And now *her* name has a whole new meaning to me."

"Yes, it does." I smile shyly in return as he pulls me into him and tightens his arms around me. He looks at me, that naughty smirk I can't resist lighting up his features and those intense eyes filled with so much emotion. He leans down and brushes a soft kiss on my lips—the kind that is nothing more than lips on lips—that is so soft, so packed full of meaning, it causes my whole body to ache in the sweetest way.

Colton pulls back and places his jacket back over my shoulders before holding his hand out to me. "Come. We should get back or people will be wondering what we've been doing." I snort loudly in the most unladylike way. As if the flush in my cheeks and glimmer in my eye won't be a dead giveaway. He squeezes my hand as we walk toward the elevator, my head still reeling from the intensity and thrill of what just happened. Colton pulls me closer into his side, a laugh falling from his mouth. "*What?*"

"A car experience," he says looking at me and raising his eyebrows.

It most definitely was. "Nope. Not even close," I tease him back at his creative yet hopeless attempt.

By some stroke of luck, we slip back into the function a moment after dinner service is announced. Colton guides me to our assigned table just as the other patrons are sitting down. He pulls out my chair for me and removes his jacket from my shoulders, placing it on the back of the chair. I catch the libidinous smirk on his face as he shakes his head at me before leaning in and whispering, "Homerun." I can't contain the laugh that bubbles up at the thought.

During dinner I watch Colton interact with the other guests at the table, championing his various causes at the same time answering questions about his upcoming race. The older women at the table are charmed by him, and the men are envious of his good looks and bucket list lifestyle.

He's such a mix of contradictions. Emotionally closed off and isolated, but at the same time so open and giving in regards to the causes he cares about. He's arrogant and overly confident, and yet has a quiet understated vulnerability that I'm getting sneak peeks of when he doesn't close himself off. He can hobnob with the extremely wealthy in this room and also understand a traumatized seven year old boy and his needs. He's brash and aggressive, yet compassionate and considerate. And my God can the man infuriate me one moment and then make me weak in the knees the next.

I smile at the checkered flag cuff links and know that only Colton could get away with making such a novelty item appear sophisticated and classy. But more than anything, I find myself staring at his hands and wondering what it is about them that I find so incredibly sexy. I watch his fingertips absently toy with the stem of his wine glass before sliding it up and over the condensation forming. My mind wanders to those fingers and their skillful mastery on other things.

When I look up Colton is watching me, an amused look in his eyes, and I know he knows my thoughts are anything but innocent. He raises the glass to his lips and takes a sip, his eyes remaining on mine.

He leans over, his lips a breath from my ear. "Every time I take a drink, I can smell you on my fingers. It's making me count the minutes until I can take my slow, sweet time with you, Rylee," he whispers. The resonance in his voice permeating every nerve in my body. "*I want to explore every delicious inch of you.*" He presses a kiss to my cheek. "*And then I'm going to fuck you senseless.*" He growls.

My core clenches and coils at the thoughts his words evoke. "*Check, please,*" I murmur, and Colton throws his head back in laughter, drawing the attention of those at our table.

We sit through the rest of the dinner and the host's enlivened speech about the cause of the evening. Colton sighs with relief when the applause ends and people start to rise from the tables. "Thank God!" he mutters under his breath bringing a smile to my face. At least I'm not the only one anxious for the nightcap to our garage rendezvous. "You ready, Ry?"

"Ready and willing," I admit, enjoying the interruption to his movement from my words.

"Willing's good," he whispers. "Wet's even better."

"I've been that way all night, Ace," I murmur in response, smiling to myself when I hear his sharp intake of air as he follows me through the maze of tables.

"Colton! Hey, Donavan!" a voice to the right yells out.

Colton curses under his breath as I turn to face him. "I'll make this quick," he says before placing a chaste kiss on my lips. He turns and walks across the room meeting the gentleman. "Vincent!" I hear Colton say in greeting as the two shake hands and slap each other on the backs like two men who are more than casual acquaintances.

I watch the exchange from afar, a soft smile on my face as I marvel at Colton and this evening's unexpected turn of events.

"That smile on your face won't last you know," a voice says beside me.

I bristle at the sound of it. *Here comes the rain to fuck with my parade.* "What a pleasant surprise," I say, my tone saccharine laced with sarcasm. I keep my eyes straight ahead, focused on Colton. "Are you having a good time, Tawny?"

She ignores my question and goes straight for the jugular. "You know he's already getting bored with you, right? Already looking for his next willing piece of ass?" She laughs low and snidely, and in my periphery I can see her turn to face me, looking for a reaction I refuse to give her. "And you know as well as I do that there are plenty of women vying for that coveted spot."

I'm riding high from Colton's revelation tonight. I feel brazen and am sick of Tawny's crap. "Oh, believe me, I know." I smirk. "But don't worry, I'm not as naïve as you think I am when it comes to Colton's needs. Little Red Riding Hood, I'm not." I hear Tawny suck in an audible breath as she realizes that I overheard her conversation. Colton glances up from his discussion and his eyes meet mine, a quizzical look crossing his face as he sees who's standing beside me. I smile sweetly back at him as if everything is under control.

It will be momentarily anyway.

"Your time's up, Rylee," she antagonizes.

I take a sip of the champagne in my hand and carefully choose my next words, my voice low and spiteful. "Well, I think it's time you get a new watch then, Tawny, because it seems to me like you're stuck in the past. You really need to get current with the here and now...because when you do, you'll see that you no longer have a say or hold on Colton's personal life."

I watch her chest rise and fall as the anger fires within her. I feel like telling her that if what she feels is anger, then I've got a fucking inferno of fury in comparison. *And I'm just getting started.* "It must suck for you, Tawny, when all you have to look forward to in life is being Colton's sloppy seconds. Thinking you're only good enough to go back to once he's tried everybody else that he thinks might possibly be better. Talk about a hit to that overinflated ego of yours."

"*You bitch!*" she sputters. "You can't fulfill his needs. You're—"

I turn quickly toward her, the look on my face stopping her words. "*Oh, doll,* I just did. Was it you he was fucking on the hood of Sex in the parking garage before dinner? I didn't think so," I patronize with a smirk, but my eyes tell her he's mine and to back the fuck off.

The look on her face is priceless: eyes wide, lips parted as she digests what I've just said. "*Colton would never...*" she huffs getting herself worked up "...the Ferrari is his baby. He'd never risk scratching it."

"Well I guess you don't know him as well as you thought you did." I give her the same catty smirk she's graced me with several times. "Either that or you just didn't mean more to him than his car." I twist my lips and look at her while her ego tries to process what I've just said. "We're done here then," I say with a laugh as I walk away from her toward Colton.

God, that felt good! Serves her right.

When I reach Colton, he extends a hand to me and wraps it around my waist, pulling me into his side as he finishes his conversation with Vincent. They say their goodbyes and as he walks away, Colton leans down and kisses me gently. "What was all that about?" he asks warily.

I angle my head to the side as I look at him and run my fingers along the line of his jaw. "Nothing...it was *inconsequential*," I tell him, scrunching up my nose at the word.

Chapter Nineteen

"Are you sure you're not too cold?"

"Uh-uh," I murmur as Colton rubs his hands up and down my arms, the ocean breeze a biting chill against my bare skin, but I don't want to ruin the moment. This evening—post garden argument—has been one that I'll never forget.

Something has changed in Colton with the evening's progression. It's not something I can put my finger on exactly but rather several things that are subtly different. The little looks he's given me. The causal touches here and there for no specific reason other than to let me know he's at my side. That shy smile of his that I noticed he's reserved for only me tonight. Or maybe it's always been there, and I'm looking at things through different lenses now that I know Colton is going to try for the possibility of an us. He's willing to try to break a pattern that he swears is ingrained in him. For me.

The pitch-black night is lit solely by the sliver of moon hanging in the midnight sky. I close my eyes, hum softly to *Kiss Me Slowly* floating from the speakers, and lift my face as the salty breeze drifts up onto the terrace where we stand. Colton rests his chin on my shoulder as he wraps his arms around my waist from behind. I melt into his warmth, never wanting him to let me go. We stand there, lost in our separate thoughts, soaking in the dark night's atmosphere, and completely aware of the underlying current of desire between us.

Baxter barks at the gate to go down to the beach, and Colton reluctantly releases me to take him out. "Do you want a drink?" I ask, my body chilled the minute his warmth leaves mine.

"Beer, please?"

I wander into the kitchen and get our drinks. When I walk back out, Colton is standing, hands propped on the railing, looking out toward the empty night, completely lost in thought. His broad shoulders are silhouetted against the dark sky—the white of his untucked dress shirt a stark visual contrast—and once again I'm reminded of my angel fighting to break through the darkness.

I place my wine glass down on a patio table and walk up behind him, the crash of the waves drowning out the sound of my footsteps on the deck. I slip my hands through his arms and torso, my front to his back, and wrap my arms around him. A second after my body touches his, Colton spins around violently, a harsh yelp echoing in the night air, his beer flying from my hands, and shattering on the deck. As a consequence of his actions, I am shoved to the side, my hip smarting against the railing. When I clear the hair out of my face and look up, Colton is facing me. His hands are fisted tight at his sides, his teeth are gritted in rage, his eyes are wild with anger—or is it fear—and his chest is heaving in shallow, rapid breaths.

His eyes lock with mine, and I freeze mid-movement with my hip angled out, hand pressing on it where it hurts. A myriad of emotions flash through his eyes as he stares at me, finally breaking through the glaze of fear that masks his face. I've seen this look before. The utter and consuming fear of someone traumatized when they have a flashback. I purposely keep my eyes on Colton's, my silence the only way I know how to let him breach through the fog that's holding him.

My mind filters back to the last morning I spent in this house and what happened when I curled up behind him. And now I know, deep down, that whatever happened to him, whatever lives within the blackness in his soul, has to do with this. That the action—the feeling of being hugged, taken, held from behind—triggers a flashback and brings him momentarily back to the horror.

Colton breathes in deeply—a ragged, soul cleansing drag of air— before breaking eye contact with me. He looks down at the deck momentarily before shouting a drawn out, *"Goddamnit!"* at the top of his lungs.

I startle at his voice as it echoes into the abyss of night around us. That one word is filled with so much frustration and angst all I want to do is gather him in my arms and comfort him, but instead of turning to me, he faces the railing, bracing himself against it once again. The shoulders I admired moments before are now filled with a burden I can't even begin to fathom.

"Colton?" He doesn't respond but rather keeps his face straight ahead. "Colton? I'm sorry. I didn't mean to…"

"Just don't do it again, okay?" he snaps. I try not to be upset by the vehemence in his tone, but I see him hurting and all I want to do is help.

"Colton what happen—"

"Look…" he whirls to face me "…we all didn't have perfect-fucking-suburban-white-picket-fence childhoods like you, Rylee. Is it really that important for you to know I'd go days without food or attention? *That my mom would force*—" He stops himself, his fists clenching and his eyes getting a far off look in them before refocusing on me. "That she'd make me do whatever was needed to ensure her next fucking fix?" His voice is void of all emotion except anger.

I suck in my breath, my heart breaking for him and the memories that plague him. I want to reach out to him. Hold him. Make love to him. Let him lose himself in me. *Anything to make his mind forget for just a moment.*

"Shit, I'm sorry." He sighs with remorse, scrubbing his hands over his face and looking up to the sky. "I find myself apologizing a lot around you." He looks back down and meets my eyes, shoving his hands in his pockets. "I'm sorry, Ry. I didn't mean—"

"It's okay to feel that way." I take a step toward him and raise my hand and place it on his cheek. He leans his face into my hand, turning it briefly to press a kiss to the center of my palm before closing his eyes to absorb whatever emotions he's processing. His acceptance of comfort from me warms my soul. Gives me hope that in time he might talk to me. His unfettered vulnerability tugs at my heart and opens my soul. Draws me in. When he opens his eyes, I look into them, searching their depths. "What happened, Colton?"

"I told you before. Don't try and fix me…"

"I'm just trying to understand." I rub my hand over his cheek one more time before I run it down and rest it over his heart.

"I know." He exhales. "But it's something I don't like to talk about. Shit…it's something no one should have to talk about." He shakes his head. "I told you, my first eight years were a fucking nightmare. I don't want to fill your head with the details. It was—*fuck!*" He pounds his hand on the railing beside us, startling both Baxter and myself. "I'm not used to having to explain myself to anyone." He clenches his jaw, making that muscle pulse. We stand in silence for a while before he looks down at me with a sad smile. "*I swear to God it's you!*"

"Me?" I stutter flabbergasted. What did I have to do with what just happened?

"Mmm-hmm," he murmurs, staring at me intently. "I've never let my guard down. Never opened myself up to…" He shakes his head, his confusion and clarity written on his face. "I've been able to block things out for so long. Ignore emotions. Ignore everything, but you? You tear down walls I didn't even know I was building. *You make me feel, Rylee.*"

I feel as if all of the air has been sucked from my lungs. His words render me thoughtless and yet inundated with thoughts at the same time. Possibilities flicker and flame. Hope sets in. My own walls crumble. My heart swells at his acknowledgement.

He purses his beautifully sculpted lips as he brings a hand up and sets it on my shoulder, his thumb aimlessly rubbing back and forth over my bare collar bone. "Feeling like this when I'm so used to living life in a blur…it's drudging up old shit…old ghosts that I thought I'd buried long ago."

He reaches his other hand out and places it on my waist, pulling me into him. I nuzzle my face into the underside of his neck, inhaling the uniquely Colton scent that I can't seem to get enough of. He wraps his strong arms around me, clinging to me as if he needs the feel of me to help wash away some of his memories.

"I've lived for so long trying to close myself off from people. From this kind of emotion…Rylee? Do you have any idea what you're doing to me?"

His words nurture the love blooming in my heart, but I know he's uncomfortable with his unexpected admission, and I don't want him to suddenly freak out when he realizes it. *Call for a pit stop.* I feel the need to do something—add some levity—to chase away his demons if just for the night. I lean into him and brush a slow, intoxicating kiss on his lips until I can feel his erection thickening against my midsection and wiggle against it. "*I think I can feel that easy enough,*" I murmur against his neck.

His laughter vibrates through his chest against mine. "So beautiful." He brings a hand up to my chin and tilts it back as he leans down and teases my lips with his. My name is a reverent sigh on his lips. His tongue caresses mine over and over, teasing me with a dance intent on complete seduction and utter surrender. I never thought it was possible to make love to someone by kissing alone, but Colton is proving me wrong.

He flutters his tongue gently against mine, the softness of his firm lips coaxing me to need more from him—to need things I never thought possible or could even exist again. His tenderness is so unexpected, so overwhelming, tears sting the back of my eyes as I lose myself in him. Lose myself to him.

"You are so breathtakingly beautiful, Ry. Not what I deserve, but just what I need." He breathes into my mouth, his hands cupping my neck. "Please let me show you…"

As if he even has to ask.

I step up on my toes and thread my fingers through the hair at the nape of his neck. I look up at him, his eyes framed with thick lashes and chock-full of all of the unspoken words his actions are trying to express. I tip my head up and bring my lips to his as a response.

I laugh as he leans down and places his arm behind my knees, picking me up and carrying me over the broken glass of his beer that's scattered all over the decking. He continues inside and carries me up the stairs into his bedroom. He flicks a switch with his elbow as we enter the room and a fire roars to life in the fireplace in the corner of the room.

He stops at the edge of the bed and places me on my feet.

"Is this the part where you take your *deliciously, slow, sweet time with me?*" I whisper, using his words from earlier.

I see his eyes spark at my words. He leans down and delves his tongue between my parted lips. "Baby, I want to enjoy every single inch of this ridiculously sexy body of yours." I feel his hands on the zipper at my back and then my skin becomes chilled from the room's air as he slowly parts my dress. He hints at the things he wants to do to me. His rasp of a voice caresses over me, matching the feel of the fingertip he trails down the path he's unzipping. I feel the tug on the fabric, and it slides down and pools around my high heels.

"Christ, woman, you test a man's restraint," he swears at me, his pupils dilating as he absorbs the entire visual of my lingerie that he's seen only in bits and pieces tonight.

I smooth my hands over the black lace piped with a fire engine red bra portion of my basque and continue down the fabric until I reach the garters attached to it. "You like?" I ask coyly, a smirk on my lips.

"*Oh, baby.*" He sucks in a breath of air closing the distance between us, his eyes devouring the sight in front of him. He wraps his arm around me and yanks me against him so we are face to face, our lips a whisper from each other's. "I more than like. *I want.*" He growls as he moves us backwards and pushes me down onto the bed.

I lean my weight on my elbows and look up at him standing before me as he unbuttons the rest of his shirt. My mouth waters and desire coils as I get an inch by inch glimpse of the magnificence beneath. The hunger in his eyes is a promise of what he wants to do to me, and it leaves me revving with need. He shrugs off his shirt, the hard-edged muscles of his chest and abdomen leave my fingers itching to touch them. He crawls onto the bed, his knees nudging my legs apart as he sits between them. His fingertips trace heated lines up and down my inner thighs. My muscles tense at the feeling and tremble in anticipation.

"Colton," I plead as his touch ignites the ache deep inside me. The need is so intense my hands snake down my abdomen and my fingers dig into the flesh at my hips in restraint. I'm bound up so tight that I need release.

"Oh yes." He groans. "Touch yourself, sweetheart, and let me watch. Show me how much you need me."

His words are all I need to throw my modesty out the window. My fingers dance down my mound, and I part myself, sighing in relief as my fingers begin to add the friction I need over my most sensitive part. Colton groans in lust as he watches, and the sound urges me on. I draw my bottom lip between my teeth as the sensation starts to pull me under.

"Rylee." He rasps out a tortured breath. "My turn."

My eyes flicker up to meet his, lids weighted with desire as I drag my fingertips over my clit one last time before pulling them away. His lips part in reaction to the moan that escapes between my lips and then curve in a wicked smile that has me arching my back, begging for more of his touch. His eyes hold mine as he leans down. I feel the gentle draw of his warm mouth on my aching hot spot and once again he drowns me. His passion swallows me whole.

Chapter Twenty

We lay on our sides facing each other, our heads propped on pillows, our bodies naked, and our current desire temporarily sated. Craig David plays softly through the speakers in the ceiling. I drink in Colton, our eyes speaking volumes despite our lips remaining silent. So many things I want to say to him after what we've just exchanged. It wasn't just sex between us. Not that it ever has been for me, but tonight especially, the connection was different. Colton has always been a more than generous lover, but how he was tonight—his slow, worshipping touch—has left me in a state of blissful daze. I find myself becoming so lost in him, so blanketed by everything that he is, that in a sense, *I have found myself again.*

I am whole again.

"Thank you." His words break our silence.

"Thank me? I think I'm the one who's just come multiple times."

The crooked, cocky grin fills me with such happiness. "True," he concedes with a nod of his head. "But thank you for not pushing earlier."

"You're welcome," I tell him, feeling like the smile on my face is a permanent fixture.

We fall silent again for a bit before he murmurs, "I could look at you for hours." I blush under the intensity of his stare, which is funny considering I should be blushing rather in regards to all of the various things he just did to please me. But in this moment I realize that I am blushing because I am completely naked to him—stripped, bared, open—and not in just in the literal sense. He is looking at me, seeing

173

into my eyes and through the guard I have lowered to reveal the transparency of my feelings for him.

I shake myself from my thoughts. "I think I should be the one saying that," I tell him, the dancing flames from the fire bathing a soft light across his dark features.

He snorts at me and rolls his eyes. Such a childish reaction from such an intense man that it softens him, makes my heart stumble that much more. "Do you have any idea how much crap I got as a kid for being so *pretty*," he says with disdain. "How many fights I got in to prove that I wasn't?"

I reach out and run my fingertips over the lines of his face and then down the crooked line of his nose. "Is that how you got this?" I ask.

"Mmm-hmm." He chuckles softly. "I was a senior in high school and had the hots for the football captain's girl. Stephanie Turner was her name. He wasn't too thrilled when the school rebel snuck out of a party with his girl." He smiles sheepishly. "I was...I had quite a rep back then."

"Only back then?" I tease.

"Smartass," he says, giving me that bashful smile. "Yes, only then." When I roll my eyes at him, he continues. "Anyway, I was quite the hot head. Got in fights constantly for no reason except to prove no one had a say in what I could do or how they could control me. I had a lot of anger in my teenage years. Because of that, the next day he got his buddies to hold me down while he beat the shit out of me. Broke my nose and fucked me up pretty bad." He shrugs. "Looking back, I deserved it. You don't touch another man's woman."

I stare at him, finding his last comment oddly sexy. "What did your parents say?"

"Oh they were pissed," he exclaims before continuing on to explain how they reacted. We talked like this for the next hour. He explained what it was like growing up with his parents, filling in little stories here and there that had me laughing at both his rebellions and his shortcomings.

We fall back into a comfortable silence after a while. He reaches out and pulls the covers up my back after noticing I've become chilled and tucks an errant curl behind my ear. "I'm proud of you," he says softly, my drowsy eyelids opening fully in question. "You walked into that storage closet tonight and didn't freak out."

I look at him, awareness seeping into me that he's right. That I didn't think twice about it. With him beside me, I was able to forget my fear. "Well I didn't actually walk into it...I believe I was *coerced*. It's the

Colton effect," I tease. "You had my thoughts focused elsewhere."

"I could do that again right now if you'd like?" he suggests.

"I'm sure you could, Ace, but..." I stop and stare at him, Tawny's bathroom conversation seeping into my thoughts. Curiosity melds with insecurity and it gets the better of me. "Colton?"

"Hmm?" he murmurs, his eyes drifting closed as his fingers draw aimless circles on the top of my hand.

"Do I give you what you need?"

"Mmm-hmm" The nonchalance of his response tells me that either doesn't understand my question or is lost to the clutches of sleep.

Her words echo in my head. "Do I satisfy you sexually?" I can't help the break in my voice when I ask.

Colton's body tenses at my words, his fingertips become motionless on my skin, and his eyes open with deliberate slowness and confusion. He stares at me as if he is looking straight into my soul, and the intensity of it is so strong that I eventually avert my eyes to watch my fingers pluck at the sheet. "Why would you ask me such a ridiculous question?"

I shrug as embarrassment colors my cheeks. "I'm just not very experienced and you—you most definitely are so I was just wondering..." My voice fades off, unsure how to ask what is in the forefront of my mind.

Colton shifts in the bed and sits up, tugging on my arm so that I have no choice but to follow suit. He reaches out and tips my chin up so that I'm forced to look into his eyes. "You're just wondering what?" he asks softly, concern etched in his features.

"How long until you're bored with me? I mean, I'm—"

"Hey, where is all of this coming from?" Colton implores as he brushes his thumb gently over my cheek.

How is it I can let this man have his way with me sexually, but right now, confronting him about my lack of experience makes me feel more naked than ever? Insecurity clogs my throat when I try to explain. "It's just been a rough night," I say. "I'm sorry. Forget I said anything."

"Uh-uh, you're not getting off that easy, Rylee." He shifts in the bed and despite my protests, pulls me so that I'm seated between his thighs—face to face—my legs astride his hips. I have no choice but to look at him now. "What's going on? What else did I miss tonight that you're not telling me?" His eyes search into mine looking for answers.

"It's silly really," I admit, trying to downplay my feelings of inadequacy. "I was in the bathroom stall and overheard some ladies talking about what a God you are in the sack." I roll my eyes for good measure not wanting his ego to get any bigger than it already is. "...And how it's obvious that I'm more than inexperienced." I look down and focus on his thumbs rubbing absently back and forth on my thighs. "How you're going to take what you want, chew me up, and spit me out. They said you don't do predictability and—"

"Stop." His voice is stern, and I can't help but look up to meet his bemused eyes. "Look, I don't know how to explain it." His voice softens and he shakes his head. "I can't really. All I know is that with you, things were just different from the start. *You broke the mold, Rylee.*"

His words elate the feelings of hope inside of me, and yet I still feel the roots of inadequacy weighing down my soul. We sit here both trying to gain our bearings on the ever-shifting ground beneath our feet. "I know," I interject, "I just—"

"You don't get it do you?" he asks. "You may not have the experience but..." He fades off trying to find the right words. "...you're the purest person I've ever met, Rylee. That part of you— that innocence in you—*it's so goddamn sexy.* So fucking incredible."

He rests his forehead against mine, pulling my body further into his. He sighs and laughs softly, his breath feathering across my lips. "You know, a couple of months ago, I might have answered you differently. But since you fell out of the damn storage closet, nothing has been the fucking same." He pauses momentarily, his fingertip trailing down the bare line of my spine. "No one's mattered before. Ever. But you? Fuck, somehow you changed that. *You matter,*" he says with such clarity that his words delve into places deep inside of me I thought could never be healed. Places and pieces now slowly stitching themselves back together.

I still as Colton's warm arms wrap around the chilled skin of my back. He pulls my hair to the side and presses his lips to the curve of my neck. The scrape of this returning stubble sends shivers down my spine. "What is it with you and jumping to conclusions tonight?" he murmurs, keeping his lips pressed against my skin. The vibrations of his lips ricocheting across hypersensitive nerves.

I shrug without explanation, suddenly embarrassed at confessing my moment of blatant insecurity to him when he so obviously showed me tonight that I'm the one he wants. Silence settles around us for a bit as we breathe each other in. "If there's something you're not getting from me—that you need—you'd tell me right?" He leans back to look at me, his hands resting on my shoulders, thumbs brushing absently over the dip of my collarbone, question in his eyes. I continue, "When Tawny said—"

Colton's eyes snaps alert. *"Tawny?"*

"She was in the bathroom," I confess and see irritation flicker across his face.

"Fuckin' Tawny," he mutters dragging a hand through his hair. "Look at me, Rylee," he commands. I raise my eyes up to meet the raw intensity in his. "Tawny's just jealous that she doesn't have a tenth of the sex appeal that you have. And the best part about it—about you—is that you don't even realize it. Do you remember that night at the Palisades?" he asks and all I can do is nod, mesmerized by his words and the soft smile ghosting his lips. "That's what I was struggling with. Why I was such an ass. How could I bring you there and treat you like everybody else when you were like no one I'd ever been with before? And then I walked over to you, and you were standing there trying to figure out what my problem was, looking so goddamn beautiful and unintentionally beguiling. And even though I'd been a dick, you stepped toward me *and gave everything of yourself* to me without a single explanation." He reaches up and traces a line down my forehead and nose and then stops on my lips. "It's such a fucking turn on, Rylee. *Like no one else I've ever been with.* No one."

I draw in a ragged breath, afraid to believe what he's really telling me. *That I give him what he needs. That things between him and I are different for him.* A first of sorts for him. I swallow loudly before clenching my jaw. If I speak right now, three words he doesn't want to hear are going to come tumbling out of my mouth. It's been an emotional night, and I'm more than overwhelmed. All I can manage is a simple nod.

"I've never had to work so hard to get something I never thought I wanted," he confesses and the words feather through me and embed themselves in my swelling heart and transparent soul.

How is it possible to feel love this intense when I thought the ability for me had died with Max?

I lean in and express the words my tangled tongue cannot, by pressing my lips to his. "Thank you," I whisper to him for the many things I don't even think he could understand even if I told him.

He pulls back and I can't miss the smirk on his devilishly sexy mouth. He raises and eyebrow at me, amusement in his eyes. *"A God in the sack, huh?"*

I can't help the laughter that bubbles up and spills out, not surprised he didn't forget. "Did I say that?" I tease as I run my fingertips down the ridges of his abdomen. I can feel his thickening arousal pulse beneath me from my touch. "Must have been a slip of the tongue."

"Oh really?" He asks with a playful grin on his lips, and a look in his eyes that tells me his sated needs are no longer fulfilled. "Tongues are funny things don't you think?" He leans in and traces my lower lip with his tongue. "They can lick like this," he whispers. "And they can kiss like this," he says branding his mouth to mine, his tongue parting my lips and dominating my mouth. He shifts us backwards on the mattress so that his weight presses deliciously on top of me.

He breaks the kiss and the lust in his eyes has desire unfurling in my belly. "And they can lick like this," he whispers before grazing his way down my neck to tease the tightened bud of my nipple. "They can tease and pleasure like this." His tongue caresses one then another before trailing down my abdomen at an achingly slow pace. My muscles flex in anticipation as he stops at the top of my sex.

He looks up at me and I catch a flash of grin. "And they most definitely..." He blows against my seam, the heat of his breath feathering over my sensitive flesh. "...love to taste like this."

His tongue laves over me and my sharp intake of air followed by a soft moan is all I can manage. My words are lost and mind is clouded from the soft slide and adept skill of his tongue.

As he consumes me. Pleasures me. Undoes me.

Chapter Twenty-One
Colton

God, she's fucking gorgeous. I can't help but reach out and pull a curl off of her cheek. The feeling—that fucking foreign feeling that's not so foreign any more—courses through me, grabs me by the balls and then hands them back to me on a platter.

Makes fear shiver at the base of my spine in a constant state of reverberation.

My fingers linger on her shoulder, touching her to make sure she's real. There's no possible way that she can be. She scares the fuck out of me. That not so foreign feeling scares the fuck out of me. But I can't force myself to walk away. From that very first encounter I haven't been able to. Shit, at first it was definitely the challenge. That smart mouth, those violet eyes, and the sway of that ass—what red-blooded male would have?

Christ. Tell me I can't have something, I'm sure as fuck going to go after it until I get it. *Game on.* I'm in it until the motherfucking checkered flag.

But then, that first time I showed up at The House—that look in her eyes that told me to get the fuck out and to not mess with *her Zander* or she'd take me down herself—everything changed. *Shifted.* Became real. The challenge ceased to exist. All I saw in that moment was myself as a kid. Myself now. Knew that she loved the broken in us. Was okay with the darkness because she was so full of fucking light. Knew she'd understand so much more than I'd ever be able to say.

That selfless soul of hers and come-fuck-me body just pulled at me, twisted through parts inside of me that I thought had died and would never regenerate. *Made me feel* when I've been so content to live in the blur around me. I mean who really does the shit she does? Takes fucked up kids—*lots of fucked up kids*—and treats them as her own. Defends them. Loves them. Fights for them. Is willing to make a deal with the devil such as myself for their benefit.

That day in the conference room when I trapped her into my little deal, I could see the trepidation and the knowledge that I'd hurt her in those fucking bedroom eyes, and as much as she knew it, she agreed for the sake of the boys, regardless of the damage it'd cause to her personally. And of course I'm a fucking bastard for wondering the whole time how sweet her pussy would taste. I mean if her kiss was that fucking addictive, then I couldn't even imagine how the rest of her body would drug me. She's sacrificing herself for her boys, and there I was thinking of my end game.

And that in itself fucked me up, forced me to keep my guard up. I knew she was going to let me have her, but had no fucking clue that first time together—when she looked at me with such a definitive clarity afterward—that she'd be able to look right into my goddamn soul. It freaked me the fuck out, stirred things within me I never wanted churned up again. Things I had accepted living a lifetime without. No one knows the things I did—the things I allowed to be done to me. The poison living inside. How I loved and hated and did unimaginable things for reasons I didn't understand at the time and still don't understand now.

And I fear every minute of every fucking day that she'll figure it out, learn about the truths inside of me and then leave me so much worse off than she found me. She's unlocked things in me I'd never intended to allow to see the light of day again. She pushes the concept of vulnerability to a whole new level.

But I can't push her away. I can't stop wanting to for her sake. But every time I try—every time I crack and she sees a glimpse of my demons—I'm scared shitless. God, I try to make her leave—even if it's only in my fucked up head—but I'm never successful. And I'm just not sure if it's because she's stubborn or because it's a half-assed attempt on my part just so I can tell myself I actually tried.

I know what's best for her is not me. Shit, last night...last night was...*fuck*. I handed myself to her. Told her I'd try when every part of me screamed in protest from the fear of being ripped to shreds by allowing myself to feel. I've always used pleasure to bury the pain. Not emotions. Not commitment. Pleasure. How else can I prove to myself that I'm not that kid I was forced to be? It's the only way I know. The only way I can cope. *Fuck* the therapists who had no clue what happened to me. My parents wasted so much fucking money on people telling me how to overcome the issues they thought I had. That I could use hypnosis to regress and overcome. *Fuck that.* Give me a tight, wet, willing pussy to bury myself in momentarily and that's all the proof I need.

Pleasure to bury the pain. So what do I do now? How do I cope with the one person that I fear can give me both? And she does, yet I still hurt her last night. I have a feeling I always will in some way or another. At some point she's just going to stop forgiving or coming back. Then what, Donavan? What the fuck are you going to do then? If I'm broken now, I'll be fucking shattered then.

I stare at her sleeping, so innocent *and mine* and fuck all why I can't stay away from her. I'm scared shitless and she fucking did this to me. She fucking grabbed ahold, forced me to listen to the silent words she spoke, and *really hear them.* Now what the fuck am I supposed to do?

My God the way she looked at me last night with eyes filled with naivety and jaw set with obstinance, asking me if she was enough for me. First of all—fucking Tawny—and then secondly, enough? I'm the one that's not enough. Not hardly. I'm fucking drowning in her, and I'm not even sure I want to come up for air. Enough? I shake my head at the irony. She stays despite, if not because of the darkness deep in my soul. A saint I'm not worthy of, shouldn't taint.

She makes a soft noise in her throat and rolls onto her back. The sheet slips down off of her chest exposing her perfect fucking tits. Fuck me. My dick starts stirring to life at the sight. It's been what, like three hours since the last time I was buried in her, and I'm already fucking ready to have her again. Addictive voodoo pussy. I swear to God.

She whimpers again and rocks her head back and forth on the pillow. I hear Baxter's tail thump at the sound and the possibility that someone might be up already. My eyes trail over her lips and back to her tits. I groan at the sight of her pink nipples pebbling from the morning chill. I really should cover her back up, but fuck me, the view's pretty fucking fantastic, and I don't want to ruin it just yet.

Her shriek scares the shit out of me. It's a piercing keening that causes my chest to tighten. She cries out again and it's a tortured sound followed by her throwing her arms up to block her face. I sit up and try to gather her against me, but she bucks back.

"Rylee. Wake up!" I say, shaking her shoulders a couple of times.

She finally wakes with a start and struggles out of my grip to bolt up in the bed. The sound of her gasping for breath makes me want to fold her into my arms and take the fear and pain that's rolling off of her in waves away from her. I do the only thing I can think of and run my hand up and down the bare skin of her back—the only comfort I can offer. "You okay?"

She just nods her head and looks over at me. And in that one glance I'm paralyzed. *Fucking paralyzed.* As a guy you're supposed to have that instinct to protect and care for. You always hear about how that's your job. It's ingrained. What-the-fuck-ever. Besides the few times when Q had some bullies at school fuck with her, I've never remotely felt that way. Never.

Until right now. Rylee looks at me and those violet eyes are pooling with tears and filled with such absolute pain and fear. I do the only thing I want to even though I know it's not enough for her, it'll assuage my needs. I reach out pulling her toward me and onto my lap before leaning back against the headboard. When I wrap my arms around her, she lays her cheek over my chest. Over my heart. And despite the calm that the feel of her bare skin on mine brings me, I can't help but keep feeling the single connection of her face over my heart.

The one place I never expected to feel again just quickened at such a simple, natural gesture. I swear that her pulse and breathing are evening out and mine are accelerating. I run my fingers through her curls, needing to do something to combat the panic I feel setting in.

First I feel like I need to protect her, take care of her, covet her. And then the simple notion of her getting comfort from my heartbeat freaks me the fuck out. Can you say pussy, Donavan? More like pussy whipped. *What. The. Fuck?* This shit is not supposed to happen to me. Telling her I'll try is one thing. But this fucking feeling taking hold of me like a vice grip in my chest? No fucking thanks.

I hear my mom's voice. It seeps into my head and my hand stills in Rylee's hair. I swear I stop breathing. "Colty. I know how much you love me. How much you need me. That you understand that love means doing whatever the other person tells you to. So I'm telling you that because you love me, you'll go lay down on my bed for me and wait like the good little boy that you are. You want food right? It's been days. You've got to be hungry. If you're a good little boy—if you love me—you won't fight this time. Won't be the *naughty* boy you were last time. If you're bruised up, the police might take us away from each other. And then you won't get anything to eat. And then I won't love you anymore."

Rylee's hand tracing absent circles on my tattoos jolts me back to the here and now. The irony in that—her touching the tattoos that represent so much—is enough in itself. I force myself to breathe calmly, try and clear the revulsion in my stomach. Quiet the tremor in my hand so she doesn't notice. Fuck. Now I know the feeling earlier really was a fluke. How can I want to protect and take care of Rylee when I can't even do that for myself? Breathe, Donavan. Fucking breathe.

"I wonder if we're drawn to each other because we're both fucked up emotionally somehow," she murmurs aloud, breaking the silence. I can't help the breath that hitches in my chest. I swallow slowly, digesting her words—realizing they're just a coincidence—but how true they ring for me.

"Well gee thanks," I say, forcing a chuckle, hoping to calm both of us with some humor. "Us and everyone else in Hollywood."

"Uh-huh," she says, snuggling deeper into me. The feeling is so fucking soothing to me I wish I could pull her inside of me to ease the pain there as well.

"I told you, a seven forty seven baby." I leave it at that. I can't force any more words out without her catching on that something's amiss with me.

She moves her hand from my tattoo to tickle through the slight smattering of hair on my chest. "I could lie here forever," she sighs out in that throaty morning voice of hers. I pray for my dick to stir at the sound. Need it to. Need to prove to myself that the unexpected reminder of my mother and my past can't affect me anymore. That they aren't who I am.

My thoughts flicker to what I'd normally do. Go call up my current flavor and use her. Fuck her into oblivion without a second thought of her needs. Use the fleeting pleasure to bury the endless goddamn motherfucking pain.

But I can't do that. I can't just walk away from the one person that I want and fear and desire and have fucking grown to need. Balls in a fucking vice.

And before I even think, the words are out of my mouth. "Then stay here with me this weekend." I think I'm as shocked as Ry is at my comment. She stills at the same time I do. The first time my lips have *ever* uttered those fucking words. Words I never wanted to say before, but know without a doubt I mean right now.

"On one condition," she says.

One condition? I just handed her my balls on a platter in exchange for

183

the whip to her pussy and she's going to add a condition? Fucking women.

"Tell me what a voodoo pussy is."

For the first time this morning I feel like laughing. And I do. I can't contain it. She just looks up at me, with those eyes that do wild things to me, like I'm crazy. "Fuck, I needed that," I tell her, leaning down and pressing a kiss to the top of her head.

"Well?" she asks in that no-nonsense tone she has that usually turns me on. And I breathe a slight sigh as I start to harden at the thought of her wet heat I plan on taking advantage of in mere moments.

"Voodoo pussy?" I choke on the words.

"Yeah. You said it last night in the garden."

"I did?" I ask, unable to hide the amusement in my tone, and she just nods her head subtly with her eyebrows arched waiting for an answer. Oh yeah. Definitely hard and raring to go now. Thank Christ. "Well…it's that pussy that just takes hold of your dick and doesn't let go. It's so fucking good—feels, tastes, everything good—that it's magical." I feel so fucking stupid explaining it. I don't think I ever have. I just say it and Becks knows exactly what I mean.

Rylee laughs out loud and the sound is so beautiful. *Beautiful?* Fuck. I am pussy whipped. "So you're telling me that I have a magical pussy?" she asks as her finger trails a circle around my nipple before looking up at me and licking her lips. I can't manage a word at the moment because all of the blood needed to supply a coherent thought in my brain has just traveled south, so I just nod my head. "Well maybe I should show you—"

The cell phone on the dresser rings—it's a different ring than her normal one—and something about it has her scrambling off of the bed in a flash. She's breathless when she answers. And fucking breathtaking. She stands at the wall of windows looking out to the beach down below, her phone to her ear, and the sun bathing her naked body in its light.

The concern in her voice pulls me from my perverse thoughts of all of the ways I can take her. Position her. Corrupt her.

"Calm down, Scooter," she soothes. "It's okay, buddy. I'm okay. I'm right here. Shhh-shhh-shhh. Nothing's happened to me. I'm actually sitting on the beach right now, looking out at the water. I promise, buddy. I'm not going anywhere." The concern in her voice has me shifting in the bed. She notices my movement and looks over and smiles apologetically at me. As if I'd be mad that she left me to talk to one of the boys. Never. "You okay now? Yes. I know. Don't be sorry.

You know that if I'm not there, you can always call me. Always. Mmm-hmm. I'll see you on Monday, okay? Call me if you need me before then." Rylee walks back toward the dresser as she wraps up her call. "Hey, Scoot? I Spiderman you. Bye."

I Spiderman you? Rylee hangs up her phone and tosses it on the dresser before walking back to the bed. My eyes roam over the line of her curves, thinking how lucky I am to have her naked and walking toward me with an extremely durable bed beneath me.

"Sorry," she says. "Scooter had a really bad dream and was afraid that I'd been hurt. That I was going to be taken away like his mom was. He just needed to make sure that I was okay. Sorry," she says again, and I swear that my fucking heart twists in my chest at her apologies for being selfless. Is she for fucking real?

"Don't be," I tell her as she climbs into the bed beside me and sits on her knees. I tell myself to ask now before I become distracted at the sight of her sitting there looking so damn obedient. *"I Spiderman you?"*

She laughs with this adorable look on her face. "Yeah." She shrugs. "Some of the boys have trouble with affection when they come to us. Either they feel like they're betraying their parents, regardless of how fucked up their situation, by having feelings for their counselors, or feelings in general had a negative connotation from whatever situation they came from… It all started with Shane really, but it kind of caught on and now most of the boys do it. We take the one thing that they love more than anything and use that as the emotion instead. Scooter loves Spiderman so that's what he uses."

I look at her with bemusement, a little unnerved that she has these kids pegged so well—me so well—if I allowed her to look close enough. She's just unknowingly fucked with my mind so much that my eyes haven't roamed south of her face to take in her gloriously naked body below as they normally would.

She mistakes the look I give her to be that I don't understand so she tries to clarify. She shifts off of her knees and situates herself closer to me. "Okay, for instance pretend you are one of my boys—tell me one thing that you love more than anything."

"That's easy." I smirk at her. *"Sex with you."*

The smile spreads on her lips and her cheeks flush. So sexy. "Well that's an answer I've never gotten from one of my boys before," she jokes, laughing at me. "No seriously, Colton, give me the one thing."

I shrug, saying my first and only love. "I love to race."

"Perfect," she says. "If you were one of my boys and you wanted to tell me you loved me, or vice versa, you'd say 'I race you, Rylee.'"

My heart stutters again at hearing her say those words, and I think she realizes what she's said the minute the words are out of her mouth. She stills and her eyes dart to me and then down to her hands twisting in her lap. "I mean..." she backpedals and I'm glad this conversation is making her as nervous as I am right now "...if you were one of the boys that is."

"Of course." I swallow, desperately needing a distraction. I reach out to trace a finger down the midline of her chest—from her neck, down between the center of her breasts, and stopping at her bellybutton.

I race you, Rylee fleets through my mind. Just to hear what it sounds like for no other reason than to see how one of the boys would feel saying it. The tightening of my chest forces me to focus on the one thing that always allows me to forget. There will be no *racing* between Rylee and I. *None.* I look up from where my finger rests on her stomach to meet her eyes. "Now, I think you were just about to show me just how magical that pussy of yours was before we were interrupted."

Chapter Twenty-Two

The ringing of my cell phone startles me awake, and in the muted light of the dawn, I fumble for it on my nightstand. "Hello?" I mumble groggily, afraid that even though it's not the designated ring, something is possibly wrong with one of the boys at The House.

"Good morning, sleepy." Colton's velvety smooth rasp fills my ears. I can hear his smile through the line, and it sends shivers straight down my spine to the tips of my toes. I'm definitely awake now.

"Morning," I murmur, sinking back into the comfort of my warm bed.

"Do you have any idea how much I wish I was tangled up with you in that bed of yours? And that I was waking up with you and having lazy morning sex rather than just calling your cell?"

His subtle yet seductive words serve their purpose as I shift in my bed to still the ache he's just unfurled in me. "I was just thinking that same thing." I sigh softly, my mind wandering to how much I already miss him. How much my body automatically responds to the sound of his voice. I look down at my cotton camisole and panties and smirk. "Considering I'm very cold and very naked and I know you'd know exactly what to do to warm me up." A little lie never hurt anyone when one was trying to keep the fires burning, right?

I hear him suck in a hiss of a breath. "Sweet Jesus, woman, you know how to make a man want," he says quietly as I hear other voices in the background and realize that he's not alone.

It's only been four days since our blissful weekend together, but it feels like forever since I've been able to touch him. He drove me home on Monday morning on his way to the airport, and since then I've had to survive on texts and phone calls that leave me bereft and acting like a love-struck teenager.

"I'll be right back," he tells someone off the speaker, and I hear the chatter fade into the background. "I'm not sure that the people having breakfast here in the hotel want to watch me rub one out because my girlfriend's so fucking hot," he chuckles that seductive bedroom laugh of his through the line and I let it wash over me.

And then I still when the one word he said breaks through my sleep hazed brain. *Girlfriend.* I want to ask him to say it again so I can hear the word that is so simple but just literally took my breath away. But it's the fact that he's said it so casually, as if that's how he thinks of me, that I don't want to draw attention to it.

I sink further into the comfort of my bed with a huge smile plastered on my lips. "How's Nashville?"

"It's Nashville," he replies drolly. "Not bad, just not home. I'm sorry to wake you up with the time difference, but I'm going to be crazy busy all day, and I wanted to make sure that I got to talk to you. To hear your voice."

His words soften my smile, knowing that he's thinking about me even though he's doing work and prepping with his top sponsor. "Your voice is definitely a better wakeup call than my alarm clock…" I falter, holding back before I say screw it and just say what's on my mind. "I miss you," I tell him, hoping he hears what I really mean behind the words. That I miss more than just the sex. *That I miss him as a whole.*

He's silent on the other end of the line for a moment, and I think maybe I've expressed too much verbalized affection for Mr. Stoic. "I miss you too, baby. More than I thought possible." His last statement is said very quietly as if he can't believe it either. I smile broadly and snuggle deeper in my covers as his words warm me. "So what are your plans for the day?"

"Hmmm…sleeping some more and then a run, laundry, cleaning house…Maybe dinner with Haddie." I shrug although I know he can't see it. "What's your schedule like?"

"Brand meetings with the Firestone team, sponsorship junkets, a trip to Children's hospital—best part of the day if you ask me—and then some formal dinner thing tonight. I'll have to check with Tawny on the exact order." He sighs as I roll my shoulders involuntarily at her name. "The days just all run together sometimes on these trips. It's all important but it's also rather boring."

"I bet it is." I laugh. "Next time you're nodding off in one, just picture what my mouth did to you last Sunday," I murmur to him in my breathiest voice. Images flash through my mind and I can't fight the smile that comes with the memory.

A strangled moan comes from the other end of the line. "Jesus, Ry, are you purposely trying to make me walk around with a permanent hard-on today?" When my only response is a contented sigh, he continues, the edge in his voice expressing his unsatisfied desire. "When I get back, I'm locking you in my bedroom for an entire weekend— tying you up if I have to—and you'll be my sex slave. Your body will be mine to use as I please." He chuckles. "Oh and don't worry Ryles, you mouth will be used and then some."

Hello, Mr. Dominant! "Why are you limiting us to just your bedroom? I believe you have numerous surfaces in that large house of yours that are usable."

The groan he emits causes need to coil inside of me. "Oh, don't worry about where. Just worry about how you're going to walk afterward." His laugh is strained and sounds like how I feel.

"Promise?" I whisper, my body heating up at the thought of it.

"Oh, sweetheart, I'd stake my life on that promise." I hear his name called in the background. "You ready, Becks?" he says away from the speaker before sighing loudly. "I gotta go but I'll call you later if it's not too late, okay?"

"Okay," I reply softly. "It doesn't matter the time. I like hearing your voice."

"Hey, Ry?"

"Yeah?"

"Think of me," he says, and I can hear something in his voice: insecurity, vulnerability, or is it the need to feel wanted? No, not wanted. He has that all of the time. Maybe it's the need to feel needed. I can't decipher it, but that little request has me heart constricting in my chest.

"Always." I sigh, a smile on my lips as the line goes dead.

I sit with the phone to my ear for quite some time, so many thoughts running through my head about Colton and the sweet and affectionate side of him. The side that I'm getting glimpses of more and more. I can't help the broad smile on my face as I hang up my phone and sink back into my bed. I will myself to go back to sleep, but thoughts of him and endless possibilities prevents it.

The next time I glance at the clock, I'm startled an hour has passed while I've been lost in my thoughts, thinking about our time together. About how in such a short time he has brought me from such maddening lows to the incredible high like I am feeling now.

I finally start to drift off to sleep when my phone rings again. "*Seriously?*" I say to aloud until I see who the caller is.

"Hey, Momma!"

"Hi, sweetie," she says, and just hearing her voice makes me want to see her again. I feel like it's been forever since I've been able to hug her. "So when were you going to tell me about the new man in your life?" she asks, tone insistent.

Nothing like getting straight to the point. "Well don't beat around the bush or anything." I laugh at her.

"How do you think I felt when I was flipping through last week's People magazine and lo and behold, I thought I saw a picture of you. So I flipped back and sure enough there you were, *my daughter*, looking absolutely breathtaking, on the arm of that tall, dark, and sinfully handsome Colton Donavan." I start to talk but she just keeps on going. "And then I read the caption and it said that 'Colton Donavan and his reported new flame heat up the night at the Kids Now charity function.' Do you know what a shock it was to see you there? And then to think that you're *dating someone* and I don't even know about it."

I can hear the shock in her voice. And the hurt over not telling her about my first date since Max. That she had to find out from a magazine. I glance over to my dresser where the copy of People sits. "Oh, Mom, don't be silly." I sigh, knowing I've hurt her by not confiding in her.

"Don't be silly?" She scoffs. "The man has donated a boatload of money to bring your project to fruition to get your attention and you're telling me I'm being silly?"

"Mom," I warn, "that's not why he donated the money." She harrumphs on the other end of the line at my answer. "No, really. His company picks one organization a year to focus on, and this year it happened to be mine. And I wasn't not telling you…things have just been crazy."

"Well, I think it's rather telling that you told me about his company donating the money for the project, but neglected to say that you'd actually met him…so?" she asks skeptically.

"I met him at the charity function," I answer without giving more away.

"And what happened at that function?"

"Have you been talking to Haddie?" I ask. There is no way she knows what to ask without having talked to Haddie.

"Quit avoiding the question. What happened at the function?"

190

"Nothing. We talked for a few minutes and then I was pulled away because of a problem with the date auction." Dear old mom doesn't need to know about the brief interlude backstage before that.

"And what was the problem?"

"Mother!"

"Well, if you'd just answer me straight the first time, we wouldn't have to play this cat and mouse game you're playing now would we?"

What is it with mothers? Are they clairvoyant? "*Okay, mom.* A date contestant got sick. I took her place. Colton bid on a date with me and won. Are you happy now?"

"Interesting," she says, drawing out every syllable, and I swear I can hear the smirk on her face in the single word. "So you tell me that I'm being silly when one of the sexiest men alive is pursuing my daughter, donating to her charity to get her attention I assume, and taking her to high profile events to show her off? Really? And how is that being silly, Rylee?"

"Mom—"

"How serious is it?" she deadpans, and I shouldn't be shocked at her frankness, but even after all of these years, I still am.

"Mom, Colton doesn't do serious," I try to deflect.

"Don't try to play it off, Rylee," she scolds. "I know you well enough to know that any man you give your time to is obviously worth it. And you wouldn't waste your time on someone that is in it for a quick lay." I cringe at her words. If only she knew about Colton's arrangements, I'm sure she wouldn't be so sure of my judgment then. "So tell me, honey, just how serious is it?"

I sigh loudly, knowing that my mother is tenacious when she wants an answer. "Honestly, from my viewpoint, it could be something. From his...well, Colton isn't used to doing the more than a couple of months type of thing. We're just feeling it out as we go," I answer softly and as honestly as possible.

"Hmmm," she murmurs before falling silent. "Does he treat you well? Because you know that they always treat you the best in the beginning of the relationship, and if it's not good in the beginning then it's not going to get any better."

"*Yes, Mother,*" I say like a child.

"I'm serious, Rylee Jade," she says, her voice implacable. She must be serious if she's using my middle name. "Does he or doesn't he?"

"Yes, Mom. He treats me very well."

I hear her warm laughter on the other end of the line, and I can tell she's relieved. "Just remember what I always say; don't lose yourself trying to hold onto someone who doesn't care about losing you." I finish mouthing the words she's saying. Words she's told me since I started crushing on boys as a teenager.

"I know."

"Oh, honey, I am so happy for you! After everything that you've been through...you deserve nothing but happiness, my sweet child."

I smile at her unconditional love and concern for me, appreciating what a great mother I have. "Thanks, Mom. We're just taking things a day at a time right now and seeing where it leads us."

"There's my girl. Always with a level head on her shoulders."

I sigh, a soft smile on my face. "So how are things going? How have you been? How's Dad?"

"All's good here. Dad's fine. Busy as ever, but you know how he is." She laughs and I can imagine her running her tongue over her top lip as is her habit. "How are the boys?"

I smile at my mom's question. She treats them like they're family too, always sending them treats or cookies or little things to make them feel special. "They're good. I think Shane has his first pseudo-girlfriend, and Zander is slowly making progress." I go through the boys and talk about each one with her, answering her questions, and I can sense another care package coming for them.

We talk for a bit more before she has to go. "I miss you, Mom." My voice cracks with my words because she might be tough and overbearing, but she only wants the best for me. I love her more than anything.

"I miss you too, Ry. It's been too long since I've seen you."

"I know. I love you."

"Love you too. Bye."

I hit call end and snuggle back into my warm bed that for some reason no one will let me sleep in this morning. I glance over at the dresser at the People and grab it. I flip it open to the marked page and there I am.

I stare at the picture of Colton and me at the Kids Now function on the red carpet. He is standing, his shoulders squared to the camera, with his hand in one pocket of his slacks and his other hand wrapped around my waist. His pocket square front and center. His face is looking toward the camera, but his chin and eyes are angled toward me with a huge smile on his face.

My eyes gravitate to the part of the picture that I love the most, the way his hand grips my hip, a possessive hold announcing to the world that I am his.

I reread the caption again and sigh. I'm so glad the press hasn't gotten a hold of my name yet. I'm not ready to be thrust in to the media circus but I know it's inevitable if I'm with Colton.

"In for a penny, in for a pound," I mutter to myself.

I hold the picture in my hand, staring at it until I talk myself into taking my run. I shift out of my bed when my phone dings a text. I laugh out loud at technology's rule over my life this morning and nonetheless pick up my phone to see Colton's name. I can't help the smile on my lips.

Thinking nasty thoughts of you in the middle of my meeting. Won't be standing for a while now. Bruno Mars – Locked Out of Heaven.

I laugh out loud, knowing the song and feeling flattered at the same time at the song's lyrics. I text him back.

So glad I could help with your boredom, Ace...it's the least I can do. Think more thoughts! TLC – Red Light Special.

I smirk as I toss my phone onto my nightstand, knowing that he's going to have a lot harder time concentrating in his meeting now.

Chapter Twenty-Three

"Stella?" I call out from the door of my office. "Stella? What happened to my schedule for today?"

I lower my very tired and aching head into my hands and rest it there while I try to figure out how to juggle everything this week: budget projections, schedules, project meetings, along with the usual daily grind. And now I can only hope that the sudden four hour meeting blocked on my schedule for after lunch is just a computer glitch. Why didn't Stella enter any details? I swear it wasn't there thirty minutes ago. Maybe I'd looked at the wrong day.

"Fuck," I mutter under my breath as I rub my temples to assuage the beginning of a headache. I hope it's not one of Teddy's endless brainstorming sessions. Our optimism had been tested earlier in the week when new budget projections showed us falling short of funding due to changes in California insurance laws. And since we've tapped every fundraising well dry, we're crossing our fingers and hoping that Colton's team pulls through with the needed sponsorships to keep everything on track. I look down at my schedule again, reining in my impatience at Stella's lack of response, and remind myself of Haddie's accusation when I'd snapped at her earlier this morning.

"Ooooh, someone's having Colton withdrawals," she chided as she added creamer to her coffee.

"Shut up," I muttered, shoving my bagel in the toaster with more force than necessary.

"I guess it's the toaster's fault you're pissy then." I shot her a glare of death, but her only response was a smarmy smile. "Look, I get it.

You're so used to getting fucked into next week that when you're stuck in this week you're beyond sexually frustrated. You've gotten used to having incredible sex regularly, and now he's been gone now for what? Nine days?"

"Eight," I snapped.

"Yeah." She laughed. "But it's not like you're counting right? And now Momma needs to *get some* to make her happy." I stifled my smile then even though my back was to her. "Christ, Rylee, it's nowhere near the real thing, but Skype the man and get yourself off if it's going to stop you from being such a bitch!"

"Who says I haven't," I responded coyly, extremely happy that she didn't see the blush creep over my cheeks as I remembered Colton's and my chat last night. *Oh the marvels of technology.*

"Well hot damn!" She slapped the kitchen table. "At least someone's getting some in this house this week." She laughed. I caved and finally turned around, my laughter joining hers. She brought the cup to her lips again and looked at me while she blew the steaming coffee cooler. "I'm happy for you, Rylee. Really happy. The man looks at you as if you're the only woman in the world." When I snorted at her telling her she's completely wrong, she just continued. "Colton's put that spark back in your eye. Made you confident and sure of yourself again. He's made you feel sexy too…don't give me that look," she told me when I narrowed my eyes at her. "I've seen the lingerie hanging to dry in your bathroom, sister, so don't even try to deny it. I love it! So when does the handsome stud get back anyway?"

"Two more days," I sighed.

"Thank God! Then you can stop being such a raving bitch!" she teased with a smile. "You've got it bad girl!"

"I know. I know." I shot her a quick smile as I stuffed my lunch into my bag, knowing the following forty-eight hours were going to drag big time. "I gotta go before I'm late. Love ya – bye."

"Love ya – bye."

I take a deep breath as I shake myself from my reverie. Haddie's right, *I've got it bad.* I turn in my chair and buzz Stella again.

"Yes?"

"There you are…hey what's up with this meeting taking up my whole afternoon?" I try to keep the irritation out of my voice, but it's hard. I've been working non-stop since Sunday and just want the afternoon to catch up.

"Um, I'm not sure."

What? Who took my overly efficient assistant and hid her? "*What do you mean you're not sure?"*

"Well…" I sense her discomfort even through her disembodied voice on the intercom. "I mean—"

"What's it for?"

"Well someone from CDE called over and asked that I clear your schedule for a very important meeting about the sponsorship program. Teddy was right here when they called and okayed it. Said he'd tell you…and I'm guessing by the sound in your voice that he didn't?"

My heart flutters at the mention of Colton's company and then deflates knowing that he's not going to be there. And then my mind starts turning and my heart accelerates because I have a feeling that this means I'm going to have to be one-on-one with Tawny and her team. Just the person I want to spend four hours confined in a room with.

"No, he didn't. Are you fucking kidding me?" I say before I can catch myself.

"Nope." She chuckles sympathetically, knowing I've been burning the candle at both ends. "I'm sorry. I know your day was packed, but I was able to move everything around. I left you a voicemail…I guess you didn't get to that either, huh?"

"Haven't even had a chance to listen to them since I first checked them this morning."

"Well at least you might get to see that hot hunk of a man hmmm?"

I laugh overtly at her comment, knowing the rumors are swirling around the office about what Colton and I are or aren't doing. I've yet to justify any of them except to say that we attended the gala together to promote the sponsorship despite what the caption in People said. I'm not sure if anyone believes me or not—and honestly I am way too busy to care—but I'm sure the water cooler has been a busy place as of late.

"Nah. When we spoke last week he mentioned that he'd be out of town for the week for some kind of promo junket," I lie.

"Too bad," she murmurs. "Looking at him during a four hour meeting would definitely put some pep in anybody's step." Her hearty laugh comes through the line, and I can hear it echo in stereo outside my office door.

"You're incorrigible, Stella. What time do I have to be there?"

"They're sending a car for you. It'll be here in just under thirty minutes."

Sending a car? Tawny probably wants to make sure I have no way to escape her evil plans for me. I snort a laugh at my thoughts and bring a hand up to cover my mouth to stifle it. "Okay, Stell…I don't like it but

I guess I have no choice, huh?"

"Nope," she agrees before I disconnect the line.

"Fucking great!" I mutter aloud before reaching for a tootsie roll in the bowl on my desk. I think I'm going to need the whole lot of them to help me cope with the rest of my afternoon.

"We're almost there," Sammy says from the driver's seat. "About ten more minutes."

"Okay. Thanks, Sammy," I murmur as I take in the beautiful interior of the G-class SUV. This must be yet another one of his collection of cars. I fight the smirk that wants to come. I don't think it matters how many he has; Sex is definitely my favorite.

Sammy glances at me in the rearview mirror, and I smile at him. I was shocked when he was the one who came to pick me up. I told him so, expressing that I was surprised Colton had left him behind on his trip. I thought that they were inseparable. Sammy had just given me a non-committal shrug without saying a word. And now my overactive imagination starts to roam on the ride over, and I begin to worry about Colton. What if he needs help to keep some crazy, irrational fan away from him and Sammy's not there to help protect him? I shake my head, telling myself I'm crazy. Colton admitted to me he was quick to throw down in his youth. I'm pretty sure he could hold his own if he needed to.

My phone beeps a text and I pull it out of my purse, a smile spreading on my face when I see it's from Colton.

Beckett scolded me for not giving you romantic gestures. RME. He says I need to give you the flowers and poetry variety. Here's the closest I get and the best we could come up with. Roses are red. Violets are blue. Sitting in Nashville. Thinking of you.

I laugh out loud at the image of Beckett and Colton sitting in Nashville having a discussion about me. I can very clearly see Colton rolling his eyes at Beckett's big brotherly recommendation of romantic gestures, all the while making up a nursery school rhyme to send to me instead. I quickly pull up the web on my phone and search for different versions of the preschool poem. After a few different links, I find the perfect one.

How sweet! And you said you didn't do romance. Be still my beating heart. Those must be some really boring meetings. Now, I have one for you. Roses are red. Violets are blue. I'm using my hand, while thinking of you. Xx.

I smirk as I hit send, pleased with my witty response and wishing I could see his face as he reads it. We drive a couple more minutes when my phone chimes again.

FYI – Dick's hard like a teenage boy. My turn—typing with one hand now: Roses are red. Lemons are sour. If you open your legs, I'll be there in an hour.

I bite back the laugh that bubbles up in my throat, squeezing my knees together to stifle the ache our little text tête-à-tête has stirred up. I look up and meet Sammy's eyes in the mirror, my cheeks blushing as if he knows what I'm reading, the dirty thoughts I'm thinking. I quickly avert my eyes and reply.

Quite the poet, Ace. Too bad you're not here. The flight's at least four hours. I don't know if I can wait that long. Might just have to take care of myself. xx Gotta go. I need my hands for other things now.

I hit send as we pull into the parking lot of a large, nondescript, gray three-story building with a mirrored glass exterior. The building spans the better part of the block, and the only marker denoting its occupants are the letters "CD Enterprises" in electric blue at the top row of windows.

"Here we are," Sammy murmurs, and my anxiety ratchets up at the thought of having to sit across from Tawny. I close my eyes momentarily and inhale a long breath while Sammy moves around to my side of the car to open my door. I need to keep my cool with Tawny because the last thing I need is to be known as Colton's bitch of a girlfriend. Thank God I had my little texting distraction to ease the dread.

Within moments he's taken me in a side entrance and leads me up the stairs to a waiting conference room. "Someone will be right with you," he says as he walks out.

"Thank you, Sammy."

"My pleasure, Ms. Thomas."

I turn and appraise the conference room I've been ushered into. There is a long, typical looking conference table in the midst of the room with walls painted a warm coffee color, but the focal point of the room is the wall opposite the doorway. It's a wall of tinted glass, and as I step closer to it, I realize that the opening looks down upon a massive garage of sorts. Around several race cars there is a flurry of activity with men moving here and there. Snap-on tool boxes in cobalt blue line one wall of the garage with a chair rail of sorts, made of stainless steel diamond plate across the midsection, with various posters and banners above it on the wall. I step closer, fascinated and feeling the energy from all of the activity below.

"Roses are red. Violets are blue." The voice at my back startles me, but I whip around knowing that rasp anywhere. "It better be only *my* hands on you."

"Colton!" His name comes out in a breathless rush of air and despite every nerve in my body tingling at his proximity, my feet remain cemented to the floor. I swear my heart rate doubles at the sight of him, and although my intention is to remain cool and mask the excitement wreaking havoc on my system, I can't help the wide grin that spreads over my lips.

"Surprise!" he exclaims, holding his arms out to the side. He steps into the room and shuts the door behind him.

It's seeing him in the flesh that makes me realize how much I've missed him. How in such a short amount of time I've gotten used to him being a part of my day-to-day life. We both take a few steps toward each other, drinking the other in. The hungry look in his eyes steals my breath and hints at things that make my center ache with liquid heat.

My eyes move to that sensuous mouth of his. It's quirked up at one corner, as if his thoughts aren't exactly pure and innocent. And I hope they aren't because then they'd be matching mine.

My body vibrates with his nearness, confirming that time has done nothing to dampen the instant pull he has on me. I surpassed stepping cautiously off of the edge of falling in love with him a long time ago and am now currently plunging headfirst.

Our eyes lock as we slowly close the distance between us, and I know it's not possible, but in that instant I swear that I see a flash of my future in his eyes. The revelation unnerves me and releases the butterflies I have flitting around in my stomach.

We stop within a foot of each other, and I angle my head up so that my eyes can remain on his. "Hiya, Ace." I smile at him, my pulse still jumping erratically.

"Ili," he mouths, that shy smile tipping up the corners of his lips. We stare at each other for a beat, and before I can process the thought, Colton's hands are fisted in my hair, yanking me forward, his lips claiming mine. He tastes of mint and urgency and everything Colton, and even though I'm drowning in him, I still can't seem to get enough. His tongue licks in my mouth and teases by pulling back and then darting back in again.

His mouth captures my moan as he lowers his hand on my back and skirts under my sweater to draw his calloused fingers against my bare skin before pressing me into the hard length of his body. And just when the kiss starts to soften and become tender, Colton's mouth dominates mine again, our hands becoming a series of touches and movements as if we can't feel enough of each other.

He breaks from our kiss, his forehead resting on mine and his breath panting against my lips. "I couldn't let you resort to your hand, Rylee," he murmurs, and I can feel his lips form a smile as they press against mine, smothering the carefree laugh his words incite. "You're mine now. I'm the only one allowed to give you pleasure."

Before I can think of a witty retort, Colton's mouth is on mine again, his tongue delving between my lips, his body pushing me backwards so my hips hit the edge of the conference table. He presses me to sit down, nudging my legs apart with his knee, and steps in between them. I am now at a height disadvantage to him, and he leans over and cups my cheeks in his hands, his tongue soothing over where he just nipped my bottom lip. I keen with need as he continues his tantalizing assault on my mouth and all sense of coherence is lost.

In an unexpected move, he pulls his face back, his hands still framing my cheeks in possession, and stares at me. His eyes swim with emotion as his jaw clenches from unspoken words. We stare at each other and pant from the need that is driving every action and subsequent reaction. Feelings I want to confess die on my lips as the pad of his thumb reaches over to graze them tenderly. Something has shifted between us, and I can't put my finger on it, but the look in his eyes tells me all I need to know: He wants me as much as I want him. Any doubts of mine that he wants another vanish with this singular look.

"I missed you, Rylee," he says softly before wrapping his arms around me and folding me into him. He places his cheek on the top of my head, his arms squeezing tighter. Hearing him say it, admitting that I am a part of his everyday life too, warms me on the inside.

"I missed you too," I murmur as I melt into the comfort of his arms, "more than I want to admit." A small sound rumbles in his chest, and I know that my words have affected him. We sit like this for a few moments, reveling in the warmth and comfort from each other that we've missed over the past week and a half; we're absorbing what we've finally acknowledged, verbalized, and are both accepting in our own ways. I plant a soft kiss over his heart without thinking. "I really like my surprise. You sure know how to spoil a girl. Thank you."

"You're welcome," he tells me, kissing the top of my head again. "I wasn't sure how your office would react if I were to waltz in and take you over the edge of your desk."

"What?" I laugh out loud as my body heats at the thought. I lean back so I can look up at his eyes. "That was your plan, huh?"

"Desperate times call for desperate measures."

"I believe you once told me that you were far from desperate," I tease, throwing his words back at him.

He chuckles softly before pursing his lips. "That was before I spent an endless amount of time, in God knows how many boring meetings, thinking about what exactly I'd like to be doing with you." A lascivious grin spreads across his lips. "And to you."

"That's a lot of dirty thoughts."

"Oh, Rylee, you have no idea."

I swallow loudly, the lust that leaps in his eyes and darkens his irises giving me a hint. "So, you planned on acting out these impure thoughts in my office? On my desk?" I arch my brow in mock disapproval, but the smirk on my face betrays me.

"Yep. I told you," he says, playing along, "I take what's mine when I want it..."

"With an audience of my co-workers?"

"Ah-huh." He grins like a mischievous schoolboy. "I'd planned on coming straight from the airport this morning but I didn't think Teddy would approve of it."

I run my tongue across my top lip as I look up at him, placing my hands behind me on the table so I can lean back on them—my shoulders arching and my breasts pushing forward. I take notice of Colton's eyes and their languorous appraisal of my new posture—his eyes heating and tongue darting out to wet his lip. "Since when do you care what people think?"

"Oh, sweetheart, believe me, I don't..." he smirks "...but we still have to preserve your reputation."

"I think that was ruined the minute I started going out with you."

"Probably." He shrugs in nonchalance. "I still think that your boss might object to his star employee being fucked on her desk."

"But your boss?" I ask playfully. "He's okay with his employees doing something like that? Here?"

A slow, suggestive smile curls one corner of his mouth, his dimple deepening. "Oh I think so," he says, leaning down and laying his hands beside my knees on the table.

"You think so? Why's that?" I ask, narrowing my eyes at him as I continue to play along.

"Oh, he has quite a vested interest in this situation here," Colton murmurs as he leans closer into me.

"Oh really?" I breathe as I involuntarily arch my back so my breasts brush against his chest. I bite my bottom lip as we stare at each other.

Colton's breath whispers over my face. "*Sometimes it's fucking great to be the boss,*" he says before lowering his lips to mine again, but this time it's an achingly slow kiss that tantalizes and torments me to the point of no return.

I want him, and I want him now. My God the man makes me crave with an intensity I never thought was imaginable. His fingers begin a slow, languid slide up my arms, my body coiling at the thought of where his talented fingers will trail to next.

I lean my head back as his mouth skims down my jaw and expose my neck for him. I reach his hip with one hand and pull him harder against me as his mouth tempts and dips below the neckline of my sweater.

"Colton." I exhale as need swelters through my core and fire spreads in my veins.

A loud beep fills the room suddenly and Colton sags against me as I hear, "Excuse me, Colton?" coming from the phone on the credenza.

"Fuck," he mutters quietly against my neck. "Yes?"

"Beckett's looking all over for you. Something about an issue with Eddie…" she trails off as if she's afraid of his response.

"Christ!" he swears aloud, his body tensing in response to her comment.

"My thoughts exactly."

"Where?"

"They're on the garage floor."

"I'll be right there. Thanks, Brooke."

The phone clicks off as Colton straightens his frame to its full height. I push myself off of the conference table as he walks over to the glass-viewing wall to look at the garage below. When he turns back toward me he has transformed from the playful lover to the consummate businessman.

"I apologize, Ry. I have to go take care of something down below. Come with me?" he asks, holding his hand out, and I'm slightly taken back. Mr. I-Don't-Do-Commitment wants to hold my hand at his work? Isn't that a little too much of a 'public display' for someone with his history?

"I can stay here if you'd like," I offer meekly, not wanting to leave his side.

He just looks at me oddly before reaching out and grabbing my hand and pulling me with him. "I'm not letting go of you, Ryles, until I get my fill of you," he warns in a promise that causes flames of desire to lick at my center, "and that may just take a long fucking time."

Chapter Twenty-Four

Beckett nods to me, the ghost of a smile curling his lips as Colton leads me from the garage floor. We make our way to a side door that Colton ushers me through, and I find us in a stairwell of sorts. "Up." Colton points as he places a hand on my back.

I ascend in front of him, his hand remaining on the swell of my backside the entire first flight. "Did I tell you how damn sexy you look today?" His voice rasps from behind me.

I look over my shoulder and smile at him. "Thank you," I reply, recognizing the salacious look in his eyes. "But I have a feeling that your view is a little jaded from a lack of sex."

The hum of appreciation in the back of his throat makes me smile. "Oh, baby, there's definitely nothing wrong with my view," he says with a chuckle. I start to go up the second flight again, but this time Colton's hands seem to be touching me in various places with every step. A soft caress up the back of my thigh. A slight brush down my bare arm. A quick tap on my backside.

I know exactly what he's doing, but it's not like he needs to stoke the embers because I'm already a wild fire of need. Knowing that he wants me like this, needing and aching for more of his touch, makes me feel wanton and willing to play the game too. I sway my hips a little more than usual as I walk across the second landing. My hand purposely snagging my hem to reveal just a trace of what's beneath it.

Colton's lightning quick as he grabs me from behind, both of his arms wrapping around me in a vice like grip. "You little minx." He growls in my ear as I feel the play of his muscles against my back. "Are you really going to tease me like that when I've been without being

204

inside of you—tasting you for way too long? Especially when you know how desperate I am to have you."

Thank God he's as needy as I am because I'm not going to be able to hold out much longer. He nips my earlobe when I try to shrug away, the need almost debilitating. "Desperation doesn't suit you. It's not like you're going to do something about it with a building full of your employees nearby?" I taunt playfully.

Colton spins me around, his body presses against mine, and his hands clasp at my lower back. The smirk on his face matches the wicked gleam in his eye. *"Oh, Ryles, didn't you know that dares like that are what rebels like me live for?"* He leans in, his lips a breath from my ear as my heart pounds against my rib cage. "I will have you, Rylee, when I want, where I want, and how I want. *It's best you remember that."*

The dominance in his voice excites me. The threat-filled promise arouses me. The feel of his body against mine vibrating with need and his hands possessing my skin cause moisture to pool at the apex of my thighs. I tilt my head up and my lips part—needing his mouth on mine desperately. From what I read in Colton's eyes, he feels the same way. The days apart have fueled our desire into a raging inferno. All I want to do is take anything and everything he can give me. The temptation of paradise at my fingertips.

I lean in to him succumbing to my craving, but before I can have a single taste, he spins me around and emits a deviously pained chuckle. "One more flight," Colton says smacking my backside before placing both hands on my waist and urging me forward. I sigh out in sexual frustration and from the ache strangling parts deep within me. I'm on my second step when I feel the cool air of the stairwell on my ass as he lifts up the back of my skirt to discover what's beneath.

I smile to myself, knowing exactly what he'll find. It was one of those mornings where I didn't feel particularly attractive, and I was grumpy because I was missing him, so I decided to make myself feel better by wearing something sexy and girly underneath. For some reason wearing lingerie always makes me walk with a little added bounce to my step when I need it. Little did I know how well that decision would pay off, but I do now when I hear Colton suck in a hiss of breath at what he finds.

"Sweet Jesus," he mutters on a pained draw of air.

I move one of my legs to prop it up on the next riser and stop as I feel his finger trace the top line of my stockings and then up the strap of my garter. I look coyly back over my shoulder at him, "Is there a problem, Ace?"

He just smirks at me and shakes his head subtly, his eyes steadfast on what I can assume is the mixture of lace and satin beneath. "Woman, you really don't play fair do you?" he exhales in a groan before tearing his eyes away to look up at mine.

"Whatever do you mean?" I bat my eyelashes at him and purposely bite my lower lip. I love watching his mouth part and his tongue dart out to lick his lower lip as his eyes darken and cloud—his stare unwavering on mine—green eyes to violet. I love knowing that I can bring him to such a state of desire without even touching him. And it's all because of him that I can do this. He makes me feel confident and sexy and desirable when all I've ever felt before is run of the mill and unable to own my sexuality.

Colton's eyes remain on mine but his fingers feather over my flesh to the edge of my panties. My muscles quiver at the proximity of his touch—so close yet so far from where I want his fingers to claim. *Where I need them to.* "Two can play this game," he murmurs as he steps closer. "I seem to recall you saying predictability doesn't suit me. Why don't I show you how absolutely right you are...*right now?*"

I bite down harder on my lip to stifle a moan as his deft fingers pull my panties aside and he slips a finger into my molten core. I brace my hand on the stair rail beside me as he pulls out, sliding up and down the folds of my sex before tucking three fingers in me. "Oh, baby, I love how wet and ready you are for me." He growls as I gasp out. "Do you have any idea what that does to me? How much knowing you want me turns me inside out?"

"Colton, please," I plead. Right now I am not beneath begging for him to fill me. To take me to that unprecedented edge that only he can help me climb at a lightning pace.

"Tell me what you want, Rylee." He chuckles as he withdraws his fingers, and I groan at the sudden feeling of emptiness.

I throw my head back. My eyes close as my body convulses with such need that its evidence glistens on Colton's hand. "You. Colton." I pant. "I. Want. You."

He runs his finger over my bottom lip before leaning in and replacing his fingertip with his tongue, darting it between my lips before pulling away. I can't help the whimper that falls from my mouth. "Tell me, baby."

"Only you, Colton."

In a flash he has me spun around, my back pressed up against the wall of the stairwell. His chest heaves and his jaw clenches as he looks at me with such intensity that I am lost to him. The outside world ceases to exist in this moment as I stand here exposed and unbidden. I am stripped physically and emotionally. I have never been more his.

Colton lifts my skirt back up, and forces my legs further apart. He smiles lasciviously as he sinks slowly to his knees, his eyes never leaving mine.

My rational thoughts should kick in now. My head should be treading atop of the waterfall of lust I'm drowning in and tell me that I'm in the stairwell at his work, but it does no such thing. Instead, my traitorous body shudders in anticipation, and when Colton notes it, his eyes spark and smile taunts as he leans into me. Within seconds a single laugh slips between my trembling lips as he rips my panties off of me effortlessly and stuffs them in his pocket. My mind and body are so focused on him, on what I need from him, that I don't give the fact that he's ruined yet another pair of underwear without a second thought.

His fingers part my folds, his eyes never leaving mine, and he closes his mouth over my nub of nerve endings. My hands fly to fist in his hair, and I fight with everything I have to not close my eyes and give into the ecstasy of his clever tongue. I want to watch him while he drives me up and over, but the sensation is so strong that it overtakes me and I arch—my neck, my head, my back—pushing my hips out so I can rock against him.

He pulls my leg up and drapes it over his shoulder before adding his fingers to the mix. They press, push, and circle inside of me. My muscles clench so tight that when my climax claims me, I feel like my body shatters in a million pieces of ecstasy. Colton runs his tongue up and back over my sex before licking inside of me, drawing out every last tremor of my orgasm.

I sag against the wall behind me, needing its support because my legs have just been rendered boneless. I close my eyes and try to calm myself, but he has just obliterated my senses with such devastation that *I've now lost a part of myself to him forever.*

"My God, woman, a man could get drunk on the taste of you." He groans as he places a soft kiss on my abdomen before rising from his knees. I open my eyes to his smug, satisfied smirk and eyes lidded heavy with desire. He leans in and kisses me forcefully, the taste of myself on his lips unexpectedly arousing.

I moan into his mouth, my hands snaking down his body to cup his erection through his pants, still wanting more, still needing more. He breaks from the kiss with a tortured groan and pulls away from me. "Colton," I murmur, "let me take care of you."

"Not here," he tells me, smoothing my skirt down and smirking as he stuffs what's left of my panties further down into his pocket. "I want to hear you scream out my name when I take you. I want to hear it when you fall apart from the things I'm going to do to you, Rylee. I want to claim you. Make you mine. Ruin you for any other man that dares to think of touching you." He grimaces from the conviction of his words.

"You already have, Colton," I breathe out without thinking, reaching out to place my fingertips to his lips. "I'm yours..." My words trail off as he stares at me, his jaw working overtime as he absorbs the words I've said.

A ghost of a smile mixed with an uncertain disbelief plays on his lips before shaking it away and pushing it aside. "I—we can't continue here with what I want to do, but this," he says, motioning to me and the wall, "will tide me over." He flashes a quick grin at me before grabbing my hand and climbing the last flight of stairs.

I follow him, knowing my heart and body are far from recovered from that little episode. Haddie's words flash through my head, and I can't help but disagree with her. When it comes to Colton, I don't just have it bad. I've drowned, been consumed, and am utterly and undeniably his.

Colton pushes open the door at the top of the stairwell, and I'm surprised to find us in the interior of a very masculine and sparsely decorated office. Assumptions aside, I know it's his because it's so similar to his office in Malibu. I step in behind him when I hear a gasp.

"Oh, Colt, you scared me half to death!" the feminine voice exclaims, and instantly my back bristles at her familiarity with him. Does the woman have to be everywhere? *Fuucckk!*

"Can I help you with something, Tawn?" Colton asks, and I swear that I hear an edge to the curiosity in his question.

Tawny straightens up from where she is leaned over his desk and straightens the papers she is fumbling with. Of course she looks flawless in her cleavage defying shirt, skin-tight pants, and freshly made-up face. The woman is absolutely, fucking perfectly stunning. Her lips form a startled *O* shape as she looks at Colton before her eyes dart over to me and then back to him. The catty, territorial girl inside of me wants her to notice the flush on my cheeks and that just fucked smirk on my face so it's reaffirmed that she's nothing more than a blip on Colton's radar.

"Sorry. You scared me." She exhales. "I was just looking for the Penzoil contract. I wasn't sure if you'd had a chance to sign it. That's all." She smiles too sweetly.

I've got a place she can shove that fake smile.

Colton looks at her for a moment as if he's trying to decipher something, but shakes his head absently. "Tawny, you've met Rylee, right?"

Tawny's eyes flit back and forth between us noting our joined hands before re-plastering the smile that has slightly fallen from her lips. "Something like that," she says as she steps out from behind his desk and walks—no, saunters—toward us. There really is no other way to describe it. Her eyes remain steadfast on Colton's. She is definitely one of those women who are acutely aware of every move of her body and its effect on the opposite sex.

If I disliked her before, I truly detest her now.

Colton gives me a warning look as he feels my hand tense at her approach. "So good to see you again," I lie, and I wonder if he has any idea of the future WWE Smackdown he's just initiated. I have to stifle the giggle I feel bubbling up at the image of Tawny and me flying off of the ropes of a wrestling ring with bad costumes and even worse moves as we fight over the trophy of Colton.

"Yes, how unexpected to see you here." She smiles, and I'm observant enough to note Colton's eyebrows raise in amusement at the obvious tension between the two of us.

He turns to me, his eyes reissuing the warning to be on my best behavior as if he knows my WWE thoughts. "As you know, Tawny here is the head of my marketing team and is actually the one who came up with the lap match sponsorship idea."

Yes, please remind me again so I don't reach across and slap her because it's so damn tempting.

"Yes," I exclaim indifferently, knowing I should thank her properly but not wanting to. I pause for a moment, but my manners finally prevail. "And Corporate Cares is appreciative of all of the hard work you've put behind this," I say with sincerity.

"You're welcome," she says, her eyes never leaving Colton's although she is addressing me. Does he not see her infatuation with him? It's so obvious it's ludicrous. "We've already landed some sponsors, but we have a few more irons left in the fire for some big name corporations. We're wrapping that up right now and most likely will get that magic number to solidify the funding for the project."

"Incredible," I say, trying to express my enthusiasm while hiding my complete disdain for her as she oozes—yes oozes, for that's what she does—her charm all over Colton.

I observe her watching Colton, and it irks me that I suddenly feel like an outsider. She turns slowly to me, a snarky smirk on her face, and I have to remind myself it was me that Colton was just doing inappropriate but hot as hell things to in the stairwell. Not her. *And with that mental reminder, I'm more than ready to play this game.*

"If you think you can contribute in any way…Rylee, right?" she asks apologetically as I just tilt my head to the side and bite my tongue at her catty barb because she damn well knows my name. "Please feel free to let me know."

"Thank you—but I'm sure that any help I could provide…would be…" I look up in thought as I search for the perfect word "…*inconsequential.*" My eyes shift from her to Colton as I speak. A smile plays at the corners of my lips, and I arch an eyebrow in question. "Don't you think, Ace?"

"Inconsequential," Colton mouths, a smirk on his lips as he shakes his head at my word choice. He holds my stare and I can see that even with this stunning woman beside me he desires me.

Me.

The air between us fills with an electricity as our gazes hold. I can sense Tawny's discomfort as she shuffles from foot to foot in the charged silence. "Thank you, Tawny," Colton says dismissing her without breaking our connection, "Rylee and I have somewhere we need to be," he concludes, standing and reaching out for my hand.

And hopefully that someplace he needs to be is in me.

Chapter Twenty-Five

"You know, Rylee, you sure are changing how I look at certain things in the world," Colton comments as we pull into my driveway.

"Why's that?" I murmur distractedly, my mind still trying to process the events of the day—that Colton is here—with me.

"I'll never wipe down the hood of my car or trudge up a stairwell again without thinking of you," he says, flashing his megawatt grin at me. "You'll forever be the one who made me look at mundane things in a new light."

I laugh out loud as he leans over to give me a chaste kiss before getting out of the car. I watch him come around the hood to open my door, and I'm suddenly shaken by his comment. A part of me smiles at the knowledge that he will never be able to forget me while another part saddens at the notion that this won't last forever. Even if we could, I don't think he'd ever accept it. The problem is that I'm the one who keeps getting pulled under, deeper and deeper. I'm the one trying to stay afloat. I'm the one who needs a pit stop.

Colton swings the door open and the comment on his lips dies when he sees the look on my face. I've tried to mask my sudden sadness, but obviously I haven't been too successful. "What is it?" he asks, stepping into the doorway of the car between the V of my legs.

"Nothing." I shrug, shaking it off. "I'm just being silly," I tell him as his hands slide up my thighs and under my skirt to where my naked sex is.

I sigh at the feathered touch of his fingertips over my skin as I look up at him. The smirk on his face draws me from my mood, and I smile back at him. "You know, we need to do something about this habit you have of ripping my panties off."

"No we don't," he murmurs as he leans down and slants his mouth over mine.

"Don't distract me." I giggle as his hands slide farther up my thighs and his thumbs brush at my strip of curls, my body arching into him in reaction. "I'm being very serious."

"Uh-huh...I prefer you distracted," he says against my lips. "And I also like you when you're very serious." He imitates my tone, causing me to giggle again.

"You're starting to put a dent in my drawers," I respond breathlessly as his thumbs graze lower this time.

"I know and I hope to be again very soon." He chuckles against the side of my neck, the vibration soothing.

"You're a hopeless case." I sigh as I run my hands up his chest and loop them around his neck before claiming his lips with mine.

"That I am, Rylee..." he sighs when we part lips "...that I am."

We enter the quiet of my house. Haddie will be working late at an event tonight so the house is all ours, and I intend to take full advantage of that. "You hungry?" I ask him as I lay my stuff down on the kitchen counter.

"In more ways than one," he smirks at me and I just shake my head at him.

"Well how about I fix us something and take care of your first hunger, get you nice and fortified, and then I'll make sure I offer up some dessert for your second hunger," I tell him over my shoulder as I bend over and peer in the refrigerator.

"Whether it's offered up or not, sweetheart, *I'll be taking it*," he says, and I can hear the smile in his voice. I forget a moment too late about my bare nether region as I'm bending over because Colton runs a finger across my naked backside before landing a playful slap on it making me jump and jarring my constant ache for him into a smoldering burn.

We eat the simple meal I've concocted in a comfortable exchange. He tells me about his endless meetings in Nashville and what he'd hoped to accomplish during them. I tell him about the progress on the project at the office as well as little tidbits about the boys' week. I find it endearing that he actually listens when I talk about the boys and that he asks questions letting me know that he has a genuine interest in them. It's important to me that he understands what a big part of my life they are.

"So why'd your trip get cut short?" I ask him while we finish up our meal.

He wipes his mouth with a napkin. "We started reviewing meetings we'd already had. It started to get redundant..." he shrugs "...and I hate redundancy."

That's not what Teagan says, flickers through my head thinking how she told me that Colton likes to dabble with past flings while in between current ones. I chastise myself for trying to sabotage a perfectly good time.

"Besides," he says, looking up from his plate to me, "*I missed you.*"

And now I feel like crap for my little mental barb. "*You missed me?*" I ask incredulously.

"Yes, I missed you," he says, smiling shyly, his foot nudging mine beneath the table to emphasize his words.

How is it four simple words from his mouth could mean so much to me? The emotionally unavailable bad boy I tried so hard to keep at arms' length, I now never want to let go.

"I could tell by the beautiful poetry you wrote me," I tease.

He flashes me a heart-warming grin that makes me want to pinch myself to know this is real and that smile is meant for me. "Those were clean compared to some of the nasty ones we wrote." He raises his eyebrows and his eyes alight with humor.

"Oh really?"

"Yep. I think I'd rather show you though."

"Is that so?" I smirk as I bite into my last strawberry.

"Yep, and we brainstormed the meaning of Ace as well."

"Oh, I can't wait to hear these..." I raise my eyebrows at him and laugh.

"Always creating ecstasy."

"Nope." I laugh. "You do know that you've made such a big deal about this that you're going to be so disappointed at the real answer right?"

He just smirks at me as I get up and start clearing the dishes, rejecting his offer of assistance. We chat about the sponsorship some until the ringing of his phone interrupts us.

"One sec," he says as he answers the phone. He holds a short conversation about something work related and then says, "Thanks, Tawny. Have a good night."

I automatically roll my eyes at the name and he catches me. "You really dislike her, don't you?" he asks, a bemused look on his face.

I sigh deeply, wondering if I want to tackle this right here and right now. She is an ex-girlfriend, friend of the family that his parents obviously love, and an important member of his CDE team. Do I really want to fight a losing battle here? If I'm going to be with Colton, I have to face the fact that she is going to be a part of his life, whether I like it or not. I twist my lips as I contemplate the right words to use. "Let's just say that she and I have had a couple of exchanges that lead me to believe she's not as innocent as she seems…and I'll leave it at that," I tell him.

He stares at me for a long time and a lopsided smile forms on his lips. "You're jealous of her, aren't you?" he asks as if he's just had an Oprah ah-hah moment.

I return the same measuring stare at him before averting my eyes and rising to wipe off the counter that I've already cleaned. "Jealous no…but c'mon, Colton." I laugh with disbelief. "Look at her and look at me. It's pretty easy to see why I'd feel that way."

"What are you talking about?" Colton asks as I hear the chair scoot out from underneath him.

"Seriously? She's a walking wet dream. Perfect in every way whereas I'm just…I'm just me." I shrug in acceptance.

Colton rests his hips on the counter beside me as I fiddle with the dishtowel, and I can feel the weight of his stare on me. "You're something else, you know that?" he says, exasperation in his voice.

"Why's that?" I ask, suddenly feeling embarrassed about revealing my insecurities when it comes to Tawny. Why did I even say anything? Me and my big mouth.

Colton pulls on my hand, but I don't budge. Someone as attractive as Colton has no clue what it's like to be insecure. "C'mon," he says, pulling my hand again without taking no for an answer. "I want to show you something."

I follow him reluctantly down the hallway to my bedroom, curious as to what he's being so adamant about. We enter my bedroom and Colton leads me to my en suite bathroom. He ushers me in so that my back is to his front. His eyes blaze into mine as his hands run up the sides of my torso and back down. On their second pass, his fingers veer over and start undoing the buttons on my sweater. Although I feel and see what he's doing in the mirror, my eyes instinctually look down.

"Uh-uh, Rylee," he murmurs, his voice a seductive whisper against my neck. "Don't take your eyes off of mine." My eyes flicker back up to his, and we stare at each other like this for a few moments, neither of us speaking. Colton's fingers finish undoing my sweater, and he steps back as he pulls it off of my shoulders. His fingers rasp across the bare skin of my lower back, and then I feel the zipper on my skirt being lowered. Colton's hands run over my waist and then slide inside the loosened waistline of my skirt. He pushes my skirt down until it clears my hips and falls to the floor.

I chance a glance down to where his hands remain in the front of my pelvis, their olive color a stark contrast to my pale skin. The look of ownership they have over my body—big strong hands lying over silk and lace and flesh—cause my breath to hitch between my parted lips.

"Eyes right here, Rylee," Colton commands as he steps up against me once more, placing his head to the right of mine. I keep my eyes fastened to his as they give a leisurely appraisal of my body and the bra, garter, and stockings I have on, sans the panties he took care of earlier. When his eyes finish their sweep, and they connect with mine again in our mirrored reflection, I see so many things swimming in their depths.

"Rylee, you are breathtaking. Can't you see that?" he questions, his hands running up my rib cage and stopping at by bra. "You are so much more than any one man could handle in a lifetime." He sweeps a finger inside the cup of one side of my bra and pushes it down so that my breast rests above the collapsed cup, my nipple already pebbled and aching for more. He moves to the other side and repeats the same process, but this time I can't help the soft moan that escapes my lips at his touch. I lay my head back on his shoulder and close my eyes at the sensation.

"Open, Rylee," he orders, and I snap them back open to his. "I want you to see what I see. I want you to see how sexy and desirable and fucking hot you are," he whispers against the bare skin of my shoulder. "I want you to see what you do to me. How you—in this body that is beautiful inside and out—cause me to come undone. *Can unravel me.*" His hands travel down to my hips before one slowly travels back up, rubbing back up between my breasts and then holding onto the side of my neck while the other travels lower to slide softly over the mound of my sex. "Can reduce me to nothing and build me up all at the same time." His words seduce me. The eroticism of the moment entices me. He completely mesmerizes me.

It takes everything I have to not close my eyes, tilt my head back, and give into the thunderstorm of sensation that he is evoking with his touch, but I am unable to due to his firm grip on my neck. His sweet seduction of words leaves me wet and wanting while the intimate connection between our gazes fills me emotionally.

"I want you to watch me while I take you, Rylee. I want you to watch each of us as we crash over that edge. I want you to see why this is enough for me. *Why I choose you.*"

His words course through me, opening locks on places deep within that I've been trying to keep guarded. My soul ignites. My heart swells. My body anticipates. I inhale in a shuddered breath, his foreplay of words successful in their pursuit of arousal. His eyes smolder with a mixture of need and desire.

"Hands on the counter, Rylee," Colton orders as he pushes me forward on the back with one hand while the other hand grips onto my hip. I can feel him hard and ready against my backside through his pants and push back into him. "Head up!" he commands, and I comply as his hand snakes south and slowly parts me.

"Colton." I gasp, fighting the natural inclination to close my eyes at the overwhelming sensations rocking through my body when he eases a finger in me and then out to spread my moisture around. I keep my eyes on his and smirk when I notice that he's having trouble with his own composure as well. The rigid tension in his jaw and fire leaping in his eyes incites me. His fingers slide up and tease my bundle of nerves while I feel him fumbling at my backside with his button and zipper. "Now," I plead, my insides unfurling into an oblivion of need. "Quickly."

I can see the wicked grin that blankets Colton's face in the crinkles around his eyes as he positions his rigid head at my opening. "Do you want something, Rylee?" he asks as he just barely pulses into me.

"Colton." I gasp, lowering my head in the painfully exquisite agony of needing more.

"Eyes!" He growls against my shoulder as he denies us both the pleasure we so desperately want. "Say it, Rylee."

"Colt—"

"Say it!" he orders, his face the picture of a man on the verge of losing control.

"Please, Colton..." I gasp "...please." And he plunges inside of me completely in one slick thrust. The unexpected movement steals my breath and catapults me with an explosion of white-hot heat.

"Oh God, Rylee." He groans wildly, his eyes turning to slits, his eyelids weighted with desire. He wraps his arms around me, his fingertips pressing into my flesh, and his cheek pressed against the back of my neck as my body adjusts to his invasion.

He places a row of open mouth kisses on the line of my shoulder and up to my ear before he straightens up and starts to move. Really move. Giving me exactly what I need because right now I don't care about slow and steady. I want hard and fast, and he doesn't disappoint when he sets a punishing rhythm that drags out inexplicable sensations from my depths with every thrust out and drive back in.

I lose myself in his steady tempo, our eyes still locked on each other. The look on Colton's face takes my breath away as his eyes darken and face pulls tight with pleasure. He reaches a hand forward to my breast and rolls my nipple between his fingers. An incoherent moan slips from my lips, the fire inside me almost too much to bear. With his one hand still gripped on my hip, he moves his other from my breast to my shoulder and pulls us against each other, my back to his front, slowing his relentless pace to grind his hips in a circle inside of me.

"Look at yourself, Rylee," he murmurs in my ear between movements. "Look how goddamn sexy you are right now. Why would I want anyone else?"

I break from his reflective gaze and look at my own reflection. Skin red from his hands. Nipples pert and pink from pleasure. The folds of my sex swollen with desire. My lips are parted. My cheeks are flushed. My eyes are wide and expressive. *And alive.* My body reacts instinctively to Colton's movements—driven by such unexpected need, fueled by such a relentless desire, and crashing into unimaginable possibilities. I look at this mysterious woman in the mirror, and a slow, sensuous smile ghosts my lips as I look back to Colton. Our eyes lock again and I acknowledge for once that I see what he sees. That I accept it.

Colton pushes my back forward so that my hands can brace on the sink as he slowly eases in and out of me several times. One of his hands maps my hip and over the front to tease my clit, and my body squeezes at the sensation, my velvet walls milking his cock.

"Fuuucckk!" He groans, throwing his head back, forgetting his own rule about eye contact momentarily. He is absolutely stunning at this moment. Magnificent like an Adonis. Head back, lips parted in pleasure, neck strained with impending release, and my name a pant on his lips. He starts moving again, picking up the pace, dragging me to the edge of ecstasy with each relentless drive. He tilts his head back up and locks his eyes on mine.

The wave pushes me higher and higher, the intensity building, my legs weakening as pleasure tightens everywhere. And just before I crash into oblivion, I can see in his face that he's past the point of no return as well.

We crash over the cusp together: eyes clouded, lips parted, souls united, hearts spellbound, and bodies drowning in spirals of sensation.

My knees buckle beneath me as my muscles reverberate with my climax. Colton's rough hands hold me in place as he empties himself into me. His hands remain tight on my hips for a moment longer, as if the single action is enough to keep us from both sliding to the floor.

Eventually I straighten up and lean back against him, angling my head back onto his shoulder where I finally close my eyes, allowing myself a moment to absorb what I've just experienced.

I am overwhelmed and emotionally shaken. I know I loved Max with everything I had, but it pales in comparison to what Colton and I just shared. Together we are so intense, so volatile, so powerful, so intimate that I don't think I've ever felt closer to another human being as I do with Colton right now. My body trembles with the acceptance of it as he withdraws slowly from me and turns me to face him.

I try to bury my head in his shoulder, to avoid eye contact with him because I feel completely stripped bare, naked, and vulnerable—more so than any other time in my life. Colton puts a finger to my chin and lifts my face up to his. His eyes search mine in silence, and for a moment I think I see how I feel reflected in his, but I don't know if that's possible. How was it a few weeks ago this man before me was a complete stranger and now when I look at him, I see my whole world?

I know Colton senses something different in me, but he doesn't ask, just accepts, and for that I'm grateful. He leans down and brushes a tender kiss on my lips that brings tears to my eyes before wrapping his arms around me. I revel in the feeling of his silent strength, and before I can even think properly, my mouth is opening. "Colton?"

"Hmmm?" he murmurs against the top of my head.

I love you. It takes everything to stifle the words on my lips. I want to scream it out loud. "I...I...that was *wow*," I recover, silently saying the other three words I want to say.

"Wow is right." He chuckles against my temple.

Chapter Twenty-Six

I awake to Colton's warm body pressed up against the back of mine. His hand cups my bare breast, and his finger draws lazy circles around its shape, over and over until my nipple tightens from his touch. I smile softly to myself and sink back into him, absorbing the moment and the emotions I'm feeling.

"Good morning." His voice rumbles against the back of my neck, and he places a soft kiss there as his hand slowly traces lower down the curve of my body.

"Hmm," is all I can muster as the feeling of him hard and ready against me already has me willing and wanting.

"That good, huh?" He laughs.

"Mmm-hmm," I respond again because there is nowhere else I'd rather be right now than waking up in this man's arms.

"What time does your shift start today?" he asks as his erection grows harder and presses into the cleft of my backside.

"Eleven." I'm on a twenty-four hour shift at The House today. I'd much rather stay in bed with him all day instead. "Why? Did you have something in mind?" I ask coyly as I wiggle my hips back against him.

"Most definitely," he whispers as he nudges his knee between my thighs from behind so I'm opened up for his hand that is slowly tickling my tender folds. "What time do you have to be at work...aahh—" I'm distracted as his fingers find their target.

"Later." He laughs against my skin. "Much later."

"Then we better make the most of the time we have." I sigh as he shifts us so I sit astride him.

"Your pleasure is my number one priority, sweetheart," he says, flashing his megawatt grin.

He reaches up and cups the back of my neck, pulling me down to him. I moan as his mouth finds mine and I become lost in the haze of lust.

"You sure you don't mind me using your razor?" Colton asks me, his eyes meeting my reflection in the mirror.

"Nope." I shake my head as I watch him from the doorway to my bedroom. A towel is fastened around his waist sitting just below that sexy V, drops of water still cling to his broad shoulders and muscular back, and his hair is in wet disarray. My mouth isn't the only thing that moistens when I look at him. The sight of him, so gorgeous and fresh from the shower, makes me want to drag him back to my bed and dirty him up all over again.

I'm not sure if it's because he's in my bathroom making himself at home with my things after a long night and early morning of incredible sex, but I know I've never thought him sexier.

I bite my lip as I walk behind him thinking how normal this feels. How domestic and comforting it is. I put my arms through my bra straps as I move, feeling Colton's eyes on me as I clasp it and adjust myself. I look up at him in the mirror and notice that he has paused, the pink handle of my razor halfway up to his face, a soft smile on his lips.

"What?" I ask, suddenly shy under the intensity of those gorgeous green eyes.

"You own more bras than any woman I've ever known," he says as his eyes home in on the one that I've just put on. It's light pink, edged in black, and does a perfect job creating just the right amount of cleavage.

His eyes flash up to meet mine, and I purse my lips at him. "I can take that several ways," I tease him. "I can be quite offended that you're comparing me to all of the other women you've been with, or I can be pleased that you appreciate my vast array of lingerie."

"I'd tell you to go with the latter." He smirks. "Only a dead man would be able to ignore your penchant for sexy underthings."

I smile brazenly at him as I hold up a matching thong that is made of lace and very little of it at that. "You mean like this?"

His tongue darts out to lick his bottom lip. "Yeah, like that," he murmurs, his eyes tracking my movements as I step into the panties. I make sure to give him a little floor show as I bend over to pull it up over my wiggling hips. "*Sweet Christ, woman, you're killing me!*"

I laugh out loud at him as I grab my T-shirt and tug it over my head. "Can't fault a girl for having a soft spot for sexy underthings as you put it."

"No ma'am." He smirks at me as he moves the razor up and clears a clean path of shaving cream under his chin—such a masculine act and so sexy to witness. I lean against the door and watch him with thoughts of tomorrows and the future running through my mind.

I thought I knew what love felt like, but standing here, breathing him in, I realize I had no clue. Loving Max was sweet, gentle, naive, and what I thought a relationship should be. Like what a child sees when they look at their parents through rose-colored glasses. Comfortable. Innocent. Loving. I loved Max with all my heart—always will in some capacity—but looking back at it in comparison to what I feel for Colton, I know that I would have been selling myself short. Settling.

Loving Colton is so different. *It's just so much more.* When I look at him, my chest physically constricts from the emotions that pour through me. They're intense and raw. Overwhelming and instinctual. The chemistry between us is combustive and passionate and volatile. He consumes my every thought. He is a part of everything I feel. His every action is my reaction.

Colton is my air in each breath. My endless tomorrow. My happily ever after.

I watch the line form between his eyebrows as he concentrates, angling his face this way and that. He's just about finished, little smudges of shaving cream left on his face here and there when he notices me.

As he wipes his face on a towel, I walk up slowly behind him and to the left, his eyes on mine the whole time. I reach out and run a hand softly up and down the line of his spine, stopping at the nape of his neck so I can run my fingers through his damp hair. He leans his head back at the sensation and closes his eyes momentarily. I want so badly to nuzzle up against his broad back and powerful shoulders and feel my body pressed against his. I hate that the horror from his past robs me—and him—of the chance to snuggle up against him in bed or being able to walk up to him and wrap my arms around him, nuzzling into him from behind—another simple way to connect with him.

I lean up on my toes and press a soft kiss to his bare shoulder while

221

my fingernails trail up and down the line of his spine. I can feel his muscles bunch and move as my touch tickles his skin, and my lips form a smile against the firmness of his shoulder.

"You're tickling me," he says with a laugh as he squirms beneath my touch.

"Mmm-hmm," I murmur, my cheek now pressed against his shoulder so I can meet his eyes in the mirror, and watch his face tense as I tease my fingernails up the side of his torso. I can't help the smile that forms on my lips as his face scrunches up to try and prepare for the graze of my fingers over his ribcage—a little boy's expression on the face of a grown man. I find my purchase and make sure to be extra thorough in my tickling.

"Stop it, you evil wench." He struggles trying to remain stoic, but when my fingers continue their relentless torture, he wriggles his body away from me.

"I'm not letting you get away." I laugh with him as I wrap my arms around him and try to prevent him from escaping.

He's laughing, the razor thrown and forgotten into the sink, his towel dangerously close to falling from his hips, and my arms wrapped around him from behind. Unintentionally, I've maneuvered him into the one position I'd just been thinking about. I know he realizes it the moment that I do because I feel his body tense momentarily and his laughter fades off before he tries to cover it up. Colton's eyes glance up to the reflection of the mirror to meet mine. The look I've seen in any one of my boys' flickers through them, and it breaks me apart inside, but as quick as it flashes there, it's gone.

Regardless of the length of time, I know how much that small concession is a huge step between the two of us.

Before I know it, Colton's twisted out of my grip and is assaulting my rib cage with the tips of his fingers.

"No!" I cry, trying to escape him but unable to. The only way I can think to get him to stop is to wrap my arms around his torso and press my chest to his as hard as I can. I'm breathless and know that I'm no match for his strength.

"Are you trying to distract me?" he teases as his fingers ease up and slide up the back of my shirt to the bare flesh beneath. The protest on my lips fades as I sigh into him and welcome the warmth of his touch and the arms that he tightens around me. I find comfort here, a peace I never thought I'd know again.

We stand here like this for some time—the length I don't know. It's long enough, though, that his heartbeat beneath my ear has slowed significantly. At some point I press my lips into his neck and simply absorb everything about him.

I'm so overwhelmed with everything. I know that he's just shared something monumental with me—bestowed a depth of trust to me—and maybe subconsciously I want to give him a piece of me in return. I speak before my head can filter what my heart says. And by the time I do, it's too late to take it back.

"I love you, Colton." My voice is even and unfaltering when the words come out. There is no mistaking what I've said. Colton's body stiffens as the words suffocate and die in the air around us. We stand there in silence, still physically entwined for several more moments before Colton unlaces his fingers from mine and deliberately removes my hands off of him. I stand still as he steps to the edge of the counter to grab his shirt and shove it over his head, an exhaled *"Fuck!"* coming from between his lips.

I follow him in the mirror and the panic in his eyes, on his face, reflected in his movements are hard to watch, but I'm silently pleading with him to look into my eyes. To see that nothing has changed. *But he doesn't.* Instead, he briskly walks past me into my bedroom without looking at me.

I watch him drag on yesterday's jeans before sitting on the bed and shoving his feet in his boots. "I've got to get to work," he says as if I hadn't spoken.

The tears that threaten fill my eyes and blur my vision as he rises from the bed. I can't let him go without saying something. My heart is hammering in my ears, the sting of his rejection twisting my insides as he grabs his keys off the dresser and shoves them into his pocket.

"Colton," I whisper as he starts to walk past me to the doorway. He stops at the sound of my voice. His eyes remain focused on his watch as he fastens it on his wrist, his damp hair falling onto his forehead. We stand there in silence—me looking at him, him looking at his watch—the chasm between us growing wider by the second. The silence so loud it's deafening. "Please say something," I plead softly.

"Look, I—" He stops, sighing heavily and dropping his hands down but not meeting my eyes. "I told you, Rylee, *that's* just not a possibility." His rasp is barely audible. "I'm not capable of, not deserving..." he clears his throat "...I've got nothing but black inside of me. The ability to love—to accept love—is nothing but poison."

And with that Colton walks out of my bedroom and what I fear most possibly out of my life.

Chapter Twenty-Seven
Colton

I can't breathe. *Fuck*. My chest hurts. My eyes blur. My body shakes. The panic attack hits me full force as I grip the steering wheel, knuckles turning white and heart pounding like a motherfucking freight train in my ears. I try to close my eyes—try to calm myself—but all I see is her face inside the house in front of me. All I hear are those poisonous words falling from her mouth.

My chest constricts again as I force myself to pull out of her driveway and make myself concentrate on the road. To not think. To not let the darkness inside take over or allow the memories to seep through.

I do the only thing that I can do—I drive—but it's not fast enough. Only on the track is it ever fast enough to push myself into that blur around me—get lost in it—so that none of this can catch me.

I pull into the dive bar: blacked out windows, no sign above the door with it's name, and a myriad of overflowing ashtrays on the window ledges. I don't even know where the fuck I am. I park my ride next to some piece of shit clunker and don't even think twice about it. All I can think about is how to numb myself, how to erase what Rylee just said.

The bar is dark inside when I open the door. Nobody turns to look at me. They all keep their heads down, crying into their own fucking beers. Good. I don't want to talk. Don't want to listen. Don't want to hear Passenger on the speakers above singing about letting her go. I just want to drown everything out. The bartender looks up, his sallow eyes sizing up my expensive clothes and registering the desperation on my face.

"What'll you have?"

"Patron. Six shots. Keep 'em coming." I don't even recognize my voice. Don't even feel my feet move toward the bathroom in the far corner. I walk in and up to the grungy sink and splash some water on my face. Nothing. I feel absolutely nothing. I look up at the cracked mirror and don't even recognize the man in front of me. All I see is darkness and a little boy I no longer want to remember anymore, don't want to be anymore.

Humpty fuckin' Dumpty.

Before I can stop myself, the mirror is shattering. A hundred tiny fucking pieces splinter and fall. I don't register the pain. I don't feel the blood trickling out and dripping from my hand. All I hear is the tinkling as it hits the tiles all around me. Little sounds of music that momentarily drown out the emptying of my soul. Beautiful on the surface but so very broken as a whole. Irreparable.

All the king's horses and all the king's men, couldn't put Humpty back together again.

The bartender eyes my wrapped hand as I walk up to the bar. I see my shots lined up by some fellow patrons, and I walk to the other vacant end of the bar and sit down. My stomach churns at the thought of sitting between the two men there. The barkeep picks up and delivers my shots to me and just stares as I place two one hundred dollar bills on the bar top. "One hundred for the mirror," I say, lifting my chin toward the bathroom, "and one hundred to keep them coming, no questions asked." I raise my eyebrows at him, and he just nods in agreement.

The bills slip off the counter into his pocket before my second shot is being tossed back. I welcome the sting. The imaginary slap to my face for how I just left Rylee. For what I'm going to do to Rylee. The third one's gone and my head still hurts. Pressure's still in my chest.

You know that you're only ever allowed to love me, Colty. Only me. And I'm the only one who'll ever really love you. I know the things you let them do to you. The things you enjoy them doing to you. I can hear you in there with them. I hear you chanting 'I love you' over and over the whole time. I know you're convinced you let them because you love me, but you really do it because you like how it feels. You're a naughty, naughty boy, Colton. So very bad that no one will ever be able to love you. Will never want to. Never. And if they did and found out all of the naughty things you've done? They'd know the truth—that you're horrible and disgusting and poisoned inside. That any love you have inside of you for anyone but me is like a toxin that will kill them. So you can't tell anyone because if you do, they'll know how repulsive you are. They'll know the Devil lives inside of you. I know. I'll always know and I'll still love you. I'm the only one that is ever allowed to love you. I love you, Colty.

I try to push the memories from my mind. Push them back into the abyss that they're always hiding in. Rylee can't love me. No one can love me. My head fucks with me as I glance down the bar. The man sitting with his back to me causes sickness to grapple though me. Greasy dark hair. A paunchy gut. I know if he turns around what he'll look like. What he'll smell like. What he'll taste like.

I toss back the seventh shot, trying to force the bile down. Trying to numb the fucking pain—pain that won't go the fuck away even though I know in my right head that it's not him. Can't be. It's just my mind fucking with me because the alcohol hasn't numbed enough yet.

I push my forehead in my hands. It's Rylee's voice clear as day that I hear in my head—but it's his face that I see when I hear those three words.

Not Rylee's.

Just his.

And my Mom's. Her lips and that ragged smile giving me her constant affirmation of the freakish horror inside of me.

The blackness has already poisoned me. There's no way in hell I'm going to let it kill Rylee too. Number ten goes down and my lips are starting to not work.

A catastrophic exit. The perfect fucking meaning to Ace. I start laughing. It hurts so fucking much that I can't stop. I'm barely holding it together. And I'm afraid that if I do stop, I'm going to fracture just like the goddamn mirror.

Humpty fuckin' Dumpty.

Chapter Twenty-Eight

"This is the way you want it to be. Guess you don't want me," I sing solemnly with my old standby, Matchbox Twenty, as I drive home after my shift the next day. I still haven't heard from Colton, but then again I hadn't expected to.

I pull into my driveway, the past twenty-four hours a blur. I should have called in sick to work as it wasn't fair to the boys to have a guardian around who's so wrapped up in their own head they weren't really present.

I've relived the moment so many times that I can't think about it anymore. I didn't expect Colton to confess his undying love for me in return, but I also didn't think he'd act as if the words were never spoken. I'm hurt and feeling the sting of rejection and am uncertain where to go from here. I took an important moment between us and fucked it up. *What to do now?* I'm not sure.

I trudge in the house, drop my bag rather unceremoniously on the floor by the front door, and collapse on the couch. And that is where Haddie finds me hours later when she walks through the door.

"What'd he do to you, Rylee?" Her demand rouses me from sleep. Her hands are on her hips as she stands over me, and her eyes search mine for an answer.

"Oh, Haddie, I screwed up royally," I sigh as I let the tears that I'd been holding back flow. She sits down on the coffee table in front of me, hand on my knee in support, and I relay everything to her.

When I finish she just shakes her head and looks at me with eyes full of compassion and empathy. "Well, sweetie, if anything's screwy, it's definitely not you!" she says. "All I can say is that you need to give him a little time. You probably scared the shit out of Mr. Free-Wheelin'-Bachelor to death. Love. Commitment. All that shit..." she waves her hand through the air "...is a big step for someone like him."

"I know." I hiccup through my tears. "I just didn't expect him to be so cold...so nonchalant about it. I think that's what hurts the most."

"Oh, Ry." She leans in and hugs me tightly. "I'll call in sick to the event tonight so you're not alone."

"No don't," I tell her. "I'm fine. I'll probably just eat a gallon of ice cream and go to sleep anyway. Go..." I shoo her away with my hands "...I'll be fine. I promise."

She just stares at me for a moment, debating whether I'm lying or not. "Okay," she says, taking a deep breath, "but just remember something...you're awesome, Rylee. If he doesn't see that...if he doesn't see everything you have to offer in and out of the sack...then fuck him and the horse he rode in on."

I give her a slight smile. Leave it to Haddie to put it eloquently.

The next morning passes without hearing from him. I decide to text him.

Hi, Ace. Call me when you have a chance. We need to talk. XO.

My phone remains silent for most of the day despite how many times I've looked at it and checked to see if I have good service. As the day drags on, my unease settles in, and I start to realize that I've probably done irrevocable damage.

Finally at three o'clock I receive a response. My hopes soar at the prospect of having contact with him.

Busy all day in meetings. Catch you later.

And then my hopes take a nosedive.

On the third day post the I-love-you disastrous confession, I get up the nerve to call his office on my way in to the office. "CD Enterprises, can I help you?"

"Colton Donavan please," I answer, my knuckles white from gripping the steering wheel.

"May I ask who's calling please?"

"Rylee Thomas." My voice cracks.

"Hi, Ms. Thomas, let me check. Just a moment please."

"Thanks," I whisper, anxiety eating at me as I hope he answers and then at what to say if he does.

"Ms. Thomas?"

"Yes?"

"I'm sorry. Colton's not in today. He's out sick. Can I take a message? Can Tawny help you with anything?"

My heart moves up into my throat at the words. If he is in fact sick, she wouldn't have had to check. She would've known.

"No. Thank you."

"My pleasure."

The past few days have started to take their toll on me. I look a mess, so much so that even make-up isn't helping. On day four I feel like I would give anything to take my words back. To take us back to the moments before where we were connected in the moment of his unyielding trust in me. *But I can't.*

Instead, I sit at my desk and stare aimlessly at the pile of work on my desk without any desire to do anything. I look up at the knock on my open door to see Teddy. "You okay, kiddo? You don't look so good."

I force a smile. "Yeah. I think I'm coming down with something," I lie. Anything to avoid the questioning look and the I-told-you-so tone. "I'll be fine."

"Okay, well don't stay too late. I think you're the last one. I'll tell Tim down in the lobby you're still up here so that he can walk you to your car."

"Thanks, Teddy." I smile. "Good night."

"Good night."

My smile fades as he turns his back from me. I watch Teddy walk to the elevators and into the open car while I muster up the courage to call him again. I don't want to come off desperate, but I am. I need to talk to him. To show him that even though I said the words, things are still the same between us. I pick up my cell phone but know he probably won't pick up if he sees my number. I opt for the office line.

On the third ring the phone picks up "Donavan."

My heart pounds in my chest at the sound of his voice. Keep it light, Rylee. "Ace?" I say breathlessly.

"Rylee?" His voice seems so far away as he says my name. So distant. So detached and bordering on annoyed.

"Hi," I say timidly. "I'm glad I got ahold of you."

"Yeah, sorry I haven't called you back," he apologizes, but he sounds off. He's talking to me in the same irritated tone that he spoke to Teagan with.

I swallow the lump in my throat, needing any type of connection with him. "Don't worry about it. I'm just glad you picked up."

"Yeah, I've just been real busy with work."

"Feeling better then?" I ask, then cringe when there's silence on the line— the pause that tells me he has to think of something quick to say to cover the lie.

"Yeah...just getting some last minute details done to try and push a patent through on one of our new safety devices."

My insides twist at his disembodied tone because I can feel it. I can feel him removing himself from all we shared together. From all the emotions I thought he felt but couldn't put words to. I try to hide the desperation in my voice as the first tear trails down my cheek. "So how's it going?"

"Eh, so-so...look, babe..." he laughs "...I've gotta run."

"Colton!" I plead. His name falls from my mouth before I can stop it.

"Yeah?"

"Look, I'm sorry," I say softly. "I didn't mean..." My words falter as I choke on getting the lie out.

The line is silent for a moment, and that's the only reason I know he's heard me. "Well that's a slap in the face," he says sarcastically, but I can hear the annoyance in his voice. "Which one is it, babe? *You either love me or you don't, right?* It's almost worse when you say it and then take it back. Don't you agree?"

I think it's the obvious derision in his voice that breaks me this time. I catch the sob before it comes out loudly. I hear him laugh with someone on the other end of the line. "Colton..." is all I can manage to say, the hurt swallowing me whole and pulling me under.

"I'll call ya," he says, the phone clicking off before I have a chance to say what I fear could possibly be my final goodbye. I keep the phone to my ear, my mind running through all of the other ways that conversation could have gone differently. Why did he have to be so cruel? He forewarned me. I guess I'm at fault all around in this case. First for not listening and then for opening my big mouth.

I cross my arms and lay my head down on my desk, groaning when I realize I've laid my head on top of the schedule his office has sent over to me. Of the events that I've been contracted to attend. With him. What the fuck did I do to myself? How could I have been so damn stupid agreeing to go along with this? *Because it's him*, the small voice in my head reiterates. *And because it's for the boys*. I pick up the schedule, crumple it up, and throw it across the room hoping for a thump at least, but the soft sound of it hitting the wall does nothing to assuage the pain in my chest.

Within moments, sobs rack my body. Fuck me. Fuck him. *Fuck love*. I knew this was going to happen. *Bastard*.

I wake Saturday morning still feeling like shit but with a renewed purpose. I get up and force myself to go for a run, telling myself it will make me feel better. It will give me a fresh outlook on things. I take the run and pound my feet into the pavement at a relentless pace to relieve some of my heartache. I arrive home, out of breath, body tired, and still feeling the ache deep in my soul. I guess I lied to myself there.

I take a shower and tell myself no more tears today and definitely no more ice cream.

I am scooping the last of the mint chocolate chip out of the carton when my cell phone rings. I glance at the unknown number, curiosity getting the best of me. "Hello?"

"Rylee?" I try to place the feminine voice on the other end of the line but can't.

"Yes? Who is—"

"*What the hell happened?*" the voice demands of me in a clipped and obviously annoyed tone.

"What? Who—"

"It's Quinlan." A small breath squeaks past my lips in shock. "I just left Colton's house. What the hell happened?"

"Wh-what do you mean?" I stammer because I can answer that question in so many different ways.

"God!" She sighs in frustration and impatience on the other end of the line. "Will you two get your shit together and pull your heads out of your asses? *Fucking Christ.* Maybe then you'd realize you two have got something real. Something that's undeniable. It would take an idiot not to see that spark between you guys." I remain silent on the other end of the line. The tears I told myself I couldn't cry, leak out of the corners of my eyes. "Rylee? You there?"

"I told him I loved him," I tell her softly, wanting to confide in her for some reason. Maybe needing some kind of validation about his response from someone that's closest to him so I don't keep replaying it over in my head endlessly.

"*Oh shit.*" She breathes in shock.

"Yeah..." I laugh anxiously "...that about sums it up in a nutshell."

"How'd he take it?" she asks cautiously. I tell her his reaction and how he's been since then. "Sounds like what I'd expect from him." She sighs. "He's such an ass!"

I remain silent at her comment, dashing away my tears with the back of my hand. "How is he?" I ask, my voice breaking.

"Moody. Grouchy. Surly as hell." She laughs. "And from the number of his friends Jim and Jack, empty and lining his kitchen counter, I'd say he's trying to drink himself into oblivion to either help forget his demons or so he can push down the fear he has in regards to his feelings for you." I exhale the breath I'm holding, a part of me reveling in the fact that he's hurting too. That he's affected by what's happened between us. "And because he's missing you terribly."

My heart wrenches at her final words. I feel like I've been in a world without light for the past couple of days, so it's welcome to know that he's drowning in darkness too. And then the part of me that acknowledges that notion doesn't want him to hurt, feels sorry for causing all of this pain with those stupid words, and just wants to make everything right again.

My voice is thick with tears and wavers when I speak again. "I really fucked up by saying it, Quinlan."

"No you didn't!" she scolds. "Ugh!" She groans. "*God, I love him and hate him so much sometimes!* He's never opened himself up to this possibility before, Rylee...he's never been in this predicament. I can only guess how he'll react."

"Please," I plead. "I'm at a loss for what to do. I just don't want to screw up and push him away further."

She is silent for a few moments as she contemplates things. "Give him a little time, Rylee," she murmurs, "but not too much time or he might do something stupid on purpose, and risk fucking up the one good girl he's ever truly cared about."

"Not Tawny..." The words are out before I can stop them. I cringe, knowing I've just openly insulted a family friend.

"Don't get me started on her." Quinlan sneers in contempt, causing a small part of me deep down to smile at the knowledge that it's not just me who detests her. I laugh through my tears. "Hang in there, Rylee," she says, sincerity flooding her voice. "Colton is a wonderful yet complicated man...worthy of your love, even if he is unable to accept that concept yet." The lump in my throat prevents me from responding, so I just murmur an agreement. "He needs a lot of patience, a strong sense of loyalty, unrelenting trust, and a person to tell him when he steps out of line. All of that is going to take time for him to realize and accept...in the end though, he's worth the wait. I just hope he knows it."

"I know," I whisper.

"Good luck, Rylee."

"Thank you, Quinlan. For everything."

I hear her chuckle as she clicks off the phone.

Chapter Twenty-Nine

Quinlan's advice still rings in my ears as I lie in bed the next morning. The pain in my chest and ache in my soul is still there, but my resolve has returned. I once told Colton to fight for us. For me. Now it's my turn. I told him he is worth the risk. That I'd take the chance. Now I need to prove it.

If Quinlan seems to think I matter to him, then I can't give up now. I have to try.

I drive up the coastline, Lisa Loeb playing on the speakers, and my mind a whirl of thoughts—what I'm going to say and how I'm going to say it—as the clouds above slowly burn off and give way to the morning sun. I take it as a positive sign that somehow when I see Colton face-to-face, he'll see it's just him and me, how it was before, and that the words mean nothing. That they change nothing. That he feels the same way and that I act the same way. And that we are us. That the darkness I feel will dissipate because I'll be back in his light once again.

I steer down Broadbeach Road and pull up to his gate, my heart pounding a frantic tattoo and my hands shaking. I ring the buzzer, but no one answers. I try again, and then again, thinking maybe he is asleep. That he can't hear the buzzer because he is upstairs.

"Hello?" a feminine voice asks through the speaker. My heart drops into my stomach.

"It's Rylee. I...I need to see Colton." My voice is a tangle of nerves and unshed tears.

"Hi, dear. It's Grace. Colton's not here, sweetie. He hasn't been here since yesterday afternoon. Is everything okay? Would you like to come in?"

The rush of blood into my head is all I hear. My breath hitches as I rest my head against the steering wheel. "Thanks, Grace, but no thank you. Just tell…just tell him I stopped by."

"Rylee?" The uncertainty in her voice has me leaning out the window of the car.

"Yes?"

"It's not my place to say it…" she clears her throat "…but be patient. Colton's a good man."

"I know." My voice is barely audible, my stomach lodged in my throat. If only he would realize it.

My drive back down the coastline is not as filled with hope as my drive up it was. I tell myself that he probably went out with Beckett and was too drunk to drive home. That he went out with the crew and grabbed a hotel in downtown L.A. after partying a little too hard. That he decided it was time for another trip to Las Vegas and is on the plane home right now.

The endless scenarios run through my head but do nothing to alleviate the ripples of fear that ricochet within me. I don't want to think of the one other place that he could be. The townhome in the Palisades. The place he goes to be with his arrangements. My heart races and thoughts fly recklessly at the notion. I try to justify that he crashed there. That he's alone. But both Teagan's and Tawny's comments flicker through my mind, feeding the endless stream of doubt and unease churning within me.

My mind fills with the many warnings he's given me. *"I sabotage anything that resembles a relationship. I'm hardwired this way, Rylee. I'll purposely do something to hurt you to prove that I can. To prove that you won't stick around regardless of the consequences. To prove that I can control the situation."*

I don't remember steering the car in that direction, but before I know it, I'm turning down his street from memory. Tears spill over and down my cheeks as I grip the steering wheel tightly. The need to know outweighing the agony of acknowledging what my mind fears. What my heart worries. What my conscience already knows.

I pull up to the curb, a small sigh escaping my lips in momentary relief when I see that none of Colton's cars are there. But then I see his garage door and wonder if it's inside. I have to know. I have to.

I push my hair out of my face and suck in a deep breath before I slide out of my car. I walk on weak knees up the pathway and into the cobblestone courtyard. My heart pounds so loudly that its thundering is all hear, all I can focus on besides telling my feet to place one foot in front of the other.

Chapter Thirty
Colton

My fucking head. I groan as I roll over in the bed. Stop pounding on the fucking drums. Please. Somebody. Anybody. *Fuck me.*

I shove the pillow over my head, but the goddamn throbbing continues in my temples. My stomach rolls and twists, and I have to concentrate on not getting sick because my head really doesn't want me to get up just yet.

Fucking Christ! What the fuck happened last night? Bits and pieces come back to me. Becks coming to get me to shake me out of the voodoo pussy funk. A funk I'm not really sure I want to be shaken from. Drinking. Rylee—wanting Rylee. Needing Rylee. Missing Rylee. Tawny meeting us at the bar for some signatures. A lot of fucking alcohol. Way too much fucking alcohol according to my head right now.

Pleasure to bury the pain.

I struggle to fight through the fuzz in my head to remember the rest. Snapshots of clarity amidst the haze. Coming back here. Palisades house closer than Malibu. Drinking more. Tawny not comfortable in her business suit. Getting her a shirt of mine. Standing in the kitchen looking at the fucking Tupperware container of cotton candy on the counter. Memories of the carnival making the ache burn.

"*Oh fuck.*" I groan as the next recollection flickers through loud and clear.

Sitting on the couch. Becks, the fucker looking no worse for the wear even though he's gone drink for drink with me, sitting in the chair across from me. His feet propped up and his head angled back. Tawny next to me on the couch. Reaching over her to the end table to grab my beer. Her reaching up. Hands around my neck. Mouth on my lips. Too much alcohol and a chest still burning with need. Hurting so bad because I need Rylee. Only Rylee.

Pleasure to bury the pain.

Kissing her back. Getting lost in her momentarily. Trying to get rid of the constant fucking ache. To forget how to feel. All wrong. So wrong. Pushing her off. She's not Rylee.

Looking up and meeting the disapproving eyes of Becks.

Fuuccckkk! I shove myself up from the bed and immediately cringe at the freight train that hits my head. I make it to the bathroom and brace myself on the sink for a moment, struggling to function. Images of last night keep flashing. Fuckin' Tawny. I look up to the mirror and cringe. "You look like shit, Donavan," I mutter to myself. Bloodshot eyes. Stubble verging on beard. Tired. And empty.

Rylee. Violet eyes begging me. Soft smile. Big heart. Fucking perfect.

I love you, Colton.

God, I miss her. Need her. Want her.

I brush my teeth. Trying to rid the taste of alcohol and misery from my mouth. I start shoving off my shirt and underwear—needing to get the feel of Tawny's hands off of me. Her perfume off of me. Needing a shower desperately. I'm just about to flick the water on when I hear a knock at the front door. "*Who the fuck?*" I grumble before looking over at the clock. Still fucking early.

I look disjointedly for something to wear, trying to shake the fuzz from my head. I can't find my fucking pants from last night. Where the fuck did I put them? Frustrated, I yank open my dresser, grab the first pair of jeans I find, and hastily shove my legs in them. I hurry down the stairs starting to button them up as I try to figure who the fuck is at my door. I glance over to see Becks passed out on the couch. Serves the fucker right. I look up to see Tawny and her mile long legs opening the door. The sight of her—T-shirt, legs, and nothing else—does nothing to me, for me—when it used to do everything.

"Who is it, Tawn?" My voice sounds foreign as I speak. Gravelly. Unemotional because the only thing I want is Tawny gone. I want her out of my house so I don't need a reminder of what I could have done. What I almost fucked up. Because it matters now. *She* matters now.

And when I step into the blinding morning light through the doorway, I swear to God my heart stumbles in my chest. There she stands. My angel. The one helping me break through my darkness by letting me hold on to her light.

Chapter Thirty-One

My knock sounds hollow on the front door. I lay my hand on it, contemplating knocking again, just to make sure. My shoulders start to sag in relief that he's not holed up inside with someone when the door pushes inwards beneath my fingers.

All the blood drains to my feet as the door swings open and Tawny stands before me. Her hair is tousled from sleep. Make-up is smudged under her bedroom eyes. Her long, tan legs connect to bare feet that stick out from under a T-shirt that I know is Colton's, right down to the small hole in the left hand shoulder. The morning chill showcasing her braless breasts.

I'm sure that the look of shock on my face mirrors the one on hers, if only momentarily, for she quickly recovers, a slow, knowing, siren's smile spreading across her face. Her eyes dance with triumph, and she licks her tongue over her top lip as I hear footsteps from inside.

"Who is it, Tawn?"

She just widens her grin as she uses her hand to push the door open further. Colton strides toward the door with nothing on but a pair of jeans; jeans his fingers are fumbling to button the fly on. His face sports more than its usual day's worth of growth, and his hair is unwashed and messy from slumber. His eyes are bloodshot causing him to flinch at the morning sunlight as it comes in through the doorway. He looks rough and reckless and as if the alcohol from the night before has taken its toll. He looks how I feel, shitty, but no matter how much I hate him in this moment, the sight of him still causes my breath to hitch in my throat.

It all happens so quickly, but I feel as if time stops and moves in slow motion. Stands still. Colton's eyes snapping to mine when he realizes who is at his door. When he understands that I know. His green eyes hold mine. Imploring, questioning, apologizing, all at once for the hurt and crushing devastation that is reflected in mine. He steps forward into the doorway and a strangled cry escapes my lips to stop him.

I struggle to breathe. I try to drag in a breath, but my body is not listening. It does not comprehend my brain's innate commands to draw in air because it is so overwhelmed. So crushed. The world spins beneath me and around me, but I can't move. I stare at Colton, the words in my head forming but never making it past my lips. Tears burn in my throat and sting my eyes, but I fight them back. I will not give Tawny the satisfaction of seeing me cry as she smirks at me from over his shoulder.

Time starts again. I draw in a breath and thoughts start to form. Anger starts to fire in my veins. Emptiness starts to register in my soul. Pain radiates in my heart. I shake my head in disgust at him. At her. In resigned shock. "Fuck this," I say quietly but implacably as I turn to walk away.

"Rylee," Colton calls out in despair, his voice gravelly from sleep as I hear the door slam behind me. "Rylee!" he shouts at me as I all but run down the path, needing to escape from him. From her. From this. "Rylee it's not what you—"

"Not what I think?" I yell over my shoulder at him in disbelief. "Because when your ex answers your door this early in the morning with your shirt on, what else am I supposed to think? " His footsteps are heavy behind me. "Don't touch me!" I yell as he grabs my arm and spins me around to face him. I yank it from his grip, my chest heaving, my teeth clenched. "Don't fucking touch me!"

Albeit temporarily, anger has replaced the hurt now. It is coursing through me like a wild inferno, emanating off of me in waves. I clench my fists and squeeze my eyes shut. I will not cry. I will not give him the satisfaction of seeing how deeply he has torn me apart. I will not show him that giving my heart away for the second time might be the biggest regret of my life.

When I look up, his eyes meet mine, and we stare at each other. My love for him still there. So deep. So raw.

So forsaken.

His eyes swim with emotion as he clenches and unclenches his jaw trying to find the right words. "Rylee," he pleads, "let me explain. Please." His voice breaks on the last word, and I close my eyes to block out the part of me that still wants to fix him, comfort him. And then the anger hits me again. At me for still caring for him. At him for breaking my heart. At her for...just being.

He runs a hand through his hair and then scrubs it over the stubble on his face. The sound of its rough scratch—the one that I usually find so sexy—does nothing but drive the proverbial knife deeper into my heart. He takes a step forward, and I mirror him taking a step back. "I swear, Rylee. It's not what you think..."

I snort incredulously, knowing the consummate playboy will say anything—do anything—to talk his way out of this. The image of Tawny snuggled in nothing but his shirt flashes in my mind. I try to quiet the other ones that form. Of her hands on him. Of him tangled with her. I close my eyes and swallow purposefully, trying to wipe the images away. "It's not what I think? If it looks like a duck and walks like a duck..." I imply with a shrug "...well then you know what they say."

"Nothing hap—"

"*Quack!*" I shout at him. I know I'm being childish, but I don't care. I'm pissed and hurting. He shakes his head at me, and I can see the desperation in his eyes. Tawny's smug smirk fills my head, her previous taunts echo in my mind, and they fuel my fire.

Colton's eyes search mine as he steps toward me again, and I retreat. I see the sting of rejection glance across his face. I need my distance to think clearly. I shake my head at him, disappointment swimming in my eyes and pain drowning my heart. "Of all people, Colton...why chose her? Why turn to her? Especially after what we shared the other night...after what you showed me." The memory of the intimacy between us as we looked in the mirror at each other is almost too unbearable to envision, but it floods into my mind. Him behind me. His hands on my body. His eyes drinking me in. His lips telling me to look at myself, to realize why he chooses me. That I'm enough for him. A sob I can't hold back escapes and is wrenching and comes from so deep within me that I wrap my arms around my torso to try and stifle its effects.

Colton reaches out to touch me but pauses when I glare at him, his face etched with pain, and his eyes frantic with uncertainty. He doesn't know how to assuage the pain he's caused. "Rylee, please," he begs. "I can make this right again..."

His fingertips are so close to my arm that it takes everything I have to not lean into his touch. Visually shunned from touching me, he shoves his hands in his pockets to ward off the early morning chill. Or perhaps mine.

I know I'm hurt and I'm confused and I hate him right now, but I still love him. I can't deny that. I can fight it, but I can't deny it. I love him even though he won't let me. I love him even through the hurt he's inflicted. The floodgates I've been trying to hold back burst and tears spill over and down my cheeks. I stare at him through blurred vision until I'm able to find my voice again despite the despair. "You said you'd try..." It's all I can manage to say, and even then my voice breaks with each word.

His eyes plead with mine and in them I can see the shame. For what, I can only imagine. He sighs, his shoulders sagging and his body defeated. "I am trying. I..." His words falter off as he removes his hands from his pocket and something falls out of one. The scrap of paper flickers to the ground in slow motion, the sun catching its reflective silver packaging. It takes my mind a moment to process what has landed at my feet—and not because I don't understand, but rather because I am hoping against hope that I'm wrong. I stare at the emblazoned Trojan emblem on the torn package, synapses slow to fire.

"No, no, no—" Colton repeats in shock.

"You're trying?" I shout at him, my voice rising as anger blazes. *"When I meant try, Ace, I didn't mean try to stick your dick in the next available candidate the first time you got scared!"* I'm yelling now, not caring who hears. I can sense Colton's rising panic—his uncertainty of how to have to actually deal with the fallout of his actions for once—and the notion that he's never had to before…that no one else has ever called him on it, made him accountable, feeds my anger even further.

"That's not what I—I swear that's not from last night."

"Quack!" I shout at him, wanting to grab him and hold him and never let him go and at the same time wanting to hit him and push him and show him how much he's hurt me. I'm on a fucking roller coaster, and I just want to jump off. Stop the ride. Why am I still here? Why am I even fighting for something he so obviously doesn't want? Doesn't deserve from me?

He runs his hands through his hair in exasperation, face pale, eyes panicked. "Rylee. Please. Let's just take a pit stop."

"A fucking pit stop?" I shout at him, my voice escalating, pissed that he's patronizing me right now. A pit stop? More like an engine rebuild. "Did you not believe in us enough?" I ask, trying to understand through the hurt. "You told me the other night that Tawny had a tenth of the sex appeal I had? Guess you chose to go slumming, huh?" I know I'm being overdramatic but my chest hurts with each breath that I take, and frankly I'm beyond caring at this point. I'm hurt—

devastated—and I want him to hurt like I do. "Did you not believe enough in me that you had to run to someone else? Fuck someone else?" His silence is the only answer that I need to know the truth.

When I finally have the courage to look up and meet his eyes, I think he sees the resignation in mine, which in turn causes panic to flicker through his. He holds my gaze, emerald to amethyst, a volume of emotions passing between us—regret the biggest of all. He reaches out to wipe a tear from my cheek, and I flinch at his touch. I know that if he touches me now, I will dissolve into an incoherent mess. My chin trembles as I turn to go.

"I told you I'd hurt you," he whispers behind me.

I stop in all two steps of my walk away from him. So much for distance, but his words infuriate me. I know if I walk away without saying this, it'll be something I will forever regret. I whirl back around to face him. "Yeah! You did! But just because you warned me doesn't mean that it's okay!" I shout at him, sarcasm dripping with anger. "Suck it up, Donavan! We both have baggage. We both have issues we have to overcome. Everyone does!" I seethe. "Turning to someone else...*fucking someone else*, is unacceptable to me. Something I won't tolerate."

Colton sucks in his breath as my words hit him like punches. I can see the torment on his face and a part of me is relieved to know that he is hurting–maybe not as much as I am–but at least I know what I thought we were wasn't all a lie. "You can't possibly love me, Rylee," he says quietly resigned, his eyes on mine.

"Well you sure tried to make sure of that, didn't you?" I say with a wavering voice. "Did you sleep with her, Colton?" My eyes beseech his, finally asking the question I'm not sure I want answered. "Was fucking her worth losing me?"

"Does it matter?" he snips back, emotions warring over his face as he goes on the defensive. "You're going to think what you want to think anyway, Rylee."

"Don't turn this on me, Colton!" I scream at him. "I'm not the one who fucked this up!"

He stares at me for a few moments before he responds, his eyes accusing, and when he does, his voice is an icy barb. "Didn't you though?"

His words are a stinging slap to my face. Callous Colton has resurfaced. Tears re-emerge and run down my cheeks. I can't stand here anymore and deal with my pain.

Something behind him catches my eye, and I glance over to see that

Tawny has opened the door. She is leaning against its frame, watching our exchange with amused curiosity. The sight of her there gives me the strength I need to walk away.

"No, Colton," I answer him sternly, "this is entirely on you." I close my eyes and breathe deep, trying to control the tears that won't stop. My breath hitches and my chin trembles at what I should have done the first night we met. "Goodbye." I whisper, my voice thick with emotion and my eyes full of unshed tears.

My heart full of unaccepted love.

"*You're leaving me?*" His question is a heart-wrenching plea that snakes in my soul and takes hold. I shake my head sadly as I look at the little boy lost inside the bad boy in front of me. Vulnerability encased in rebellion. Does he have any idea how irresistible he is right now? What a wonderful, empathetic, caring, passionate man he is? How he has so much to give someone, to contribute to a relationship, if he just conquers his demons and lets someone in?

How can I even be thinking of that right now? How can I be worrying about how my leaving will hurt him when the heartbreaking evidence is at my feet and within my sight?

His eyes dart frantically as panic sets in. The pain is too much to bear. Hurting him. Him hurting me. Walking away from the man I love when I never thought it was possible to feel this strongly again. Walking away from the man who's set the bar that all others will be compared against. My chest squeezes as I try to control my emotions. I need to go. I need to walk to the car.

Instead, I step closer to him, the drug to my addiction. His eyes widen as I reach up and run my fingers gently over his strong jaw and perfect lips. He closes his eyes at the feel of my touch and when he opens them I see devastation welling there. The sight of him coming silently undone squeezes something in my chest. I step up on my tiptoes and kiss him oh-so-softly on the lips, needing one last taste of him. One last feel of him. One last memory.

One last fracture in my shattered heart.

A sob escapes my mouth as I step back. I know this will be our last kiss. "Goodbye, Colton," I repeat as I take in everything about him one last time and commit it to memory. *My Ace.*

I turn on my heel and stumble down the pathway, blinded by my tears. I hear my name on his lips and push it from my head, ignoring his plea to come back, that we can fix this, as I force my feet to move to my car. Because even if we fix it this time, with Colton, there will always be a next.

"But, Rylee, *I need you...*" The broken desperation in his voice stops me. Undoes me. Breaks the parts of me that aren't yet broken. Tears into my depths and scorches me. Because for everything that Colton isn't, there is so much that he is. And I know he needs me as much as I need him. I can hear it in his voice. Can feel it in my soul. But need isn't enough for me anymore.

I stare at the ground in front of me and shake my head. Not able to turn to face him because I won't be able walk away from what I see in those eyes of his. I know myself too well, but I can't forgive this. I squeeze my eyes shut and when I speak, I don't recognize my own voice. It's cold. Absent of all emotion. Guarded. "Then maybe you should have thought of that before *you needed her.*"

I tell my body to leave as Colton sucks in a breath behind me. I yank the door open and throw myself into my car just in time to succumb to all of my tears and the endless hurt. And it hits me. How alone I've been over the past two years. How until I had to walk away from Colton, I didn't realize that he's the only one that's been able to fill that void for me. Has been the only one that has made me whole again.

I don't know how long I sit there, emotions exploding, world imploding, and heart breaking. When I can compose myself enough to drive without crashing, I start the car. As I pull from the curb, Colton is still standing there in my rearview mirror with a wounded look on his face and regret dancing in his eyes.

I force myself to drive away. From him. From my future. From the possibilities I thought were a reality. From everything I never wanted but now don't know how I'm ever going to live without.

Chapter Thirty-Two

My feet pound the pavement to the driving beat of the music. The angry lyrics help relieve some of the angst, but not all of it. I make the final turn on the street to reach my house and just wish I could keep running right on past it—past the reminders of him that blanket my house and overload my phone on a daily basis.

But I can't. Today is a huge day. The corporate big wigs are visiting, and I have to present the final details of the project as well as give the requisite dog- and- pony- show Teddy wants for them.

I've thrown myself into preparing for this meeting. I've pushed aside—or tried to as best as possible—the sight of Tawny's face as it flickers smugly through my mind. I've tried to use work to drown out Colton's voice pleading with me, telling me he needs me. I've tried to forget the sun glittering off of the foil packet. Tears well in my eyes but I push them back. Not today. I can't do this today.

I jog the last couple of steps up the front porch and busy myself with my iPod so I'm able to overlook the newest bouquet of dahlias sitting on the doorstep. As I open the door, I pluck the card from the arrangement without really looking at the flowers and toss it in the dish on the foyer table already overflowing with its numerous unopened and identical counterparts.

I sigh, walking into the kitchen and scrunching my nose at the overbearing smell of too many unwelcome flowers that are scattered randomly throughout the house. I pull out my earbuds and lean into the refrigerator to grab a water.

"Phone?"

Haddie's contemptuous voice startles me. "Jesus, Had! You scared the shit out of me!"

She eyes me with pursed lips for a moment as I chug down my water, her usually cheerful countenance has been replaced with annoyance. "What? What did I do now?"

"Sorry if I worried about you." Her sarcasm matches the smarmy look on her face. "You were gone a lot longer than usual. It's irresponsible to go running without your phone."

"I needed to clear my head." My response does nothing to lessen her visible irritation. "He calls and texts me constantly. I just needed to escape from my phone…" I gesture to the ludicrous amount of flower arrangements "…from our house that smells like a damn funeral parlor."

"It is a little ridiculous," she agrees, scrunching up her nose, her features softening as she looks at me.

"Asinine is what it is," I murmur under my breath as I sit at the kitchen table to untie my shoes. Between the one to two bouquets delivered daily, with cards that go unopened, to the numerous text messages that I delete without reading, Colton just won't get the hint that I'm done with him. Completely. Over him.

And regardless of how strong I try to sound when I say those words, I'm quietly falling apart at the seams. Some days are better than others, but those others—*they are debilitating.* I knew Colton would be hard to get over, but I just didn't know how hard. And then to add to the fact that he just won't let me go. I haven't spoken to him, seen him, read his texts or cards, or listened to the voicemails that are sapping up the memory of my phone, but he remains relentless in his attempts. His persistence tells me that his guilt really must be eating at him.

My head has accepted the finality of it; my heart hasn't. And if I give in and read the cards or acknowledge the songs he refers to in his texts depicting how he feels, then I'm not sure how resolute my head will remain with its decision. Hearing his voice, reading his words, seeing his face—any of them will crumble the house of cards I'm trying to reconstruct around my broken heart.

"Ry?"

"Yeah?"

"Are you okay?"

I look up at my dearest friend, trying to hold it together so she can't see right through my false pretense, and bite my bottom lip to quell the tears that threaten once again. I shake my head and push it back. "Yeah.

Fine. I just need to get to work."

I start to stand up and shuffle past her, wanting desperately to avoid the Haddie Montgomery pep talk. I'm not quick enough. Her hand reaches out and holds my arm firm. "Ry, maybe he didn't…" she stalls when my eyes meet hers.

"I don't want to talk about it Haddie." I shake her hand loose and walk toward my bedroom. "I'm going to be late."

"All set?"

I glance over at Teddy as I finish my final run through of my Power Point presentation on the conference room screen and make sure that my smile reflects confidence. In case Teddy's heard the rumors, I can't let him know that anything is amiss between Colton and I. If I do, then I know he'll fret about losing the funding. "Definitely. I'm just waiting for Cindy to finish running off copies of the agenda to place on the top of the binders."

He steps into the room as I refasten a diagram to an easel. "I'm sure you noticed that I adjusted and added a couple of items on the agenda. It doesn't affect your portion but—"

"It's your meeting, Teddy. I'm sure whatever you added is fine. You really don't have to run any changes by me."

"I know, I know," he says, looking at the slide up on the projector screen, "but it's your baby being presented to the bigwigs today."

I smile genuinely at him. "And I'll get them up to speed. I have my updates, budget projections, estimated schedules, and everything else relating to the project updated and ready to present."

"It's you, Ry. I'm not worried. You've never failed me." He returns the smile and pats me on the back before looking at his watch. "They should be here any minute. Do you need anything from me before I go down to meet them?"

"Not that I can think of."

Cindy passes Teddy on his way out of the conference room. "Do you want to see the agendas first or should I just lay them out on top of the binders?"

I glance up at the clock, realizing that time is slipping away from me. "You can just lay them on the binders. That'd really help. Thanks."

I clean up my mess, get my presentation back to the beginning slide, and just escape the conference room to stash the unneeded items back in my office when I hear Teddy's resonating voice down the hallway. Time to put my game face on. "And here she is," he booms loudly, his voice reverberating off of the office hallways.

I stop, hands full of items, and smile warmly at the stuffed suits. "Gentlemen." I nod my head in greeting. "So glad to have you here. We can't wait to get you up to speed on the project and get your input." I look down at my overloaded hands and continue, "I just need to go put this stuff away real quick, and I will be right back."

I dash into my office, throw the items on top of my desk, and take a quick minute to check my appearance before making my way back to the conference room. I enter right as Teddy starts addressing the group before him. Trying not to interrupt his welcoming comments, I sit in the first seat available at the front of the massive, rectangular table without looking around at the room's occupants behind me.

Teddy rambles on about expectations and how we will be exceeding them as I square up the papers in front of me. The agenda being the top paper, my eyes travel over it dismissively since I know it like the back of my hand. And then I do a double take when I notice one of Teddy's changes. Right beneath my time slot, the words, "CD Enterprises" mars the page.

My heart stops and pulse races simultaneously. My breath pauses and I begin to feel light headed. *No! Not now.* I can't do this right now. This meeting means too much. He can't be here. Panic starts to overwhelm me. The rush of blood fills my ears, drowning out Teddy's words. I slowly lay down the paper and place my hands in my lap, hoping that no one notices their trembling. I lower my head and close my eyes tightly as I try to steady my breathing. How stupid was I to assume that he wouldn't be here? After all, his donation and sponsorship program are the reason our hands are hovering over the *go* button. I've been so wrapped up in avoiding him and being conveniently sick for some of the other functions that I was supposed to attend, I completely shut out the possibility from my subconscious.

Maybe Colton didn't come. Then of course that means Tawny would most likely be sitting here. I'm not sure which one would be worse. When I can't stand it anymore, I take a fortifying breath, and raise my eyes to scan the occupants of the room.

And I immediately lock onto the pale green irises of Colton whose attention is focused solely on me. The house of cards surrounding my heart flutters to the ground and all of the air punches out of my lungs at the sight of him. No matter how hard I tell myself to break eye contact, it's like a car accident. I just can't help but stare.

Only because I have intimate knowledge of his face, do I notice the subtle differences in his appearance. His hair is longer, the scruff is back around his jaw, slight shadows bruise beneath his eyes, and he seems slightly unkempt for a man who's always so well put together. I drag my gaze over his magnificently stoic face and am drawn back to his eyes. It is on this second pass that I realize the usual mischievous spark that lights them from within is absent. They look lost, sad even, as they silently plead with me. I see his jaw tic as the intensity in his eyes strengthens. I tear my eyes away from him, not wanting to read the unspoken words he is conveying.

After what he did, he doesn't deserve a second glance from me. I close mine for a beat to try and blink away the tears that threaten, telling myself that I have to keep it together. I have to keep my composure. And regardless of what I tell myself, images of Tawny barely covered by Colton's T-shirt flash through my head. I have to bite back the sickening pang in my stomach and fight the urge to leave the room. My shock at seeing him here slowly churns itself into anger. This is my office and my meeting, and I can't let him affect me. Or I at least have to give the pretense of it anyway.

I clench my jaw and shake away my misery as Teddy's voice slowly seeps through the buzzing in my brain. He's introducing me and I rise on wobbly legs to make my way to the front of the conference room, all too aware of the weight of Colton's eyes locked on me.

I stand at the front of the room, thankful that I've rehearsed my presentation numerous times. My voice breaks as I begin, but I slowly find my confidence as I continue. I make sure to meet the eyes of the suits as well as avoid one set of eyes in particular. I channel my hurt and anger at him and his actions—and him just being here in general—to fuel my enthusiasm for the project. I speak of CD Enterprises and their monumental contributions, but never once look in his direction. I finish my presentation smoothly and succinctly and smile at the group before me. I answer the few questions that are posed and then gladly take my seat as the same time that Colton rises from the table and makes his way to the front of the room.

I fiddle with the papers in front of me as Colton addresses everyone. I curse myself for my last minute entrance into the meeting and my proximity to the front of the room. He is so close to me that his clean, woodsy smell lingers in the air and wraps itself into my head, evoking memories of our time together. All of my senses are on high alert, and

I'd give anything to be able to leave the room right now.

It's torture to have the person inches from you that makes you love inexplicably, desire desperately, despise viciously, and hurt unfathomably, all in the same breath.

I doodle aimlessly on my papers trying to distract myself as the rasp of his voice pulls at me. My eyes desperately want to look at him—to search out a reason or explanation for his actions, but I know that nothing will erase the images in my head from that day.

"In partnership with Corporate Cares, CD Enterprises has gone down every avenue possible to ensure the largest sum of donations. We've knocked on all doors, called in all outstanding favors, and answered all incoming phone calls. *Everyone gets equal attention.* No one is overlooked as we've found in projects past, that usually when you least expect it, someone will come along—someone that you might have originally written off—and they will be the one that ends up turning the tide. Sometimes the one that you assumed would be *inconsequential,* turns out to be the one that *makes all the difference.*"

My eyes reflexively flash up to Colton's on the word that holds so much significance between us. Despite the audience, Colton's eyes are transfixed on mine as if he's waiting for any reaction from me to tell him that I've heard his private innuendo. That I still care. And of course I played right into it. *Damn it!* The emerald of his eyes bore into mine and the muscles play in his jaw as our stare lasts longer than is professional, the message within his words registering in my psyche.

A diminutive smile curls up the corner of his mouth as he breaks his gaze from mine to continue. And that little smile, that little show of arrogance that proves he now knows he still affects me, both pisses me off and overwhelms me. Or is he trying to tell me that I'm the one who matters to him? I'm so confused. I don't know what to think anymore.

The one thing I am sure of is that I refuse to be *that girl.* The girl that we all look at and think is stupid because she continually goes back to the guy that is always doing wrong by her—screwing around behind her back, leading her on, telling her one thing while doing the other. I have a backbone, and as much as I want Colton—as much as I do love Colton—I value the things I have to offer someone too much to let him or any guy trample me and my self-esteem. I just have to keep telling myself this as his voice seduces my ears, trying to draw me back in and strengthening his hold over me like nothing I've ever experienced.

"And such a phone call came in yesterday to my office. And by no means are we done with our fundraising efforts, but with that unexpected phone call, I am pleased to announce that in addition to the funds already pledged by CD Enterprises, another two million dollars has been confirmed in donations for the completion of your project."

A collective gasp echoes through the room with Colton's declaration. Voices buzz with excitement and the knowledge that our project is now fully funded, that all of our hard will work come to fruition.

I hang my head down amidst the commotion and squeeze my eyes shut as the roller coaster soars me up and then yanks me back down. I can't even begin to process the gamut of emotions coursing through me. On one hand, all of my efforts on behalf of my boys will pay off in a monumental way. More kids will benefit from the program and have the chance to become positive contributors to society. On the other hand, Colton is the one handing me this victory. *Talk about irony.* I'm being handed everything I've dreamed of on a professional level by the one person that I want more than anything in the whole world, but can't have on a personal level.

As much as I fight the emotions, they are just too much to bear. I'm overwhelmed. The flip-flopping between hurt and anger and misery has exhausted me. A tear slips down my cheek, and I hastily dash it away with the back of my hand as my shoulders tremble from the threat of so many more. The pain of having Colton just within reach and yet so far away from me is just too much. Everything is too fresh. Too raw.

I've lost myself so much to my emotions that I've forgotten my surroundings. When I come back to myself, the room is silent. I keep my head down, trying to pull myself together when I hear Teddy's hushed voice. "It's meant everything to her. She's put her heart and soul into this...you can't fault her for being overwhelmed."

I hear murmurs of agreement, and I'm relieved that my coworkers have mistaken my visible emotion as elation in respects to the good news on the project rather than as a result of my personal heartache. I force a thready smile onto my lips and look up at the room of people despite the tears pooling in my eyes. I meet Teddy's gaze, warmth and pride reflected on his face, and I smile sheepishly at him, playing into the charade. *Anything to escape from Colton.* "If you'll excuse me, I just need a moment," I murmur.

"Of course." He smiles softly as does the rest of the room, assuming correctly that I need to go pull myself together but for all of the wrong reasons.

I rise and calmly walk to the door, leaving a wide berth to where Colton stands, and exit the room. I can hear Teddy's voice congratulating everyone and declaring the meeting over seeing as there is no need to brainstorm how to secure the remainder of the funding anymore. My pace quickens as the distance increases from the conference room. I hold up my hand to Stella, effectively dismissing her, as she calls out my name. I make it to my office and shut the door in the nick of time before the first sob tears from my throat.

I let them roll through me as I lean against the wall opposing the door. I've tried to be so strong and hold them in for so many days, but I can't anymore. I'm disappointed in myself for still caring about him. Upset that I still want him to think about me. Pissed that he can affect me in so many ways. That he still makes my heart swell for him while my head acknowledges that he turned to Tawny when things between us went beyond the mandated Colton dating stipulations.

I ignore the gentle knock on the door, not wanting anyone to see me in such a wrecked state. The person persists and I try to rub away the tears from my cheeks knowing it's useless. There is no way I can hide my crying jag. I snap my head up as the door opens and Colton slides inside, shutting it behind him and leaning against it.

I'm staggered by his presence in my office. He dominates the small space. It's one thing to try and get over him when he's not tangible, but when he is right in front of me—when I can touch him with my fingertips—it's that much more unbearable. Our eyes lock onto each other's and my mind whirls with so many things I want to say and so many things I fear to ask. The silence is so loud between us it's deafening. Colton's eyes are saying so much to me, asking so much of me, but I'm unable to respond.

He pushes off the door and takes a step toward me. "Rylee…" My name is a plea on his lips.

"No!" I tell him, my quiet yet useless defense against him. "No," I say again with more resolve as he takes another step. *"Don't do this here, Colton. Please."*

"Ry…" He reaches out to touch me, and I bat his hand away.

"No." My lip trembles as he stands inside my personal space. I look down at the ground. Anywhere but his eyes. "Not here, Colton. You don't get to come into my work—*my office*—and take the one place that has been keeping me sane after what you did to me and taint it." My voice breaks on my last words as a tear escapes and makes a path down my cheek. "Please…" I push against his chest to try and gain some distance, but I'm not quick enough because he grabs my wrists and holds them. The jolt of electricity still remaining between us has me gritting my teeth and fighting back more tears.

"Enough!" He grates out. "I'm not a patient man, Rylee. Never have been and never will be. I've given you your space, dealt with you ignoring me, but I have half a mind to tie you down to your chair and force you to listen to me. Keep it up and I will."

"Let go!" I yank my wrists from him, needing to break the connection.

"I didn't sleep with her, Rylee!" He grates out.

"I don't want to hear the sordid details, Colton." I have to stop him. I can't listen to the lies. "Two words, condom wrapper." I'm proud of myself for the quiet steel in my voice. Proud that I can process a thought when my insides are shredding.

"Nothing happened!" he snaps harshly at me as he paces the small confines of my office. "Absolutely nothing!"

"I'm not one of your typical airheads, Colton. I know what I saw and I saw—"

"Jesus fucking Christ woman, it was just a goddamn fucking kiss!" His implacable voice fills the room.

And empties my heart.

I force myself to swallow. To unheard what he's said. "What?" I ask, disbelief dripping from my question as he grabs the back of his neck and pulls down on it, a grimace of regret on his face. "First you swear that nothing happened. Now you're telling me that it was just a kiss. What next? You're going to tell me you forgot that your dick accidentally slipped into her? The story keeps changing, but I'm supposed to believe that this time you're telling the truth?" I laugh, hysteria mixed with the hurt bubbling up. "Last I checked, you didn't need a condom to kiss someone."

"It's all just a misunderstanding. You're totally blowing this out of proportion and I—"

A knock on the door jolts us from our bubble. It takes me a moment to find my voice and sound composed. "Yes?"

"Teddy needs you in five," Stella says timidly through the door.

"Okay. I'll be right there." I close my eyes momentarily, resigning my soul to this continuous anger and hurt.

Colton clears his throat; his face clearly conflicted between forcing me to hash this out and allowing me to retain my dignity here at work. Reluctantly he nods his head in defeat. "I'll go, Rylee. I'll leave, but I'm not letting you run away from this—from us—until I get to have my say. This is by no means over. Understood?"

I just look at him, missing him so desperately but unable to wrap my head around telling him I love him and then him running into another woman's arms. Unable to accept the ever-changing story about what happened between him and Tawny. I nod my head once, panic fluttering through my body when I realize that as much as I need distance, a part of me is relieved to know that I will get to see him again. It's a silly thought seeing as the sight of him churns my stomach and causes my heart to hurt, but you can't undo the addictive haze of love.

Tears well in my eyes as I brace myself when he leans in and places a lingering kiss on the top of my head. Chills dance up my spine despite my initial reaction to pull away from him in self-preservation.

He holds my head to his lips for a moment so that I can't squirm away. "I had to see you, Rylee. I moved Heaven and earth to get that sponsorship so that I could call Teddy and tell him to let me present today." My breath hitches at his words. I can feel his throat work a swallow as I drown in him despite the pain he's inflicting. "It's killing me that you won't talk to me—that you won't believe me—and I'm not sure what to do with how that makes me feel." He pauses but keeps his cheek against my head, and I know opening up like this is difficult for him. "*I can still feel you, Rylee.* Your skin. The way you taste. Your lips when you smile against mine. Smell the vanilla you wear. Hear your laugh…you're everywhere. You're all I can think about."

With those parting words, Colton turns and leaves my office, shutting the door behind him without looking back. I nearly cave. I nearly give into the urge to call his name and go back on the promises I made to myself long ago about what I deserve in a relationship. The memory of Tawny in his doorway draws me back to myself. Allows me to keep the slippery hold on my resolve.

I exhale slowly, trying to locate my composure because his words have undone me. They were the words I needed to hear weeks ago. The words I needed to hear in response to telling him I loved him. But now I'm just not sure if they're too late. My stumbling heart says they're not, but my sensible head says yes as it tries to protect my vulnerable feelings.

After a few minutes, I stop trembling and freshen up my make-up in time to participate in a smaller conference with the bigwigs from corporate. During the meeting, my cell phone vibrates signaling an incoming text, and I grab it quickly as to not interrupt the conversation. In my fleeting glance, I see the short text from Colton.

Sad by Maroon 5 - x C

I know the song. A man talking about the two paths of a relationship. A man admitting that he chose the wrong one to take.

That he never said the words she needed to hear. That he realizes it now that she's gone.

I take a small victory in knowing he's affected by the turn of events, but it doesn't feel good. Nothing about this situation feels good.

I hate that I want him to hurt as much as I do. I hate myself for wanting him even when he hurt me. And more than anything, I hate that he made me feel again because right now I just wish I could go back to being numb.

I pull myself from my thoughts and wonder for the hundredth time if Colton really misses me or if he's once again trying to repair that fragile ego of his from being rejected.

Regardless, he's a big boy and big boys have to take responsibility for their screwed up actions. He says nothing happened but it's hard to believe when I saw them wearing the same pieces of a matching outfit.

Consequences. I'm sure that's a word he's never had to own up to before. I don't plan on responding, but I do just for measure.

I Knew You Were Trouble – Taylor Swift.

Chapter Thirty-Three

"So you're still not going to talk to him?"

"Nope." I put the Xbox game back on the shelf, trying to remember if Shane has it already.

"Nope? That's all you're going to give me?"

"Yup." I furrow my brow in indecision as I look around the various possible presents at Target.

"Are you going to say more than one word for an answer?"

"Hmm." I stall for a moment. "What do you get a sixteen year old boy for his birthday?"

"Beats me. I realize avoidance is really your thing right now, but you're an idiot if you think that you're going to be able to steer clear of him at the race."

"I've done a pretty good job so far and after yesterday, I've got enough of a reason to keep avoiding him," I shrug, not really wanting to have this conversation with Haddie. I just want to get Shane's birthday present, and then go home and shower before my shift and Shane's birthday party.

I hear Haddie's loud sigh of frustration but ignore it. "Ry, you've got to talk to him. You're miserable. You said yourself he said nothing happened."

I snort in jest. "'He' being the operative word Haddie." I say, turning to her, a chill in my voice as a result of her constant meddling in regards to how I'm handling the relationship that I no longer have with Colton. "Put yourself in my shoes. Let's say that you went to talk to the guy you're seeing and some long-legged bimbo, the one who has made it crystal clear to you in previous conversations that she wants your man, opens his door. In the morning. The only thing she is wearing is his T-shirt. *Definitely no bra.* And your boyfriend comes to answer the door, buttoning up his jeans, happy trail showing *and then some* to let you know that he was naked just prior to that moment. You realize that Long-Legged-Bimbo is most likely wearing the T-shirt that is missing from your boyfriend's bare chest. You ask said boyfriend what the hell is going on, and you can see his mind trying to figure out how to explain what you've just seen." I shove another game back on the shelf. "As he's denying nothing happened, a condom wrapper falls from his pocket. He still claims nothing happened. I believe the actual words he used were absolutely nothing happened, but push him a little—get him flustered—and oops, out slips that it was just a kiss. Only a kiss. I guarantee if I push him a little harder, more truths will spill out. *Nothing happened my ass!*"

"There could be a perfectly good reason…" she throws in there but stops when I glare at her.

"That's what I thought."

"I just hate seeing you like this." She angles her head at me and twists her lips. "Look, I understand where you're coming from, Ry, I do. I really do, but I wouldn't be a good friend if I just sat back and watched you make a mistake. I think you're so upset—and rightfully so—at what happened that you're not seeing the forest through the trees right now. You need to talk to him and hear him out. I mean the guy is still chasing after you relentlessly."

I raise my eyebrows in agitation, my feathers automatically ruffled. "Guilt will do that to you," I mutter as I move on looking at other possible gift options.

"It will," she agrees, "but so will being falsely accused of something." I peer up from the case of iPods and accessories, meeting her eyes. She reaches out and places a hand on my upper arm. "I've seen the way he looks at you. I'm watching his non-stop attempts to get your attention. Shit, he's been to our house three times in the last week trying to get you to listen to him. I'm not going to lie to him anymore for you and tell him you're not home. I know you're scared to let him back in again, but I think that fear might be healthy. The man's got it bad for you. Just like you do him. Please, keep that in mind."

I stare at her for a moment and then turn back to the case, needing a minute to digest what the one person that knows me better than anyone else has just said. "I'll think about it," is all I can manage. "Am I missing something here? Why are you pushing this so hard when you are the queen of moving on to the next guy when there is the smallest transgression let alone the guy screwing someone else? I just don't get it."

"Because he makes you happy. He challenges you. Pushes you outside your comfort zone. Makes you feel again—both good and bad—but at least you're feeling. How can I not when in the short time you've been together, you've come back to life again?" She throws a box of cereal in the cart I'm pushing. "I know I'm supposed to side whole-heartedly with you because you're my best friend, but I'm holding out hope."

I try and let her words sink in. "You didn't see what I saw, Haddie. And let's face it, words mean nothing. One minute he says nothing happened and then the next that it was just a kiss, but you know what? Something did happen, and I'm not just talking about between him and Tawny. I told him I loved him—and the something that happened was him running away and turning to another woman." My voice cracks on my last words, my resolve weakening. "I understand that he might have issues because of his past—I get that. Running away for a while to figure your head out is one thing, but running to another woman? That's unacceptable."

"I've never known you to be so hard on someone. To not give him the benefit of the doubt. From what you said, he seems to be as miserable as you are."

"We're done here," I tell her, and I mean more than just the shopping. I don't want to listen to her sympathize with Colton any more. I roll my eyes on a sigh as Haddie steps in front of the cart to block me.

"A man like Colton isn't going to wait around forever," she warns. "You need to figure out what you want or else you're going run the risk of losing him. Sometimes when you love someone, you have to do and say things you never thought you ever would—like forgiving. It sucks donkeys, but that's just the way it is." She steps to the side of the cart, her eyes steadfast on mine. "There's a fine line between being stubborn and being stupid, Rylee,"

"Hmpf," is all I manage to say in response, pushing the cart past her, but her words hit their target. I blow out a long breath as I fight back the tears threatening and the images that flood my memory. I struggle to figure out where exactly that line is. At what point do I actually open myself up and listen to Colton's explanations with the possibility of believing him? And at what part of that process do I become stupid for either forgiving or not forgiving him. Am I willing to let the man I love walk away on principal alone?

It's a no win situation, and I'm so sick of thinking about it and dwelling over it. Seeing as how I will be spending time with him and his team in St. Petersburg starting Thursday, I think I'll have more than ample time to dwell some more on it then. Right now, I just want to buy Shane his birthday present and go enjoy his party without the complication of Colton's presence.

Fuck! I groan internally. I'm being a coward and I know it. I'm just so afraid to forgive and get hurt again. To get sucked up in the tornado that is Colton and be hurled back into emotional suicide. I laid myself out bare and he chewed me up and spit me out just like Tawny said he would. But what if Haddie's right? What if I'm fucking this up? What if he didn't do it?

And it's in the middle of my self-deprecation that I look up and my eyes catch the latest issue of People. And there he is—the current cause of my misery and schizophrenic emotional state—gracing the cover of the magazine. A candid shot of him and Cassandra Miller together at a party.

The pang hits me in a flash and I do my best to recover quickly. Unfortunately I've been getting good at it over the past few days.

"As miserable as I am?" I question Haddie, sarcasm rich in my voice. I try to tear my eyes away but they won't budge. They scrape over every detail of the picture. "Yeah he looks like he's really suffering."

Haddie sighs in exasperation. "Ry, it was a charity auction. One that you were supposed to attend as his date if I recall, and I read online that he showed up alone."

I swallow the lump in my throat. It's bad enough to think of him with Tawny, but now I have to push the image of Cassie out of my head too. "Arriving alone and leaving alone are two completely different things," I respond wryly, forcing my eyes from the cover.

"Ry—"

"Just drop it, Haddie," I say, knowing I'm being irrational but so beyond caring any more.

Haddie and I chat about everything but Colton as we leave the store, our earlier conversation tucked away for me to ponder later and a new set of noise canceling head phones and an iTunes gift card for Shane under my arm. Haddie and I are a few feet from my car when I hear, "Excuse me, Miss?"

I glance at Haddie before turning to the voice at my back, suddenly grateful that Haddie asked to accompany me on my errand. There is nothing more unnerving to a female than a random man approaching you in a parking lot when you're alone. "Can I help you?" I ask the gentleman as he nears me. He's of average height with a baseball cap covering his longish brown hair and eyes masked behind a pair of blacked out sunglasses. He looks completely normal, but he still makes me uncomfortable. Something about him seems familiar, but I know I've never met him before.

"Are you...no, you couldn't be?" he says in a uniquely sounding grate of a voice while shaking his head.

"Excuse me?"

"You look like that young lady that was featured in the paper with those orphaned kids and that racing guy. Was that you?"

His comment surprises me. I look at him for a moment thinking how to best respond and trying to figure out why he'd remember that particular article. Odd but possible. "Uh...yeah."

He just tilts his head and despite not being able to see his eyes behind his dark lenses, I get the distinct feeling that he is running his eyes over the length of my body and it unnerves me. Just as I'm about to say screw this and get in the car, he speaks again. "What a great program you have there. Just thought I'd let you know."

"Thanks," I say absently as I climb in my car, dismissing him and breathing a sigh of relief when he walks away without another word.

Haddie looks over at me, concern etched in her eyes. "Creepy," she mutters, and I can't help but agree.

Chapter Thirty-Four

"*Not yet!*" I chastise Shane as he begs again to open one of his presents.

"Oh c'mon, Ry," he flashes his lady killer grin at me. "Can't I at least open one?"

"Nope! No presents are being opened until after cake. You have to make a wish first!" I smirk as I finish the last portion of dinner clean-up. "Besides, you already opened the presents from your friends last night when you all went to the movies."

"Can't fault a guy for trying," he says as he sits on a barstool.

"What'd you guys see?"

His eyes light up like a normal sixteen-year-old boy at the mention of his coed movie night out, and it warms my heart. This kid is a heartbreaker, and I remind myself to speak to Jackson about having a little man-to-man with him about being responsible. "That new zombie movie. It was way cool!"

"Mmm-hmm…did Sophie go with you guys?" His cheeks redden at her name, and I know that Jackson definitely needs to have that chat soon.

Shane fills me in on the details about his evening while the rest of the boys are outside with Dane, Bailey, Jackson, and Austin—the other counselors here to help celebrate. They are decorating the patio area for the birthday party, as is our practiced tradition here at The House.

"Okay, we're ready for the birthday boy!" Austin announces as he enters the kitchen. Shane rolls his eyes at the babyish idea of a birthday party, but I know deep down he secretly enjoys the fuss.

We head out to the patio where streamers and balloons hang

haphazardly yet affectionately. It's obvious that the younger boys helped with decorating. A cake sits on one table and another has a small gathering of birthday presents on it. Shane smiles brightly at the sight and at the chorus of cheers that erupt when he walks through the doorway.

We visit for a bit and play childish party games because for these kids nothing is silly. They've missed out on numerous ridiculous traditions in their lifetimes, and we want to try and provide such things for them here. After pin the tail on the donkey, we decide it's time for cake.

"Oops, I forgot the party plates," Bailey whispers to me as she places seventeen candles on the cake.

"I'll get them!" Scooter pipes up.

"No! I've got them," I say quickly as Bailey looks at me oddly. "All the stuff for the Easter baskets are in the same cabinet," I whisper to her, not wanting Scooter to accidentally see the Easter Bunny's secret stash. She just smiles and calls him back to help her.

It takes me a while to get the plates out of the cabinet in the garage because I move and re-stash the Easter garb onto a higher shelf and place some stuff in front of it for better hiding. Austin is walking down the hall to find me when I come back in the door from the garage to the house.

"Everything okay?" he asks, his English accent turning the corners of my mouth up a tad. He really is the epitome of handsome with his blond hair and golden skin and very serious girlfriend whom I've come to call a friend.

"Yeah." I smile. As we walk through the great room and out toward the back door, he slings an arm over my shoulder and pulls me close into his side to whisper what he got Shane for his birthday as we walk onto the patio. I laugh out loud as he tells me about his gag gift and then his real gift, when I refocus my attention on the party. And although it is completely innocent, Austin's mouth is nuzzled into my ear divulging his birthday present secrets when I raise my head and surprisingly meet Colton's eyes across the yard.

I feel like the world falls out beneath my feet, my heart staggering in my chest and breath catching in my throat. His comments mingled with Haddie's mix and meld in my head, and every part of my body and soul wants every part of his right now. I want the complications gone, the images in my head of him and Tawny to vanish, and to just be back to where we were with him shaving in my bathroom with the pink handle of my razor in his hand.

And as much as I want to see him again regardless of the pain his presence causes, I can't find it in me to forgive what he did. Wouldn't it just happen again?

His eyes hold mine for a beat, shooting daggers at Austin and his arm draped on my shoulder, before turning back to his conversation with of all people, intern Bailey. Yes, that Bailey. The girl I believe he'd messed around with prior to helping me out of the storage closet that first night we met. And even though Colton keeps glancing over at me, Bailey is clueless, all of her blatant flirting focused solely on him. My stomach revolts when I see her place a hand on his bicep and smile suggestively up at him.

"Someone didn't get the memo," Dane whispers in my ear as Austin goes to help Ricky with something.

"What?"

"Bailey didn't seem to get the memo that Colton's no longer on the market."

"She can have him." I snort, rolling my eyes as I see him dart another glance over at me. Dane looks at me oddly, and I realize that I've let our little no-longer-seeing-each other predicament slip. I've purposely kept what has happened quiet, not wanting anyone at the company to get wind that Colton and I are at odds so it wouldn't get back to Teddy. It's really been easy since I never spoke about it anyway; rather I just let the rumors run without confirming or denying them.

"Uh-oh." Dane smirks, always one for juicy gossip. "Sounds like trouble in paradise."

"Paradise is most definitely not the word I'd use to describe it," I murmur, unable to take my eyes off of Colton. "Try a sinking ship without life preservers and a whole shitload of issues."

"Everybody's got issues, honey. Too bad he doesn't swing my way because I could definitely take care of any mommy issues he may have by making sure he tends to *my big daddy issue* if you catch my drift." He wags his eyebrows playfully.

"Eew gross!" I slap his shoulder but burst out laughing. I can't help it. It's the first good laugh I've had in weeks, and it feels good to just let go.

"I have a feeling there are going to be fireworks in St. Petersburg, and it's nowhere near the fourth of July." Dane snickers.

I have a serious case of the giggles, my catharsis over my pent up emotions happening at the oddest time, and several of the boys look at me as if I've lost my marbles. "Okay...c'mon you guys," I say, struggling to contain my laughter, "it's time to cut the cake."

Everyone gathers around the table, Shane sitting in front of the cake as we light the candles and sing to him. His face full of excitement when he closes his eyes to make his wish, and I wonder what it is he is hoping for. The cake is cut and everyone is enjoying a piece, so I slip inside to bring the ice cream back to the freezer and clean off the knife. I shut the freezer door and jump out of my skin when I see Colton standing there in the kitchen.

"*Who's the Brit?*"

"Jesus! You scared me!"

I keep my hand on the refrigerator handle, unsure what to do as we just stare at each other. Several times over the past few weeks, I've wished that I could rewind time and take back those three little words that I'd said, but I realize right now in this moment—as he stands before me so achingly beautiful inside and out—that I don't think I would. I did love him. I still love him. And he needed someone to tell him so that at some point in the future he can look back and accept the fact that he is worthy of such a love. I just don't know if I'm willing to stick around and accept the pain that I'm positive he'll inflict on the person willing to assert such a notion.

"Sorry." He smirks halfheartedly, but the smile never reaches his eyes. Rather, I sense irritation and impatience from him. "*Who is he?*" he demands again, and there is no masking his annoyance now. "Is he with you because you sure looked cozy? You moved on awfully quick, Rylee."

Every part of me that sagged in relief at seeing him here tonight is now bristling with irritation. Who the hell does he think he is coming here and accusing me of having a date? If he thought this was the right way to start our conversation, he's sadly mistaken.

"Seriously, Colton?" I roll my eyes using Shane's word, not wanting to deal or spend the time to assuage Colton's fragile ego. When he just stands there and stares at me, I relent for the sake of not making a scene despite the jealous, alpha-male tantrum he's throwing. "He's a counselor here." I huff out.

He angles his head and stares at me, muscle ticking in his jaw, eyes piercing. "*Have you fucked him?*"

"That's none of your goddamn business." I sneer at him, anger rising as I try to brush past him.

He reaches out and grabs my bicep, holding me in place so my shoulder hits the middle of his chest. I can feel the rapid beat of his heart against my arm and hear his uneven breathing as I stare straight ahead. "Everything about you is my business, Rylee." A disgusted snort is my only response. "Did you?"

"Hypocrite. Unlike you, Ace, I don't make a habit of *fucking* the people that work for me." I tilt my chin up and look into his eyes to let him see the anger, hurt, and defiance brimming in mine. The grimace he emotes on his otherwise stoic countenance lets me know I've made my point. We just stand like this for a moment, staring at each other. "Why are you here, Colton?" I eventually ask with resignation.

"Shane invited me to his birthday party." He shrugs, taking his hand from my arm and shoving both hands deep into the pockets of his jeans. "I couldn't let him down just because you refuse to see me."

What can I say to that? How can I be mad at him for being here, when he's here for one of the boys?

"And because..." He runs a hand through his hair and steps back while he struggles to figure out what to say next. He blows out an audible breath and is about to speak again when Shane comes barreling into the house.

"We're going to...open presents now," he finishes after looking back and forth from Colton and me, his brow furrowing with uncertainty as he tries to figure out the dynamic between the two of us.

I inhale deeply; glad to be saved because I don't think I'd made my mind up on what to do just yet. My heart tells me I want to listen to him, understand what happened, and figure out where to go from here. But my head, my head tells me, *"Quack."*

"Presents!" I repeat as I walk out of the kitchen and brush past Colton without acknowledging his comment.

Shane's excitement is more than contagious to the rest of us bystanders as he opens his gifts. His eyes are full of excitement, and his smile reflects a teenager who feels loved. I stand on the fringe of the crowd, watching the action and reflecting a bit on what a good job we're doing here with these boys. It's odd how sometimes it just hits you, and right now is one of those moments. I lean against the beam of the patio cover as Shane lifts his last present up and shakes it as the little ones yell out what they think it might be.

It's a flat rectangular box that I hadn't seen on the table before, and I take a step closer to see what it is, my curiosity getting the better of me. Shane rips the paper off and when he opens the box, a card slides out. He turns the card over in his hand, and when he sees nothing on the envelope, he shrugs and tears it open. I watch his eyes widen and his lips fall open as he reads the words inside. His head snaps up and he searches the partygoers to meet Colton's eyes. *"Seriously?"* he asks, incredulity in his voice.

I'm curious as to what's written in the card and my sight focuses on Colton's as a shy smile spreads across his lips, and he shakes his head, "Seriously, Shane."

"You're shittin' me?"

"Shane!" Dane snaps out at him in warning, and Shane's cheeks turn red as he blushes at the reprimand.

Colton laughs out loud. "No, I'm not. Keep your grades up and I will. *I promise.*"

Still mystified as to what the two of them are talking about, I ease out of the shadows and walk up to Shane. He holds the card out for me to see. The card is a typical birthday card, but it's the penmanship inside that makes my heart flop.

Happy Birthday, Shane! What I remember the most about turning 16 is wanting desperately to learn how to drive…so this card entitles you to driving lessons—from me. (I get to pick the car though…and the Aston is off limits). Have a good one bud. —Colton

I look down at Shane who still seems like he can't believe that a famous race car driver has offered up to be his behind-the-wheel instructor. And I see in his eyes the self-worth that Colton has given him in this one offering and bite back the tears that burn my throat. He doesn't offer him something of material value that he can buy easily, but rather gives Shane something much more valuable—*time.* Someone to look up to. Someone to spend time with. Colton understands these boys so well and what they need at what times, and yet he can't comprehend what I need and how I feel about what I walked in to.

Shane gets up and walks over to Colton and shakes his hand to thank him before passing the card to everyone to show them what it says. I look away from observing Shane to see Colton silently watching me. I just shake my head softly at him trying to convey my appreciation for his well thought out gift. He holds my gaze as he slowly walks over to me. I bite my bottom lip in hesitation. My body is filled with a civil war of emotions, and I just don't know what to do anymore.

Colton places his hand on my lower back, the contact sending my nerves dancing even more than they already are. His signature scent envelops me, and I reflexively part my lips, craving the taste of him that I've missed so much.

He leans in to me and asks for the second time tonight, "Can we speak for a moment?" His rasp fills my ears and the warmth of his breath feathers over my cheek.

I step back from him, needing distance to keep a clear head. "Um…I don't think it's a good idea…The House isn't the best place to…" I fumble with the words.

"Don't care. This won't take long," is his only response as he steers me the fringe of activity on the patio. The short reprieve gives my mind time to think. To rationalize. To decide. "I'm talking, you're listening. Understood?"

I turn to face him and look up at the lines of his magnificent face partially hidden by the shadows of the night. My angel struggling between the dark and the light. I take a fortifying breath before I open my mouth to speak, options and indecision swirling around with mixed emotions. "Colton…" I begin before he can speak and when I see the annoyance flash across his face, I decide to change tactics. Try to protect my heart from further devastation even though it's crying in protest over what I'm about to do. "There's nothing to explain." I shrug; swallowing down the lump clogging my throat so the lies can prevail. "You made it clear from the beginning what was between us. I mistook our physical chemistry for love." Colton's eyes narrow and his mouth falls lax at my words. "*Typical female mistake*. Great sex doesn't mean love. Sorry about that. I know how much you hate drama, but I realize that you're right. *This would've never worked*." I grit my teeth, knowing this is for the best as I watch the confusion flicker across his face. "It's not like we were exclusive. What you did with Tawny is your business. I may not like it, but that's the breaks right?"

If I write him off, it might make having to work together less awkward for the both of us despite knowing deep down that having to be beside him when my heart still desires him—*hell, when every cell in my body wants him in one way or another*—will be brutal.

Trying to prevent the memory of the wounded look in those crystalline green eyes, I start to turn away from him, moving so he can't see the welling tears or my trembling chin. He reaches out and holds his favored spot on my bicep. "Get back here, Rylee…"

I squeeze my eyes shut at the forlorn sound of my name from his lips and try to infuse nonchalance in my voice when I actually find it. "Thanks for the good time. It was real while it lasted." I shrug my arm out of his grasp, and only when I open my eyes to walk away do I see Shane watching the interaction, concern in his eyes at the expression on my face.

Colton mutters a curse beneath his breath as I walk away under the pretense of going to help clean up. Rather than going in to the kitchen to wash dishes, I walk right past it and go into the counselors' room. I sit on the edge of one of the twin beds there and hold my head in my hands.

What did I just do? I try to catch my breath, my conscience and my heart not agreeing with what my head decided was the best course of action. I fall back on the bed and rub my eyes with my hands, a litany of curses falling quietly from my lips as I chastise myself. A soft knock is at the door and before I can sit myself up, Shane pokes his head into the open doorway.

"*Rylee?*"

"Hey, bud." I sit up and the smile I think I'm going to have to force comes naturally at the look of concern on his face. "What's up?" I ask as I pat the spot on the bed next to me. I can tell something is bugging him.

He shuffles over and sits down next to me, eyes angled down as he laces and unlaces his own fingers. "I'm sorry." He breathes.

"For what?" I'm usually pretty good at following the moods of the boys, but I'm thrown here.

"I just...you've been sad...and he makes you happy...usually...so I invited him so that you'd be happy again. And now you're sad...and it's because of him. And I..." He clenches his fists and grits his teeth.

Shane's discomfort is obvious as it hits me what he's saying. My heart breaks as I realize that he's invited Colton here to try and cheer me up without knowing he's the reason I've been so somber the past few days. And then I feel guilty because I obviously did let my relationship with Colton affect my work. I reach out and squeeze his hand.

"You didn't do anything wrong, Shane." I wait until he raises his eyes to mine—eyes of the man he's becoming but still reflecting the unsettled little boy deep inside. "What makes you think I've been sad?"

He just shakes his head, tears starting to collect at the corners of his eyes. "You just have been..." He stops, and I wait for him to finish the thought I can see working its way to his mouth. "My mom was always so sad...always so upset because it was just us two...I never did anything to help...and then..." *One day you found her dead with the empty bottles of pills beside her bed.* "I'm sorry, I was just trying to make things better...I didn't realize he's the one who made it worse."

"*Oh, sweet boy,*" I tell him, pulling him into my arms as a lone tear slides down his cheek. My heart swells with the love I have for this boy, so much older than his years for unfathomable reasons but with such a tender heart, trying to make me feel better. "That is one of the nicest things that anyone has ever done for me." I lean back and frame his face in my hands. "You, Shane—you and the rest of the boys in our family—are what makes me happy on a daily basis."

"Kay... Well, I don't have to accept his present if it upsets you," he offers without a hesitation.

"Don't be silly." I pat his leg, the gesture touching me. "Colton and I are fine," I lie for good measure. "He's just being a guy." I get a slight smile out of him with that line despite his eyes still reflecting uncertainty. "Besides, think how cool it'll be to tell all of your friends that a real race car driver taught you how to drive!"

His grin widens, "I know! It's so cool!" And once again we are back on even footing. He stands and starts toward the door, my little boy who is growing up so fast.

"Hey, Shane?"

"Yeah?" He stops at the door and turns around.

"Happy birthday, buddy. *I football you* more than you'll ever know."

A sheepish smile spreads across his face, his hair flopping down over his forehead when he just shakes his head and looks at me. "I'm sixteen now. We can stop with the whole football thing." He pushes his hair out of his eyes as they meet mine. "I love you too," he says before shrugging as only a sixteen year old can and walking away. I stare after him with a smile plastered on my face, a heart overflowing with love, and tears of joy pooling in my eyes.

Chapter Thirty-Five

The beautiful Florida sunshine feels magnificent on my skin and elevates my spirits. Arriving a day earlier than needed in St. Petersburg, I have taken full advantage of the ever-present warm weather and lavish pool of the Vinoy Resort and Golf Club. The home base of CD Enterprises and Corporate Cares for the next few days. There's nothing like relaxation and the touch of sun on my skin to rejuvenate me before my official duties and the whirlwind that will ensue tomorrow.

It's not that I mind the crazy schedule—in fact, I look forward to meeting and thanking the people that have helped make the project a reality—it's that I will have to stand side by side with Colton to show the unity between our two companies. There are photo ops and sponsorship appreciation events among other things before the actual race on Sunday.

I cringe at the thought of my schedule—my close proximity to Colton—seeing as how I was able to avoid him the rest of the night at Shane's party and therefore didn't follow through on my promise to talk with him. I'm sure my due will come tomorrow when I see him, but for now, my head swims of sun and relaxation.

Rihanna's *Stay* plays in my earbuds, the lyrics hitting a little too close to home. Wanting to forgo getting sunburn on the first day here, I gather my belongings and head back toward the room.

I step into the empty elevator, and just as the door starts to close, "Hold the elevator!" echoes off of the marbled walls of the lobby. A hand sticks in the small space between the moving door and the wall, and it immediately retreats back open. I suck in a breath when a very sweaty, extremely delectable Colton jogs his way into the elevator. His momentum dies when his eyes meet mine.

A pair of sweat soaked gym shorts ride low on his hips while the top portion of his torso remains bare. His tan is darker, no doubt from his work out in the bright sun, and sweat glistens off every inch of his bared skin. My eyes wander helplessly over the well-defined ridges of his abdomen, the intricate markings of his tattoos, and to where rivulets of sweat drip down into the deep V that travels below his waistband. I swallow reactively at the memory of my hands mapping those lines and the feel of them bunching beneath my fingertips as he buries himself in me. I drag my eyes away and up to those magnificent pools of green that stare at me with a somber intensity.

Of all of the elevators in the entire frickin' resort, he has to pick this one?

A cautious smile turns up the corners of his mouth as he steps farther into the elevator toward me. He knows I'm affected. "Glad to see you got in okay."

"Yeah…" I clear my throat, finding it difficult to make my thoughts form into words when the temptation is so painstakingly clear in front of me. "Yes, I did. Thank you."

"Good," he says, eyes locked on mine.

The doors start to close again, and when a gentleman starts to walk in, Colton breaks our visual connection and steps in front of him, spreading his arms across the entrance. "Sorry, this elevator's taken." His voice that denotes that there is no arguing the matter.

I start to protest as the doors close and Colton whirls around to me, his predatory glare matching the posture of his body. "Don't even start, Rylee…" He growls, silencing me as he takes a step toward me. His chest is heaving and I'm not sure if it's a result of the exertion from his run or because of our close proximity. His dominance of this small space is all consuming. "This ends right now."

He takes another step closer, his jaw clenched, his eyes unforgiving as they leave mine and roam over my bikini-clad torso. My swimsuit seemed to provide more than adequate coverage when I bought it, but standing here in an elevator with Colton's eyes scraping over every single curve of my body, it feels indecently suggestive. And I know it's because even though he's not touching me—even though I'm hurt and want nothing to do with him—my body remembers all too well the havoc he can wreak on my system with the simple graze of his fingertips or caress of his tongue.

I tell myself to snap out of it. To remember what he did to me, but it's so damn hard when his heady after-workout scent is dominating the small space. The ache resurfaces deep within my body at the sight of him, creating desires I know only he can satisfy. The man's pull on me is relentless, even when he doesn't even realize it. "Now's not a good time, Colton."

He chuckles a sliver of a laugh, but his face doesn't depict a single trace of humor. He takes a final step toward me, my retreat leaving my back pressed against the wall. He leans forward and presses his hands on either side of me, boxing me in. "Well, you better make it one, Rylee, because I really don't care. This ends right here, right now. Non-negotiable."

My breath hitches, betraying my false façade as his body brushes against mine. The heat of his skin radiates off of him and into me. His lips are mere inches from mine. All I'd have to do is lean forward to feel them. To taste him again. And then I realize that this is exactly what he wants. He wants to remind me physically so I forgive and forget about what happened emotionally.

Wrong tactic to use with me.

I want him—God yes I want him—but not on these terms. Not with lies still hanging between us. Not with the hurt from his deception poisoning my heart.

We breathe each other in, our eyes unwavering, and I'm proud of myself for holding my own. "I think you've forgotten how good we are together," he grates out in frustration when he realizes that I'm able to resist him.

I angle my head and look at him. "It's easy to forget when Tawny opens the front door of your whorehouse with nothing but your T-shirt on, Ace." I sneer, timing it perfectly so my last word coincides with the elevator's ding to our destined floor. I take the sound as my cue and duck quickly beneath his hands, bolting into the hallway to the sounds of a cursing Colton. I should know better by now how fast he is, but my mind is jumbled with everything else.

I can hear his footsteps behind me as I fumble with the keycard into my room. I think I may be in the clear, but the minute I have the door open, his hand slams against the door forcing it open with a bang. I don't even have a moment to yelp before he spins me around and crashes my back against the wall with the full force of his body.

"*Then let me remind you,*" he growls, and in my surprised state, I barely register his words, but they seep into my fuzzy conscience the moment before his lips claim mine. It's amazing that regardless of how long it's been—how hurt I am—when we connect, I feel like I'm home. A home currently set ablaze, but a home nonetheless. His mouth fervently possesses mine, and his hands map over every inch of my exposed flesh. Kneading. Stimulating. Possessing. I get lost in his taste; his touch; the low groan emanating in the back of his throat; the hard length of his body pressing into mine as one hand wraps around the waterfall of curls down my back and holds me captive to his mind-altering onslaught.

It takes a moment for my mind to work through the chaos and the bang of arousal he's just created between my thighs. I struggle out of the desire-induced haze that renders my body boneless. *Shit! Shit! Shit!*

"*No!*" It's a broken, strangled cry but a cry nonetheless. I push forcibly on his chest, tearing his mouth from mine. "I can't. I just can't! This doesn't fix anything!"

I stand there staring at him with our chests heaving and pulses racing—a sure sign that our chemistry still remains—and his more than addictive taste still on my lips. His hands are wrapped around my wrists, holding my hands against his damp and alluring chest. "Rylee..."

"No!" I try again to push against his chest, but my strength is no match for his. "You don't get to just take what you want, when you want it."

"My God, woman, you are driving me insane!" he mutters into the air.

"Why? Because you got caught?"

"You have to do something wrong to get caught!" he shouts, releasing my wrists and pushing away from me, his face a mix of exasperation, frustration, and unsatisfied desire. "*Nothing! Fucking! Happened!*" His voice bellows around the empty room and echoes in the emptiness of my hurting heart.

"*Tigers can't change their stripes, Ace.*"

"You and your fuckin' tigers and ducks," he mutters before turning his back and walking farther into my room and away from me.

"Don't forget jackasses!" I shout.

"Goddamn frustrating, pig-headed woman!" he says to himself before turning back around.

The man is infuriating, thinking he can just waltz in here and kiss me senseless so that I forget everything else. "C'mon, since when does the infamous ladies' man, Colton Donavan, resist a half-naked woman?" I sneer, taking a step toward him, infusing sarcasm in my next comment. "And to think you were even generous enough to offer her the shirt off your back." I snort. "With a track record like yours, I'm sure you offered what was in your pants as well. Oh, I'm sorry—we know you did because you made sure it was jacketed up. Nothing happened? Just a kiss? *And I'm supposed to believe that?*"

"Yes!" he shouts loud enough to make me wince. "Just like I was supposed to believe your excuse at Shane's party. It was bullshit and you know it."

"Don't you dare turn this on me!" I yell at him.

"You really believe that we were just sex?" He grates out, jaw clenched, voice challenging.

"Oh, were we something more?" Sarcasm drips from my words.

"Yes goddamnit!" He pounds his fist against the wall, "and you know it!"

I take a step toward him, anger overriding any intimidation I normally would have felt. "Well by you acknowledging it, it just makes what you did even worse?"

"What did I do, Rylee? Tell me exactly what I did!" He shouts at me, stepping well within the realm of personal space.

"Now you want to rub it in? You want to shove my face in it by making me say it out loud? Fuck you, Colton," I shout at him, anger starting to snake through my body and permeate through the hurt.

"No. I want to hear you say it. I want you to look in my eyes and see my reaction for yourself. What did I do?" he commands, giving my shoulders a slight shake. "Say it!"

And I refuse to. I refuse to watch the little smirk that I know will play at the corners of his mouth if I obey him so instead I say the only thing that comes to mind. "*Quack!*"

"Now you're just acting like a child!" Exasperated, he releases me and shoves his hand through his hair before taking a few steps from me to control his temper.

"A child?" I sputter, shock radiating through me. Talk about the pot calling the kettle black. "A fucking child? Look who's talking!"

"You," he says with a sneer and an arch of an eyebrow, "the child throwing the goddamn tantrum. The one so wrapped up in your own head, that you don't realize your little fit is for all of the wrong fucking reasons."

I stare at him for a moment, our eyes locked on one another's and I realize that we're tearing each other apart and for what? We obviously can't get past this. Me accusing. Him denying. "This is such a waste of time," I say quietly, a single tear slipping down my cheek and resignation in my voice.

He takes another step toward me, and I just shake my head at him, unable to let go the tumultuous emotions inside of me. How can I love this beautiful man before me and despise him at the same time? How can I crave and desire him, all the while wanting to throttle him? I sag against the wall as I try to process everything that I was afraid of happening transpire.

"Why was she there, Colton?" I stare unflinchingly into his eyes, asking but not really wanting to know the answer. His eyes look down for a moment, and his hesitancy makes me miserable. I gather every ounce of hurt I have in my voice, and when I speak, it drips with it. "I told you that cheating was a deal breaker for me."

"Nothing happened." He throws his hands up as the image of Tawny legs, hard nipples pressed against his T-shirt, and her smug smile flickers through my head. "*What is it going to take to make you believe me?*" The sound in his voice takes me by surprise. As if he really can't believe my doubt in him. Haddie's comments flicker through my mind, but I push them away. She wasn't there. *She didn't see what I saw.* She didn't see Tawny tousled from sleep with that victorious siren's smile across her swollen lips. The condom wrapper fluttering to the ground like a nail sealing the coffin lid shut. "Rylee, Tawny came to the house. We were drunk. Things got out of control. It all happened so fast that—"

"Stop!" I shout, holding up my hand, not wanting to hear the gory details that I know for sure will break my heart even further. "All I know, Colton, is that you pushed me to open up—to feel again after everything that happened with Max—and I did exactly what you said. I trusted you, despite my head telling me not to. I allowed myself to feel again. *I gave everything of myself to you.* Was willing to give so much more…and the minute you got spooked, you ran into the arms of another woman. *That's not okay with me.*"

He leans back against the wall opposite me, and we just stare at each other, sadness smothering the air between us. I can see him struggle with something but push it back. "I don't know what else to say, Rylee…"

"Saying nothing and running away are two completely different things." He pushes himself off of the wall and takes a step toward me. I shake my head at him. The fact that not once has he acknowledged that I told him I loved him slingshots into my head. He's here trying to make things right, but he can't acknowledge the words I spoke to him. *This is so fucked up.* "I could've lived with you saying nothing. I could've accepted you running away. But you ran into the arms of another woman. I can't bring myself to trust that it wouldn't happen again. You made your choice when you slept with Tawny."

His shoulders sag and his eyes flash with fire at my words before settling with defeat. "*I need you.*" The unhindered honesty behind his words strikes me and twists my heart.

"There's a fine line between wanting me and needing me, Colton. I needed you too." *And I still do.* "But you obviously needed her more. I just hope she was worth it." I choke on the words and shake my head. Anything to try and erase the sound of his voice saying he needs me. Anything to prevent the doubt from creeping in.

Hurt propels my thoughts. Devastation controls my actions. "I think it's best you go." I whisper, forcing the words past my lips.

He just looks at me, pools of green silently pleading with me. "You've made your choice then...." His voice is broken. Silent. Resigned.

I can't bring myself to agree with him. My body is a riot of conflicting answers, and saying it out loud will just add permanence to something half of me wants over and done with while the other half would kill to have a second chance at. There is nothing left for me to say. But I say it anyway.

"Yes, I have. But only because you did it for me."

"Rylee..."

"And mine's no longer you."

I break from his gaze and stare at the floor. *Anything to get him to leave.* He stands staring at me for a time, but I refuse to raise my head and look at him.

"This is fucking bullshit, Rylee, and you know it," he says evenly to me before turning to walk out. *"I guess you don't love the broken in me after all."*

The sob catches in my throat at his words and it takes everything I have to stay on my feet. And even standing proves to be too much because the minute I hear the door close, I slide down the wall until I hit the floor.

The tears come. Hard, jagged sobs that shudder through my body and steal little pieces of my soul with each one. His parting words echo over and over in my head until I know for sure that I'm the one that's broken, not him.

Doubts creep through. Sorrow sets in. Devastation reigns.

Chapter Thirty-Six

I slip back into my hotel room for a quick respite before the next event occurs. I tell myself that I just need to take a breather, but I know for a fact that I'm just being a coward and avoiding Colton as I've done for the better part of the day. He's been nothing but cordial in front of others but aloof when no one is watching. Hurt is evident in his eyes, but then it's prevalent in mine as well.

In one of the rare instances that we were alone, I tried to talk to Colton about his parting words to me. I wanted to tell him that I do love the broken in him—that I still want the parts of him that he's hiding away and afraid to let out—but when I opened my mouth to speak, he just dismissed me away with a glacial glare. His patience has obviously run out. It's what I wanted, so why do I feel like I'm dying inside.

What am I doing? *Am I making a huge mistake?* I press the heels of my hands to my eyes and sigh. Having him move on should make me happy. Should make me relieved that I don't have to put up with the "let me explain" routine. Then why am I so utterly miserable? Why do I have to swallow the huge lump in my throat every time I think of him or look at him?

I'm screwing this up. Maybe I need to listen to him. Give him the chance to explain. Maybe if I know the whole story it will help me push through this pain and move on once I hear all of the sordid details of his night with Tawny. And I think these details are exactly what I fear…but what if there are no sordid details? What if everything Haddie has been pushing into my ears is legitimate?

What if I'm in the wrong?

Crap. I am screwing this up. I can't even think straight—thoughts fragmenting in a million directions—but I know I'm fucking this up.

My cell phone chirps a text notification, and it drags me from my schizophrenic thoughts. It's a text from Dane about Zander. I dial him immediately. "What's wrong?" I ask in response to his greeting.

"He had a pretty rough night, Ry." He blows out a loud sigh. "Actually talked about that night. It was his dad, Ry. And he swears that he saw his dad in his window last night. Freaked out. Literally. But Avery was in the room with him, and she said that there was no one there."

"*Oh God!*" is all I can say, imagining the fear tearing through his little body.

"Yeah…Avery did a great job with him though. In fact, he hasn't left her side all day."

"Is he still talking?" My mind immediately thinks of all of the progress he's made in the past month. Of how in therapy he's started drawing pictures depicting what happened that horrific night and started piecing it together for both his counselors and the authorities. A set back like this could wipe all of that away and then some.

"Not as much but it's still fresh in his mind. I'm just keeping Avery with him. The two of them have really bonded."

"Do I need to come home? I can…" Guilt spirals through me. I should be there with Zander right now. Comforting him. Helping him through this. Holding him.

"Don't be silly, Ry. We've got it covered. I just know how you like to know everything about the kids when it happens."

"You're sure?"

"Positive," he reiterates. "How's it going resisting the Adonis? Is the ship still sinking or are you diving into his bits of paradise?"

I can't help the smile that forms on my lips. "You've been talking to Haddie, haven't you?" His silence is the only answer that I need. Resigned and needing someone to bounce things off of, I reluctantly respond. "It's…confusing." I sigh.

"Men always are, babe."

I laugh. "I don't know, Dane. I know what I saw. I'm not stupid. But between Haddie telling me I'm being stubborn and Colton's non-stop denial, I wonder if I'm making a mistake. I just don't get how one plus one doesn't equal two."

He just makes a non-committal sound on the other end of the line while he thinks. "Shit, Ry, not everything is black and white if you know what I mean. What does it hurt to hear him out?"

I breathe out audibly, fear snaking through me that I really might be wrong. That I might already be too late. "My pride."

"Sugar, maybe you should be holding on a little tighter to that Adonis instead of your pride. That'll just cause you to end up alone with lots of cats."

A silence settles between us, his words striking a little closer to home than I care to admit. "Yeah...I know."

"Then get off your ass and do something about it! A gorgeous man like that isn't going to wait around forever regardless of how delicious you are. Shit, I just might try to turn him."

I laugh again; always appreciative of Dane and his unsolicited advice that no doubt puts me in my place. Crap! I thank him quickly and hang up, my mind made up. I scramble quickly, slipping my practical outfit over my head, and grab the sexiest dress I have in my suitcase.

In the time I've had to sit and think about everything, I've reapplied my make-up and given myself a pep talk to regain some of my confidence. I'm not sure what I'm going to say to Colton, but I have to say something. I have to fix the damage of this cluster-fuck that we're continually finding ourselves in.

It's time for me to put on my big girl panties.

I figure if I can speak to him quickly, then I can make some plans to see him afterward and talk things through. I double-check my reflection in the mirrors of the elevator. My quick change has done wonders for both my appearance and my attitude. I head toward the ballroom where the event of the evening is taking place. An event that I had not been scheduled to attend, but I don't care. I have to do this now.

I can't wait any longer. I can't waste another minute clutching to my pride.

And besides, I really hate cats.

The evening's event is a charitable cocktail party where people pay the requisite donation and get the rights to say they had drinks with the elusive Colton Donavan. As much as I'm thrilled that the funds will be going toward a local St. Petersburg organization for orphaned children, I have a hunch that the attendees of this evening's event will be more concerned with trying to grab Colton's attention—or rather what's in his pants—than the kids their money will be helping.

I take a deep breath as I walk. My mind's made up. I need to talk to Colton. Tonight. I need to either bury this or take a chance, trust him, and listen to what he has to say. Believe him when he tells me that he didn't sleep with Tawny—that he'd never cheat on me. I silently rehearse the words I want to say. Nerves jingle in my stomach. I smooth my hands over my dress, turning the corner to the foyer leading to the ballroom and stop dead in my tracks when I come face to face with the one person I have dreaded seeing this entire trip. The one person I am most certain that Colton has purposely kept my eyes from even catching a glimpse of.

"*Well isn't this an unexpected surprise,*" her unmistakable voice chides, causing the hairs on the back of my neck to stand up. It takes everything I have from launching myself at her. From slapping that smug, smarmy smirk off of her face and showing her how I really feel about her.

And I'm just about to lay into her when the gentleman passing by catches my eye and nods at me, a murmured, "Rylee," on his lips—a corporate sponsor.

I nod back at him, forcing a slight smile in greeting, knowing that as much as I'd like to attack Tawny right here and show her what I think of her, I can't commit the professional suicide that would result from it. And I know that Tawny knows it because she works her tongue in her cheek as her smirk widens.

"What?" she says, looking me up and down. "You're finally ready to forgive Colton for his indiscretions?" She quirks her eyebrows, so much more than contempt dancing in her eyes. And it's not lost on me that the word 'indiscretions' is plural. I stare at Tawny, so many things I'd like to spew at her running through my mind. I physically have to clench my fists to prevent them from reaching out and slapping her. Anger is so thick in my throat that words don't come. Feelings—emotions—hatred overwhelms, but words don't come.

"Did you think he'd change just for you, doll? Maybe you should ask him *what* or should I say *who* he's been up to these past couple of weeks." A sliver of a laugh escapes her botox enhanced lips as she takes a step closer. "Neither Raquel nor Cassie nor..." she raises her eyebrows with the insinuation of herself "...had any complaints in your absence."

Her words shock me at first and then catapult me into fury. "Go to Hell, Tawny," I grit out as I take a step closer to her, infringing well inside the bounds of her personal space. My hands shake. My blood rushes. She has singlehandedly replaced my hope of reconciling with

281

Colton with unfiltered ire and absolute despair. What should I expect? She's the one who took it from me in the first place.

I'm done. So fucking done. Just when I had worked myself up to believe that I was the one in the wrong—place the blame for all of this heartache on myself—here comes the truth, slapping me in the face. My hope splinters and falls to the ground around me.

"You know what?" I sneer, wanting to shove her up against the wall behind us and wrap my hand around her throat. "I don't care who gets him anymore, but sure as hell, *I'll make certain it's not you!*"

She laughs coyly, my words not affecting her. "Well big shock, sweetie, you've already fucked that up since Colton's mine for the rest of the night." She smirks, winking at me before turning and walking off. I stand there watching her back as she retreats, and I can't even begin to process my whirlwind of thoughts.

He's been with other women? This whole time he's been trying to win me back, he's been screwing his exes? Teagan's words from the gala come back to me. *What an ass I am.* I actually believed him that he wanted me back. *That he was willing to change for me.*

The Big Bad Wolf definitely has tricked Little Red Riding Hood.

The all too familiar feelings of hurt turned into rage course through me. Before, where I would have run and hidden, right now—right now—I want to unleash my fury on Colton. Unload on him and tell him exactly what I think. And although it's not the right time or place, my feet obviously don't give a flying fuck because before I know it I'm pushing through the entrance into the ballroom.

A woman on a mission.

When I enter, the venue is already full of patrons, seeing as this is one of the hot tickets for this evening. I scan the crowded room to try and catch a glimpse of Colton. It's not hard—my body always seems to know just where he is regardless of location—but the congregation of people at the far corner, bordering on a small mob, confirms the hum that buzzes through my body.

A buzz at this point and time I wish would electrocute itself and die out because I'm done. *I'm so fucking done.*

I stalk across the room, my heart thumping in my chest, noting that cleavage, legs, and form fitting seem to be the dress code of the evening. I hear Colton's laughter erupt from mob causing me to roll my shoulders and my stomach to churn.

As I approach the gathering of people, I swear the group parts with my approach and opens up to highlight the spectacle before me. Colton stands amidst a crowd of women who willingly seem to adhere to the dress code of *easy*. He is completely relaxed and obviously the unyielding center of attention in this circle. Both of his arms are casually draped over the two women at his sides with one hand holding an empty snifter.

Something about his smile seems off. His eyes aloof. Something missing from his expression. Maybe this is just Colton in full, public persona mode. Or maybe, by the looks of the empty snifters on the table behind him, he's drunk.

I stand from a distance watching the display of estrogen edged with desperation, my rage building, and just when I'm about to walk up and interrupt the little gathering, Colton looks up and his eyes lock onto mine. Some unnamed emotion flickers through them, but it's gone before I can really comprehend it. I take a step forward as a diminutive smile ever so slightly turns up one of the corners of his mouth. And very slowly, very deliberately, Colton leans down to the blonde on his right—his eyes still on mine—and proceeds to kiss her. And I'm not talking a peck on the lips. I'm talking a full-blown kiss.

Green eyes all the while held steadfast on mine.

I think my mouth drops open. I think a feeble squeak even escapes from between my lips. I know that all of the blood rushes from my head and into my veins. "Fucking bastard!" The words fly from my mouth, but they are so low, so grated, that I'm unsure if anyone even hears them.

I turn my back on him and rush from the room. The image burned in my mind of what I just saw. The bimbo's face flickers and changes to Tawny. To Raquel. To the faceless, nameless others that Tawny threw in my face. I blow past a server, not caring that I almost topple his tray in my wake, and push through the closest exit I can find.

The tears that scorch the back of my throat threaten, but the anger firing through me burns them out. I have so much pent up rage—so much hurt—that I don't know what to do. I walk toward one end of the empty room I've found myself in to find no exit.

A bubble of hysteria slips out as the song on the fucking speakers assaults my ears as I try to calm myself and look for a way out other than back through the ballroom. *Slow Dancing in a Burning Room.* Like that song couldn't be any more perfect at this fucking moment.

I press my hands against a table in the hall and try to catch my breath. The replay of his mouth on that skank, so blatantly in my face, makes my stomach turn. What the hell am I doing here? Trying to reconcile? *Who is this woman that I've become?* And I was willing to compromise my own morals for him? I hear the door open behind me.

283

I try to straighten up and dash away the tears from my eyes.

"Rylee…"

I glance back at Colton, so completely done with him. How many times am I going to walk headfirst into heartbreak without learning from my own stupidity? "Go away, Colton! Leave me alone!"

"Rylee, I didn't mean it."

This time I turn around. Colton stands a few feet from me, hands shoved deep in his pockets, shoulders hunched, eyes utterly apologetic. But I'm not falling for it this time. I cross my arms across my chest, a useless protection over my heart. "*Fuck you*! For someone so hung up on me, you sure do move fast, *Ace*! You definitely earned the nickname now!"

His eyes search mine, questioning my comment, but he doesn't ask it once he notices my fists clenching and unclenching in anger.

"It's not what you think, Rylee."

"I'm so sick of hearing you say that! *Not what I think*?" I say, raising my voice. "I just watched you shove your tongue down some bimbo's throat and it's not what I think?" How stupid does he think I am? I start to laugh. Really laugh. Almost in hysterics, the push and pull of emotions from the day almost too much to bear. "Oh wait. You didn't mean to with that skank, but you did with *all of the others of your BBB that you fucked* while trying to win me back? Pretending it was me you wanted? Just tell me one thing, Ace…did you get a good laugh at my expense?"

Colton grabs my upper arm, his fingers digging in to my skin. His grip is so tight that when I try to recoil from his touch, I can't. "What. The. Fuck. Are. You. Talking. About?" he says quietly. "Who—"

"Raquel. Tawny. *Who else, Ace?* Cassie? Did they give you what you needed? Sit on their knees patiently and kiss your feet *like a good girl should?* Take what you give and shut the fuck up otherwise? Did you order the flowers for me in between screwing them?"

Colton's fingers grip harder to the point that I think I'll have bruises tomorrow. His eyes pierce into mine. "Do you mind explaining to me—"

"I don't have to explain anything to you!" I yank my arm from his grasp. "To think I was coming down here to try and fix things between us. To apologize for being stubborn. To tell you I believed you." I shake my head in defeat, and I start to walk away but turn back. Hurt consuming every fiber of my being. "Tell me something…you said they weren't whores, but you pay Tawny a salary right?" I arch my brow and I know by the look on his face that my implication is understood.

"She works for me," he says, releasing one of my arms and shoving his hand through his hair. "I pay her because she does her job. I can't fire her because you don't li—"

"Yes. *You can.*" I scream at him. "And it's not that I don't like her. *I fucking hate her! You fucked her, Colton. Fucked! Her!* I think your choice is pretty fucking obvious. Don't you?"

"*Rylee…*"

"You know what, Colton? You make me sick. I should've trusted my gut instinct when it came to you the first time around. You really are nothing but a whore."

When I stop and wipe the tears from my eyes that I didn't even realize were flowing, Colton still remains standing there, his face stoic and his eyes hard as steel. When he speaks, his voice is low and unforgiving. "Well if I'm going to be accused of it—lose the one girl I choose because of her misperception and absolute obstinance—*then I might as well do it.*"

I stop mid-motion at his words. So sarcastic. So accusatory. I meet his eyes and my breath catches in my throat before closing them and taking a deep breath as his comment sinks in. My world spirals in black, looping with confusion that just became quite clear. It's the first time that he hasn't denied sleeping with her. He didn't confess—I didn't hear the words come from his mouth—but he didn't deny it either. Pain staggers through my chest as I focus on trying to breathe—on trying to think—but he just keeps talking. My fractured heart shatters and splinters into a million pieces.

"This is how I'm used to dealing with pain, Rylee. I'm not proud of it, but I use women to cover up the hurt. I lose myself in them to block everything out." He hangs his head for a second as my mind tries to grasp the shock waves his words create.

He's just told me two things, and I'm not sure which one my scattered mind can focus on. His admission causes his comment from several weeks ago to float into my head. The comment he made in my house the morning after our first time sleeping together. How his 747 of baggage makes him crave the sensory overload of physicality—the stimulating indulgence of skin on skin. *But why?*

And at what point is a convenient explanation just a bullshit excuse for a playboy caught in his own lies? An opportune way for the man who always gets what he wants, to well, get what he wants. I can love the broken in him, but I can't accept the lies any more.

"You told me the other day that we're over. I'll be the first to admit it's fucked up, but I'm coping the only way I know how," he says.

285

I search his face, looking so far within him that it scares me. I can see the pain in his eyes. Can hear the hesitation and utter shame in his confession. *Is this what I want?* A man who every time we have an argument or every time he gets spooked about our relationship turns to someone else? Runs off to another woman to help lessen the pain? I told him I loved him. I didn't tell him I want to marry him and be the mother of his unwanted children for God's sake.

"So you're telling me that I'm so important to you that if you bag some unmemorable chick, you'll forget me?" I shake my head at him. "That if we're together, every time the going gets tough you'll run off with Tawny or another willing candidate? *Gee, you're really building the foundation of a great relationship here.*" He tries to interrupt me, but I just hold up my hand to stop him. "Colton..." I sigh. "Coming to talk to you tonight was obviously a mistake. The more you talk, the more I'm really starting to realize I don't know you at all."

"You know me better than anyone!" he shouts, taking a step closer as I take one back. "I've never had to explain anything to anyone...I'm not doing a good job at it."

"You can say that again," I snip back at him.

"Let's get out of here and talk."

"Colton?" a seductive female voice calls to him from over my shoulder. Everything in my body tenses at the sound. Colton's face blanches.

"Out!" He grates between gritted teeth at her.

I unclench my jaw and take in a deep breath. "Talking's overrated. Besides, it's obvious you found someone to help you bury the hurt." I nod my head toward the door behind me. "And you know what? I think it's time I try it too." I shrug. "See if finding a guy for the night fixes everything like you seem to think it does."

"No!" The pained look of desperation on his face upsets me, but I'm so far past caring right now. So far past feeling. So numb.

"Why not? What's good for the goose and all that," I say, adding another animal to the imaginary menagerie I'm building as he just stares at me. One last look. "Enjoy your cocktail party, Ace."

Chapter Thirty-Seven

I wander aimlessly around the resort for what feels like an eternity. I watch the sun sink into the horizon, snuffing out the light of the day like the emotions darkened in my heart. Sadness overwhelms me but it's nothing new since I've been there the past few weeks anyway. I think it's worse because I allowed myself to believe that when I went to Colton, he'd accept why I was upset and that would be it. I never thought he'd play the idiotic game he did to purposely try and hurt me further.

I replay his admission to me over and over in my mind. His acknowledgement that he uses women to bury his hurt. On one hand I understand him a bit better now, but on the other it tells me that I really know nothing of his past—of the things that make him who he is.

But he's so in denial—or maybe so used to getting away with things—that he doesn't even realize the excuses he's giving for his actions are inexcusable.

As I take a seat on a bench in one of the many gardens of the hotel, my phone rings. I look down, debating on answering it, but know that this might be the one person that might help me get my head on straight.

"Hey, Had," I say, trying to muster up as much normalcy as possible.

"What happened?" Her insistent tone rings through the phone line loud and clear. I guess I failed at fooling her.

The tears come. They don't stop. When they eventually subside, I relay the events of the evening. Haddie speaks. "That's the biggest bunch of bullshit I've ever heard."

What? "Come again?"

"Well first of all, Tawny. She's just a jealous bitch trying to get to you and she succeeded!"

"Whatever..." I blow my nose, completely dismissing Haddie's remark.

"Seriously, Ry...that's like *Bitch 101*. If you can't have the guy, make the girl the guy wants doubt him so that you can have him." She sighs loudly. "I'm not proud to say it, but I've done the exact same thing before."

"Seriously?" My mind starts to comprehend what she's saying.

"Rylee...for a smart girl sometimes you're really dumb."

"Way to add insult to injury, Had."

"Sorry, but it's true. You're so wrapped up in your own head right now that you're not seeing it from the outside. If Colton wanted to fuck around, then why would he pursue you relentlessly? The guy's got it bad for you, Ry. Tawny's just one of those devious bitches that's going to get her due sometime. I hope Karma kicks that bitch's ass sooner than later."

I start to hear what Haddie is saying. When the hell did dating become so complicated? *When the someone you're dating is so incredibly worth the fight.*

"I hear what you're saying, Haddie, but what about tonight then? The kiss. The...he cheated on me." I breathe the last part out.

"Did he though?" she says, and it lingers on the line between us.

"Fucking Christ, Haddie! You're not helping me here." I squeeze my eyes shut and pinch the bridge of my nose.

"I'm not in your shoes, Ry. I can't tell you what to do—what to feel—all I can tell you is to use your gut instinct." She sighs. "Women are vicious bitches and men are confusing bastards—you just have to figure out which of the two you trust the most."

"Fuck!" I groan, feeling less resolved than when our conversation began.

"Love ya, Ry."

"Love ya, Had."

I hang the phone up and walk some more along the edge of the golf course thinking about Haddie's comments and lack of advice. I wander around the grounds of the resort, attempting to stop my mind from thinking, but I'm unsuccessful. I walk past one of the hotel cocktail lounges and uncharacteristically find myself turning into it and taking a seat at the bar. The lounge is not overtly busy, but it's not quiet by any means either. Both the bar and the various tables are peppered with patrons, some alone and others coupled here and there.

It's not until I take a seat that I realize how much the arches of my feet ache from my heels and my aimless wandering. I look up at the clock on the wall and am astounded to see that over two hours have passed.

I lean into the back of the chair and shake my head at the day's chain of events that have hit me like a head-on collision. I order a drink and take a long sip on the straw as my attention turns to the television in the corner to the right of me. Of course the channel is on something or other pertaining to the race tomorrow—the whole city has been transformed for the road track—so I can understand why the television is tuned to it. Unfortunately for me, the panel of men on the program discuss one Colton Donavan and review his highlights from last year. Images of the number thirteen car at various venues flash on the screen. I swear I can't escape the man no matter where I go.

Without thinking, I lean forward as I hear the announcers mention Colton's name. "Well, Leigh, Donavan seems to be lighting up the track this week," one announcer says. "He's been like a man on a mission the way he's barely letting up in the turns in his practice runs."

"He's obviously worked on his skills in the off season because it's definitely showing. I'm just wondering if he's running a little too hard. Going in with a game plan that's a little too aggressive for the race tomorrow," the other announcer observes. "Maybe taking too many risks. He's definitely driving like a man scorned for sure though." The other announcer laughs, and I just roll my eyes at the comment.

"If he runs laps tomorrow like he did today, he's set to break a course record."

The screen flashes to the media headshot of Colton and then flashes back to the highlights. Ludacris' *The Rest of My Life* plays as the background music during the spotlight of Colton's testing runs, and I shake my head for I couldn't think of a more fitting song.

I sigh heavily and take another draw on my straw, averting my eyes that are drawn to the sight of his face on television.

"Rough day?"

I turn to face the masculine voice that has spoken to my left. I'm in no mood for company really, but when I see the set of chocolate brown eyes filled with compassion framed by a rather handsome face, I know that I can't be rude. "Something like that," I murmur with a slight smile before turning back to my drink, just wanting to be left alone. My nervous hands start to shred tiny pieces of my napkin apart. "Another please?" I motion to the bartender as she walks past.

"Let me get it," the man beside me says.

I look over at him again. "That's really not necessary."

"Please, I insist," he tells the bartender, sliding his card across the counter to start a tab, which makes me a bit uncomfortable seeing as I don't plan on being here long enough to have a tab.

I stare at him again. My eyes take in his clean-cut appearance and attire but are drawn back to his eyes. All I see is kindness. "Thanks." I shrug.

"Parker," he says, holding his hand out.

"Rylee," I reply, shaking his hand.

"You here for work or pleasure?"

I laugh softly. "Work. You?"

"A little of both actually. Looking forward to the race tomorrow."

"Hmpf," is all I manage as I focus back on shredding my napkin. I realize I'm being rude, but I'm really not in the mood to make polite conversation with someone that possibly wants more than just a drink and quick chat at the bar. "I'm sorry," I apologize, "I'm not much company right now."

"It's okay," he says wistfully. "Whoever he is…he's a lucky man."

I look over at him. "That obvious, huh?"

"Been there, done that before." He chuckles as he takes a long sip of his beer. "All I'll say is the man must be an idiot if he's willing to let you walk away without a fight."

"Thanks," I resign, a flash of a smile lighting up my face for the first time since I've met him.

"Wow! There's a smile," he teases, "and a beautiful one at that!"

My cheeks flush as I avert my eyes and take a drink of liquid courage. We talk idly about nothing in particular for a while as the lounge slowly fills up and the night progresses. At one point Parker scoots his stool closer to mine as we're having trouble hearing each other over the increased noise. He's easy to talk to, and I know that if we were in another place and another time, I'd enjoy his casual attempts at flirting with me, but my heart's just not in it so his harmless attempts remain unreciprocated.

I've had a couple of drinks, and a slow hum is buzzing through my system—not enough to stifle the hurt from the day but just enough to allow me to forget for sporadic moments of time. My attention is drawn to loud laughter outside the open entrance to the lounge, and when I look up, I stifle a gasp as my eyes meet Colton's. We stare for a beat, and then I see his eyes narrow in on Parker and the angle of his body leaning in to hear me over the noise.

I hear Beckett and Sammy shouting in the background over the noise, and I pull myself away from Parker when I hear Colton growl. I search through the shifting crowd and see Beckett in front of Colton, hands pressed against his chest as Sammy stands behind him, restraining him by the shoulders. Colton is not looking at them at all. His eyes are boring holes into mine as he works his jaw back and forth on gritted teeth, muscles straining in his neck.

I look back at Parker, who has heard the distraction in the hallway but can't see anything with his line of sight. He looks to me and shakes his head. "Let me guess," he says with a resigned laugh. "He's come back to fight for you?"

"Something like that," I murmur.

I hear more shouting as I look back toward the door and the rest of the patrons have taken note of the chaos ensuing. The noise level has hushed some as all of the onlookers stare and I hear Beckett shout, "No! You've got other priorities, Wood!" before I see Colton break free from his grip and stalk through the crowd that parts for him without hesitation.

Parker has since taken note of the scuffle in the hallway, and when he sees who is bearing down on us, I hear him suck in a breath. "That's the guy?" he says incredulously, with a mixture of fear and astonishment filtering through his voice simultaneously. "Colton fuckin' Donavan? *Christ, I'm dead!*" He groans.

I stand up from the stool and step in front of him. "Don't worry. I can handle him," I tell him confidently, but when I catch a glimpse of the unadulterated rage reflected in Colton's eyes, I question if I can.

And I'm sure it's the numerous cocktails under my belt and buzzing through my system, but the thought sends an unexpected thrill through me regardless of the events of the past couple of days. Something on his face besides his anger pulls at parts deep within me. It's that look in his eye. The one that says he's had enough. That says he's going to waltz into this room, pick me up, throw me over his shoulder, and take me somewhere to have his way with me. In those few seconds before he reaches me—as I watch the muscles bunch beneath the fitted fabric of his shirt—every part of me below the waist coils with desire. I am so not into the cave man thing, but damn if the man doesn't make a woman want like no other.

And then when he stops in front of me, those cold, calculating, emerald green eyes visually pin me motionless, and my mind regains control of my traitorous body, pushing my libido to the wayside. "What the fuck are you trying to pull, Rylee?" he growls, low but it resonates above the chatter of the bar.

I hear Parker shift restlessly behind me. Without looking, I reach my hand back and pat his knee to tell him I've got this. "What business is it of yours?" I respond flippantly, the alcohol allowing me to reflect the courage that I really don't feel.

I'm ready for his hand as it reaches to grab my arm, so I yank it out of his reach before he can grasp it. We stare at each other, both seething for the same reasons. I see Beckett approach us with trepidation in his eyes and Sammy not far behind him.

"I don't like games, Rylee. I won't tell you that again."

"You don't like games?" I laugh with disgust. "But it's okay for you to play them?"

He leans in, his face inches from me, his alcohol laced breath feathering over my face and mingling with mine. "Why don't you tell your little boy toy he can run along now before things get even more interesting?"

Knowing that we have both been drinking and should stop this little charade before we can't turn back should make me walk away—but rational exited the building a long time ago, leaving crazy and scorned to reign. I shove against his chest as hard as I can to get him out of my face, but he just grips my hands and pulls me with the momentum that I've caused. *"You. Arrogant. Conceited. Egomaniac!"* I shout brokenly at him, unconsciously giving him the meaning behind his nickname, but I know he doesn't catch it. I fall against him and the action draws even more stares from the crowd around us. Our chests rise and fall with our angry, harsh breaths as we both clench our jaws in frustration.

"What the fuck are you trying to prove?" he grits out.

"I'm just testing your theory," I lie.

"My theory?"

"Yeah." I scoff. "If losing yourself in someone helps get rid of the pain."

"How's that working for you?" He smirks.

"Not sure." I shrug nonchalantly at him before I reach back and tug on Parker's hand. I know I shouldn't involve him any further. It's extremely selfish of me to use him in this, but Colton makes me bat-shit crazy sometimes. "I'll let you know in the morning." I raise my eyebrows at him as I take a step past him.

"Don't you walk away from me, Rylee!"

"You lost the right to tell me what to do the minute you slept with *her.*" I sneer at him. "Besides, you said you like my ass…enjoy the view as I walk away because that's the last you'll be seeing of it."

Within moments, so many things happen that I feel like time stands still. Colton lunges at Parker, pulling him so our hands disconnect. In that split second I hate myself for involving Parker in our bedlam, and when I look at him I try to convey that thought with my eyes alone, I see Colton's arm cock back to throw a punch. Before it surges forward, Sammy has his arms around Colton, preventing him. I start yelling at Colton, throwing everything but the kitchen sink into my accusations. I feel an arm close around my shoulder, and I buck it off but to no avail. I turn my head to see it's attached to Beckett. He shoots me a warning glance as he forcefully leads me out of the bar.

Chapter Thirty-Eight

By the time we reach the elevator, the burst of adrenaline has subsided, burning off the remaining alcohol in my system. My entire body starts to shake. The emotion of what just transpired overwhelms me. Makes me realize the crazy-ass woman I just became in a public place that I in no way recognize. Of how I involved an innocent guy who didn't deserve the wrath of Colton bearing down on him for no reason. I feel like I've just stepped out of a scene from Bravo's Real Housewives, and I was the star attraction.

My knees give way as everything—having Colton, not having Colton, wanting Colton—becomes too much.

"No you don't," Beckett says as he tightens his grip around my waist before I slide to the floor. I take his lead as he nudges me out of the elevator and toward my room. My insides are numb with hurt and bewilderment. I glance up at him as he just shakes his head at me and murmurs so quietly that I think he's talking to himself. "Jesus Christ, woman, are you purposely trying to push every single one of Colton's buttons? Because if so, you are damn well succeeding!"

He holds his hand out when we reach my room, and I fumble in my purse for my keycard and hand it to him. He unlocks it and pushes open the door for me, pressing a hand to my lower back to usher me in.

I walk immediately over to my suitcase start yanking dresses off of hangers and shoving them and anything else I can find into the suitcase, hysterical tears spitting out every chance they can.

"Uh-uh. No way! Don't you dare, Rylee!" Beckett shouts from behind me as he sees what I'm doing. I just ignore him, throwing, shoving, stuffing. Beckett's protests continue, and I yelp out as I feel his arms circle around me from behind me, holding my arms down, trying to tame my hysterics.

He just holds me awkwardly, hushing me like a tantruming child who needs soothing. He embraces me as I break down and succumb to the tears and the heartbreak of the day. And to what will never be.

"I thought you guys were trying to figure this out. *Could figure this out.* You're both miserable fucks apart."

"And we're miserable when we're together as well," I whisper. Tears he can't see fill my eyes again, and I just shake my head at him. "He needs to concentrate, Becks. I'm...this...is a distraction he doesn't need right now."

"That's a fucking brilliant statement if I've ever heard one...*but what does that mean, Rylee?*"

I wipe a fallen tear off my cheek with the back of my hand. "I don't know...I feel like I don't know anything anymore...I just need some space from him to be able to think and figure it out."

"So what? You're going to pack up and leave without him knowing? Sneak out?" He breathes out as he paces the room in front of me. "Because that's just so much better, right?"

"Beckett...I can't..." I mumble, "I just can't..." I grab the handle of my suitcase and start to pick it up.

Beckett yanks it out of my hand, stepping around me to grab both of my shoulders and gives them a hard shake. "Don't you dare, Rylee. Don't you fucking dare!" he shouts at me, anger now firing in his veins. "You want to leave him?"

"Becks..."

"Don't you *Becks* me. On any other day I'd tell you that you're just as big of a fucking coward as he is...that both of you are so goddamned stubborn you'd rather cut off your noses to spite your faces. You didn't work your shit out? I get it. I really do. It happens." He sighs loudly, releasing me and walking a few feet from me before turning around and getting back in my face. "But by you walking out, Rylee, you're fucking with my team—my driver—this race—*my best friend.* So suck it up and pretend for me. At least pretend until the race starts. That's all I ask. You owe me that much, Rylee." When he speaks again, he's eerily calm and full of spite. "Because if you can't do this for me, so help me God, Rylee, if something happens to him...it's on you!"

I swallow loudly, my lips falling lax as I look at Beckett, a one-man army on a mission. "Look, Ry, I know it's easier for you to do it this way...to leave this way...but if you love him—if you ever loved him? You'll do this for me. If you leave, it's too dangerous...I can't have

Colton flying close to two hundred miles an hour tomorrow with his head focused in la-la land thinking about you instead of being focused on the goddamn track." He grabs my suitcase and sets it back down.

All I can do is look at him through blurred eyes and with a hurting heart. He's so right on every level, and yet I don't know if I can find it within me to pretend. To act like I'm unaffected when the sight of Colton causes my breath to hitch and heart to twist. When we continually tear each other apart and purposely hurt one another. I cry out a strangled sound, hating the woman that I've become in the last few days. Hating Colton. Just wishing that I could be numb again even though it felt so damn good to feel again. But if I can't have him—have my beautifully damaged man—then I'd rather be numb than live in this endless abyss of pain.

Beckett sees the hysteria surfacing—sees the moment that I realize how much I actually love Colton and the devastation I foresee on the horizon—and mutters, "Motherfucker!" in exasperation at being the one left to tend to my irrationality before calmly walking me over to the bed and pushing my shoulders down. "Sit!" he orders.

He squats down in front of me, the motion much like a parent does to a child, and it makes me realize what a good guy Beckett really is. He reaches out and puts his hands on my knees, looking me squarely in the eye.

"He fucked things up, right?" All I can do is nod my head, my throat clogged with emotion. "You love him still, correct?"

I tense at the question. The answer comes so willingly into my mind that I know even though I love him—that loving him will most likely bring me a truckload of continual hurt—it's just not enough. "Beckett...I can't keep doing this to myself." I lower my head, shaking it as my breath hitches again.

"Remember when I told you that Colton was going to push you away to prove a point?" I nod my head, listening to him but really just wanting to be by myself, wanting to take my suitcase with items sticking out of it at all angles and make a mad dash to the airport—back to structure and predictability and a life without Colton.

And that thought alone robs me of every emotion possible.

Beckett squeezes my knees to get me to focus back on him. "*Right now is that time, Rylee.* You need to push away everything in your head. Clear all of the assumptions out and think with your heart. Just your heart, okay?"

"I can't do it anymore, Becks—"

"Just listen to me, Ry. If you really love him, then keep knocking on that fucking steel gate he has around his heart. If he's really worth it to you, you'll keep at it." He shakes his head at me. "The damn thing's got to give sometime, and you're the only one I think is capable of doing it." When I just stare at him with my mouth lax, he just shakes his head at me. "I told you, you're his lifeline."

I just stare at him, unable to speak, trying to digest his words. Am I his lifeline? Can I possibly be his lifeline? I feel more like a weight dragging us toward the bottom of the ocean than a lifeline. And why does Beckett keep telling me to clear all assumptions?

"That can't be. Love doesn't fix—"

I'm startled from my thoughts from a knock on the door. I start to stand but Beckett just pushes back down on my shoulder and goes to answer it. When he opens it, I see Sammy shoves Colton through the door before Beckett slams it shut.

Despite everything Beckett said, just the sight of Colton ignites my temper. I'm off the bed in a flash the minute he stalks into my room. "Uh-uh! No way! Get that egotistical asshole out of here!" I shout at Beckett.

"Fuckin' A, Becks! What the fuck is this?" he yells, confusion in his voice. He glances down at the haphazard packed suitcase and grunts. "Thank Christ! *Don't let the door hit you in the ass, sweetheart!*"

I step toward him, fueled with fury and ready to detonate.

"This is over here and now!" Beckett's voice booms at us like a parent scolding his children. We both stop mid-motion as Beckett turns toward us, exasperation on his face and obstinance in his stance. "I don't care if I have to lock you in this fucking room together, but you two are going to figure you're shit out or you're not leaving. Is that understood?"

Colton and I both start yelling at him at the same time, and Beckett's voice thunders over ours. "Is that understood?"

"No way, Becks! I'm not staying in this room another second with this asshole!"

"Asshole?" Colton whirls on me, his body mere inches from mine.

"Yeah! Asshole!" I sneer.

"You want to talk about assholes? Try that stunt you pulled with bar boy back there. I believe you claimed the title right then, sweetheart. "

"*Bar boy?* Wow, because having a harmless drink is so much worse than you with your gaggle of whores earlier, right?" I shove at his chest, the physicality of the action giving me a small iota of the release that I need.

Colton steps back from me and walks to the far side of the room and back, blowing out a puff of air from his lungs. My room feels small with Colton eating up the space, and I just want him gone.

He looks over to Beckett and shoves his hands through his inky hair. "She's driving me fucking crazy!" Colton yells at Beckett.

"You'd know all about the *fucking part* seeing as you fucking Tawny is what started this whole thing in the first place," I scream back at him.

Since Colton is standing beside Beckett, it's hard not to notice the completely dumbfounded look on his face. "What?" Beckett stutters.

"What? He didn't tell you?" I grind out looking at Beckett, my fists clenched as images flash through my head. "I told the asshole that I loved him. He bailed as fast as he could. When I showed up at the Palisades house a couple days later, Tawny opened the door. In his T-shirt. Only his T-shirt." I focus completely on Beckett because I can't bring myself to look at Colton right now. "Colton didn't have much more on than that either. Told me nothing happened. But that's a little hard to believe with his notorious reputation. Oh and the condom wrapper in his pocket."

I finish my little rant, for some reason wanting to show Beckett what an ass his friend is, as if he didn't know it already. Trying to explain to him why I have a case of the crazies right now. But when I stop, the look I expect to see is not there. In its place is utter confusion, and when he turns to look at Colton, it morphs into incredulity. "Are you fucking kidding me here?"

Now I'm confused. "*What?*"

Colton growls. "Leave it, Becks."

"What the fuck, man?"

"I'm warning you, Beckett. Stay out of this!" Colton steps chest to chest with Beckett.

"When you start jeopardizing my team and the race tomorrow, then it becomes my business…" he shakes his head at him. "Tell her!" he bellows.

"Tell me what?" I shout at the both of them and their damn man code.

"Beckett, she's like talking to a goddamn brick wall. What good will it do?"

Colton's words hit my ears but don't really seep in. I'm so focused on Beckett's reaction that I don't hear them.

"She's right. You're an ass!" Beckett snickers with disbelief. "You won't tell her? Fine! Then I will!"

In a heartbeat Colton has Beckett pressed against the wall, his hands pressing against his chest, his clenched jaw inches from his. I suck in a breath at the sound of Beckett's back hitting the wall, but I notice that he has no reaction otherwise to Colton's temper. "I said leave it, Becks!"

They stare at each other for a few moments, testosterone oozing between them in two entirely different ways: Colton's with force and Beckett's with a simple look. Finally Beckett raises his hands and shoves back against Colton's chest. "Then fucking fix this, Colton! Fix! It!" he shouts, pointing at him before yanking the hotel room door open and slamming it behind him.

Colton expels a litany of curses as he paces back and forth the length of the room with his hands clenched and his temper flaring.

"What was that all about?" Colton ignores my comment and continues to wear a path in the carpet in front of me, refusing to meet my eyes. "Damn it, Colton!" I stand in his path. "What don't you want me to know?"

The eerie calm in my voice stops him momentarily, his head down, jaw clenched. When he lifts his head to look into my eyes, I can't get a read on what underlies the anger I see boiling over on the surface. "You really want to know?" he shouts at me. "You really want to know?"

I step up to him, confronting him, standing on my toes to try and stretch my height to be eye level with him. "Tell me." Fear snakes up my spine at what I might hear. "Are you that goddamn chicken shit you can't fess up and just admit it? I need to hear it come out of your mouth so that I can get the fuck over you and get on with my life!"

He angles his head down and looks unflinchingly into my eyes, green to violet. My chest hurts so bad breathing feels impossible as time stretches.

His voice is quiet steel when he speaks. "*I fucked Tawny.*" His words float out into the space between us but stab sharply into my heart.

"You coward!" I scream, pushing against him. "You goddamn fucking coward!"

"Coward?" he bellows. "Coward? What about you? You're so fucking stubborn that you've had the truth staring you in the face for three fucking weeks. You're up there so high and mighty on your goddamn horse you think you know everything! Well you don't, Rylee! *You don't know shit!*"

His words that mean to hurt and push me away just fuel my temper even more, egging me on. "I don't know shit? Really, Ace? *Really?*" I step closer to him. "Well how's this? I know a bastard when I see one," I seethe.

We stare at each other, both so willing to hurt the other that we neglect to see that we're both tearing the other apart for the same reason. *"Been called worse by better, sweetheart."* He smirks, taking another step toward me, the smarmy look on his face setting me off.

Before I can think, my hand flashes out in front of me to connect with his cheek. But Colton's quicker. His hand jerks up and grabs my wrist mid-flight, our chests bumping against each other from our momentum. My wrist is locked in his hand and when I start to struggle away from him, he takes his other hand and grabs hold of my free arm that's flailing. I'm frustrated and struggling against him, and I hate him so much right now that my chest hurts. His face is inches from mine, and I can hear his exertion in the breath that pants against my face.

"If you were done with me…had your fill of me? You could have just told me!"

He looks at me, face strained as he holds my arms from pummeling him. "I'll never have my fill of you." And then before I can even process what he's doing, Colton's mouth crashes against mine. It takes me a moment to react, and I'm so angry—so furious with him—that I buck against his hold and tear my mouth from his.

From the taste I crave but the man I hate.

"You want rough, Rylee?" he asks, my head not comprehending his words but my body reacting instantly. "I'll give you rough!"

And from one beat to the next, Colton's mouth crushes down on mine and takes every sensation in my body hostage for his sole manipulation. His hands still grip mine as I struggle to refuse his kiss, trying to push him off and away from me. Regardless of how much I thrash my head, his lips remain on mine, tiny grunts of satisfaction coming from deep within his throat.

I try desperately to deny the desire that starts to seep through the anger-induced haze in my brain. I try to reject the ache deepening at the apex of my thighs from the taste of his tongue melding with mine. I attempt to fight the pebbling of my nipples at the firmness of his chest as he brushes against mine.

Rage turns into desire. Hurt expels into yearning. Absence fuels our fervor. His touch blocks out all rationality. A soft moan catches in my throat as his mouth continues to tempt and torment every spot of my lips and within.

At some point Colton realizes that I'm struggling against him not to get away but rather to touch him. He releases my wrists and my hands go immediately to his chest where they fist into his shirt, aggressively pulling him into me. His hands, now free, are on the move, mapping the lines of my curves over and over again as our mouths convey the unbridled desire we still have for one another.

Every action and reaction reflects urgency. Necessity. Hunger. Longing. Desperation as if we're afraid that at any minute we're going to be pulled away from one another to never experience this again.

Colton brings a hand to cup the rounded curve of my butt as he jerks me into him while the other holds my neck still. I don't even realize that the moan in the room is from me when the hard length of his arousal rubs against the V of my thighs as he pushes us backwards to the dresser behind me. He lifts me up and settles my backside on the top of it, pushing my dress up my thighs as he steps between my legs, all the while continuing his mind-numbing dexterity to my lips and tongue.

I lock my legs around his hips, pulling him farther into me. I know this is wrong. I know that after what he just told me, I shouldn't be here doing this with him. *But I am so sick of thinking.* So sick of wanting him when I know we don't belong together. Our two completely different worlds just don't mesh. But I am so tired of missing him. So tired of wanting to hear his voice when I pick up the phone. So tired of needing him.

So tired of loving him without being loved in return.

I need this connection with him. I need the silence in my head that the all-encompassing feeling of him against my skin brings to me. There is a peace in the physicality of it all that I never realized before. A peace that I know Colton has used over and over in his life to numb his pain.

And right now, I need to numb mine.

I know its temporary, but I turn myself over to him. To the feel and taste and sound and smell of him. My troubling, all-consuming addiction. I willingly let myself get lost in him to forget for just a moment the pain I know I'll feel when we're no longer one.

I grip the waist of his shirt and pull it up over his head; our lips break for the first time since we've reconnected with each other. Immediately after the material is gone, we crash back together again. He tugs the straps of my dress off of my shoulders as his mouth laces open mouth kisses down the line of my neck and to the lacy edge of my bra. I cry out in shock and need as he yanks down one of my bra cups and closes his mouth over my nipple. I throw my head back at the sensation while one of my hands fists in the hair at the back of his neck. The burn in my core turns into a raging inferno directing my free hand to fumble with his belt and undo his pants.

I successfully unzip them, shoving my hands between the cotton of his briefs and his heated skin. I grab his rock hard erection in my hands, and he groans at the feeling of my skin on his flesh. His hands are instantly on my thighs, shoving my dress up higher and yanking my dampened thong to the side. He slides a finger along my seam, and I buck my hips at the feeling of his fingertips on me again. I press my hips into his hands, greedy and unashamed to lose myself in the pleasure. I cry out as he slips a finger into my core and then spreads my wetness around.

Before I can open my eyes and notice the absence of his fingers, he enters me in one fervent thrust. We both cry out as he stills and seats himself as far as possible within my wet heat. My walls clench around him as I adjust to the over-fullness of him within me. The muscles in Colton's shoulders strain beneath my hands as he tries to hold onto his control. I feel it slipping—know that he's a man about to snap—so I take the reins and start to move against him, moving my hips to tell him to go. Urging him to lose his control. To be rough with me. I don't need foreplay right now. All I need his him. I've craved this for the past couple of weeks, and he feels so damn good right now I don't need anything else to push me over the edge.

Colton grips his fingers, bruising the flesh at my hips, and holds me still on the edge of the dresser as he pistons his hips into mine. Over and over. Drive after delicious drive.

"God, Rylee!" He moves relentlessly within the confines of my thighs. He brings his mouth down and devours mine again, his tongue mimicking the actions below. And from one kiss to the next he pulls me into him, cupping my ass so we remain connected as he lifts me up and turns me around so we fall onto the bed behind us.

His mouth claims mine as he finds his rhythm again. I can feel the pressure building—can feel the conflicted bliss just within my reach—and grab the back of Colton's neck and hold his mouth to mine as I drink him in. "You. Feel. Incredible," he murmurs against my lips.

I can't speak. Don't trust myself to. Don't know who I am right now. So instead I just I arch my back into him so I can change the angle of my hips allowing him to hit that nerve-laden spot deep within, over and over.

Colton knows my body so well already—knows what I need to bring me to climax—that he takes the hint of the subtle repositioning. He rears back onto his knees, grabs my legs, pushes them back, and places my feet flat against his chest. The angle allows him to surge even deeper, and I can't hold back the moan of utter rapture as he bottoms out inside of me before pulling back out slowly and driving back in.

I look up at him, a sheen of sweat on his face and shoulders with my pink painted toenails bright against his tanned torso, and I meet his eyes. I hold his stare as long as I can until it's too much for me to bear; it's the first time since we've met that there is nothing guarding the emotion flickering through his eyes. It's too much for me to comprehend—too much for me to think about when all I want to do is lose myself in this moment and block out everything else. To lose all train of thought.

I throw my head back, my eyes closed and hands gripping the sheets beneath me as the sensations threaten to overtake me. Colton must sense my impending release from my rapid breathing and the tightening of my thighs.

"Hold on, Ry." He pants. "Hold on, baby." He plunges into me, picking up his pace until I can no longer hold it back.

"Oh God!" I cry out as my body fractures into a million pieces of mindless pleasure. Release surging though me and consuming my every breath, thought, and reaction. The continual pulsing of my orgasm milks Colton to his climax. He cries out my name brokenly and throws his head back, welcoming his own release and jerking harshly within me. When he comes back to himself, I am still catching my breath and my thoughts with my eyes closed and my head angled back. I feel him remove my feet from his chest, and without breaking our connection, flanks his body over mine, resting his weight on his elbows propped on either side of me. He brings his hands to the side of my face and cups it, running his thumbs gently over the skin on my cheeks.

I can feel his breath feathering over my lips—know that his eyes are staring at me—but I can't bring myself to open mine yet. I need to get a hold on my emotions before I open my eyes because no matter how wonderful that just was, it doesn't fix anything. It doesn't take away the fact that he ran away when I told him I loved him. It doesn't erase that he slept with Tawny to bury the very idea that someone might actually want more than just an arrangement with him. All it solidifies is that we can have incredible, mind-numbing sex.

And numb—right now—is how I feel.

I can feel the weight of Colton's stare, but I can't bring myself to open my eyes because I know the tears will fall. He sighs softly and I know he's trying to understand me and what's going on in my mind. He leans his head down and rests his forehead on mine, his thumbs still caressing the line of my jaw softly. "God, I missed you, Rylee," he murmurs softly against my lips.

It's harder to hear those words from his lips than it is to accept that we just had sex. The vulnerability in the way he says them with his rasp of a voice tugs at my heart and twists in my soul. I think maybe the idea that he's had sex with numerous people but most likely never murmured those words to anyone before is what gets to me.

"Talk to me, Ry." He breathes into me. "Baby, please talk to me," he pleads.

It's now that a tear slips out of the corner of my eye and slides down my cheek. I just keep my eyes shut and shake my head subtly, emotions warring violently inside of me. Our connection is enough to fix things for him. Not for me. *How can I ever trust him?* How can I ever trust me? This girl who sleeps with someone after they cheat on her—that's not me. How can I live and love him knowing I have to constantly walk on eggshells because I fear that if I say anything to spook him, I'll drive him into the arms of someone else?

For him, this is a reconciliation. For me, it's a last memory. My final goodbye.

I hate myself terribly. Hate that I used him to try and soothe the pain that I know is going to own my heart and soul in the weeks and months to come. I hate that just as he seems to be needing me, I can't bring myself to need him anymore. I can't lose the *me* that I've just found—that ironically he's just helped me find. Look what he's doing to me. To the person I'm becoming. I'm a fucking neurotic lunatic around him. And yes—*God yes, I love him*—but love's definitely not worth it if it's one sided and this is the return I get.

He pulls back and kisses the tip of my nose, my chin trembling as I hold my realization in. "Tell me what's going on in your head, Ry?" he urges as he laces tender kisses along the track of my lone tear and then up to both of my closed eyes before back to my lips. Such tenderness from a man that swears he can't feel has me fighting the opening of the floodgates. And even though he hasn't withdrawn from me, I sense that he feels like he's losing our connection for as his lips brush mine again, he presses his tongue to part between them. He licks slowly into my mouth, his tongue dancing tenderly with mine, expressing his desire for me with a subtle, gentle desperation.

I respond to him and his unspoken request, needing this connection to hold on to everything I feel for him even though I know it's just not enough anymore. Unreciprocated love never is. Eventually Colton ends the kiss and sighs when he pulls back and I keep my eyes closed.

"Give me one sec," he says to me. I wince as he slips out of me, *one now becoming two*, and I feel the bed dip as he pushes himself up off of it. I hear the water running in the bathroom. I hear his footsteps come across the bedroom and am startled as he takes a warm washcloth and cleans me ever so gently before padding back into the bathroom. "Baby, I desperately need a shower. Give me a minute and then we need to talk, okay? *We have to talk.*" He brushes another kiss to my forehead, and I feel the bed dip again as he rises from it. I hear the shower start and hear the stall click closed.

I lie there in silence, my head humming with so many thoughts it's starting to hurt. Do I love this man so magnificent, yet so damaged? Without a doubt…but where I used to think love conquers all, I'm not sure of that any more. He may care for me in his own way, but is that enough for me? Is always wondering when the other shoe is going to drop what I want in my relationship?

I've spent the past two years numb to emotion—fearing what it would be like to feel again—and now that I found Colton, and he's made me do just that, I don't think I can go back to how I was before. Merely existing, not living. Can I really be with Colton and hold back everything inside of me bursting to finally get out? I don't think I want to revisit that life of void. I don't think I can. I'm just not sure if he'll ever be able to accept my love. I squeeze my eyes shut and try to tell myself that we can overcome all of this. That I can be strong enough and patient enough and forgiving enough to wait him out while he tackles his demons and accepts the love that I've offered. But what if he never does?

Look at the two of us tonight. We purposely hurt each other. We purposely used other people to get back at the other. Tried to tear each other apart. That's not healthy. You don't do that to someone you love or care about. My mom's words flicker through my mind. About how someone always treats you the best in the beginning of a relationship, and if it's not good in the beginning, then it's not going to get any better. If the past twenty-four hours is any indication, then we definitely aren't going to make it.

We are passionate, fiery, unyielding, and intense when we're together. In the bedroom, that leads to immeasurable chemistry; in the relationship arena, that leads to disaster. And as heavenly as it would be to contain Colton to the bedroom so he could have his way with me over and over, that's just not realistic.

The tears come now and I don't have to hide them anymore. They rack my body and tear through my throat. I cry and cry until I have no more tears for the man just within my grasp yet so incredibly far away. I close my eyes momentarily and steel myself for what I'm about to do. In the long run, it's for the best.

And I move without thinking. Use the numbness to guide me before

I can't bring myself to do this. Colton's right. He's broken. *And now I'm broken.* Two halves don't always make a whole.

I fucked him—yes, it was most definitely fucking because there was nothing soft or gentle or meaningful about it—especially after he admitted to me that he fucked someone else. *Tawny of all people.* That's not acceptable to me. Ever. But when I'm near him—when he dominates the air I breathe—I compromise on things I never would otherwise. And that's not a way to exist. Compromising everything of yourself when the other person compromises nothing.

I catch the sob in my throat as I have trouble pulling my clothes on. My hands are trembling so badly I can barely slip my clothes to their proper position. I steal a glance in the mirror and it stops me in my tracks. Pure and utter heartbreak is reflected looking back at me. I force my eyes to look away and grab my suitcase as I hear Colton drop something in the shower.

I wipe the tears that start to fall in their familiar tracks down my cheeks. "Bye, Ace. I love you," I whisper the words to him that I can't say to his face. That he'll never accept. "I think I've always I loved you. And I know I always will." I open the door as quietly as possible and slip out of the hotel room, luggage in hand. It takes me a moment to physically release the door handle because I know once I lose the connection, it's over. And as sure as I am about this decision, I'm still shattering into a million pieces.

I take a deep breath and let go, grab my luggage, and start to make my way toward the bank of elevators, tears flowing freely.

Chapter Thirty-Nine

The descent of the elevator feels like it takes forever as my tired eyes and heavy heart force my feet to stand, urge my lungs to breath. Try to figure a reason to move. I knew that getting over Colton would be hard—absolutely devastating—but I never in a million years imagined that the first step would be the hardest.

The doors ping and open. I know I need to hurry. Need to disappear because Colton will try and track me down and drag this out.

Then again, maybe he won't. Maybe he got his quick fuck and he'll let me go. It's not like he's easy to figure out, and to be honest, I'm so tired of trying. Thinking one thing and him doing another. If I've learned one thing being with Colton, it's that *I know nothing*.

I rub my face, trying to blot the tears from my cheeks but know that nothing is going to lessen my damaged appearance. And frankly, I don't have enough left in me to care what people think.

I know I've been here for a couple of days, but my mind is in such a haze that it takes me a second to figure out which way I need to go to find the main entrance in order to catch a cab. I have to walk out through a garden and then into the main lobby. I see it and start shuffling toward it, all of my luggage overflowing and awkward. I'm in a state of numbness, telling myself that I'm doing the right thing—that I've made the right decision—but the look in Colton's face as he buried himself in me—raw, open, unguarded—haunts me. We can't give each other what we need, and when we do we only end up hurting each other. One foot in front of the other, Thomas. That's what I keep telling myself. As long as I keep moving—keep my mind from wandering—I can keep the questioning panic that is just beneath the

307

surface from bubbling up.

I make it about twenty feet into the garden, empty at this time of the night, and I'm struggling desperately to keep moving.

"I didn't fuck her."

The deep timbre of his voice causes the words to slice through the still night air. My feet stop. My head says go, but my feet stop. His words shock me, and yet I'm so numb from everything—from needing to feel and then not wanting to feel then to emotional overload—that I don't react. *He didn't sleep with Tawny?* Then why did he say that he did? Why did he cause all of this heartache if nothing happened? In the back of my mind I hear Haddie telling me that I'm so stubborn I didn't allow him to speak—didn't allow him to explain—but I'm so busy trying to remind myself to breathe that I can't focus on that. My heart thunders in my chest, and I find myself completely at a loss for what to do. I know his words should relieve me, but they still don't fix *us*. Everything that seemed so clear—conflicted yet clear—no longer is. I need to walk away, but I need to stay.

I want and I hate and more than anything, *I feel.*

"I didn't sleep with Tawny, Rylee. Not her or any of the others you accused me of," he repeats. His words hit me harder this time. Hit me with a feeling of hope tinged with sadness. We did this to each other—tore each other apart verbally and played stupid games to hurt one another—*and for no reason?* A tear escapes and slides down my face. "When I heard the knock at the door, I grabbed an old pair of jeans. Haven't worn them in months."

"Turn around, Ry," he says, and I can't bring myself to do so. I close my eyes and take a deep breath, emotions running rampant and confusion in a constant state of metamorphosis. "We can do this the easy way or the hard way," he says, his implacable voice closer than before, "...but have no doubt, *it will be my way*. You are not running this time, Rylee. Turn around."

My heart stops and my mind races as I slowly turn to face him. And when I do, I can't help the breath that catches is my throat. We're standing is this garden full of exotic plants with exploding colors but by far the most exquisite thing in my line of sight is the man standing before me.

Colton stands in a pair of blue jeans and nothing else. Bare feet, bare chest heaving with exertion, and hair dripping with water that runs in rivulets down his chest. He looks as if he literally stepped out of the shower, noticed I was gone, and chased me. He takes a step toward me, his throat working a nervous swallow, and his face a mask of conviction. He is utterly magnificent—breathtakingly so—but it's his eyes that capture me and don't let go. Those beautiful pools of green just hold mine—imploring, apologizing, pleading—and I'm frozen in the moment.

"I just need time to think, Colton," I offer as a justification of my actions.

"What is there to think about?" He blows out a loud breath, a harsh curse following right after. "I thought we were…"

I stare at the paint on my toenails; flashbacks flit through my mind of them on his chest not too long ago. "I just need to think about us…this…everything,"

He steps closer to me. "Look at me," he commands softly, and I owe him this much regardless of how much I fear seeing the look in his eyes. When I raise my eyes to meet his, searching mine in the full moonlight, I see worry, disbelief, fear, and so much more in the depths of his eyes and as much as I want to look away—to hide from the damage that I'm about to cause—I can't. He deserves better than that from me. His voice is so soft when he speaks that I barely hear him. "Why?" It's a single word, but there is so much emotion packed behind it that it takes a minute for me to find the words to respond.

And it's the same question I need to ask him.

"If this is real, Colton…we're supposed to complement each other—make each other better people—not tear each other apart. Look at what we did to each other tonight." I try to explain. "People who care for each other don't try to purposely hurt one another…that's not a good sign." I shake my head, hoping he understands what I'm saying.

His throat works as he thinks of what to say. "I know we've made a mess of this, Ry, but we can figure this out," he pleads. "*We can get us right.*"

I close my eyes momentarily, tears spilling over as I remember where we are and what tomorrow signifies. "Colton…you need to focus right now…on the race…we can talk later…discuss this later…right now you need to get your head on the track where it belongs."

He shakes his head emphatically at me. "You're more important, Rylee."

"No, I'm not," I murmur as I avert my eyes again, silent tears endlessly sliding down my cheeks now.

I feel his finger on my chin, guiding my eyes to look back at his. "If you leave, it's not just to think. You're not coming back, are you?" He stares at me, waiting for a response and my lack of one is his answer. "Did us—you and me—earlier not mean anything to you? I thought

309

that..." his voice drifts off as I can see it dawning on him "...you were getting closure. That's why you were so upset," he says, talking more to himself than me. "You were saying goodbye weren't you?"

I don't respond but rather just keep my eyes fixed on his so maybe through his pain he can see how hard this is on me too. It would be so much easier if he raged and threw something instead of these soft pleading words and eyes filled with disbelief and hurt.

"I just need some time to think, Colton," I finally manage, repeating myself.

"Time to distance yourself to make it easier on you is what you really mean, right?"

I bite the inside of my cheek as I carefully chose my next words. "I—I just need some time away from you, Colton, and the disaster that we've made of the past couple of days. You're so overpowering—so everywhere—that when I'm near you I become so lost in you that it's like I can't breathe or think or do anything on my own. I just need a little time to process this..." I look around before turning back to him. *"Time to try and figure out why we're so broken..."*

"No, Ry, no," he insists, the rasp in his voice breaking as he brings his hands up to frame the sides of my face at the same time he bends his knees to bring us inches apart, eye to eye, thumbs caressing over the line of my jaw. "We're not broken, baby...we're just bent. *And bent's okay*. Bent means that we're just figuring things out."

I feel like my heart is going to explode in my chest as he recites my words—the lyrics of the song I once said to him—back to me. It hurts so much. The look in his eyes. The raw simplicity in his explanation. The pleading conviction in his voice. The subtle irony that the one person who doesn't ever "do the relationship thing" is giving the advice here on how to fix one.

Ours.

I just shake my head at him, my mouth opening to speak but closing again to just taste the salt of my tears when I can't find the words to answer him. He's still bent down, eye level with me. "There's so much that I need to explain to you. So much I need to say...so much I should have already said to you." He breathes out in a desperate plea. Colton puts both hands up on to the back of his neck, elbows bent, and paces back and forth a few steps. My eyes follow him and on his fourth pass, he grabs me without preemption and crushes his mouth to mine, bruising my lips in a kiss teeming with desperation. And before I can regain my footing beneath me, he tears his lips from mine, hands on my shoulders, eyes boring into mine. "I'll let you go, Rylee. I'll let you walk away and out of my life if that's what you want—*even if it fucking kills me*—but I need you to hear me out first. Please, come back to the room so I can tell you things that you need to hear."

I take a deep breath as I stare at his eyes, inches from mine and pleading with me for some scrap of hope. The rejection is on my tongue, but for the life of me I can't get it past my lips. I drag my eyes from his and swallow, nodding my head in consent.

The room is dark except for the light of the moon. In the space between us on the bed, I can make out Colton's shadow. He's on his side, head propped on his angled elbow, staring at me. We sit like this in silence for a while—him staring at me, me staring at the ceiling—as we both try and process what each other is thinking. Colton reaches out hesitantly and takes my hand in his, a soft sigh escaping his lips.

All I can think to do is swallow and keep my eyes fixed on blades of the ceiling fan above as they rotate endlessly.

"Why?" My voice croaks as I speak for the first time since we've come back to the room, asking the same question he's asked me. "Why did you tell me that you slept with Tawny?"

"I...I don't know." He sighs in frustration as he shoves a hand through his hair. "Maybe because since that's what you thought of me—expected of me without even letting me explain—then maybe I wanted you to hurt as much as I did when you accused me of it. You were so sure that I slept with her. So sure that I'd use her to replace you that you wouldn't listen to me. You shut me out. *You ran away*, and I never got a chance to explain that whole fucked up morning to you. You wouldn't let me...so a part of me felt like I might as well give you the affirmation you needed to think of me like the bastard-asshole that I really am."

I remain silent, trying to process his rationale, understanding and not-understanding all at the same time. "I'm listening now," I whisper, knowing full well that I need to hear the truth. Need it all laid out on the table so I can figure out where to go from here.

"I truly didn't know how alone I was, Rylee," he starts on a shaky breath and for the first time, I can sense how nervous he is. "How isolated and alone I've made myself over the years, until you weren't there. Until I couldn't pick up the phone and call you or talk to you or see you…"

"But you could, Colton," I reply, confusion in my voice. "You ran from me…not the other way around. I was the one sitting and waiting for you to call. How could you think otherwise?"

"I know," he says softly. "I know…but what you said to me—*those three words*—they turn me into someone I won't ever let myself be again. It triggers things—memories, demons, *so fucking much*—and no matter how much time has passed, I just…" he fades off, unable to verbalize what the words *I love you* do to him.

"What? Why?" What in the hell is he talking about? I want to scream at him, but I know that I have to have patience. Look where my obstinance has gotten us thus far. Verbalization is not his strong point. I have to just sit back and be quiet.

"Ry, the explanation—when, as a kid, those words are used as a manipulation…as a means to hurt you…" He struggles and I so desperately want to reach out and hug him. Hold him and help him through it, so maybe I can understand him better—comprehend the poison he says sears his soul—but I refrain. He looks at me and tries to smile but fails miserably, and I hate that this conversation has robbed him of that brilliant smile of his. "…it's too much to go in to right now and probably more than I'll ever be able to explain." He exhales on a long, shaky breath. "This, talking right now, is more than I ever have…so I'm trying here, okay?" His eyes plead with me through the shadow of darkness, and I just nod at him to continue. "You said those words to me…and I was immediately a little boy, dying—wishing I was dead—hurting inside all over again. And when I hurt like that, I usually turn to women. *Pleasure to bury the pain*…" My free hand grips the sheet beside me for the little boy that was in so much pain he'd rather die and for the man I love beside me that's still so haunted by it and for what I fear is going to spill from his lips next. His confession. "*Usually*," he whispers, "but this time, after you, there was no appeal in it. When the thought crossed my mind, it was your face I saw. Your laugh I missed. It was your taste I craved. *No one else's*." He shifts onto his back, keeping his fingers still laced with mine as my heart squeezes at his words. "Instead, I drank. *A lot*." He chuckles softly. "The day before…everything happened…Q came by my place and read me the riot act. She told me to clean myself up. Told me to find some friends other than Jim and Jack to hang out with. Becks showed up an hour later. I know she called him. He didn't ask what was wrong—he's good like that—but knew I needed some company.

"He took me out surfing for a couple of hours. Told me I needed to clear my head from whatever was fucking it up. He had to assume it had something to do with you, but he never pried. After we surfed for a while, I told him we needed to go out, hit a couple of bars, something to make me numb." He rubs his thumb softly back and forth over our clasped hands, and I turn onto my side so now it's me watching him staring at the ceiling. "We did and in the process, Tawny called and had some documents she needed me to sign since I hadn't been in the office for several days. I told her where we were and she showed up. I signed the documents and the next thing I knew, a couple of hours had passed and all three of us were shitfaced. Lit like you wouldn't believe. We were closer to the Palisades house, so I had Sammy drive us there and figured we'd pick up their cars in the morning.

"We walked through the front door, and I realized that I hadn't been there since that night with you. Grace had been there of course—the shirt I'd thrown on the couch before we..." He fades off remembering. "It was folded neatly on the back of the couch for me to see the minute I entered the house. My first reminder. When I walked into the kitchen, she'd taken the cotton candy and it was sitting in a container on the counter. I couldn't escape you—even drunk, I couldn't escape you. So I drank some more. Tawny and Beckett followed suit. Tawny was uncomfortable in the clothes she had so I grabbed a shirt for her so she could be more comfortable. We were all sitting in the family room. Drinking more. I was trying anything to numb how much I needed you. I don't remember the exact sequence of events, but at some point I reached for my beer and Tawny kissed me..."

Those words hang in the darkened room like a weight on my chest. I grit my teeth at the thought even though I'm appreciative of his honesty. I'm starting to think that maybe I don't need to hear all of the story. That in this case truth might not be the best policy. "Did you kiss her back?" The question is out of my mouth before I can stop it. I feel his fingers tighten momentarily around mine, and I know my answer. I worry my bottom lip between my teeth as I dread hearing the confirmation come from his lips.

He sighs again and I can hear him swallow loudly in the quiet of the room. "Yes..." he clears his throat "...at first." Then he falls silent for a few moments. "Yes, I kissed Tawny back, Rylee. I was hurting so much and drinking wasn't helping to numb it anymore...so when she kissed me, I tried my old fallback method." I audibly suck in my breath and try to pull my hand from his but his grip remains firm. He doesn't allow me to pull away from him. "But for the first time ever, I couldn't." He

313

turns on his side again so that although the darkness of the room doesn't allow us to completely see each other, I know that he is staring into my eyes. He reaches his free hand up to run the backside of his fingers over my cheek. "She wasn't you," he says softly. "*You ruined casual for me, Rylee.*"

I sniffle at the tears burning the back of my throat, and I'm unsure of whether they're a result of the fact that he did try to start something with her or if they're because of his reasons why he couldn't. "I told you I loved you, Colton, and *you ran away*. Basically into the arms of another woman," I accuse. "A woman who has harassed and threatened me no less in regards to you."

"I know…"

"What's to say you won't do that again, Colton? What's to say that the next time you get spooked you won't do the same damn thing?" Silence falls around and between us, wiggling its way into the doubts in my head. "I can't…" I whisper as if talking normally is too much for the words I'm about to utter. "I don't think that I can do this, Colton. I don't think I can let myself believe again…"

Colton shifts suddenly in the bed and sits up, grabbing both of my hands in his as I fall onto my back. "Please, Rylee…don't decide yet…just hear the rest of it out, okay?" I can hear the desperation in his voice, and it undoes me for I know exactly how it feels when that tone is in your voice.

That was the same one I had right after I told him I loved him.

We sit there and his hands hold mine—our only connection despite feeling as if he is the only air that my body can breathe. I feel the tension radiate off of him as he tries to put the thoughts swarming in his head into words.

"How do I explain this?" he asks the room as he blows out a loud breath before beginning. "When you race, you're going so fast that everything outside of your car—the sidelines, the crowd, the sky— everything becomes a big, stretched out blur. Nothing specific can be identified. It's me in the car, alone, and everything outside of my little bubble is part of the blur." He stops momentarily, squeezing my hands to stop the nerves trembling through his as he regroups to try and explain better. "Kind of like when you're a kid and you spin in circles…everything in your line of sight becomes one big continuous image all blurred together. Does that make sense?"

I'm unable to find my voice to answer him. His anxiety seeping into me. "Yes," I manage.

"I've lived my life for so long in that state of blur, Rylee. Nothing is clear. I never stop long enough to pay attention to the details because if I do then everything—my past, my mistakes, my emotions, my demons—will catch up to me. Will cripple me. It is always easier to live in that blur than to actually stop, because if I stop, then I might actually have to feel something. I might have to open up to the things I've always protected myself against. Things ingrained in me from the shit that happened to me as a kid. Shit that I don't ever want to remember but that I constantly do." He releases one of my hands and scrubs it over his face. The chafe of the stubble against his hand is a welcome sound to me, a comforting one.

"My past is always there, just on the edge of my memory. Always threatening to overwhelm me. To drag me back and pull me under." I can hear the emotion thickening in his voice, and on impulse, reach out and grab his hand again. I squeeze it—a silent sign of support for the hell inside of his head. "Living inside of that blur is like living in a bubble. It allows me to control the speed I'm going…to slow down if I need a breather, but to never really stop. I've always been in the driver's seat…always in control. Always able to speed up, push the limits, when things get too close…

"And then I met you…" The astonishment in his voice is raw and honest and tugs so deep within me that it causes me to sit up, so I'm now cross-legged with my knees pressing against his. His hands find mine again and squeeze them tightly. "The night I met you it was like a firecracker shot out of that blur of color and exploded above me. So bright and so beautiful…and so hostile…" he chuckles "…that I couldn't look away even if I tried. It was like life slammed the brakes on me and I'd never touched the pedal. I was immediately drawn to you, to your attitude, to your refusal of me, to your wit…to your incredible body." I can feel him shrug unapologetically at the last comment, and I can't help the smile that curls up my lips or the hope that begins to bloom in my soul. "…to everything about you. That first night you were a spark of solid color to me in a world that's always been one big mixed blur of it."

Words escape me as I try and process what he's telling me. Just when I've made up my mind one way, he says something so poignant and achingly beautiful that I can't help but feel my heart swell with love for him. Colton accepts my silence and reaches out to cradle my head in his hands before he continues. The tenderness in his touch brings tears to my eyes. "That first night you created a spark, Rylee, and every day since then, you've allowed me the strength to slow down long enough to see into the blur I've always feared. Even when I don't want to do it, your quiet strength—knowing that you are there—pushes me to be a better person. A better man. Since you've come into my life, things finally have definition, specific colors assigned to them...I don't know..." I can hear his struggle, and I turn my face into the palm of his hand and kiss it there softly as he sighs. "I don't know how else to explain it, but I know that I can't go back to how I existed before. *I need you in my life, Rylee.* I need you to help me continue to see the color. To slow things down. To allow me to feel. I need you to be my spark ..."

He leans in and brushes his lips so softly, so tenderly against mine. "Please be my spark, Ry..." he pleads as the words cause his lips to brush against mine.

I lean in and press my lips against his, instigating the kiss to go deeper by slipping my tongue into his mouth because the words and thoughts in my head and heart are so jumbled that I'm afraid to speak. Afraid that in this moment of his revelation—that if I pour out what's spilling over in my heart—I will overwhelm him. So instead, I pour it all into my kiss. He gathers me to him, cradling me in his lap while he worships my mouth in the way that only he knows how. The reverence in which he breathes my name between kisses causes a tear to slide down my cheek.

"I might not be able to tell you the things you need to hear with the traditional words you need to hear them in, but I swear to God, Rylee, *I will try.* And if I can't, then I'll show you. I'll show you with everything I have—anything it takes—where your place is in my life," he murmurs to me, shattering every last form of protection I have guarding my heart.

He just stole it completely.

And I just more than willingly handed it over.

He wraps his arms around me and buries his face in my neck, holding me tightly for a long while, his vulnerability palpable. My mind thinks in sensations and emotions and shuts all sensibility out so that I can just enjoy this unguarded side of Colton that is such a rarity. I breathe in the scent of us mixed together. I feel the beat of his heart against my chest. The warmth of his breath against my neck. The strength of his arms as they hold me tight. The scrape of his scruff against my bare skin. The comfort his presence brings to me by just being near. So many things to absorb—to pack away for another day—so I can remember them when I need them the most.

Because I know that being with Colton—staying with Colton—loving Colton—guarantees that I will need these memories at the most random of times to help me get by in the trying ones I know will inevitably come.

"I'm drowning here. Your silence is killing me. Can you say something? Throw me a lifeline please?" he says and the comment has me immediately thinking of Beckett's words on the way to Vegas and earlier to me.

"C'mon," I whisper to him as I run my hands up and down his back. He pulls me tighter and nuzzles deeper into the underside of my neck. "You have a long day tomorrow. It's late. You need to get some sleep."

His head startles back and in our close proximity I can see the crystalline green of his eyes—their clarity, their utter shock, their acceptance—of my unspoken words. "You're not leaving?" he asks so brokenly. "You're staying?"

I catch the sob that almost escapes my throat with his words. That I think he's worth it. His hands run over my face and down the curve of my shoulder and back up. Touching to make sure that I really am before him—flesh and blood and accepting of him. Accepting the journey that he wants to try and take with me.

"Yes, Colton. I'm not going anywhere," I'm finally able to say once the burn in my throat dissipates.

He holds my head with both hands and leans in to press a sigh of a kiss against my lips before wrapping his arms around me and pulling me tightly into him. "I don't want to let you go just yet," he murmurs against my temple. "I don't think I ever will."

"You don't have to," I tell him softly as I lay down on the bed and pull him down with me. He shifts so that we are both on our sides, bodies pressed together, arms wrapped around each other, and my face nuzzled in his neck now.

We've been quiet for some time, the silence around us not so lonely anymore, when Colton sighs out a soft sound of contentment and then murmurs, "*A chance encounter.*" He plants a kiss on the top of my head and clears his throat. "I don't know what it meant before me, but to me, now, it means a chance encounter. One that's changed my life."

I snuggle in closer to him, planting a soft kiss at my favorite spot beneath his jaw, my heart overflowing with love and my soul brimming with happiness.

After some time of just absorbing each other and our new found balance, his breathing slows and evens out. I sit there for some time, just breathing him in, feeling his warmth, and my heart lodges in my throat when I realize that my decision was never really mine to make. It was made the minute I fell out of that damn storage closet and into his life.

I turn onto my side so I can watch him. My chest physically hurts as I stare at the beautiful man he is inside and out. He looks so peaceful in sleep. Like he can finally rest from the demons that chase him so frequently while he's awake. So much like the dark angel I think of him as that's breaking through the inescapable darkness to grasp and hold on to the light. His spark of light.

Chapter Forty
Colton

For the first time in a month, the riot in my head is quiet as I sleep. Nightmares are non-existent. The events of last night flicker through my head as the morning hour pulls me from slumber.

That and the feel of Rylee's weight settling over me.

I groan involuntarily as she sinks down, sitting astride me. The heat of her pussy has me straining to be released from the sheets she's now pinned against my body. Talk about sweet fucking torture.

Fuck me if this isn't the best wake-up call ever.

Fingertips feather up my abdomen, circle around my nipples, and then trail back down to my hipbone. "Good morning," she whispers in that rasp of hers before pressing a soft kiss against my lips. Her fingers continuing to tease my skin. To taunt me with the drug to my addiction.

I grunt a response and squint open my eyes to find one of the most terrific sights I have ever seen. Tits—Rylee's tits to be exact—full and pert with pink nipples hardened in arousal dominating my line of sight. I take a moment to admire God's greatest creation ever before I drag my eyes away and scrape them over the rest of her sun-kissed skin to meet her eyes.

Those eyes.

The ones that have held me captive and owned parts of me I never even knew existed since that first moment they looked up at me amidst a mass of fallen curls.

"Good morning," she says again, her sleepy eyes hold mine and a sluggish smile tugs up the corners of her mouth.

I feel like my heart beats for the first time. She's real and she's here. Relief floods me. Today may be the first race of the season, but waking up with her, here with me after all the shit from the past couple of weeks? I've already fucking won.

I cock an eyebrow up at her as her fingers tickle further south, my cock pulsing up in response to her touch. "It is good indeed," I grumble needing my mind to catch up with my body that's already revved and raring to go. "Any time I can wake up with a sight like this, is indeed a good fucking morning." I can't help the smile that curls up my lips. Fuck she's gorgeous.

And mine.

Seriously? What the fuck did I do to deserve her? Hell has most definitely frozen over.

"Well," she says drawing the word out into a purr. "We seem to have a dilemma here?"

"A dilemma?"

"Yes, I seemed to be underdressed and you Mr. Donavan, you seem to be very overdressed."

I quirk an eyebrow up at her, all systems fully awake now, and more than ready to go. "I think you look fucking perfect." I shift some and prop the pillow further under my head so that I most definitely do not miss a single thing from the vision in front of me. "But you think I'm overdressed, huh?"

"Most definitely," she says, "and I think it's time to fix the situation." She shifts her weight, and I can feel her fingers scrape over my hips as she pulls the sheet down. Fuck if she's not teasing me. My cock springs free from the confines of the sheet and it aches for her to touch it. To be buried in that sweet heat of hers. I watch her look at my cock and when she licks her tongue over her bottom lip it takes everything I have to not pin her to the bed and take what that mouth is tempting.

"Oh, there is most definitely a situation." She smirks and her eyes look up to meet mine, lust and mischief dancing beneath her lashes.

"And how do you suggest we fix it?" I ask enjoying the role of temptress she's playing despite my balls desperately begging for release.

She reaches out and wraps her hand around my cock. *Fuuuccckkk that feels good.* I lay my head back and drown in the sensation of her fingers on my tortured flesh. She strokes me with slow, even strokes that feel so fucking good it takes everything I have to not put my hand on top of hers and urge her to go faster. To pump harder.

When it comes to Rylee, begging is not beneath me.

"Well, it is race day, and I can't exactly let my man go to the track without fixing this little problem we have here."

I flash my eyes open and take in the arch of her eyebrow and taunt on her lips. "Oh baby, *there's nothing little about it.*"

She moves forward, her hand still on my cock but tits back front and center in my view as she leans in close to my face. "There isn't?" She angles her head watching my mouth fall lax as she works her dexterous fingers back up my dick. All I can do is bite my lip in response and shake my head as she pays special attention around its crest. Talking right now is not an option. "I guess I'll have to find out for myself then. Don't you think?"

I stare at her. Take all of her in as she kneels over me—cheeks flush, eyes dancing, and mouth tempting—and I can't believe after how bad I fucked up, that she's still here. Still fighting for us. My fucking saint.

A reply is on my lips—and fuck if I remember what it is because it flies from my mind the minute she sinks down onto my cock.

Wet fucking heat. Pleasure swamps me the instant I feel the velvet grip of her tight pussy wrapped around me. From the bottom of my spine all the way to the top of my sac tightens in a tingling surge of eye-roll into the back of your head type of ecstasy.

"Sweet Jesus!" I groan out as she seats herself root to tip and stills so that she can adjust to my invasion.

"No, not Jesus," she murmurs as she leans in and slips her tongue between my lips adding torment to her tantalization. "But I can still take you to Heaven," she whispers against my lips.

And then she starts to move. Up and down. Her slick, wet heat spasming over my cock with her every rise and fall. Skin on skin. Soft to hard. Hers and mine. So fucking good.

Fucking Rylee.

My fucking voodoo pussy.

Shit. *I stand corrected.* Now this—Rylee's voodoo pussy—is God's greatest creation.

Ever.

And motherfucker if Rylee wasn't right.

She does feel like fucking Heaven.

I shove my legs into last night's jeans, knowing I need to get my ass in gear. I'm excited for the day ahead of me—for the organized chaos and the rev of the motor at my command—but I'm just not ready to share Rylee yet. Not ready to burst this bubble around us and step into the blur.

I look over at her as she shoves her arms through her T-shirt and I shake my head. What a fucking shame to cover those perfect tits up. But I have to admit, I kind of like the idea of a T-shirt with my name emblazoned on it pressed against them. Staking a claim.

A sharp knock sounds on the door and before either of us can respond the door is shoved open. "You guys decent?"

Beckett walks in, fire suit on but the sleeves are tied around his waist.

"And if we weren't?" I ask a little miffed. What the fuck if Ry wasn't dressed yet? Or even worse, laid out beneath me naked and moaning. So not fucking cool. It's not like Becks and I haven't been drunk and fucking women in the same room before—but fuck—this is Rylee we're talking about here. My spark.

"How the fuck did you get in here?" I ask and he knows I'm pissed at the intrusion. And of course being fucking Becks, he smirks a little knowing smile to let me know he's just testing the waters. That he's pushing my buttons to see where she and I stand.

Beckett looks back and forth between Rylee and myself before tossing the key card on the bed. "From last night," he says in explanation to his room access. "You guys good now?" He looks over at Rylee, eyes holding hers for a beat, and I can see him searching her face to make sure that she is in fact okay. That we worked our shit out. Fucking Becks. He may be a cocksucker but he's the best fucking wing man a guy could ever have.

"Yeah, we're good now," she answers him and the soft little smile she gives him has me shaking my head. Could she be any more perfect?

"Good," he states glancing over at me with a cat ate the canary grin, eyes telling me *it's about fucking time.* "Don't let it happen again."

I just shake my head at him as I rise from the bed and start buttoning up my jeans. I glance over to Rylee and notice her eyes watching my fingers trail over the ridged lines of my bare abdomen. The look in her eyes has me wanting to lock Beckett out and drag Rylee to the floor—or shove her up against the wall—I'm not picky and frankly beggars can't be choosers—until I get my fill of her.

Then again, that might take a long-ass time. I don't think I'll ever get my fill of her.

"No time for that lover-boy." Becks snorts when he sees the look Ry and I exchange. I have half a mind to tell him to get the fuck out so that I can get one more taste to last me through the race. Especially when I look over and see her cheeks flushed at being caught thinking naughty thoughts.

"You've got fifteen minutes before we leave. Make the most of your time." He winks at Rylee and I know she's dying of embarrassment right now.

Oh I fucking plan on it.

The air vibrates with anticipation around me as we walk through the pits. The guys are checking and making sure that everything is in order and ready for the green flag, but let's face it, they're just busying their hands to keep from looking nervous. And I fucking love that my crew gets nervous about a race. Lets me know they care about it as much as I do.

I should be nervous, but I'm not. I look over at Rylee beside me and squeeze her fingers that are laced with mine. She's the reason that I'm not. Fucking Rylee—the balm to soothe all problems: nerves, nightmares, broken souls, and healing hearts.

My new superstition number one—her beside me.

She smiles at me, eyes hidden behind her sunglasses, and the sexiest fucking smile on those lips.

Out of habit I walk over to the car where it's parked in front of my pit row designation and rap my knuckles on the hood four times. Superstition number two down. Rylee looks over at me and quirks an eyebrow. I just shrug in response.

Superstitions are stupid fucking things but hey, whatever works.

"Why the number thirteen?"

She's referring to the number on my car. My unlucky, lucky number. "It's my lucky number." I tell her as I wave at Smitty passing by.

"How unconventional." She smirks at me, pushing her sunglasses up into her hair and tilting her head to the side, her eyes steadfast on mine.

"Would you expect anything less of me?"

"Nope. Predictability doesn't suit you." She shakes her head and drags her bottom lip through her teeth. Fuck if that's not sexy. "Why thirteen?"

"I've defied enough odds in my lifetime so far." I lean back against the car behind me. "I don't think a number's going to change my luck now." *And it's the date of the day my Dad found me.* The thought unexpectedly flashes through my head, but I don't say it—just think it—not wanting to put a damper on the moment.

I tug on her hand and pull her against me, needing to feel her. The soothing balm to my aching soul. She lands solidly against me, and I swear more than our bodies jolt.

My fucking heart does too. It jolts, trips, falls, tumbles, freefalls—no that's not it—it *crashes* into that foreign fucking feeling pulsing through me.

I lean down, needing a taste of her. I slant my lips over hers and revel in her sweetness. The move of her tongue. The taste of her lips. The scent of her perfume. The quiet moan she sighs into me.

The claiming of my heart.

My God. The woman is my fucking kryptonite. How did this happen? How did I let her own me? More importantly and fucking shocking, *I want her to own me.*

Every fucking piece of me.

Game over baby.

She's my motherfucking checkered flag.

Chapter Forty-One

"Don't I get my good luck kiss?" Colton looks over and smirks at me as he pulls his lucky shirt over his head and throws it on the couch behind him. *My God.* The man knows how to knock the wind out of me. He stands before me, that arrogant as sin grin spreading his mouth wide and his eyes reflecting all of the dirty things he'd love to do to me right now.

And the thoughts are not unreciprocated.

"Good luck kiss? Or good luck..." I let my words trail off, raising my eyebrows at him, my eyes licking their way over the bronzed skin and defined lines of his naked torso and stopping at those completely devastating lips. I let my gaze rest on his amused sparks of green as he watches me appreciatively take in the sight of him.

He quirks his eyebrow up as he unties the loose sleeves of his fire suit around his waist. "Good luck what?" he teases as he takes a step toward me and leans over, bracing his hands on either side of the arms of my chair.

I look up at him and feel a million miles away from where the two of us were twenty-four hours ago. I feel like it was a really bad dream but am oddly glad it isn't. There is something between us now, an ease or contentment I guess, that has shown us we can muddle through. That we can fight and love and despise, but in the end, *we can find us again.* That we can use each other's pleasure to bury the pain.

"Not sure...I've never done this race thing before..." I smirk as I give into the temptation—take what really is mine now—and tease my fingertips up his chest and tickle them along his jaw until they find their way into his hair.

He dips his head down and captures my mouth with a languorous exploration of his tongue against mine. The slide of my fingertips over his skin. The hum of approval deep within his throat. My soft sigh he breathes in and deepens the kiss. He shows me how he feels about me with an underlying urgency and complete veneration.

The pounding on the motor home door has me jerking back from Colton and him swearing one of his favorites as he looks over at it. I look up at him and allow the emotions to flow through me, welcome them in their still dreamlike state. My achingly handsome rogue standing before me, *really is mine.*

"Showtime?" I ask on a sigh.

"Checkered flag time, baby." He smirks and presses one last, chaste kiss against my lips. I catch him by surprise as I cup the back of his neck and slip my tongue between his lips and just take. Take everything I've needed and wanted and been too afraid to ask for over the past few months. And although I catch him by surprise, he gives unflinchingly without questioning. I end the kiss and pull back a fraction to look into his eyes—telling him without words how much he just gave me. A smile ghosts his lips, that lone dimple I love deepening, and he just shakes his head at me, trying to figure out what that was all about.

"Checkered flag time, baby." I smile at him as I rise from the chair. He reaches behind him and tugs on a new T-shirt—an endorsement T-shirt—to wear beneath his fire suit now that the requisite lucky T-shirt has been worn for the superstitious allotted amount of time. I glance over at the clock and am struck by the nerves that start fluttering when I realize that there's only a short time left before the cranking of the engines while he seems so calm and collected.

"Don't worry," Colton says bringing me back to the here and now, not realizing that I had pressed a hand to the butterflies in my stomach. "They'll hit me the minute we walk out of the RV." He points to my stomach and then nods his head toward the door before shoving a hat on his head. *His lucky hat.* And I smile softly when I realize it's the same hat that he wore on our date to the carnival.

Mr.-I'm-So-Sure-Of-Myself wore his lucky hat on our first official date. As if my heart could swell any more.

"You ready?" he asks as he walks a few steps and then turns and holds his hand out to me.

"Hey, Ace?" Colton stops with the door ajar and looks back at me with curiosity. Time for me to show him just what's waiting at the finish line. I'd found the skimpy pair of black and white checkered panties that have *Revved and Raring* embroidered across the butt at a little novelty store back at home. With the state of things between Colton and me, I'm not sure why I'd even brought them on the trip, but obviously with last night's turn of events, I'm glad that I did. His eyes widen as I unzip my shorts and wiggle my hips, pushing them down so that he can see a hint of the lace and checkering on the fabric. "This is the only checkered flag you need, baby."

His smile widens and the open door is forgotten as he strides two steps back toward me and yanks my body against his. He stops a moment and stares at me, mouths a whisper apart and emotion brimming in our eyes before he crashes his lips to mine in a kiss of pure hunger and carnality. He breaks away just as suddenly as he starts it and looks at me with a smirk. "You can bet your ass that's one checkered flag I'm definitely claiming."

Chapter Forty-Two
Colton

I can feel it.

That complete certainty that hits you like a fucking freight train on very few days in your life. I have it today. I feel it today. It's in the air circling around me as my head flickers here and there through what I need to do today when I hit the track and the rubber connects. Stay clear of Mason—the fucker's got it out for me—like I knew he had his sights on that barfly last year. It's not like he was waving a flag or anything staking his fucking claim. Bad blood is never good on the track. Never. Stay high and tight through turns two and three. Binders light. Pedal heavy. Bring it in low on one. I keep repeating my responsibilities in my head, over and over. My way of making sure that I don't have to think down the chute. Just react.

Today I'm taking the checkered flag, and not just those dick hardening panties that fucking Rylee has on. *Sweet Christ, am I claiming that flag.* But I can feel it. Everything feels right with the world, and shit, maybe I'm being a pussy but that *right* feeling started when I woke up with Rylee wrapped in my arms, head nuzzled under my neck, lips pressed to my skin, and heart beating against mine.

Right where she's supposed to be.

I take a bite of another of my pre-race superstitions—a Snicker's bar—and look up to search her out. She's sitting quietly out of the way toward a corner, and her eyes lock with mine immediately. Her lips form that shy smile that turns me motherfucking inside out, and instead of the fear that usually snakes through my system, I feel settled. At ease.

328

Can you say fucking pussy to the whip? But you know what? I'm okay with it because I'm pretty sure she'll be gentle with me. Won't crack it too hard. Well, unless I want her to.

"Wood?" I turn and look at Beckett.

Now Becks on the other hand is still going to hand my ass back to me in a hand basket once the stress of this race is over and he realizes it's minutes before a race and I'm thinking about my fucking voodoo pussy. *My fucking Rylee.*

I flash a quick smile at Ry before I turn to Becks. "Yup?" I say as I stand and begin the routine of zipping up my suit.

Getting ready to race.

Getting ready to do the one thing I have always loved.

Getting ready to take that motherfucking checkered flag.

Chapter Forty-Three

There is so much to take in. So many sights and sounds to assault and overwhelm. Hand over my heart, I stand beside Colton as the national anthem is sang on the stage at our backs. Flags wave. The breeze blows. The crowd sings. And my nerves go into overdrive for the man beside me that has transformed into an intense, introspective man as he focuses on the task at hand.

He reaches out a free hand and places it at the small of my back as the camera crew makes its way down the line of drivers standing on pit row with their crew and significant others at their sides. The fact that he's trying to comfort me in a moment strictly about him warms my insides. I'd tried telling him that I could sit in the pit box during the anthem—that it wasn't a big deal to me—but he refused. "I've got you now, sweetheart, I'm not letting you out of my sight," he'd said. Argument won. Hands down.

Fireworks boom as the song comes to an end, and all of a sudden pit row is a flurry of activity. Crews going to work to try and make all of their hard preparation come to fruition for their driver. Men descend around Colton before I can wish him one last good luck. Ear buds are stuffed in and taped down. Velcro is fastened. Shoes are double checked to make sure nothing will interfere with the pedal. Gloves are pulled on and situated. Last minute directions are given. I allow myself to be led from the craziness and am helped over the wall by Davis.

"Rylee!" In all of the complete, organized chaos, his voice rings out. Stops me. Starts me. Completes me.

I turn around and face him in all of his suited up glory. His white balaclava is in one hand and helmet in the other. So achingly handsome.

330

So damn sexy. And all mine.

I look at him confused since we already had our moment of privacy in the motor home. Did I do something wrong? "Yeah?"

His smile lights up. A solid figure standing still while everyone else moves in one big blur around him. His eyes hold mine, intense and clear. "*I race you, Ryles,*" he says in a voice that's implacable and unwavering amidst the swirling chaos.

My heart stops. Time stands still and it feels like we're the only two people in the world. Just a damaged boy and a selfless girl. Our eyes lock and in that exchange, words that I can't shout out in the chaos between us are said. That after the little he explained last night, I know how horribly difficult it is for him to utter those words. That I understand he's telling me he's still a broken child inside, but like my boys he's giving me his heart and trusting that I will hold it with gentle, compassionate, and understanding hands.

"I race you too, Colton." I mouth to him. Despite the noise, I know he hears what I've said for a shy smile graces his lips, and he shakes his head like he's trying to understand all of this too. Beckett calls his name and he gives me one last glance before his face transforms into work mode. And I can't help but just stand there and watch him. Love swells, overwhelms, and heals my heart that I once thought was irreparable. Fills me with happiness over the man that I can't tear my eyes away from him.

My storm before the calm.

My angel breaking through the darkness.

My ace.

My chest reverberates as the cars fly down the backstretch. Fifty laps in and I'm still a nervous wreck, my eyes flicking between the track and the television monitor in front of me when the cars are at my back and out of my sight. My knee jiggles, my fingernails have been picked clean of nail polish, and the inside of my lip has been chewed raw. And yet Colton's voice comes through confident and focused at the task at hand every time he speaks on the headset I'm wearing.

Each time he talks to Beckett or his spotter I feel a trickle of ease. And then they hit a turn, cars side by side—masses of metal flying at ungodly speeds—and that trickle of ease turns into a pound of anxiety. I check the monitor again and smile when I see "13 Donavan" under the number two spot fighting his way back to the lead after a pit stop prompted by a caution.

"Dirty air ahead," the spotter says as Colton comes out of turn three and heads toward traffic a lap down.

"Ten-four."

"Last lap fastest yet," Beckett pipes into the conversation as he studies a computer screen several seats down from me that's reading all of the gauges in number thirteen. "Doing great, Wood. Just keep her steady in that groove you've got. The high line has a lot of pebbling already so stay clear."

"Got it." His voice strains from the force of the car as he accelerates out of turn number one.

There is a collective gasp from the crowd as a car comes into contact with the wall. I turn to look, my heart jumping in my throat, but I can't see it from our position. I immediately look to the monitor where Beckett is already focused.

"Up one, Colton. Up!" The spotter yells in my ears.

It all happens so fast but I feel like time stops. Stands still. Rewinds. The monitor shows a cloud of smoke as the car that hits the wall first slings back down the track at a diagonal. The speeds are too fast so the remaining cars are unable to adjust their line in that quick amount of time. Colton had once told me you always race to where the accident first hits because it always moves afterwards due to the momentum.

There's so much smoke. So much smoke, how is Colton going to know where to go?

"I'm blind," the spotter yells, panicked as the mass of cars and the ensuing smoke is so large that he can't direct Colton. Can't tell him the safe line to drive with his car flying close to two hundred miles per hour.

I watch his car fly into the smoke. My heart in my throat. My prayers thrown up to God. My breath held. My soul hoping.

Chapter Forty-Four
Colton

Motherfucker.

The smoke engulfs me. The blur around me now gray with flashes of sparking metal as cars collide around me. I'm fucking blind.

Don't have time to fear.

Don't have time to think.

Can only feel.

Only react.

Daylight flashes on the other end of the tunnel of gray. I aim for it. Not letting up. Never let up. Race to where the crash was.

Go, go, go. C'mon, one-three. C'mon, baby. Go, go, go.

The flash of red comes out of nowhere and slings in front of me. No time to react. None.

I'm weightless.

Lifted.

Weightless.

Spiraling.

Spinning.

White knuckles on the wheel.

Daylight again.

Too fast.

Too fast.

"Fuck!"

Chapter Forty-Five

I see Colton's car rise above the smoke. It's up on the nose. Spiraling through the air. I hear Beckett yell, "Wood!" It's only one word, but the broken way he says it has lead dropping through my soul.

I can't react.

Can't function.

Just sit in my seat and stare.

My mind fracturing to images of Max and Colton.

Broken.

Interchangeable.

Chapter Forty-Six
Colton

Spiderman. Batman. Superman. Ironman.

The End

Stay tuned for the conclusion of Rylee and Colton's story
in the third and final book of The Driven Trilogy,
CRASHED

Acknowledgements

Wow! Where do I even begin to start? When I started this writing journey a little over a year ago, it was more of a challenge to myself. Can I do it? Not only can I do it, but can I create a story that creates visceral reactions in the reader and at the same time makes them fall in love with Rylee, Colton and their story? When I finished Driven, I liked it—but that meant nothing— the question was, would you, the reader, be taken by it?

Never in a million years did I expect that response to be yes! At first I thought it was a fluke to be honest. I knew I was in love with Rylee and Colton and the boys—but that was a given—and then the messages and emails and posts started coming in. You actually loved them as much as I did—my damaged alpha and heartbroken heroine. I've always thought the job of an author is to make the reader feel in extremes—and you all let me know that I did just that, broken Kindles and all. (Seriously, I've received pictures of broken Kindles after they were thrown at the ending of Driven). So more than anything, thank you to my readers. Thank you for taking a chance on this independent author and her debut novel—flaws, grammatical errors, and all. Thank you for talking about Driven, recommending it to your friends, creating FB pages and posting reviews anywhere and everywhere to help get the word out. You have no idea how much that kind of support means to a self-published author such as myself. So once again, I thank you from the bottom of my heart. I've read in numerous places that the second book of a trilogy is often the downfall—full of filler, fluff, and no real plot—all I can say is, I hope that Fueled lived up to and exceeded your expectations.

To the bloggers—the women who put endless hours into reading our books (good and bad), reviewing them, making collages for them, and promoting the hell out of them, just because of their love of books. For most of them, it's their second job—the one they actually like— and they don't do it for money or recognition, but because they love to be transported to another time and place. I'm not trying to kiss-up to them here, but rather thank them, because if it weren't for their tireless passion, most of you would have had no idea that a book called Driven existed. So to the bloggers, thank you for pushing, promoting, joining

Colton's Cuties (aka the Driven Street Team), reviewing, and supporting the trilogy in general. Driven may have been a great story, but without you guys and your continued support, it might have lost momentum—so thank you!

There are few necessary shout outs I must make, and it doesn't mean that other bloggers are less important, but just that these particular ones have helped me enormously in some way or another. Jenny and Gitte from Totallybooked: Where do I begin with you two? Thank you so much for answering the ridiculous PM's from this newbie and treating me with the same respect as you would a New York Times best selling author. I appreciate the late/early chats, endless stickers, and words of wisdom—your kindness is immeasurable and your support astounding. I'm telling you, it's the J&G effect! To Liz Murach with Sinfully Sexy Book Reviews: thank you for hosting a kick ass release week tour. Wow! Between the cover reveal and the actual tour, you knocked my socks off. Thanks to Autumn and Julie at AToMR for their incredible blog tour in September—as always, pure class. Thanks to Emily Kidman with TheSubClub for the endless encouragement and always when I seem to need it the most.

There are so many more bloggers to thank that I can't even begin to list them all, but I'll try, and if you've been left off, please note that it's only because my brain is overtired from looking at this computer screen. So thank you to Donna at The Romance Cover, Tray at the BookHookers, Jessy at Jessy's Book Club, Sandy at The Reading Café, Meagan at Love Between the Sheets, Ellen at The Book Bellas, Michelle at The Blushing Reader, Stephanie at The Boyfriend Bookmark, Mary with Mary Elizabeth's Crazy Book Obsession, Lindsay with Beauty, Brains & Books, Liz with Romance Addiction, Stephanie with Stephanie's Book Reports, Alicia at Island Lovelies, Jen at TheBookBar, Kimberly at Book Reader Chronicles, Jess at A is for Alpha, B is for Books, Stephanie at Romance Addict Book Blog, Cara at A Book Whores Obsession, Amy at Schmexy Girl Book Blog, Autumn at The Autumn Review, Lisa at The Rock Stars of Romance, Jennifer at Wolfel's World of Books, Kim at Shh Mom's Reading, Jamie at Alphas, Authors, & Books Oh My, Books by the Glass, and soooo many others I can't even remember....Thank you, thank you, thank you!

Another set of thank-yous is owed to my beta readers. When I released Driven, I had no idea what a beta reader was. Only three people had read it before its release and I think if I'd had beta readers, the main criticisms I received with Driven, would never have made it to the final product. So to my beta readers Willy Schilling, Jennifer

Mirabelli, Josie Melendez, Jodie Stipetich, Melissa Allum, Kim Rinaldi, Emily Kidman, Autumn Hull, Beta Hoo, and Beta Haw: Your opinions, remarks, and comments were invaluable to me and to the final version of Fueled. I appreciate your brutal honesty, the time you put in, and the second pair of eyes. You've helped to make the finished product that much more...

To my editor Maxanne Dobbs of The Polished Pen, thank you for taking the time to read and re-read my llllooonnnnggg book and helping me try to pare it down as much as possible. I didn't like you too much when you told me Rylee was coming off as a bitch—but I'm glad you did because those adjustments made a difference in the reader's empathy and lowered their frustration level. To Deborah at Tugboat Designs—killer cover once again...and to think that we got it right on the first attempt! Thank you! To Stacey with Hayson Publishing, thanks for formatting Fueled on such a short notice! You surpassed all expectations. To Jennifer at Polished Perfection, thank you for the second and third set of eyes!

To my A.C.E. contest winners – thank you for being a part of Fueled! In the Las Vegas scene at TAO, Colton and Beckett guess what Ace means, and these lovely ladies get the credit for those guesses: Lysette Lam for Colton's guess of "attractive, charming, and exquisite" and Sandy Schairer for Beckett's guess of "all consuming ego." Thanks to everyone who participated in the contest, I had some good laughs over your definitions.

Music plays a huge part in my books, so thank you so much to the many artists for their talents in which I used their songs as inspiration to write several scenes. Nothing sets the mood for writing like a certain song. Special thanks to Matchbox Twenty, Rylee's go-to therapy music and of course, as Colton so politely said, "Fuckin' Pink" – thank you for the inspiration behind one of the most important lines of the book!

To my Son for watching old school Spiderman movies on Netflix— over and over ad nauseum—having those as the background to my writing provided me with the other two most meaningful quotes in this book. May you never have to repeat superheroes. Ever. I Spiderman you bud!

To my baby girl: thank you for typing on my working copy of Fueled as often as you could. My betas thought I had randomly typed license plate numbers mid-paragraph—nope, that was just CJ making sure she's heard! I love you crazy girl!

To my oldest daughter: thanks for trying to sneak a peak at my screen every chance you can because now, you can read, and Mommy's nervous about what you just might be reading on her computer. Thanks for your patience and unending questions in regards to "do people really read what you're typing?" Let's hope they do. Love you too bug!

To my husband: Thank you for being patient during this whole process. Thank you for inventing places to take the kids so that I get a few hours alone here and there to write uninterrupted. Thank you for being okay (well mostly) with take-out or food from a bag because I need to get a scene finished. Thank you for not complaining that laundry takes a whole lot longer now and the house is a little bit messier. Thank you for going to bed by yourself several nights a week while I stay up and then fall asleep with Colton instead. (Sorry ladies, it's one of the perks of being the author!) Thank you for understanding that the computer is now glued to my fingertips and the woman who never forgot anything, is now a tad bit absentminded—just blame it on those damn people in my head. I love you!

To my family and friends: thank you for your unending support and my random ramblings about people who exist in my head and in the hearts of all of you readers.

Names are funny things to pick in a book. For instance in Driven and Fueled, my kids names make an appearance. I usually opt for names that I really like or ask my oldest daughter for a random name she wants to make her feel a part of the whole experience…but there is one name in particular in Fueled that holds special meaning in our house right now. The name is Parker—the kind man in the bar that kept Rylee company. My seven-year-old daughter has had the sweetest little boy in her class the past two years. In April, sweet Parker was diagnosed out of the blue with stage 4 nueroblastoma. His little body is currently fighting as hard as he can to beat this horrible disease and his mom and dad are superheroes right along with him, doing anything and everything they can to raise money to help his fight https://fundrazr.com/campaigns/fUHge …so I decided to give a quiet shout out to Parker in Fueled to let him know we are all thinking about him. If anyone in your life has been touched by cancer, you know what it's like…so if you get a chance, stop by and give him a few words of encouragement on Facebook at Team Parker for Life with a little '#Fueled' so he knows we're all pulling for him!

My final comment will address what I'm sure will be flooding my email and Facebook page when you finish reading this book, when is Crashed going to be released? I do not have a set date yet. I'm sorry, but I refuse to give a date and then have to adjust it and push it back a few months from now. I've been frustrated when authors do that and I don't want to make you feel that way. Rest assured though that Crashed will be the final book in the trilogy. The story of Rylee and Colton will be completed.

Are you still thinking about that ending? Thought so. Feel free to join 'The Driven Trilogy Group' on Facebook where you can discuss like crazy (spoilers and all) with other people that have finished it. The link is: https://www.facebook.com/groups/394768807306804/

Thanks again for reading. I hope you enjoyed Fueled.

I race you!

K.

About the Author

K. Bromberg is that reserved woman sitting in the corner that has you all fooled about the wild child inside of her—the one she lets out every time her fingertips touch the computer keyboard. She's a wife, mom, child rustler, toy pick-er-upper, chauffer, resident web-slinger, LaLaloopsy watching, American Girl doll dressing multi-tasker of all things domestic and otherwise. She likes her diet cokes with rum, her music loud, and her pantry stocked with a cache of chocolate.

K. lives in Southern California with her husband and three children. When she needs a break from the daily chaos of her life, you can most likely find her on the treadmill or with Kindle in hand, devouring the pages of a good, saucy book.

<u>Fueled</u> is K. Bromberg's second published novel and is the highly anticipated second book of "The Driven Trilogy." <u>Driven</u> was her well-received debut novel and Book #1 of the series.

Contact K. Bromberg at:

Email: Kbrombergwrites@gmail.com
http://www.kbromberg.com
http://www.amazon.com/-/e/B00CRSG9EE
https://facebook.com/authorkbromberg
http://www.goodreads.com/Kbromberg
http://pinterest.com/kbrombergwrites/
@KBrombergDriven
@ColtonDonavan

Made in the USA
Lexington, KY
03 November 2014